T0357148

THE GREAT PYRAMIDS

COLLECTED STORIES

THE GREAT PYRAMIDS

COLLECTED STORIES

FREDERICK BARTHELME

FOREWORD BY BRET EASTON ELLIS

Arcade Publishing • New York

Copyright © 2025 by Frederick Barthelme

All rights reserved. No part of this book may be reproduced in any manner without the express written consent of the publisher, except in the case of brief excerpts in critical reviews or articles. All inquiries should be addressed to Arcade Publishing, 307 West 36th Street, 11th Floor, New York, NY 10018.

Select stories in this collection originally appeared in the *New Yorker*, *New Orleans Review*, *North American Review*, *Chicago Review*, *Esquire*, *Kansas Quarterly*, *TriQuarterly*, *South Carolina Review*, *Playboy*, *Gentleman's Quarterly*, *New American Short Stories II*, *Fiction of the Eighties*, *Epoch*, *Ploughshares*, *Antioch Review*, *The Southern Review*, and the *Land-Grant College Review*.

Arcade Publishing books may be purchased in bulk at special discounts for sales promotion, corporate gifts, fund-raising, or educational purposes. Special editions can also be created to specifications. For details, contact the Special Sales Department, Arcade Publishing, 307 West 36th Street, 11th Floor, New York, NY 10018 or arcade@skyhorsepublishing.com.

Arcade Publishing® is a registered trademark of Skyhorse Publishing, Inc.®, a Delaware corporation.

Visit our website at www.arcadepub.com.
Please follow our publisher Tony Lyons on Instagram @tonylyonsisuncertain

10 9 8 7 6 5 4 3 2 1

Library of Congress Cataloging-in-Publication Data is available on file.

Jacket design by Brian Peterson

Print ISBN: 978-1-64821-123-2
Ebook ISBN: 978-1-64821-124-9

Printed in the United States of America

Author's Note

This collection represents about half of the stories I have written and published over the years. It was curated by the publisher and my editor, Bruce Wagner, to whom I would like to express my appreciation for their work on this volume.

Contents

FOREWORD

Frederick Barthelme's short stories began appearing in *The New Yorker* in 1981 when he was thirty-eight—he was born in 1943 in Houston, Texas. A collection of these stories, *Moon Deluxe*, was published in 1983. This was followed by two novels—*Second Marriage* (1984) and *Tracer* (1985) and another collection in 1987, *Chroma*. The novels *Two Against One* in 1988 and *Natural Selection* in 1989 rounded out the decade. In the 1990s, as for books, he only published novels along with a nonfiction work written with his brother, Steven—a memoir about gambling. (Another brother was the famed postmodernist novelist and short story writer Donald.)

His early work in the short story was perhaps most impactful, as it offered us a new way of seeing things, changing our ideas about form and structure and content. Barthelme was part of a group of writers that were briefly but immensely influential during the early 1980s and this included Mary Robison (especially *An Amateur's Guide to the Night* in 1983), Amy Hempel (*Reasons to Live* in 1985), Jayne Anne Phillips (*Black Tickets* in 1979), Bobbie Ann Mason (*Shiloh and Other Stories* in 1982), and of course the Gordon Lish edited stories of Raymond Carver, which started it all: *Will You Please Be Quiet, Please?* (1976) and *What We Talk About When We Talk About Love* (1981), as well as the stories Carver reconstructed in *Cathedral* (1983) and this was all presaged by Ann Beattie whose short stories from *The New Yorker* in the 1970s are often cited as the beginning of this movement, though her early style, like Carver's, changed radically over her career, as did those of most of these writers.

In the mid-to-late 1970s and throughout the 1980s minimalism became a dominant movement in burgeoning literary circles, especially among college students, who either became enamored by these stories because of their brevity or maybe because they thought they could so easily emulate these masters—they found out it wasn't very easy at all. Raymond Carver became the most popular practitioner of this minimalist style with the stripped-down approach of his early stories—some of them edited against his will by his editor Lish, who sometimes helped Carver, and maybe sometimes didn't.

When *Moon Deluxe* appeared, I was a sophomore at Bennington College in Vermont and the work seemed unworldly—a radical departure, a confirmation of something that was in the air, and as with Ann Beattie's early stories and Carver's, the collection asked: what is a short story? Reading *Moon Deluxe* didn't remind me at all of *The Stories of John Cheever*, a massive and massively popular collection that appeared in 1978 and sold a gazillion copies—everyone seemed to have it and it won not only The National Book Award but also the Pulitzer Prize—and this giant tome with its famous orange cover, almost 700 pages long, was a reminder of Cheever's genius, dotted with at least half a dozen of what were considered some of the greatest American stories of the twentieth century. Cheever was from a different world and a believer in something that the minimalists—emerging from the haze of Vietnam, the end of the '60s, Watergate, the Bicentennial, a recession, punk rock—did not. Cheever was rooted in an American tradition that has never fully left the landscape. George Saunders, probably the most widely read living American short story writer, is much closer to Cheever than he is to Barthelme or any of the minimalists despite his postmodern flourishes.

Moon Deluxe reminded me of the jolt I felt about seven years earlier when I read Hemingway's first collection *In Our Time* (I hadn't wanted to—it was a class assignment at my prep school) and realized while reading it that writing was about style, about consciousness, and not just plot, a clever story, "interesting" characters, drama connected to an obvious epiphany with a "beautiful" sentence tying everything up where the reader says 'Oh yes, this is the world I know, yes, I recognize this" and is somewhat reassured that their outlook and experience has been confirmed. Hemingway shook that notion up—and though his stories did have plot and movement, interesting characters, were clever, and contained drama, it was the way they were being told that shocked me: a style so stripped-down that the sentences seemed practically biblical in their cadences. The realization that a story could be told in this manner—what was left out was as important as what was left in—a kind of existential ambiguity—was a flash of lightning in my consciousness, forever altering the way I read fiction and the way I located style as the primary—if not the only—meaning of a work. Every story has been told but the way a story can be told has not. This is called having a voice.

Moon Deluxe wasn't as stripped down as Hemingway or those first two Carver books—which were arguably as influential to a generation of young American writers as The Velvet Underground or The Sex Pistols were to young musicians—but we could locate a similar signal. (Later, Denis Johnson's *Jesus' Son* in 1992 would add a new but connected sound to this signal and become almost as much of a touchstone as Carver's collected work.) The stories in *Moon Deluxe* were fuller and more detailed—entrancing to some of us, bewildering to those expecting a throughline from what was now seen as the classicism of Hemingway (and Fitzgerald and Faulkner) to the classicism of John Cheever. The minimalists, like Barthelme (whether he wants to be labeled that or not), unlike the punks, weren't a rebuke to Cheever's craftsmanship and talent, his "professionalism," but simply a different way of approaching the short story, redefining what it could be, taking it out of what some might have felt were the now moldy environs of the "classic" *New Yorker* short story and morphing it into something else. And it was *The New Yorker* that was the key hub where almost all of these new writers were being published—the magazine had heard the signal too: that things were changing, and because of a generation's particular experience, the writers were looking at the world in new ways. Ann Beattie was the precursor of this: creating an alienated sense of drift in the short stories she published in the magazine in the mid-1970s that were unlike anything else in that moment.

A microscopic attention to mundane detail, a fleeting style, characters ungrounded and unmoored, a narrative that wasn't obvious, a story that never announced itself, things just happened, there was no obvious epiphany—if there was an epiphany you had to find it.

These were not stories that moved from A to B to C to D. These were often stories, as Barthelme has said, that began at C then moved to F then back to E and then to M and to K and then to A. Many of these stories were sometimes told in second person present ("You drive the Buick to the 7-Eleven and then walk in where you buy a bag of Cheeto's and the clerk says hello to you"—a made-up example) which is something Jay McInerney would use in his iconic novel of that period, *Bright Lights, Big City* (1984), by far the most popular work of minimalism from the early '80s, even though McInerney moved toward a grander, more all-encompassing approach, from the shadow of Raymond Carver toward the romanticism of Fitzgerald.

Barthelme's stories as well as his two novels from that period, especially *Tracer*, felt new—the "style" offered a mystery that made you question: what is a short story. What you've been taught a short story should be—this wasn't it, but this is a short story, too. We were dropped into the middle of something, details accumulated, seemingly random, but you also sensed not so randomly. On the surface these stories were usually shorter than what we may have been used to but also had a pleasing simplicity—the minimalists were very easy to read—just snapshots of a moment in a life, present tense, now, filled with brand names and given a cinematic sheen mostly notable because there was a new lack of interiority to so many of these stories which again made them mysteriously beguiling. Made up of only imagery and dialogue the stories felt closer to screenwriting than prose but the writing was so suggestive, so casual-seeming but not, that whenever you started thinking this the thought evaporated.

The stories in *Moon Deluxe* and *Chroma* acquired a hypnotic quality as you kept reading, wondering: where are we heading? But they were told simply, without the purposeful obfuscation of postmodernism—these were recognizable characters in a recognizable America trailed aimlessly by a miniaturist highlighting the banality of their lives: the erasure of obvious drama, the erasure of purpose, the conversations wheeling to nowhere, the story looping in on itself—becoming lightly absurdist with flashes of lyricism: a movie theater marquee, sodium lights in a parking lot, the color of the sky at sunset, swimming pools. Reading *Moon Deluxe* and *Chroma* you felt a statement was being made, an attempt to connect the reader to the daily monotony of life and realizing it on the page within a certain style that conveyed the monotony but wasn't monotonous itself: a kind of literary trick that unearthed the mystery beneath the banality—that rescued the stories and these lives—from actual banality. Everything was mildly amusing but never laugh-out-loud funny—Barthelme was too chilled-out for that. The randomness of the stories was contained within an assured stylistic voice—these stories were obviously written. But that C to F to M to E approach eliminated all the throat clearing and exposition that came with more classical attempts at the form—and this was welcomed. Barthelme just dropped us into a situation and allowed the reader to figure who these people are and why they—and we—were here; there was no editorializing, there was no judgement. They weren't manipulative and Barthelme never told you how to feel.

Barthelme's stories were always narrated by, or from the third person POV, of white resolutely heterosexual middle-aged men—invisible, not apathetic, but with no clear goal—having inconsequential conversations with characters that were barely more than just names. For the most part the stories ran together undifferentiated creating an unbroken mosaic—they were about mood and an abstracted sense of place, despite the specificity of brand names—and yet the lack of interiority and description gave the stories a strange kind of timelessness that they might not have had if a more traditional approach had been taken—the stories wouldn't have worked; their DNA was elsewhere. The stories were about men and always elusive women—potential love interests with the promise of sex but often platonic—sometimes from afar in a chain restaurant or a Safeway supermarket—one of Barthelme's most famous stories from the early '80s where he dares to present as many brand names as possible (Oreos, Sara Lee, Tab, Pepperidge Farm)—or in close proximity in one of an endless series of modern apartment complexes (every character lives in an anonymous condo) along coastal towns and suburbs in the new American South.

The passivity of the men and the presentation of how they watch—and react or don't—to women was the core of most of the stories, with a mid-life sadness misted over everything. Nothing felt pre-planned and you had no idea where a story was heading.

They ended abruptly—the only closure being a series of words that formed a sentence or a line of dialogue—which activated the reader into reconsidering what they just read. Barthelme went way beyond ambiguity into a state of almost punk refusal to "explain" anything, to give it an obvious meaning: this exclusion of emotional detail and interiority was purposeful. He presented what seemed like an airless, impossible world and then we were stunned as we kept reading by the actual reality of it. Barthelme's purpose, unlike his older brother Donald, was not satirical—the style was too strenuously neutral; what Barthelme refers to as "small ball," the "close focus," the "ordinary life." But how do you capture the mundanity of ordinary life—all the little moments of inconsequentiality—without becoming mundane and inconsequential? The stories suggested and replicated the randomness of this life but in a very specific style and Barthelme argued: this is a valid way of seeing the world. And this was the alchemy that Barthelme ultimately achieved—the transformation. Even when you were aware that nothing was really going on you weren't distracted by that because that was the meaning—well, it was and it wasn't—and you found yourself floating along with Barthelme's style, where a story suddenly ended with the words "your black Mazda" and you heard, or didn't hear, a sonic boom. There was also a gentleness to these stories that bordered on whimsy but never tripped into it—the style was too hard-edged, angular, clean. Barthelme became more expansive as he aged and the stories grew more complicated, more expressive, crankier, and we read more about a character's thoughts and how he feels—always a male Barthelme's age. And no matter where a story landed—how lost or negated someone felt—Barthelme was never a downer because at heart he was almost always a hidden optimist.

Now, almost four decades after *Moon Deluxe* and *Chroma* were published, it was a powerful experience rereading this career-spanning collection—these stories that seemed so new and mysterious to us when they first started appearing and that different voice announced itself sending out signals we responded to—it all came back. And though I felt older, different, reshaped, I can remember with a lasting clarity, flashes of Barthelme's influence on both *The Informers*, a collection of short stories I wrote during 1982–1986 while a student at Bennington, as well as my first novel *Less Than Zero* from 1985.

> *The only light in the room is from outside, a mercury vapor street lamp that leaves the shadow of the Levolors stretched along one wall, broken by a gladiola on the pedestal where we always put outgoing mail. The shadow has a flicker to it.*

Reading so many sentences like this, decades later, is the haunting reminder why.

—Bret Easton Ellis
October 2024

PART ONE

Aluminum House

You stand by the door. Two men slide a woman on a stretcher into the open back of a dusty truck on a cheap street in Mexico City, where you have lived much of your life, and you watch the woman's fingers tighten on an old, painted comb, her face turned oddly back and up, her lips a thin violet. Adriana, your sister, says, "She's dead now," and you sigh and reply, "Stupid! Look at the hands!" But you know that Adriana is right. The truck moves—too slowly—and the old woman's flesh bounces unpleasantly. Birds swing out of the sky and toward the windscreen, then flash away. Adriana sits on a metal chair, her eyes low, the knot of her tie neatly imperfect, and draws a heart on the scummy glass, then turns the heart into a picture of blue hills, then into spectacles on a narrow-faced man. "I expected this," she says, "something like this, anyway. We'll go to the airport directly—tell the driver, hurry, we're stopping." Something catches your eye and you swivel toward the window, but at that moment a laundry van, black with a baby painted on the door, passes between you and what had caught your attention. Adriana says, "I knew this was going to happen."

You don't remember your father. In the cab the attendants pass a single brown cigarette back and forth, each puffing vigorously in turn. You tap the small window and tell the driver that the old woman is dead, that you want to go to the airport, but at that moment a fat man steps on the running board and the driver turns abruptly, gesturing toward the passengers, toward you. The fat man moves along the side of the truck and, holding his hand to the window to shunt the glare, peers inside, and the three bright rings on his fingers snap against the glass. "Doctor," he says, and thumps himself on the sternum. "She's dead," Adriana shouts back. "We're taking her to America."

The airplane is no longer shining, except a wing flap, a few panels near the hatch which have been replaced, and you sit by the woman, tucking the loose sheet, pushing and pulling the sheet, brushing dust away from the woman's completely covered face. You remember that you are nine years your sister's junior, and think that much is lost to you by that fact and accident, and that what is lost will not be recovered—a plain thought which, along with the recurrent image of a painfully pretty young man talking with attractive women in department stores, troubles you during the flight to Tampa, and the following flight to Fort Myers. Finally there is a waiting hearse and a soberly dressed man and a rented sedan for you and your sister to drive away in, and you do that, drive away to the motel and take a room on the second floor overlooking the pool which is full of children who remind you of yourself, inevitably. Adriana talks to your father's nurse on the telephone, then leaves, and you decide to take a walk. The day is cool, sticky, the air from the coast makes a thin mask on your face. The frame buildings you see remind you of buildings you've seen before, but you know they are not the same buildings. The people at the Gulf station seem familiar to you: they walk in circles around huge cars which have boats attached, and there are children in the cars, and gaily clad mothers, and men in starched green shirts. At the café there is a waitress with a bouffant and a second waitress who is quite old, and the two women sit together at a table near the window and look out at you as you walk past. The neon sign above the parking lot is off and opaque and white against the afternoon sky.

The funeral is brief and like a thousand others: at a given moment on a certain day in a particular place a woman is packed into the ground and suddenly, briefly, remembered. You know none of the mourners, and Adriana does not know them, but she speaks to each old man and woman softly, touching and being touched in an oddly objective way. Heads turn repeatedly toward the dark hole in the ground. You notice that the machinery used to lower the casket is safely out of sight beneath pads of false grass. "Let's go," Adriana says when all the mourners have gone. "His house isn't far from here, we can walk." She turns you at the edge of the cemetery and you walk in empty midmorning streets lined with bungalows, white, well-kept bungalows.

"I don't feel well," your sister says, and she takes a straight chair in the living room, reaching for a magazine. You follow the young nurse along a squat hallway and into your father's bedroom. He is small, frail, curled in the bed like a garden slug. His arms are immensely thin, bare, and dust white. When he spies you he pushes his queer body back into the pillows and tells you to sit. He has some things to tell you, some many things. He is an old man, older today than yesterday, older tomorrow than today. You are not to interrupt him with questions. You sit tensely on a chair close to the bed in the low-ceilinged room there in Florida and listen, for the first time in your life, to your father. He is an old and moral man, he believes in doing right even though it is hard to do right in this world and even though in this world right means many things. It is easier to learn as a child, and he learned, and he has not forgotten. He has been sick for several years, bedridden since his sixty-first birthday, the celebration of which was too much for his heart, and his skin bruises easily now and the bruises are uglier than they were once. He is cared for in his decline by a woman, young and very pretty, very womanly—your sister, Adriana. Before the stroke he could not stand her company because of the thoughts a father has and cannot avoid because a father is a man. He never saw her, never spoke to her. But now that he has accepted half of death, he has found life, now he looks at her hair, at her skin, and he takes the simple pleasures. Your father pauses and you wonder if you should correct him, point out that you and Adriana have only just arrived, that the woman who cares for him is a nurse, but you decide against telling him, and pull your chair closer to the bed, place your hands on the bit of sheet he has thrown aside.

He goes on. He should tell you something about life, about his life: he has a pan for his toilet and a second pan for his bath, it's clumsy, but with your sister's help he is comfortable—but that is not what he wants to tell you. You watch the old man struggle with the top of a tall clear bottle from which he finally manages to retrieve the inevitable pill, which he takes without water. The effort seems to drain him and he falls back into the pillows, his eyes shut and his breathing thick. You hear him say, wheezing, that he watches her breasts like a boy watches the breasts of the women who visit his mother—it's not good. He allows himself to imagine her breasts, her sweet curved belly, the lank of her young legs, he gives himself an increasing clarity and vividness in thoughts of touching her slightly, even accidentally, in those places he imagines to be so beautiful, so dark and gardenlike—your father stops talking and closes his eyes, remembering what he remembers, and then, as if on cue, the nurse reenters the room clutching a battered copy of Willa Cather's *My Antonia*, and she sits on the bed opposite you and takes your father's hand and begins to swing it, pivoted at his elbow, gently in a short arc above the bed.

"You're a fine young man to come to see your father all the way from South America," she says.

(1980)

BLACK TIE

At midnight Paul says, "Shh! Be quiet!" He shakes Katherine's shoulder; she jerks awake. She is beautifully draggled, her hair lank, sparkling across her temple to her cheek.

"What?" she says.

"Shh! Quiet! I heard something."

"Paul," she says, removing his hand from her shoulder, "there are no burglars, there is no junkie, the escapees are all escaping in some other direction. Less than four percent of the population is burglarious—the odds are good. Go to sleep."

He pushes a hand at her face, wags a finger back and forth, accidentally catches her on the chin.

This makes her angry.

"The criminals are interested in diamonds and animals, but as you suspect, Paul, there are many with eyes only for you." She goes to the bathroom and returns with a Sucrets, three aspirin, a glass of salt water, a heating pad, a jar of Vicks VapoRub, two Rolaids, a tablespoon of Gelusil, a wet washcloth, and an antiphlogistine. "Here," she says.

He is quiet for a minute, then says, "I feel better already."

"Ah, don't be silly," Katherine says. "I'm beginning to think you aren't serious."

"I know," he says. "I know. Does everyone else know?"

"Who's paying attention?"

"Oh . . . forces of evil, governments, friends."

She looks at Paul with a curious look: "What is evil?"

"Let's go out," he says.

"Out? Where? It's dark! No."

They get into the car and drive out Telegraph Street toward the bridge, the country, the fields of corn and the flocks of crow. The midnight air is thick and heavy and wet; Katherine rolls her window halfway up; the pearl highway lamps hang above them and slide by, green flying circles over the hood and into the glass, one after another.

Katherine says, "I liked freeways until they became popular. They're nice in movies. Want to go to a movie? No, I guess it's too late. We should take a trip, Paul. Do you want to take a trip? No, I guess not. Are we going to sing on this drive?"

"You feel okay?" Paul says.

"You mean, do I need a change? Is my life unfull? Should I get involved? Well, no. That view has fallen from favor. Meaning must be found in the self, Paul, only I looked there already."

"With small success," he says. "We could use some singing."

"Recognition of our signal, anyway."

She sticks Paul in the side with the tire gauge, using it like a false knife the blade of which slips into the handle when the knife is pressed into service.

"Maybe riches," Katherine says, "and . . . slaves?"

She puts the tire gauge away, takes out the map, opens it, puts it in her lap, and holds it there while she gets a Pentel out of the glove compartment. Rolls her window down. Turns on the map light.

"Alignment?" she says. "Is that it?"

"Formerly, I was loath to align. I'm still sort of loath to align. I mean, I don't know."

"Let me get this straight, Paul," she says. "I want to get this straight. You desire alignment, so-called. However, you want to specify . . . what? Income? Caste?"

She marks a bomb pattern on the map, makes airplane noises, flies her hand over the target, runs into bad weather, drops the bombs.

"How I feel. I want to specify how I feel."

"Well, how do you feel?"

"Better," he says. "I guess I feel a whole lot better than I used to. Still, we've smiled and slept, and laughter's been ours, but inadequate. We've tried bitterness and public angst, we've tried to not pay attention, we've told carnival jokes and fiddled the bull fiddle—with twenty-odd fingers into the act you'd think our double stop would be out of sight, but you'd be wrong. Our double-stop technique is the envy of no responsible players. Piano people only nod, graciously; tenormen hoot and honk and hack and hum. How do I feel? I feel we will not learn."

She sighs: "The way we were born, what we have done."

Paul turns the steering wheel of the car so that the car rolls right into the bright lights of an all-night filling station.

"Where are we?" Katherine asks.

"I smell gas," Katherine says.

The attendant stares at Katherine. He is sitting on a stool in his glass booth on the island where the gas pumps are. Paul stares at the attendant. When Katherine goes to the ladies' room, the attendant watches her go. Then Paul asks for two dollars' worth of regular gas.

"Sure, okay," the attendant says. "Regular gas."

Paul gives the man a five-dollar bill, then walks to the station's edge where the concrete, lovely and smooth, gives way to weeds, piled tires, a sweeping horizon of poles, black rectangles, high skeletons, hot distant lights, and running wires. Paul stands there.

The attendant hands Paul three dollars and a strip of Black Gold trading stamps and an eight-ounce glass with a rendering of the National Dance Company of Siberia in action frosted on its side.

"Thanks," Paul says.

"Sure, sure," the attendant says. "Where you headed?"

"Carnegie-Mellon, if the weather holds."

The attendant nods and Paul looks at the sky. Katherine returns with two RC Colas, three candy bars, and a package of peanuts. As she gets into the car the attendant bends to watch. She waves the peanuts at him.

"You got a ways to go yet," the attendant says to Paul. "Best take it slow."

Paul thanks him and starts the car. Katherine puts an unwrapped Snickers in Paul's mouth, an open RC Cola on the seat between his legs, and she drops the peanuts on the glove compartment door.

"The thing that has been lost," she says, "is faith—you remember faith? But, Paul, it's not so bad; we could ease into it—a book, a fiery fire; intrigue, immorality, faraway places—it might work."

"No, no, no, no," he says.

"Oh, right. I forgot. We must cast our seed carefully. However, Paul, the wayside can be quite pleasant in spots. Look there! And . . . what's that? You see, a flight of nightbirds. How pretty. We'll be all right, Paul. We can start, we can build a new life, a new time. Where is imagination? Spirit? Will?"

"Frittered," he sighs, "away."

"Oh, pooh," she says.

He turns off the highway, down an unmarked road; dust rises into the air. Paul stops half a mile in, facing the highway; the night is full of cries, howls, jingles and jangles. Short drifts of wind bring the sizzle of tires on the highway.

"We don't belong here, Paul," she says. "It's fake."

He opens his door and puts his foot in the doorjamb and takes a drink of RC and rolls his head back and gargles his throat.

She says: "Makes me nervous, you know? Feels fishy. We can't stay here, Paul. We have to go back. Nobody lives here. We don't live here."

The panel lights glow a favorable green.

Paul says: "Some troubles are worse than ours, probably. I like it here, Katherine, it's nice—these fields, the dark, the breeze, the size."

"The battery," she says.

"You're lovely, Katherine. You're lovely and you're right—the battery. Yet here, our failure seems small; we're not doing so bad, we have a grace here on our knees—screw the battery. Let's get stranded. Let's stay."

"Bugs."

"I forgot about bugs."

Paul takes the key out of the lock and pushes the light knob and flips the blinker back and forth and rocks the wheel and puts his heel on the black button in the doorjamb.

"We should help somebody."

"How about me?" she says. She gets out of the car and walks around in the field. Then she comes up on Paul's side of the car and twists his foot.

"Sometimes," he says, "a thing is as beautiful as its name."

"True," she says. "But Paul, your rigor's misplaced. There are only two questions. The first question is: Hope? The second question is: What happened? As to the first question I'd say yes—I mean, what've we got to lose? And on the second and more interesting question, I give up. We're frightened. From fear we infer guilt. And we are the judge, Paul. And we are the jury. We are the prosecuting attorneys, the witnesses, and the court-appointed lawyers for the defense. We are the Department of Corrections, the slam. And the warden and the guards guarding. And Paul darling, when the tomahawk swings, it's our hand in sweat on the shank, us on the block."

"Discomfort," he says. "Responsibility."

"I think so, yes. Plain old responsibility."

"Well," he says, "I don't think what has been lost has been lost at all, Katherine, I think it's been hidden."

"Ahh, don't be silly, Paul. Start the car."

He starts the car. She tosses her RC into the ditch and gets in the car and they drive to the highway and head home. Katherine puts away the tire gauge, and the map, and the pliers, and the Pentel.

The moon is full.

At the house she helps Paul close the garage door. They stand in the driveway: she hugs him.

"This is okay," she says. "Wind, street—coming home, Paul. Not a bad finish; not a bad world. I mean, right?"

Paul says: "I like you, Katherine."

"And why not? I walk, talk, ambulate, somnambulate, fox trot—why not like me?"

(1982)

DOMESTIC

Marie watches her husband from the porch of their bungalow, leaning against the open screen door as he digs in their backyard. The sun is out and warm, although it is fall, and late afternoon. They have been married eight years.

"Albert," she asks, "why are you doing that?" She is not entirely sure what it is that he is doing, but has asked that question already with unsatisfactory result, so she has opted for the question of motive.

"Why?" Albert says. He always repeats her questions.

He has been digging in the yard since eleven that morning, without a break, and his wife has come out of the house to ask him if he would like an early dinner. He straightens and pushes the long-handled spade into the dirt. "Marie, I am doing this because this is what I like, this is something I like, digging this hole. There are too few things in this life that are in and of themselves likable, and for me this is one of them. This is valuable to me and from this I derive pleasure. You might say I enjoy working with my hands, although that isn't the whole thing, not by a long shot." Albert stops to wipe his brow with a dime-store neckerchief, then turns to look at the hole he has dug, to gauge his progress. "Did you have something in mind?" he asks, turning back to his wife.

"Why don't you come have dinner now," Marie says, waving a fly away from her face.

He points to the sky and reaches for his shovel. "Got some light yet," he says. "Best use it."

Marie suddenly feels stupid for having suggested dinner at four o'clock in the afternoon, and feels angry that her husband has made a fool of her again, in another one of the small ways that he often makes a fool of her, and she snaps, "Well, I don't like it, frankly," and goes back inside.

After watching him from the kitchen window for a few minutes, Marie climbs the hardwood stairs and flops on the king-size bed in the bedroom, on her back, her arms outstretched. Even with her arms and legs spread, she is swallowed up in the huge mattress, enveloped by it, unable to touch the edges. She looks straight up at the ceiling and tries to imagine a great battle from the Middle Ages pictured there—horses, and cannon, and armor—but sees instead a lone knight in black chain mail astride an equally black horse, riding backward, bent over inspecting the rump of the animal. "Oh Lord," she says, and she rolls off the bed and reaches for the telephone. She calls her mother.

"What're you doing, Mama? How are you? I haven't talked to you in such a long time."

"I talked to you Thursday, Peaches. Is something wrong between you and Albert?"

"Mama! You always think that. And don't call me Peaches, please."

"Marie," her mother says, "you didn't call me two thousand miles across this great continent to ask me the time of day in the middle of the afternoon on the long-distance telephone, I know that don't I?"

"Albert is digging in the backyard is why I called," Marie says. "I don't know why—it isn't even Saturday."

"Your father dug, Peaches."

"This is different, Mama. And don't call me Peaches."

"So you called me now when the rates are high to tell me that your husband and the father of your eventual child is in the backyard digging a hole? Is that all you have to say to me? And you want me to believe that nothing is wrong in your marriage?"

Marie looks out the upstairs window at the bent white shoulders of her husband, watches as he hoists a small mound of dirt, gazes at the shovel's attenuated arc. "It's a serious problem, Mama, or I wouldn't have called. You know what happened to Papa."

"That was different, Peaches. Your papa went a little crazy, that's all. I suspect it ran in his family. When he bought the P-38 for the neighborhood kids, when he cut the hole in the roof of the den, remember? There were reasons, there were explanations— Papa was always up to some good. And, by the way, have you asked about me yet? How I am and what I'm doing out here all alone on this barren coast? No you have not. Maybe if you had brought that Albert out here last summer like I asked you to, I could have straightened him out, and you wouldn't have this terrible problem you have right now, which, if I may say, doesn't sound all that terrible from this distance."

"Thank you, Mama," Marie says.

"Don't start with me, young lady," her mother says. "I'm just trying to help. A mother has an investment in a daughter, as you might well learn one day if that Albert ever gets his head out of the clouds and gets down to business like a real man."

"I have to go now, Mama," Marie says.

"Of course you do, Peaches. You should've gone before you called, if you get my meaning. And, by the way, thank you very much, I'm getting along fine. Mr. Carleton is coming over this evening, and we're going to walk down by the water and maybe take in a show at the Showcase, if you want to know, just by way of information."

"Mr. Carleton?"

"Yes. And if you want my advice you'll stop your whimpering and get out there with a shovel of your own, if you see what I mean."

•

Albert and Marie live in a small suburb near Conroe, Texas. All of their neighbors own powerboats which, during the week, clutter the driveways and front lawns. Albert and Marie do not own a powerboat, although Albert does subscribe to *Boats & Motors*, a monthly magazine devoted to powerboating. Marie is small, freckled, delicate, blonde. Albert is overweight.

That evening, when he finishes digging and comes inside for dinner, Marie presses the question of the hole. "I can't stand it anymore, Albert," she says. "You took a day off from work and you spent the whole day outside digging a hole. If you don't explain this minute, I will leave you."

He looks at her across the dinner table, fatigue and discomfort on his face in equal measures, then pushes an open hand back over his head, leaving some strands of hair standing straight up in a curious peak. Finally he looks at the pork chop on his dinner plate and says, "I love the work, Marie. I love the product. For many years I have been interested in holes—how many times have I pointed out a hole to you when we drive to the store? A hole for telephone equipment, or for a gas line, or for the foundation of a great building? And, of course, I need the exercise, don't I? Marie, there are many wonderful holes in life—dogs dig holes, as do other animals. Pretty women dig small holes on weekend afternoons—can't you understand?"

"I think you're being foolish, Albert," she says, twisting a silver chain around her fingers until the tips of the digits turn purple. Then she unwinds the chain and twists it again, on new fingers. "You may even be silly. Still, you are my husband, and even though you have not provided me with any children, I love you. What are you going to do with this hole when you get it dug?"

Albert's eyes go suddenly very dark, flashing. "Ha!" he says, thrusting himself out of his chair, his arm at full extension, his fork teetering between the tips of his fingers. "You see? *You* are the foolish one! *You* ask stupid questions!" With that he slaps the fork flat onto the table and rushes upstairs to the bedroom, slamming the door behind him.

Marie sighs deeply and continues the meal alone, chewing and thinking of Albert's fingernails, which looked to her like tiny slivers of black moon.

In the morning, after Albert has gone to work at the airline, Marie takes her coffee to the hall table where she sits staring at the telephone for a long time. The hands of the electric clock on the table fly around the clock's face, making a barely audible whir.

An airplane passes overhead, through the clouds.

In the distance, there is a siren.

Marie begins to cry, falling forward on the table, her arms folded there and cradling her head. Between sobs she whispers, "I don't want my husband to dig this hole, I don't want my husband to dig this hole. . ."

The telephone rings. It is her friend Sissy, now a secondary school teacher in Vermont. Marie begins to tell Sissy the story of Albert and the hole, but is unable to make her objection clear, and Sissy responds unsympathetically. Marie is surprised that she isn't clearer about why she is upset by Albert's behavior, and instead of listening to Sissy, she gazes at Albert's university diploma which is framed and mounted above the hall table and wonders why she can't explain herself more clearly.

Finally she says, "I don't know why this upsets me so much, it's silly really." But she has interrupted Sissy's explanation of Albert's behavior, and Sissy insists on finishing the explanation.

"A metaphor," Sissy says, "works in a lot of ways to release the feelings of an individual, opening that individual to expressions which are, for some reason, closed to him. Albert may simply be depressed, and the physical digging is for him a model of the emo-tional digging that's going on, see what I'm saying? Reflects his dis-affection, or something. Maybe he's bored?"

"I see what you mean," Marie says, and she marks another min-ute gone on the pink pad in front of her, a horizontal stroke crossing four vertical strokes.

"Why don't you dig some, too?" Sissy asks. "Seems like that'd be more to the point."

"I've been thinking about that," Marie says.

"Don't think," Sissy says. "*Do.*" Then, her voice rising with relief and new interest, she says, "We're on strike up here, that's why I'm home today. I know it's terrible for the kids, but business is business, right? Besides, they're probably grateful."

"Strike?"

"Yeah," Sissy says. "We're going to bury the bastards if they don't pay up. There've been promises—it's real complicated, but we're up against the school board and an old jerk named Watkins who'd just as soon see us work for room and board. Anyway, we've been out three weeks and no end in sight. I've got a little money tucked away, so it's all right. Maybe you ought to get a job yourself, give you something to take your mind off Albert. I mean, you never worked at all after we finished school, did you?"

"I worked in that hospital," Marie says.

"Oh that. That wasn't work, darling, that was recreation. Try getting an office job these days. Maybe you should take a graduate course? Or pottery, pottery's always good."

•

When Albert returns from work he goes directly into the yard to work on the hole. Marie watches him from the porch for a few minutes, then goes outside and sits in the passenger seat of their Plymouth station wagon, with the door closed, watching her husband. When, after twenty minutes of sustained digging, he stops to rest, she leans out the car window and says, "You're making this to hurt me, aren't you? I know. I know you, Albert."

"Maybe you're right," he says, looking at the hole. "About knowing me, I mean."

He climbs out of the hole, and Marie gets out of the car. They walk to the house together, side by side, their arms bumping into each other as they walk. He is thirty-nine years old. She is younger.

"I want to watch television tonight," he says. "And then make love. What do you say?"

"You're not trying to hurt me?"

"No, I'm not," he says, and he links arms with her and together they turn to survey the yard.

"But," she says.

"It'll be beautiful," he says. "Just wait."

Marie glances at the neighbor's crisp green bushes, then nods tentatively. "It's hard to understand."

They stand for a moment together on the concrete steps of the porch, then go into the house. Albert washes his hands in the kitchen sink while Marie burns the hairs off the chicken they will have for dinner.

"Why can't we refurbish an old house like everybody else?" she asks. "Or refinish furniture together?"

Albert looks at her and grins. "I lied about the television," he says, and he reaches for her with his hands still soapy, staggering across the kitchen, Frankenstein fashion.

She glares at Albert as hard as she can, then giggles and runs up the stairs very fast. At the landing she stops and leans over the rail and shouts, "I'm not having a baby, Albert!"

She slams the bedroom door, and Albert, who has followed her from the kitchen still acting out his monster role, allows his shoulders to slump, and sighs, and moves on up the stairs. He taps on the bedroom door with a knuckle. "Marie?" he calls through the door.

"What if it rains, Albert?"

"What?"

"My mother doesn't like you," Marie shouts. Then, a little less loudly, "Sissy likes you, but Sissy's ugly."

"What? Who's Sissy?"

"But you can't dig that hole anymore, or I will not do anything you want me to do," she says, still shouting as he enters the room.

"What are you talking about?" he asks.

"Promise me that you won't," she says. "Promise it's over."

"Oh Jesus," Albert says. "Forget the hole for shit's sake. It's just a hole. Jesus."

"Maybe it's just a hole to you, but it's more to me—it's something I don't want you to do—promise, Albert, please."

Marie is on the bed, her knees held tight by her arms up under her chin. She isn't smiling. Albert stands in the doorway with one hand still on the knob. "I just want so see what's under there," he says.

"You don't mean that," Marie says.

"I'm going downstairs to watch television," Albert says.

Much later, Marie tiptoes down the stairs to see what Albert is doing. He is asleep on the couch in front of the television set, and, seeing him asleep, Marie squats on the stairs and weeps.

•

The following morning Marie eats a late breakfast alone on the porch, staring at the hole through the screen door. It is a cool day, cooler than yesterday, and she feels the closeness of winter, sees it in the graying sky, smells it in the scent of the morning air. The leaves on the trees seem darker to her, as if mustered for a final battle with the season. Taking a fresh cup of coffee in her striped mug, she goes down the steps into the yard. She walks in circles around the hole there, sipping her coffee and surveying the perimeter of their property—the fragment of an old stone fence, a willow, some low bushes with unremarkable fat leaves. The lot is a little more than half an acre—large, Albert has said, for this particular development.

At first she gives the hole a wide berth, almost ignoring it, but as she completes her third circle, she bears in toward it, stopping a few feet from its edge at a point on its perimeter farthest from the house. The hole, she observes, is about five feet in diameter and four feet deep. The sides are cut at ninety degrees to the horizontal, and the bottom of the hole is very flat. Albert's spade is jammed into the spreading pile of dirt that borders the hole on the side away from the driveway. She drops to her knees in the still-damp grass of the lawn and then leans forward over the edge of the hole, looking to see what's inside. "Nothing," she says, "just nothing." She tosses the dregs of her coffee into the hole and watches the coal-colored earth turn instantly darker as it absorbs the liquid. "I don't know what Albert is so smug about," she says. "Just a damn hole in the ground, for Christ's sake." Marie walks forward on her knees and then pivots her legs over the edge and into the hole. Now she realizes that the hole is a little deeper than she had thought, that it is very nearly five feet deep. Standing in the hole she can barely see over its edge and her coffee mug, which is now only inches from her nose, looms very large. She bends to inspect the wall of the hole and finds there only ordinary dirt and a few small brown worms, working their ways across what is for them a suddenly brighter terrain. Above her the sky is going very dark, and the rain is no longer a suggestion, it is a promise. This makes her excited and nervous at once—like a child, she is seduced by the prospect of passing the rainstorm outside, in the splashing mud of the hole, in the cold of the water on her skin. Like an adult, she is apprehensive about getting out of the hole, about tracking the mud into the house, about the scrubbing that now seems inevitable. She looks at her hands, then her arms, then her feet and knees—all muddied—and her pink dressing gown, which is marked and smudged in a dozen places. "Oh my," she mutters. "I suppose I'd better not." But she doesn't make an effort to climb out of the hole, and instead sits down abruptly on the bottom, leaning her back against the dirt wall.

The rain comes. Fitfully at first, the few surprisingly large drops slap into the hole with what is to Marie a charming music. Then the storm is upon her and suddenly her gown is soaked through, showing darker brown where the cloth is stuck to her skin. Under her legs she feels a puddle beginning to form, then sees it, its surface constantly agitated by the rain. She pops the shallow water with the flat of her hand, and the dark splashes stain her gown, and she laughs, and she wipes thick strands of hair away from her face with a wet palm, laughing and splashing the water all about her, and then she begins to sing, in a very wonderful voice, "The Battle Hymn of the Republic," because she has always been a soldier in her heart.

(1982)

MOON DELUXE

You're stuck in traffic on the way home from work, counting blue cars, and when a blue-metallic Jetta pulls alongside, you count it—twenty-eight. You've seen the driver on other evenings; she looks strikingly like a young man—big, with dark, almost red hair clipped tight around her head. Her clear fingernails move slowly, like gears, on the black steering wheel. She watches you, expressionless, for a long second, then deliberately opens her mouth and circles her lips with the wet tip of her tongue. You look away, then back. Suddenly her lane moves ahead—two, three, four cars go by. You roll down the window and stick your head out, trying to see where she is, but she's gone. The car in front of you signals to change lanes. All the cars in your lane are moving into the other lane. There must be a wreck ahead, so you punch your blinker. You straighten your arm out the window, hoping to get in behind a van that has come up beside you, and you wait, trying to remember what the woman looked like.

Half an hour later you pull into the parking lot of the K & B Pharmacy. Inside you look at red jumper cables, a jigsaw puzzle of some TV actor's face, the tooled-leather cowboy belts, a case of cameras and calculators, the pebble-surfaced tumblers on the housewares aisle. At the medical supplies you try on several different finger splints, then stare at a drawing on a box containing some kind of shoulder harness designed to improve the posture. You look at toolboxes, opening the fatigue-green plastic ones, then the cardinal-red metal ones. You pick up a plumber's helper and try it out on the floor, surprised when it pops loose by itself—it reminds you of a camel getting off its knees. Near the stationery, you face a shelf of ceramic coin banks shaped and painted like trays of big crinkle French fries smothered in ketchup.

"Go on—buy one," says a girl walking by.

You turn and watch her shoulders; you do want something, suddenly, so you go back to the medical supplies and select Curad bandages, because the package is green. On the way to check out, you pick up a red toolbox. You buy these things.

Leaving the parking lot, you drive too fast and nearly hit a teenager, whose hair is straight down her back to her knees. She glares and gets into a grape-colored Porsche.

At the Creekside you go in through your patio gate, because it's closer to the assigned parking.

"Edward?" says a voice from outside the patio. "It's Eileen." You knew it was Eileen, a neighbor two apartments down, a divorcee. She's older, and you like her because she's easy to get along with.

"Hello, Eileen," you say, turning to face her, not sure exactly where she is along the cedar fence.

The slats wobble, and then Eileen's stiff hair, like a giant black meringue, rises over the top of the fence. "Bad traffic?" she says.

"Not good," you say, stooping to pick up the paper, which is stuck upright in the dirt of the flower bed.

She is teetering a little; you wonder what she's standing on to look over the fence. Then, glancing quickly over her shoulder, she almost whispers, "Do you want to come over later? I mean after you get settled? I have a friend for dinner. Two friends, in fact."

"Can I leave early, Eileen?"

She grins and nods rapidly several times, shaking the fence. "I knew you were the answer. See you at seven-thirty?" She waves and drops abruptly out of sight.

Inside, you spray a lettuce head with cold water and strip away the outer layer, dropping the brown-edged leaves into the Disposall. You pull fresh leaves, rinse and sugar them the way your mother did when you were a child, then eat, looking at the local news.

When you finish, you drop the small lettuce into the crisper at the bottom of the refrigerator and go upstairs. You look at your teeth in the bathroom mirror. They need brushing. You strip, start the water for a bath, and carry your clothes into the bedroom. You stand in front of the full-length mirror for a few seconds, looking at your skin.

Phil, Eileen's boyfriend and the owner of a local Mexican restaurant, opens her door. "Hello yourself," he says. "Come in. Ivy says you haven't been around much. Why'd you wear a coat—trying to make me look bad?"

You don't know why he calls her Ivy.

She is sitting on the arm of the couch, turned toward the door. "Hi," she says, her body so twisted, her arms and legs so tightly intertwined, that you think it must hurt her to sit that way. "Come and meet Lily."

As Eileen stands, you see Lily, her blonde hair smooth around her head like a soft hat. She wears green slacks, a red belt, a shiny violet undershirt, a white jacket. She quickly slips one hand into a baggy pocket and extends the other. "Amazing," she says. "I'd swear I've met this man somewhere before."

Phil and Eileen laugh; you shrug in what must look like an odd way and take her hand.

"She moved into Carmen's apartment," Eileen says, eyeing you. "He and Carmen had a thing," she says to Lily. "Only a small thing, but definitely a thing."

"Well, congratulations, son," Phil says, hitting you on the back. "Let's hope the record goes unblemished." He widens his eyes at you.

"Yes, let's," Lily says.

Phil wraps an arm over your shoulder, steering you to a glass-topped cart crowded with new liquor bottles. "Let's see," Phil says, grabbing a bottle by its neck and twisting it around so he can see the label. "Is it Scotch?" He turns the bottle so you can see the label.

"That'll be fine."

"You need to try bourbon, son." He twirls his stubby forefinger around in your drink and thrusts the glass at you. "Drink up. The night is young."

Phil retires to the kitchen to prepare his part of the dinner; Eileen gives you a little shove toward Lily, then follows Phil, who is opening and closing cabinet doors.

Rain starts popping on the patio, and you go to the window, pushing the drapes away from one edge of the glass.

"My roommate knew Carmen," Lily says. "That's how we got here."

"Your roommate?"

Lily turns toward you, and there's something odd about the way she looks you over. "Yes—Tony. Antonia, really. She loves this place—the palms, the walks, the tilework. Tony's an architect. It's all junk, but she likes it anyway."

The two of you watch bubbles slide down the window. In the background Phil and Eileen are laughing.

Finally, she says, "We can probably leave right after dinner, don't you think? I stayed the last time—Phil's magic tricks were funny."

At the table, Eileen hands you a bowl heaped with discs of fried potato—Phil's specialty. "Lily's just back from England," she says.

"Oh, yes?" you say, inadvertently passing the potatoes to Phil without taking any for yourself.

"Visiting my brother," Lily says.

"Lily's brother is one of those music types," Eileen says. "He has a band and pink hair."

"One of my people has *blue* hair," Phil says, putting a circle of potato into his mouth. "Nice kid, actually."

"Rudy doesn't have hair anymore," Lily says.

Phil belches agreement through his napkin and nods his head vigorously, like a horse. "Know what you mean," he says. Then, to Eileen, "Tell them about your sister, Ivy."

"Well," Eileen says, balancing her fork on the edge of her plate, "my sister's always been a bit of a problem in the family, you know—nothing serious, just a little more difficult than the rest of us. She has Raynaud's disease: circulation. Last winter, Mother noticed that Heather's palms were discolored—they were orange. Mother got very worried. She urged Heather to go to the doctor; Heather wouldn't go. Mother was telling us about this on the telephone all the time, and pretty soon she had us thinking Heather was going to lose her hands—that's what you have to do with Raynaud's, amputate. This went on for almost two months.

Telephones ringing all over the country. My brother calling me, and me calling Mother, and Julie—that's my other sister—calling, and David and Mother—"

"They get the idea," Phil says.

"So finally Mother forced Heather to see Dr. Shigekane, this tiny Japanese surgeon who did Mother's stomach and do you know what happened?"

"Carrots," cracks Phil.

Eileen nods. "Shigekane told her to quit eating carrots."

"See," Phil says, "the orange from the carrots was rubbing off on her hands, into the skin." He holds up a thick palm and pops the first finger of his other hand into it. "It was just too many carrots."

After coffee, Phil takes off his shoes and urges you to do the same. "Feels great," he says.

Lily says she has to get home and asks if you want to walk with her.

"I'd walk her myself," Phil says, "but Ivy'd never forgive me."

"I may not anyway," Eileen says, forcing a crisp little smile. Then, to you, "Now Edward, remember, she's just a young girl."

At the door, Lily kisses Eileen's cheek; Eileen laughs.

"Good to see you," Phil says, waving from the couch, where he's slumped, his green-stockinged feet propped on the glass coffee table.

Outside, the air is sweet and dense after the rain, the sidewalks are still wet, and as the two of you bend to go under a tree limb that hangs low over the path, Lily slips her hand into yours. When you turn to look, she lets go. All around you the building lights are glittering, reflecting through and off slick trees. Coming to a set of steps and a branching in the path near the pool, you say, "Sorry. Not thinking again. Do you want to walk?"

"You're not anxious to rush to my apartment and keep your record intact?"

"A persuasive argument. But we could walk first." You pluck some red berries off a bush that presses out over the sidewalk, then flick the berries, one by one, like marbles off your thumb.

Lily watches their flight, then drops quickly down the four steps and catches one of the berries in the air. Out of Eileen's bright apartment, framed by the bushes and the curving walk, Lily seems more comfortable.

"Sure," she says, juggling the berry awkwardly from hand to hand. "Let's take a walk. You can give me the tour. I haven't taken a walk with a man for God knows how long."

"We don't have to go."

"Don't be silly." She stops playing with the berry and motions for you to come down the steps. "It's a lovely night. Besides, I have something to tell you about as we walk—me. Can you stand it?" She loops her arm inside yours when you reach the bottom of the steps, then marches you off along the path leading away from the swimming pool. "Now, I don't want you to get upset by this," she begins, patting you encircled arm, and then she starts a rambling account where she was born, what her parents were like, where she went to school, how much she loves her brother Rudy. You walk on concrete and through wet grass, across parking lots, up and down steps, into more than one cul-de-sac, along the tiny creek after which the site is named. In all of Lily's story—which is punctuated by tugs on your arm, jokes, and laughter—there is nothing upsetting.

You're lost when you emerge from a tunnel of crape myrtles into a courtyard glowing with green light from the pool.

"You knew," you say. "You tricked me into taking you home."

"Isn't ours," Lily says. "The pool, I mean. This is the big one; we're next to the small one. Anyway, you're supposed to know this place better than I do."

You look at the staggered wood-and-stucco buildings. "Well, they all look alike. It's part of the charm, isn't it?"

"And confusing. We go this way," she says, skirting the deeper end of the pool.

"My feet have begun to squish," you say, stopping her. "Don't move—listen." You take several steps, exaggerating the movement like a mime.

"I don't hear them," Lily says.

"They didn't do it that time. Wait a minute."

But as you try to make the watery noise, Lily walks away. "You can dry them at the house," she says. "Come on. I told Tony I'd be back by nine, and it's already ten."

"So you're a little late," you say, jogging a few steps to catch up with her. "What's the big deal?"

"Tony," she says. "That's what I've been trying to tell you."

Antonia is the woman you saw in traffic; she's huge, extraordinary, easily over six feet. Taller than you. Her skin is glass-smooth and her pale eyes are a watery turquoise, Her hair is parted on one side, and brushed back flat to her scalp. She answers Lily's abbreviated knock wearing khaki shorts and a white T-shirt with "So many men, so little time" silk-screened in two lines across the chest.

"Irony," Lily says, pointing at the shirt. "Tony, meet tonight's Mr. Lucky."

"Come in," Antonia says. "Oh—I saw you today. You remember? In the car?"

Her thick lips are burnt red, pouting, traced with little cracks— she's stunning.

The apartment looks like the inside of a fifties-movie spaceship. It's almost empty. The few pieces of furniture are curiously placed, the walls are washed with light from track fixtures in the ceiling, and a serving cart stands in front of the sliding glass door. Two thick aluminum poles lean dumbly into one corner. A grainy photograph, the size of a window, shows a man with a black fedora and cane rolled up in a rug in a small room whose only other occupant is a wolf. At the far end of the apartment there are speakers the size of steamer trunks. There are no magazines or papers anywhere in the room.

"Would you like a drink?" Antonia says. "This is wonderful."

"His feet are wet, Tony," Lily says. She stands on her tiptoes and pecks the taller woman on the cheek. "He needs to take his shoes off."

"How about brandy?" Antonia says. She guides you to the squat Art Deco sofa, which is upholstered in fabric that looks like a yellow satin packing quilt. The sofa is squarely in the center of the room, facing the brightly lighted patio.

"Fine," you say. "Good."

"I'll bring a towel down when I come," Lily says from the foot of the stairs. "I'm going to change real quick."

"Don't be silly," you say, but she's already going up the steps.

"If they're wet, you'd better take them off," Antonia says, heading for the white wood cart, which has giant platter wheels on one end.

"What is that?" you ask, watching her bend to pull a bottle off the cart's bottom shelf.

"Just some junk cognac we got last year."

"No, I mean the cart there."

"Oh. It's a famous table—do you like it?"

"Certainly is crazy."

She laughs, stepping back to look at you. "I suppose it is. Maybe it's good." She hands you the snifter and pours a half inch of cognac. "That enough?"

"Fine," you say.

She looks at the label. "You always seem so fierce. You stare at me, you know. In the car sometimes. Have you been with Lily all night?"

"Don't answer that," Lily says, coming back into the room. "It's the brandy routine." She takes the seat beside you on the sofa and looks at Antonia. "Two years ago Tony's grandfather, who was a war correspondent or something, sent us this bottle of cognac—very fancy, very special. Both of us hate the stuff, so we've lugged the damn bottle with us everywhere, waiting for the chance to use it on some bobo. The trouble is, the stuff is too fancy, nobody ever heard of it."

"It's very nice," you say.

"Might as well be Ripple," Antonia says mournfully. Then she laughs. "I wouldn't drink it if I were you. Maybe you should put it on your feet."

"She's flashy," Lily says, shoving her friend away. "Isn't she flashy?"

"I can take a hint," Antonia says. "You two want to be alone, I can see that." She returns the bottle to its place on the cart, then goes to the turntable. "Young love, true love," she warbles softly as she thumbs through a stack of records.

"Funny, Tony," Lily says. "Why don't you come over here and sit down like a normal person?"

"I'm trying to find the *right* record for this moment," Antonia says. "If I don't find it, I'm going to have an episode. Oh, this is horrible, I think it's happening, Lily, I can't stand it. Lily—what record? What music? What? Quick, grab my hands, grab my feet."

"Tony," Lily says, smiling at you. "We have a guest."

"I know it, I know," Antonia says. "Quick! I can't touch another record. I'm slipping away."

Lily gets up and goes to the turntable, takes Antonia's wrists, walks her robot style back to the sofa, and sits her down.

"I feel better," Antonia says. "I definitely feel better now."

Lily stands beside the sofa, gently. straightening Antonia's boyish hair. "That's the whole show," Lily says. "Another great performance."

"I don't know what I'd do without you," Antonia says. "Edward's not a threat, is he? You're not a threat, are you, are you, Edward?"

"I don't guess so. To my dismay."

"What a wonderful thing to say," Lily says. She combs Antonia's hair with her fingers, drawing it into funny points behind the ears.

"What about me?" Antonia says, reaching up for Lily's hands. She looks at you. "Or say I can come too—otherwise I'll feel left out."

Lily presses her fingers over Antonia's eyes, bends forward, and whispers, "You'll be the guest of honor, Tony. You'll have the best seat in the house."

"I feel better," Antonia says. She pulls Lily's hands away, turns them, then kisses the sharp nails.

"I'm going," you announce. You get up from the sofa, brush the thighs of your jeans, then push your hands into your coat pockets.

You wonder what it would be like if they invited you to stay the night, to sleep on the splendid yellow couch, to have a hurried breakfast with them before work, to be part of their routine.

For a second nobody moves and then Antonia falls sideways on the sofa and turns onto her back, her knees folded over the sofa arm farthest from you. She reaches up and grabs your wrist through your coat, looking at you upside down. "I should have smiled, I guess," she says. "I should have just smiled." When she releases you, her arms fall behind her on the couch and the T-shirt pulls out of the waist of her pants, showing the dark curves of her stomach, the lemony hair below her navel.

Both women walk you to the door, lead you out into the courtyard, walk ahead of you a few steps toward the pool. You follow, looking at their backs, then at the low sky. "This is crazy," you say when they stop by the small diving board.

"I see that," Lily says.

"You do?" Antonia says.

Then, one after the other, the women kiss you with their lips awkwardly, resolutely shut. You circle the diving board, turn, and walk backward across the courtyard, watching Lily and Antonia, hand in hand, vanish into their apartment. There is a moon. You can definitely feel the water in your shoes. Pool lights are waving on the sides of the buildings.

(1982)

Box Step

Ann is pretty, divorced, a product model who didn't go far because of her skin, which is very fair and freckled. After lunch, she comes into my recently redecorated office—the company has done both of its floors in charcoal carpet, ribbed wallcovering, chipboard-gray upholstery, and gunmetal Levolors; the windows were already tinted. "I feel like I'm inside a felt hat," she says, waving a manila folder to indicate the room. "Your socks don't match, Henry." She points to my feet, which are balanced on the taupe Selectric II, then holds the folder out at arm's length. "The arrangements. You want to check me?"

The arrangements are for a regional sales meeting we've scheduled for the Broadwater Beach Hotel, in Biloxi; with the meeting still two weeks off, the preparations are complete. We picked Biloxi because of the beach, the Gulf, the rest of that; Ann did most of the work.

"What I really need is a new game."

She tosses the folder on my desk and stands by the window, smoothing her salmon-colored skirt with both hands. "What happened to the Ant Farm?"

"Died. The ants ate parts of each other. The parts they didn't eat they carried around—it wasn't fun."

She swings one of the gray Italian visitor's chairs around to face the window. "People don't have Ant Farms anymore anyway."

"I put it in the closet."

She nods, then puts her handbag on the corner of my desk and sits in the chair. "We should get a radio."

"I want you to come for drinks," I say, rolling my executive armchair to the window to inspect my socks. She meant they don't match each other.

"Is that a good idea?"

"I need help with these," I say, pointing to the socks.

"I'm flattered." Her skirt splits over her knees as she crosses her legs. She looks outside at a wet tree and at the startlingly bare office park. There's a seam in her hose across the open toe of one of her apricot pumps. "But you hate drinks, I'm vulnerable, and it's unseemly."

"Probably damage our working relationship." In the three months since Ann started working for me, she's been to my apartment once, to get a signature on some papers the week after my tonsillectomy; having her in the apartment made me nervous.

Karl Peters, a coworker who wants to be a supervisor, sticks his head in my office door. "Hard at it?" he says, cracking his knuckles by pressing his fingers against the metal doorframe.

"Not me," Ann says. "I'm watching this rain and planning a giant party tonight at Henry's."

Peters hitches up his slacks, steps into the doorway, then turns sideways and leans against the frame. "You're serious? Hank's having people to his house?"

"No," Ann says, not looking away from the window. She doesn't like Karl; he knows it and can't leave her alone.

He wags a thumb at her back and gives me a knowing grin with lots of beige teeth. "I'd like to bring you know who, but I guess she's working." Then he slaps the wall and says, "I'll be there at eight, ready for anything."

When he's gone, I say, "Earth to Ann," and she twists her head backward over the chair to be sure we're alone.

"He's a spook," she says. "Why'd you invite him? Now you have to invite somebody I like or I'm not coming. I'll go to the movies instead."

I swivel the chair through a complete circle. "Maybe Amos. You like Amos, don't you? I like Amos."

"He's wonderful, but I want somebody else, too. What about Gillian?"

Gillian's my older sister. Ann talks to her on the phone every week when she calls to see how I am. Gillian sells real estate out of a room in her house on Short Bay Street; she's single and the black sheep, and the only member of my family it is always a pleasure to see.

"Okay. What's Amos's number? You call Gillian." I pick up the receiver. "Karl won't come anyway. I promise."

"I play hostess? Are we sure about this?"

"We could go out."

"Maybe next week," Ann says.

I call Amos and invite him for after dinner. He says he'll talk to his wife and get back to me. "He's going to ask Felicia," I tell Ann.

"She'll probably hate me. Are you sure Karl won't come? I'm nervous."

"Me too, all the time. I don't know why."

•

I have a new dinosaur, a toy eight inches tall with an oddly human torso and perfectly proportioned legs. On its belly, in a small raised script, the word "Continental" curves over an embossed crown. The toy is a rubbery dirt-black with green trim, which looks sprayed on, and red eyes. At home with Ann and Gillian I turn it upside down, spilling wonton soup and rice out of its hollow inside onto my place-mat. I ask the dinosaur if it wants a Gelusil, then wipe the toothy mouth with a napkin. The women laugh.

"He's a jerk," Gillian says.

"He had too much to eat," Ann says. She starts to clean up the mess I've made, but I elbow her away and clean it myself, wiping at the soup with a napkin, sweeping the rice into my palm from the edge of the polyurethaned white-pine tabletop.

"Henry I mean," my sister says.

Ann walks across the room and sits on the Victorian sofa. "He's a trifle nervous, the Hulk is, socially."

"That's not attractive," Gillian says. "Hulk."

"Can we get this cleaned up before the guests arrive?" I say, waving my fistful of rice at the dinner table.

"Do our best, Chief," Gillian says. She carries her plate to the kitchen.

Ann gets off the sofa and comes up to me with her palm out. "The rice, please." I give her the rice and the soupy napkin, then take the dinosaur into the bathroom to rinse its throat.

Amos and Felicia are early. I answer the door, follow them into the living room of my apartment, then do the introductions. Felicia's making fun of Amos. "He's wearing this Izod shirt, did you notice? He's very style-aware."

Gillian hugs Amos and frowns over his shoulder at Felicia. "I think he looks nice. The shirt's yellow."

"So this is Ann," Felicia says, shaking hands with Ann. "We hear a lot about you at our house." Felicia does an ugly little twist of her lips and then turns away, looking around the apartment.

"Hi," Ann says.

Amos picks Ann off the floor, twirls once, and puts her down on the sofa.

"Aren't you afraid you'll break her bones?" Felicia says.

"She's got bones like a horse," I say.

Felicia makes a face at me. "That's exactly what I mean, Henry."

Gillian says, "He doesn't mean the leg bones, Felicia, he means the other horse bones."

"Right," I say.

"Just beer for me," Amos says. He's in the corner of the room, looking at the zither, which is balanced on top of one of the natural-finish stereo speakers. He plucks a few strings, then looks at himself in a mirror mounted on the wall. "This reminds me of something," he says.

The doorbell rings. Ann pops up from the sofa and starts for the door. "Who's that? Is that Karl?"

"I hope so," Felicia says. She's leafing through an *Artscanada* from a stack of magazines on the coffee table. She turns to see Ann leave the room, then says, "What's so special about her?"

Amos sits on the sofa next to Gillian, who's brought a tray of Löwenbräu bottles and Pier 1 glasses. "My Felicia," he says, pointing to his wife.

Ann has a conversation at the door, but in the living room we can't quite hear what is being said. Amos hands a bottle of beer and a glass to Felicia and sits down again, taking a second bottle off the tray. He drinks from the bottle, then throws his arm over the back of the sofa and sighs. "This is nice," he says.

Felicia walks around the room filling her glass, ducking her head to suck the foam before it drips on her hand.

When Ann comes back from the door, she says, "Paper boy. I told him we take already."

"We?" Felicia says.

Gillian makes a little snorting sound. "Some of us are crazy for friendship."

Amos points around the room at the pictures and the few pieces of furniture. "You've changed it again, Hank. How come you're always changing it?"

"He doesn't want anybody to know what it looks like," Ann says. "I guess."

"This is new," Felicia says. She's standing in front of a framed Hockney print. "This one of those fifteen-dollar things he did a million of?"

"Wow," Gillian says, wiping her mouth with her wrist.

Amos slides forward on the peach-colored sofa and turns to look at Gillian. "So, what's new in real estate?"

"Henry got a new dinosaur," she says, nodding toward the toy, which is on its back legs, poised, on the dining table.

"Yeah," Amos says. "I saw it first thing when I came in. Is it yawning? Where'd you get it, Henry?"

I hold up the dinosaur. "T.G. & Y. Where else?"

Felicia wheels around and stares fiercely at me. "That's clever, Henry," she says, and she picks up her tan purse and stalks out, slamming the apartment door as she goes.

"Mistake?" I say.

"I'd better go after her," Amos says. He gets up from the couch and clicks his bottle back onto the tray. "It's nothing, Henry. I'll tell you about it tomorrow."

I walk him out; when I come back, Gillian is stretched on the sofa, unscrewing the cap of a new beer, and Ann is sitting at the table eating raisins out of a big red box.

"What's that about?" Gillian says. "They okay?"

"I guess. What did I say?"

"Said you bought this dinosaur," Ann says, picking up the toy. "That's all I heard." She gets up from the table, taking the dinosaur with her, and starts dancing, doing the box step, with the toy her partner. She hums and circles the room like a girl in a cowboy movie anticipating her first gala. When she's finished, she holds the dinosaur at arm's length, then pulls it to her and kisses it solidly on the jaw. "You're light on your feet," she says to the toy. "Or whatever these things are."

•

At nine the next morning Karl is sitting on the edge of Ann's desk, sipping coffee from a gray company mug. "Sorry I missed the party, Hank. I hear Felicia threw a fit."

"Don't look at me," Ann says.

I look at her. "Did we get the mail yet?"

She points at my open office door. "Karl was telling me that he went to a topless bar last night," she says. "All the women looked like me. He's going back tonight."

I look at Karl. He pushes off the desk, puts his mug on the blotter, and straightens his vest.

"And he thinks my underclothes don't fit."

"She's mad at me," Karl says, shrugging. "By the way, how's the meeting? Everything set?"

When I nod, he says, "Great," and walks off quickly. Ann follows me into my office. The mail is stacked in two piles on my desk. I start throwing away the junk while she adjusts the blinds to cut out the morning sun.

"Julio called last night," she says. Julio is her ex-husband, a photographer; he lives in Atlanta. "He wanted to know all about you."

"He should get together with Felicia. Where'd you put the base-ball game?"

She bends across the desk and tries to open one of the drawers, but the desk is locked. "There," she says, tapping the drawer.

"So you told him what? About me I mean."

"I told him you weren't just a jerk." She pushes back off the desk, straightening the mail as she does so.

Amos comes in, carrying a small glass vase with two flowers in it. He presents the flowers to Ann.

She makes a joke out of the present, but it's obvious that she's touched. "Thank you," she says, leaning forward to kiss him on the cheek.

I unlock my desk and open the drawer Ann pointed to; the three-year-old electronic baseball game is in its box at the back of the drawer. "You want to play me, Amos?" I push the remaining mail to one side and point to the chair opposite mine. "Just one inning, what do you say?" I switch the game onto automatic for some practice, but even that's too hard for me. I miss several pitches.

Amos comes around behind my desk to look over my shoulder. "Sorry about last night," he says. "Connie—you remember our daughter Connie, don't you? Well, she's living with the manager of this T.G. & Y. over here on Snap Street—the one where you got the dinosaur, I think—and anyway, Felicia's upset. Connie's quit school again, and the guy's been married a couple of times—it's not a great deal."

A pitch goes right by my batter, making the third out, and I switch off the machine. "I'm sorry, Amos."

"Felicia has her abandoned with a kid already," he says. "I don't like it either, but—" He raises his hands and shakes them at the ceiling, goes back around the desk, and looks out the door at Ann, who is standing by her desk, facing away from us. "She won't be mad, will she? Ann I mean."

"Don't be silly. She likes you."

"I hope so," Amos says.

Ann's skirt is made out of a shiny red fabric that looks as if it could be used for space suits. She's wearing a transparent chiffon blouse and her usual three-inch heels—today they're opera pink. When Amos leaves, she catches me staring at her and makes a fish face.

•

At four o'clock I ask Ann to give me a ride home. "I was going shopping," she says, putting the papers on her desk into stacks, and putting objects—the tape dispenser, the stapler, the pencil holder—on top of the stacks. "I'll go to a movie, maybe." She tucks a rose straw handbag under her arm. In the parking lot I get into her new Ford sedan, banging my knees on the dashboard because she has the seat pulled so far forward.

The theatre is small, one of four in a storefront that's part of a shopping center near the office—the shopping center where I got the dinosaur. By the time we get inside, the four-twenty show has started. Ann leads the way in the darkness, carrying popcorn and Coke. Halfway to the front she stops and steps aside. "Here," she whispers. I take the second seat in and she takes the aisle. The seats are dark plush—blue, or purple—and they rock. As the screen brightens after the credits, I see that there's no one else in the theatre. We hand the popcorn back and forth, staring at the screen.

After the movie we stop outside the theatre to look at the coming-attractions posters. It's just beginning to get dark, and the streetlights are lime against the pale sky. The store signs have come on, blinking in oranges and blues and bright whites; along Snap Street the cars have amber and red running lights. The parking lot has fresh yellow lines on new blacktop, and off to the right clear bulbs dangle on black wires over Portofino's Fine Used Cars.

"Pretty," she says, looping her arm through mine and pulling us off the curb toward her car.

"Wait a minute," I say. "I'll be right back. I'll be just a minute." I trot along the edge of the parking lot in front of the stores; when somebody honks, I jump up onto the curb and go along the covered walkway in front of the big display windows, slapping at the square metal columns that support the overhang.

Amos's daughter is the only person in the T.G. & Y.: she's tall and thin, with jagged-cut almost silver hair and punk-rock makeup. I say hello and tell her I don't know how I failed to recognize her yesterday.

"I recognized you," she says. "Did you want another dinosaur?"

"Sure." We walk down the aisle to the toy dinosaurs. Yesterday they were all jumbled together, but someone has straightened them, arranged them in flat-footed rows, so that the thirty or so rubber toys stare straight at us, scarlet eyes glaring, jaws wide, square white teeth silhouetted against dark throats.

"Which kind did you want today?"

I wonder why I've forgotten the names of the dinosaurs.

"Mr. Pfeister?"

"I think—one of these." I pick up a fleshy green dinosaur with a double line of large triangular fins running down its back. "You like this one?"

Connie giggles, then stops suddenly and stares at the toy in my hand. She seems nervous, and she doesn't know what to say; she wants me to leave. I stroke the toy's head as if it were a cat's. Finally Connie says, "Yeah. That's my favorite."

As we walk toward the cash register, I toss the toy from hand to hand, almost dropping it once because of the fins. Ann has pulled the car up along the curb in front of the T.G. & Y.

"You want a bag for him?" Connie asks.

"I don't think I need a bag, really." I strip the price tag off the dinosaur's foot and press the adhesive square onto the cuff of my shirt. "What's the tax on a dollar ninety-nine?"

"Twelve cents. It's two-eleven."

I give her two bills and drop two nickels and a penny into her cupped palm. When she starts to go behind the register, I grab her shoulder. She turns around, not sure what is coming next; I smell her perfume, which I think is the same one Ann wears. "I talked to Amos."

"I know," she says. She looks sad, resigned. "They talked to me. I don't know what to do about them."

I look outside at Ann, sitting in the Ford, her head turned toward the street, and I watch a short woman usher two small kids into the store. "Here's the answer: Do what you want and have an okay time. You can change it all later if you want to."

The woman with the kids has stopped just inside the door. She stares at us, pulls a can the size of a deodorant spray out of her purse, and advances, pointing the nozzle at my head. "You'd better ease up," she says. "You'd better just back off."

Connie is laughing—she can't stop laughing. A skull-and-crossbones is printed on the label of the can the woman is waving at my face. I let go of Connie's shoulder, but Connie doesn't move. "No, no," she says to the woman. "We're all right. Mr. Pfeister's a friend—really he is." Connie grins and wraps her arm around my back, pressing her cheek into my shoulder. "He works with my father," she explains to the woman.

"You're sure?" The woman is wary, reluctant to put away her weapon. "I can still blast him if you want me to."

Connie shakes her head.

"Well, it was hard to tell at first, the way he was holding you." The woman caps the spray can and drops it into the crinkle-finish plastic purse strung over her shoulder. "No offense, guy."

I shrug and show her the dinosaur. "Can't be too careful."

There's a click-click on the window glass; it's Ann, standing on the sidewalk, making a gesture that I take to mean "What's going on?" I wave at her and say, "Be out in a minute," and she does a puppet-like step and starts for the car.

"Is that your wife?" Connie asks, pointing outside.

The woman with the can moves off toward the back of the store to collect her kids, who are riding the cheap tricycles in circles around the inflatable swimming pools.

"Yes." I fluff the collar of Connie's blouse, then look at Ann. "Yes, it is."

Connie goes behind the counter and starts punching buttons on the register. When the cash drawer slides out, she catches it with her hip and slaps my two bills into the dollar compartment. "She seems very nice. When did you get married?"

"Recently. A couple of months ago. She was my secretary."

"No kidding?" Connie grins pleasantly, then reaches under the counter and pulls out a white T.G. & Y. bag, which she holds open alongside the register. "Do you mind?" she says. "It's store policy. Nothing goes out without a bag."

•

Ann drives us to a restaurant on the edge of town. I tell her about Connie and the manager, and about the woman with the aerosol; she smiles and then laughs. The restaurant is an old house that somebody has recently redone, extending it out in back over a shallow ravine. It's called the Blue Crab, but it has an automobile-size lobster hovering over the entrance. We get a table by a window and, because Ann is hungry, order at once. There are blue lights strung over the ravine.

She looks at the lights and at the flat, peanut-butter-colored water below them. "This isn't so bad," she says.

"Thanks."

"I mean, it's at least possible." She shakes her head a couple of times and fingers the clean black dish ashtray. "So—you want me to teach you to smoke?"

"I forgot something," I say, sliding my chair away from the table. I go out to the car and retrieve the T.G. & Y. bag from the floor in the front seat; there's a little chain of perspiration on my forehead when I get back to the table and make the presentation. The appetizers arrive. Ann loosens the staple at the top of the bag with her fingernail, hands me the receipt, opens the bag, and peers inside.

"I deserve this," she says.

She takes the dinosaur out, hops it onto the table, and stands it up between our place settings. The toy rests on its hind feet and tail; the fins on its back gleam; it looks as if it's singing. Ann shakes hands with the dinosaur the way one shakes hands with a dog; then she feeds it one of her tiny white shrimp. She says, "Welcome to America, Reuben."

"Welcome to Romper Room," Felicia says. She and Amos and Karl and his wife have come up alongside our table.

Amos moves behind Ann and puts his hands on her shoulders. "You guys want to join us? They've got to have a table for six somewhere." He scans the room, still holding Ann's shoulders.

Karl starts to introduce his wife, but she stops him and says, "Hi, I'm Celeste Peters. You're Henry's Ann?" She reaches past her husband to shake hands with Ann, then nods at me. "Hello, Henry."

"Why don't you join us?" Karl says. "You can't work all the time."

"We're not working, Karl," I say.

Ann reaches up and rubs the back of Amos's hand. "We had to go see this Amy Irving movie," she says, looking up at Amos. "He's sick for Amy Irving."

Karl snickers and slaps me on the back. "What he needs is a visit from the Girl Fairy. No offense, Ann."

Amos moves back to Felicia and puts his arm around her waist. "Well, we can't stand here all night. Let's get a table and eat. I'm starved." He nods at me as he guides Felicia away.

The four of them follow a short Chinese waiter off toward one of the other rooms in the restaurant. The guy who's sitting immediately behind Ann turns around and frowns at me, then watches Amos and the others walk off. When he's made his point, he turns back to his table.

The food arrives, and we eat without saying much. Ann repeatedly glances over her shoulder; I push my snapper around on the plate, and after ten minutes I signal the waiter. He comes with the check and is very careful—sliding his little tray onto the thick white tablecloth—not to upset the dinosaur.

●

It's two hours to Biloxi. I drive. The highway is white and empty, and Ann falls asleep sitting sideways in the passenger seat. The Ford seems to float on the road; I like the sound of it—sealed and moving fast through the narrow landscape. I go in through Gulfport, then along the water until the Broadwater Beach sign comes into view. The parking lot needs repair; the car hits a hole and the jolt wakes Ann, who yawns discreetly as I steer into a space between two Volvo station wagons. When we get out of the car, there's a terrific wind blowing in off the Gulf, bending the palm trees and a big live oak that looks as if it must be two hundred years old. The wind pushes our clothes around; we have to lean into it just to get to the outer edge of the parking lot for a look at the beach. Some cars go by. Out over the water there's a helicopter with a police-type searchlight that flicks on and off at intervals; now and then I hear the thuck-thucking of the helicopter blades. High-school kids run back and forth across the four lanes between the hotel and the beach. They go by in groups—mostly all boys or all girls—yelling to each other, waving beer cans. Some of them are wearing cutoffs, school jerseys, and beat-up running shoes; others have on high-waisted white slacks and open Hawaiian shirts. The wind is loud; when it hits, it feels thick on my skin. A couple of blocks away, on the water side of the highway, there's a large, turreted building, a souvenir palace, bright against the dark sky, all lighted up with colored floodlamps—salmon pinks and hot violets—and, surrounding it, an elaborate miniature-golf complex of castles and spaceships, with monsters guarding the holes. On the roof, shuttling back and forth over the tops of the letters in "Souvenirs," a hugely swarthy 3-D pirate in pirate boots and polka dots brandishes a neon cutlass and cackles mechanically. Ann takes a close look at my face, then at the pirate's, loops her arm through mine, and yanks me into the traffic.

(1982)

Fish

Sally meets me in the driveway. "It's great you're back," she says. She's tall, willowy, tailored. "I'm going to a German movie at the university, but I'll be home right after. Will you be here?"

"Sure," I say. "You look great." I watch her get into her car, a red Audi four-door.

I've just rented a house from her younger brother and he's invited me to dinner. He comes out waving a rolled-up newsmagazine. "Already?" he says to her. "He hasn't even moved in yet, Sally." He kisses the magazine and waves it at her, and she gives him a drop-dead smile.

He comes down the concrete steps and stands alongside me in the drive. When she pulls away he puts an arm on my shoulder and pokes me in the stomach with the magazine. "There's a thing about elephants in here. You want to read it?"

"Sure. What's it say?"

It's cool for October, but Minor's wearing shorts. He insists we eat on the deck behind his house. His legs are bony and pink. "Go on and wear your coat if you're chilly," he says. "Sally's got everything set. All I've got to do is pop it in the microwave. I want to have a drink first, though." I follow him into the house and then out onto the deck. He puts a wedge of lime on the rim of his glass and points to the white director's chair next to his. "Check out the natural beauty," he says, waving toward the backyard.

A bug twice the size of my thumb is skittering up the side of the swimming pool. He hasn't filled the pool since last year, he tells me. He stares straight across the yard. There are pads of fat under his eyes. "So what do you think of the color?"

44

"Terrific," I say.

The walls of the pool are dark blue. He had it drained and painted by some kids from the junior high school, friends of a friend's daughter, he tells me. They worked a long time to get the color just the way Minor wanted it. They even built a model and painted it, then filled it with water to be sure of the color. "Sally can't pass up a movie. She says I should go with her." He sticks a couple of fingers in the waistband of the shorts. "You like elephants? You ought to take that article home with you. It's incredible what's happening to elephants."

"I want to read it," I say, pouring myself a glass of tonic. We sit on the redwood deck for a few minutes looking out into the yard.

"So, Ben, we haven't had a chance to talk. What've you been up to? What is it—ten years? Fifteen?"

"Seems longer," I say.

"Know what you mean," he says, nodding seriously. "Same here. I bought this place originally for Mama and Dad, but they moved to Tampa in seventy-eight, so I took it over. I had a restaurant and a shop, but I quit that—figured I could do better. I've sold a lot of glass animals, Ben. I started buying property in seventy-five. Sally lived in the yellow bungalow next to you there, after I bought it, but then she married this guy Paul, an art director, and they moved to Atlanta. She came back after the divorce."

"She looks good," I say.

Minor laughs and pulls at the leg of his shorts. "Always did."

I finish my tonic and pour another half glass. "So, how many houses do you have?"

Six," he says. "You know, she wanted to marry you. Everybody got crazy about that—what were you, seventeen? So Sally threatens to quit school and get an apartment." He picks at the fly of his pants. "After you went to college there was this guy named Frank. He did better than you."

"What do you mean?" I stick my hands into my coat pockets, but I can't stop myself from shivering.

"You know what I mean," Minor says. "He got her right there in the garage. First time out." Minor squeezes his neck. "You chilly? It's cold out here, isn't it?"

"I'm freezing, as a matter of fact."

He snorts and stands up, tossing the ice from his drink out into the pool. "I felt bad for you when I saw that," he says. "Really."

The kitchen is a narrow room with a four-bulb fluorescent light fixture mounted on the ceiling. The wallpaper is marigolds and buttercups. There's a round butcher-block table pushed into one corner of the room. "It's easier to eat in here, I guess," Minor says. "Anyway, I want to keep an eye on the microwave. You know about microwaves?" He hustles around the kitchen, selecting dishes, checking the food already in the oven. In a couple of minutes he serves two pale-looking steaks and some cut green beans that have golden spots all over them. "Think I overdid these," he says, rolling beans onto my plate. "They should taste okay though. See if they're crunchy."

I spear a couple of beans, avoiding the splotched ones. "Good," I say. "What about cable? You get cable out here?"

He picks a bean off my plate and chews thoughtfully. "Crap," he says. "This ain't crunchy." He scrapes my beans back into the casserole. "You go ahead and start. I'll do up something else." He plants a shoe on the garbage can pedal and dumps the beans into the can.

"Sure," I say, cutting the steak. "We had this great cable TV in Ohio—thirty channels. Incredible stuff. The Playboy channel, three superstations, everything. Twenty-four-hour sports—you get that?"

"Nope." He touches the microwave key pad, setting the oven to defrost and cook frozen broccoli. The oven chirps every time he touches a number.

"I guess I'll get by without it," I say. "I didn't use it that much."

He points at the microwave. "We're interfering at the molecular level," he says. "You're going to love this broccoli."

The phone rings. Minor takes the receiver off the wall and says hello, bending to look inside the oven. He listens for a minute, then puts his palm over the mouthpiece and says, "It's Sally. She and her friend left the movie and they want us to go eat at Cafe 90."

"Sure," I say, waving my fork. "It's up to you—you haven't eaten yet."

"Forget it," Minor says into the phone. "We're staying put."

By the time he's ready to eat I'm on my second cup of coffee. He puts a sprig of broccoli on a butter plate for me.

"Very nice," I say, trying the broccoli. "Very tender."

"Does anything," he says, his mouth full of steak. "Anything. Bacon, eggs—bake you a potato in five minutes. You want a potato?"

I hold up my hands. "Not tonight, thanks."

"I'm not pressing," Minor says. "You don't want a potato, that's fine with me. I'm just being polite." He finishes the piece of steak he's chewing and cuts the rest of the meat on his plate into bite-size sections. When that's done he looks up, stares at me for a minute as if he's trying to recall who I am. "You probably don't even like broccoli."

"Sure I do. Broccoli's one of my favorites."

Minor's face is bloated and tight. "Crap. That's crap. You're almost squirming there, you know that? Doesn't make any difference to me. I'm set up. I got my houses, Sally—you're the renter." He wags a hand at me, wiping his mouth with a yellow napkin. He gets a quart of Miller beer from the refrigerator and takes a drink, then points the bottleneck at me. "You want beer?"

"Yes." I dump the last of my tonic into the sink and start to rinse my glass.

He looks at the ceiling. "Why don't you just get a new glass, huh? We've got glasses. Check the cabinet."

I get a mug out of the cabinet, and he pours the beer.

"You want to sit in here?" he says when I sit down again. "We don't have to sit in here. Why don't we sit in the other room?"

"Sure. Great. Let's sit in there. What the hell. You don't want to go to the bar?"

"No," he says, heading into the den.

The only light in there is green and comes from a twenty-gallon fish tank under one window. Minor climbs into a recliner and a small footrest pops out from under the seat. He points to the matching sofa. "She'll be home quick enough."

I sit on the sofa arm and look into the aquarium. The filtering system is bubbling, but there aren't any fish. "Hobby?" I say, touching the glass.

"She won't feed 'em. I try, but sometimes I'm late getting home, this and that." He twists his head to look at the aquarium. "I've got one angel left, stuck in the castle—see the castle? Went in a month ago and now he can't get out. I drop food on him but I figure he'll belly-up pretty quick." Minor wipes his forehead and takes another drink from the quart. "Look on the side there, see if you can see in that window in the turret or whatever it's called."

The castle is four shades of green and two of pink. There's an opening as big as a stamp in one side, and through the opening I see the stripes on the fish, which is tilted at about forty-five degrees. The gills flap a little. "He's breathing," I say.

"Look at his eyes."

"I can't see his eyes. All I can see is his side."

"Bang the glass."

I tick on the glass with my fingernail and the fish jerks a couple of times. Then one eye appears in the hole in the castle wall. "There he is," I say. "He looks sick."

Minor sighs. "I told her to get him out of there last week, but I guess she didn't."

"You want me to do it?"

He squints at me, then shrugs. "I guess you'd better leave him alone. He's probably grown or something." He gets up and comes over to the aquarium. "I don't know why she couldn't just take care of this," he says, sticking a hand into the water. He uproots the castle, and the fish slips out and into a tangle of aquarium grass, its body still leaning.

"Hiya, pal," Minor says, looking down into the tank. He replaces the castle, twisting it into the dirty white rocks to seat it securely. "Looks like a little dead guy, doesn't he?" He pinches some food into the tank above where the angelfish is swimming, then closes the cover and returns to his chair. "He wasn't the pretty one to start with. Really. You know what I'm saying?"

Sally is four years older than Minor, my age. "I'm glad you stayed," she says when she comes in. "He told me you were taking the house, but I thought he was messing around."

"Who's this 'he' you're always talking about?" Minor says.

She ignores him. "Minor says he feels very close to you. He says you might as well be family."

"Not quite what I said, Piggy."

"Oh hush, Minor." She pulls her sweater over her head and arranges her hair with her fingers. She's wearing a white T-shirt with "Girl" stitched in red above the small pocket. "He always calls me Piggy when he gets mad," she says, looking at Minor. "It's his way of telling me that I'd better watch out. Anyway, Betty wanted to come back with me, to meet you, but her boy has a fever so she couldn't. I told her we'd have you and she for dinner one night soon."

"Betty's your class-B divorcée," Minor says.

Sally makes a small ticking sound with her lips and rolls her eyes. "This one," she says, pointing a thumb toward Minor, "wouldn't know a divorcée from a koala bear." She reaches under the shade of a floor lamp and turns on the light. "How come it's so dark in here?"

"I let the fish out," Minor says, motioning toward the aquarium.

"Well thank God for that," she says. She goes to the aquarium and bends to look inside. "Poor baby's nearly dead, it looks like."

She reaches for the fish food but stops when he says, "I already did that."

"Fed him too?" She looks at me. "He's a take-charge kind of guy, my brother." She waves at the angelfish, then turns around and shakes her head. "I'm getting something to eat before I faint. You want anything? A sandwich?"

"Nope," he says.

I pick up the magazine that has the elephant story in it. "We just ate, thanks."

"He explained the microwave, I'll bet," she says.

Minor makes a face at her back as she disappears into the kitchen. "How was the movie?"

"The seats were hard and the sound was awful," she says. "The guys behind me were arguing with the guys behind them about smoking grass in the theatre. That's why we left. This one guy leaned over to me and whispered something, and I thought he said he was going to burn my hair off. He must've had a speech defect. What he said was could he borrow a lighter. What's with the beans in the garbage?"

"We had a bean problem," Minor says. "I did broccoli instead."

"It was very tender," I say.

Sally comes out of the kitchen carrying a tiny glass of milk and a plate of crackers, cheese cubes, and apple slices. "I hate broccoli, but my friend Ann makes me eat it because she says it kills cancer. I just love Ann. She's so great even he likes her, don't you?"

Minor crosses the room to look at Sally's plate, then wags his head. "Maybe we should get her and Betty over together and let Ben take his choice, how's that?"

"Maybe he'll want both of them," Sally says. "How come you ate so late?" She balances a cheese cube on a cracker and puts the cracker into her mouth. "Oh, never mind. I don't want to know."

"You," he says. "Ben and you. That's the reason."

"Too bad we didn't stick together," she says to me. "Paul was a lizard."

"She hates her ex-husband," Minor says. "She likes to hate people."

"Uh-huh," Sally says, holding the milk glass close to her lips. "Pete Rose I totally hate."

"That's so easy," Minor says. He's standing in front of the aquarium.

"I'll bet Pete Rose smells funny," she says.

Minor yawns. "I'm real tired."

"Now wait a minute," she says. "I just got here. I haven't had a chance to talk yet."

"I ought to go on," I say, flipping through the magazine. "I've got elephants to do."

Minor squats and leans his forehead against the aquarium. "I hate this fish," he says. "Can we get rid of this fish? He's driving me nuts."

"Maybe we could give him away," Sally says.

Minor rubs his nose on the glass and starts to say something but then stops and swivels around on his heels, looking at me. Sally looks too. The two of them look at me as if I'm the answer to their prayers.

(1983)

Cut Glass

A man in a room in a hotel in a city which is strange to him, a dark room, although it is night: he stands at the window looking out at the lights of the city. He is happy to be alone, although he can imagine being unhappy for the same reason. He loves the carpet in the room, the dresser, the coat hangers, the wallpaper, the padded headboard of each double bed. He has not seen the city except from the window; he has avoided every sight pictured in the hotel's Guide to Chicago; he will leave knowing the city no better than when he came.

He will do what he is doing: stand naked in the darkened, rented room and look out the window in peace and quiet and in pleasure.

Now he pushes away from the glass, dials Cold on the climate control, slips into the large bed, and pulls the yellow sheet and the thick spread to a point just below his nostrils.

Watching the local news on television he recalls visiting the city as a young man, recalls walking past a barber shop in which a barber was fighting with a customer. The barber knocked the customer down. Remembering this makes the man want to leave Chicago. He is uneasy. He closes the curtain and returns to bed but cannot sleep, so sits up and stares at himself in the mirror mounted on the opposite wall.

A blonde woman says hello to him in the hallway. Her voice is cracked and slow, her breath is sweet, and when they stand together at the window in his room he marvels at her suppleness. Having noticed the dark pleasant scent of her breath he becomes worried about his own, and the conversation that is carried on is carried on with both of their faces near the glass, their breathing apparent on the pane. When he turns, finally, to brush his lips against her forehead he does not breathe, but she restrains him there, his lips on her skin, and he is forced to exhale into her hair, which smells heavenly.

She laughs then and pulls away, moving toward the dresser to make herself a drink. He watches her back as she skirts the corner of the bed; he admires her; the dress she is wearing is stylish and light, and it moves as if caught by wind as she walks.

"I want to undress now," he says.

"I don't mind."

He starts to unbutton his shirt, wondering if she has told him the truth. When the shirt is open and out of his pants he feels strongly that she has not, that it is the wrong thing to do, that undressing will reduce the moment if not the whole experience, and he decides not to continue. She asks why he has stopped.

"I'm not used to this. Ordinarily I am alone here."

Light is coming from the bathroom door which is slightly ajar, coming from behind the woman, and he sees that she is lovely in her own shadow.

"Do I make you nervous?"

"Anyone would," he says. Then, thinking that this answer might offend her, he adds: "Yes. You in particular."

"I am nervous too. But it's pleasant, don't you agree? I'll go if you like."

"No. Well—not yet, not yet."

She goes into the bathroom. The man switches the television off and on several times, quickly, then undresses and gets into the bed nearest the window, stretching his legs and feet toward the corners of the mattress.

"Usually I'm here alone," he shouts into the darkness, toward the bathroom.

When she is into the second bed he says "Usually I'm alone," then feels foolish for having repeated himself and pushes his hand out in the direction of the bed she is in. It is an uncomfortable moment because when his hand first reaches her bed she does not know that it is there and he has to pat the mattress to get her attention. Then, after a time, in the darkness of that hotel room in a city with which he is by choice unfamiliar, he feels cool wetness between his fingers and feels her blonde hair softly fallen on his wrist, and he realizes that she is kissing his hand with her tongue, and laughing.

In the morning at the newsstand she says: "This is as far as you go."

"Yes. But I fly a lot. All over. I have a friend to meet today, upstairs."

"A friend?"

"Not a woman."

She leaves and he buys copies of *Domus* and *Abitare* from the clerk and returns to his room, to the chair by the window. He studies the magazines carefully, taking pleasure in the lovely homes on mountainsides, in canyons, homes of very modern design, homes in which plainness is elevated to unbearable beauty.

The woman calls the hotel from her office. He has opened the window and there is the smell of spice, of cinnamon, in the room.

"I'm coming back tonight."

"Good."

"Do you know who is dead? Sartre."

"I know."

"I think it's very curious that Sartre is dead, don't you?"

"I suppose he should be. Dead, I mean."

"Exactly."

He takes a long bath and goes back to the window with a towel around his waist, a towel draped on his shoulders, and a towel over his head. There are people walking in the street and along the waterfront, brightly colored people, and the wind has shifted, and he can no longer smell the spice.

When she returns they shake hands and then she laughs and pulls him into an embrace, kisses the still-wet hair behind his ears.

"Hello," she finally says.

He notices that she looks tired, that her dark skin is rougher than he remembers, that her hair is more brown than blonde and less well cut than he thought.

"You're marvelous," he says.

She turns from the window. "Thank you."

"My friend," he says, looking past her toward the Hancock silhouette against the closing sky, "my friend is not my friend anymore. He has gone crazy, I think."

She says: "Do you have a cigarette?" and he imagines that she sounds like a wonderful movie actress.

"In my jacket." He is pleased that she will leave her scent in the pocket of his coat.

She stays at the window with both hands in the waistband of her jeans.

"I want to smell your hands," he says.

Smiling she pulls her hands out of her waistband and walks to him holding her hands out palms upward. He takes the hands in his and bends his face to them, smelling the palms, backs, wrists, each in turn, inhaling deeply, slowly, each in turn, until she moves both hands up against his eyes. She holds them there, pressed tight, and he is made acutely aware of the shape of his face, of his cheekbones and the bones over his eyes, and of her hands, slight, almost skeletal, hard.

"I like this very much," he says.

He tells the woman that he has decided to stay in Chicago, that he wants her to stay with him, at the hotel.

"Can I do that?"

"Don't pretend to be silly."

The night is deeply hazed; lights out the window are ringed with glares in which they can see small rainbows. The man and the woman sit on the two beds, talking little; he does not drink so much as he did the first night, she does not drink at all. They sit watching the mist tighten on the glass.

She brings two suitcases and a tote and fills the bathroom with her scents, her perfumes and soaps. The following day, while she is at work, he goes through her things as if they were pieces in a treasure, touching them softly, turning bottles against light, savoring, gently tracing outlines of objects with his fingers.

He is in the bathroom when she returns.

"What's going on?"

"Just a minute," he says through the locked door.

She drops her coat on the chair and her attention is drawn to the view: the day is crisp, even cold, and looking out the window she realizes that from that vantage it is not possible to tell exactly what the weather is, that it could as well be warm and overcast, or humid, or even bitterly cold, much colder than it actually is. What is most curious to her about this is that something so obvious should have gone unnoticed.

The man comes out of the bathroom with her beige dress.

"Playing with my dress?"

"I want you to wear it again." He drops the dress on the bed behind her.

Automatically unbuttoning her blouse and tugging it loose from her pants, she hands it to him as one might hand a shirt in need of ironing to a valet. "I suppose you'll want this right away."

He stretches out on her bed and drops the blouse over his face. "It looks funny through this," he says. "You're vague-looking."

"Swell. I called at half past three."

"Many magical things happened."

"The message lamp is still blinking."

"Let it blink all night, I like it."

"Why do you stay here? It gets on my nerves, it already gets on my nerves. It doesn't work like this, people don't do things this way."

"They would if they could."

"You can't even tell what the weather's like."

"Sure I can; it's cold. I felt the glass."

"It's not just the weather, for God's sake."

They sit in silence. He watches the goosebumps appear on her naked shoulders, then disappear, then appear again; she looks out the window at the graying sky.

When he wakes up the next morning she is packing.

"I don't understand," he says.

"You understand."

"Right, I understand. But I think you're wrong."

He sits up in bed and sniffs the air, twists his head back and forth. "The smell, the scent—is that you?"

"Who else?"

"No, I mean it's new, isn't it?"

"Yes."

"Where'd you get it? Was it here?"

"Bought it yesterday, downstairs."

"It's wonderful," he says. "Everything we need right in the building."

She kisses him softly on the cheek and he holds her, puts his arms around her.

"This is awkward," he says.

She pulls free of him and walks to the door. He looks at the window, stares at it, at its whiteness and the way it seems to push itself into the room.

"It's very pretty," he says. "To see it close like this is very pretty."

She lines her cases at the door and takes a last look at the room. It is snowing. Flat spots of white slip down and across the window. The buildings of the city are obscured by the dense snow and the glass has the look of a wall. She dials room service then sits beside the man on the bed, and they wait, and the bellman comes, and she gives him bills, and he takes the bags away.

(1980)

SAFEWAY

First you see the woman's beautiful hair, steel gray and cut to brush the shoulders of her vanilla silk blouse. She is thin and too elegantly dressed for the supermarket. Her coat is folded neatly over the center of the shopping cart handle. You pass behind her and stop thirty feet away, facing the low-fat milk, for a second look. You shove the half gallons around, reading the dates on the cartons without registering them. She is standing on one foot, leaning on the yellow handle of her basket, studying some generic-brand product.

She skips the next aisle, leaving you there to read the labels on two spaghetti sauces.

You go to the front of the store, see where she is, keep your distance—skip aisles, slip by her with a preoccupied expression on your face, compare products—until the two of you have made one complete turn through the market. When she stops in the far corner to look at the whole fryers, her basket is still relatively empty; yours contains only two quart bottles of Tab. You pull a folded envelope from your shirt pocket to check your list.

The first aisle in from that side of the store is bread and cookies. There you stop near the back, staring at the Oreos. From that position you can watch her when she leaves the chickens.

Up front, you can see two checkout counters, and beyond them, through the plate-glass windows, the late-winter afternoon. It has been raining all day; you are wet, your coat is spotted, your hair is slick and dark. A college-age couple comes down your aisle very fast; he is wearing an ankle-length raincoat, she a gray hooded sweatshirt and a pair of faded khakis, soaked at the cuffs. She starts to put a

57

loaf of wheat bread into their cart; he stops her, pointing at the white bread.

"Get the Colonial," you hear him say.

"This is natural," she says.

"I don't care," he says. He tries to snatch the bread out of her hands.

"I don't ask much," she says, pulling away.

The young man sighs melodramatically. "Okay—you get yours, I get mine."

She looks past her boyfriend's shoulder at you, raising her eyebrows. The couple passes you, two loaves in the basket, still arguing breads. They are playing, having a good time.

The woman leaves the poultry cooler and comes down your aisle, looking directly at you. She is tan. Without thinking, you reach out, grab a box of cookies, pull it off the shelf, and drop it into your basket: Nabisco gingersnaps. The woman smiles prettily. Her hair, which is darker than you'd first thought, with many thin streaks of gray, moves so gently as she moves, and so regularly, that when she stops her cart and, with the long fingers of her left hand, lifts the hair slightly and draws it back, it falls strand by strand until it comes to rest again, in perfect order.

You look at her shoes. They are high-heeled, buff colored. "Hi," you say.

She doesn't stop, only pushes on toward the front of the store.

You race in the opposite direction, trying to get the waffles and the *TV Guide* and find her checkout line for a last look, but the store is out of the waffles you want, Kellogg's, so you take the house brand— small squares in a clear plastic bag.

Only three checkers are working; the woman is not in any of the lines. You linger at the magazine mini-rack on the end of one of the unused counters, thumb through a current *People*, waiting, feeling foolish.

She arrives unexpectedly out of the aisle behind you—soaps and toiletries—and as she gets in line behind two men, you catch a trace of her scent, delicate and flowerlike, almost jasmine.

You drop *People* into its wire slot and pick up *TV Guide*, then push your basket into line behind hers. You stare at the back of her head, the glistening hair, and at her shoulders, noticing, where the fabric is tight to her skin, the precise, shallow relief of straps.

She looks into her basket, then turns suddenly to you. "Will you go ahead of me? I forgot something. I'll just be a second."

You move forward, taking her place. The two men, wearing Wranglers and colorful nylon jackets over T-shirts, glance at you. With your left hand you pull the woman's basket in behind you until it's touching your leg. The taller of the two men drops his checkbook onto the counter and waits for the checker to ring a pack of cigarettes and several quart bottles of Miller beer; the checker moves the bottles, punching the repeat button on her cash terminal with a fingertip, her pink lips counting the repetitions.

The glass in the store windows is covered with transparent tinted Mylar—blue; waiting for the woman to return, you look at your reflection. You tug on your collar and straighten your tie, then look at the reflections of the two men. One of them is short, heavy, tough looking, with a jowly face and a couple of days of beard. He looks unclean in the blue glass. His stringy blond hair hangs in chunks from under a straw cowboy hat creased into a tight wedge. The second man is taller, better looking. You look from the window to the man—his face is smooth, but still there is a shadow; his teeth are perfect. The ugly man is talking.

"I don't know why I came in the first place," he says. He squeezes the brim of his hat, pushes it back from his forehead.

"Fletcher," the second man says, "calm down. I didn't promise anything."

"Of course not," Fletcher says. "Of course you didn't promise anything. Why should you? You can't deliver."

The checker takes the tall man's check, looks at it closely, turns it upside down on the top of her terminal, stamps it with a rubber stamp, carefully fills in the new blanks. You push your basket forward, bumping into the counter, then unload your few purchases— the bottles of Tab, the waffles, the *TV Guide*, and the gingersnaps. You arrange these in a neat row at the end of the rubber conveyor belt. Then you see a small, peculiarly shaped bottle of maraschino cherries in your basket. You don't remember taking the cherries, and you don't remember the cherries' having been in the basket before you started shopping. You pick up the jar and examine the label, noting that these are cherry halves, stemless, "packed in natural juices." You stare at a high stack of toilet tissue cartons, feeling the weight of the jar in your hand.

You are standing in the line like that, thinking, trying to remember, when the woman returns.

"We match," she says, showing you a jar identical with the one you are holding.

"Are these yours?" you ask. "They aren't mine. I found them in my basket, but I'm sure I didn't buy them." For a minute you wonder if you took the jar out of her basket, but then you realize that you could not have—her basket is behind you.

"Thank you," she says, and she takes your jar. Then, waving her hand toward her basket, she says, "Was there anything else you wanted?" Both of you laugh at this small joke, and you point at her food, saying, "That, and that, and that looks pretty good," but as you point, and as you laugh nervously, you are thinking of her lips, her startling rust-colored lipstick, her fair skin, her severe cheekbones, and the light white down on her cheeks; you are thinking about the lovely hair, perfectly proper, perfectly behaved, waving softly around her head and shoulders as she laughs; you are thinking about her slim waist and about her ankles in their ultra-thin straps.

The moment passes. The woman opens her purse and begins fiddling with something inside it; you turn back to the counter and rearrange your purchases, thinking how foolish your Tab and gingersnaps and *TV Guide* must look.

The man in front of you is staring at your frozen waffles. He smiles. It is not a pleasant smile meaning "Yes, the flesh is weak" but a smile more on the order of "This poor bastard is buying frozen waffles": his opinion of your entire life is instantly communicated. He is waiting for the checker to finish with his check, and the checker is on her tiptoes, scanning the store for the manager.

The one called Fletcher picks at his teeth with a green toothpick, hissing occasionally to determine whether or not he has cleared the gaps; he nudges his friend with an elbow, jerks his head toward you, then whispers something. The taller man pivots, looks past you at the woman.

This makes you angry; you move forward, toward the counter, hoping to block his view of her. Then, to see how she reacts to the man's glance, you turn to her, but she is looking away toward the special racks of Pepperidge Farm products.

Then Fletcher taps your shoulder and whispers, through a twisted little smile, "Roy told me before we came that it'd happen here, but I didn't believe him. I told him you don't want to let 'em dig those flashy brown nails into your rump—you want to get one that speaks Japanese or something, else you end up singing Disney disco tunes off the TV the rest of your life." He lowers his voice more and says, "His woman's got juice for brains is the problem; you got to squeeze her chin to make her grin, and if you don't look out, she won't wash herself all over—she'll end up with little scabs of chocolate pudding on her chest, here," and he pops himself on the chest.

Roy turns around at this point, shrugs at you, and says to his short friend, "Listen, Fletcher, why don't you go sit in the truck?"

"What?" Fletcher says. "I was just telling this fellow about the best day of your marriage; I mean, he needs to know, Roy. You can see he's on a need-to-know basis, can't you?" Then Fletcher looks at you. "Roy put a cast on her leg up to here"—he draws his hand like a blade across his upper thigh—"told her to look sexy, and shot her with his OneStep. Ain't that right, Roy?"

"That's right," Roy says to you.

"She's there with this cane his grandfather or somebody brought back from Europe after the Great War, and she's leaning on the cane with both hands, you see what I mean?" Fletcher says, suggesting the posture with his own. "And she's in front of a big Confederate painting with this look on her face, but Roy here don't show the picture to just anybody. I mean, he shows it to me, but we're friends maybe twenty years now—right, Roy?"

"Sure, sure," Roy says, and he's looking past you again, at the woman.

You're thinking of her, too, but you've got the idea that Fletcher is going to tell his story no matter what, that if you try to shut him up he's going to grab your shoulder, spin you around, and tell you, so you're trying to let it go.

"Listen," Roy says to Fletcher, dropping an arm around the thick man's shoulder and turning him back to the counter. "Maybe we ought to mind our own business, huh?"

"I feel bad," you hear Fletcher say. "I don't feel so hot."

The woman is still digging in her purse, pulling papers out and wadding them into a tight ball in her hand. The papers are mostly white, a few are yellow; they look like charge receipts. You grab your frozen waffles and wave them at her, hoping to lighten the moment, turn it into a mutual appreciation of some kind. "Not for me, of course," you say. "The kids—the kids demand them."

You put enough sarcasm into your voice so that the woman will understand what you are after: a little conspiratorial recognition, a small pleasure; but she seems to take you seriously. Looking up from her purse, letting her pretty smile open across her face, she shakes her head and shrugs, as if agreeing with you about the childishness of children. This is not the response you had hoped for, but it will do. You slide your basket away from the counter so that she can move forward, and when she does, you think about resting your hand on the uppermost chrome bar of her shopping cart, looping your fingers through the wire mesh—but you decide against it.

Fletcher has gotten impatient. Unzipping his yellow nylon jacket with one hand, he points the other, fingers folded to make a gun, at the checkout girl. "Listen, honey, I don't feel good at all," he says. "What is this crap? I'm taking this to the truck."

The girl is very young, maybe sixteen or eighteen, very tall and very skinny, wearing an ill-fitting rust-orange-and-brown smock; her makeup is smeared at the outside of one eye, but the cheap look of her face is strangely attractive to you. She is afraid of Fletcher and nervously fingers the midget gold pen attached by a retractable cord to a disc on her lapel.

"We're not supposed to let things—" she begins, looking frantically at the kid in the checkout enclosure two down. "The manager was here a minute ago. If you can wait, I'll go find him."

"We'll wait," Roy says.

The girl almost jumps out from behind her terminal, half running and half walking toward the manager's office.

Fletcher says, "I'll dance with that one, Roy. I'll have her wearing rubber pants in no time."

"Take it easy," Roy says.

"Those lips are so thick they got muscles you can't even imagine. Like crawling on oysters."

You stand there with your frozen waffles still in your hand, looking over the top of the chewing gum rack at a huge nurse in a crisp white uniform waddling along behind a basket stuffed with meats and paper towels.

The woman behind you bends over the handle of her basket and picks up a package of Sara Lee frozen cinnamon rolls, holds this up for you to see, looks quickly from you to your waffles and back to her rolls. "I know what you mean," she says. "My husband loves them." And she and you stand for a moment waving frozen pastries at one another, smiling, while you think about the mention of her husband.

Then Fletcher's voice, loud again, comes from behind you. "I wouldn't eat that crap for anybody."

"Excuse me?" you say, almost automatically stepping backward.

"I said that crap'll kill you." He points at the waffles.

"We know," the woman says. "That's what we were saying."

"They were saying that to each other," Fletcher says, pulling on Roy's jacket. "Get it?"

"Are you a nutritionist?" the woman asks, leaning to her left to look around you.

"He's a plumber, lady," Fletcher says. "We're both of us plumbers, but we know how to eat."

"So what's going on these days in plumbing?" she says. "What's all this PVC-pipe business?"

"Sorry," Roy says. "Forget it."

Fletcher tugs his hat over his eyes and pushes past you to get to the woman. "She's rich," he says, and he reaches up and runs a stiff finger along the woman's cheek.

She does not move, only stares at him.

"Jesus," you say to Roy. "Can't you control him?"

Fletcher says, "I like the checker better anyway. This one, you give her two weeks and she'll be wanting money for new panties. The other one, you wrap her ass around a thirty-dollar bicycle seat and you can stand her on her head in a mirror for life."

The checker is returning from across the store, walking slowly, pinching her smock, pulling it down in front.

"Here comes your friend," you say to Fletcher.

She slides into her booth, waves the check, and says, "It's okay. I'm sorry it took so long. The manager was out on the loading dock talking to the architect about renovations. It'll just be a minute now." She sticks a button on her terminal with the point of her pen.

"Hey," Fletcher says, pulling on Roy's arm. "Hey, I think I'm going to take me a little walk—you take the beer, okay?"

"It's wet outside."

"I like wet," Fletcher says, walking out backward.

"It's the cash over," the checker says to Roy. "That's the problem, that's why I had to get the okay." She counts twenty-five dollars into Roy's hand.

He folds the money over his thumb, then turns to the woman. "I'm sorry," he says. He squints at you and goes out the double door.

The checker begins with your cookies, pressing a button on the terminal and slipping the box to her left, calling out the price in a soft, childlike voice.

You start to say something to the woman behind you, but the conveyor belt suddenly lurches forward, knocking a bottle of Tab off the counter. It bursts when it hits the floor, spraying her thoroughly. Her blouse is soaked—the entire area beneath her breasts clings to her stomach. She takes two steps backward and stands there with her arms outstretched like a scarecrow, shaking her hands and looking down at her chest. All other activity in the supermarket seems to stop; your aisle is stared at like a traffic accident. Then you are surrounded by boys mopping and being solicitous, and everyone is laughing. The woman is laughing. The manager, who appears from nowhere, is laughing and trying to blot dry her blouse with a yellow sponge. The checker is laughing and at the same time apologizing. The boys are laughing as they fall to their knees in order to clean up the mess. Someone goes to get another bottle of Tab, and while the lane is still crowded with people, while everyone is still laughing, the checker shoves your purchases to the foot of her counter, where yet another tall, thickset, smiling teenager stuffs the goods into a brown sack.

You stop by the ice machine just inside the door to let a small boy in a silver costume of some kind run by you; he jumps with both feet onto the rubber pad that controls the twin sliding-glass doors. He runs out and back in twice, his Suzuki violin case slung over his shoulder like a toy rifle, then attaches himself to the leg of a middle-aged woman who is holding a transparent shopping bag, standing on the covered walk outside the store and gazing at the fine slate-gray rain. She is startled by the boy, and turns quickly to scold him; but then, almost as quickly, she stops scolding and smooths the child's hair as if unable to resist his charm. In the far corner of the parking lot, just across the street from the Pee Wee baseball diamond, you see Roy getting into the cab of a three-quarter-ton gold pickup truck; the truck is backed against the curb under a tall light, facing the store. Shoppers are starting their cars, which suddenly steam at both ends; the steam and the dark sky, the rain, and the water thrown off by windshield wipers give the parking lot a close, magical look.

"Well, we can't simply stay here," your woman says. She has come up behind you, her smallish sack of groceries held against her chest.

"Oh, hello," you say. You turn too fast, hitting her shoulder with your forearm. "I'm sorry," you say.

"Two's a charm," she says, laughing softly. "Who's watching the store?"

Before you can reply, two nuns in brilliant blue habits start to walk out the door but, on seeing that it is still raining, stop suddenly. One of the nuns, quite a bit older than her companion, stands on the pad, and the doors slide open to the hiss of the outside. She turns to you and says, "Will it ever end?"

You look at the ceiling and say, "No," and the nun gathers her robes into a bundle at her knees and motions for the younger one to follow.

When they are out and the door is closed, the woman beside you says, "They make me nervous."

"All that beautiful blue," you say. "My name is Fred."

"Well, Fred, how do you do?" She frees one hand from her package and thrusts it at you. "I'm Sarah Garner."

"Hello, Sarah."

"Wet, isn't it? Still, I don't know why none of us has an umbrella."

"I was thinking that myself," you say, although you aren't thinking that at all. You're thinking about her perfect hair—for it to be so perfect, she has to *know* it's perfect. "Actually, I have one, but it's in the car."

"Ditto," she says. "I didn't remember until I was deep in peanut butter."

"Right," you say, laughing too abruptly, too loud.

People are coming into the store, shedding rain gear, stomping feet as they pull shopping baskets out of the rack and wheel off in the direction of the produce. Sarah Garner puts her groceries down on the brick ledge at the bottom of the huge blue window you are both standing in front of, then lights a cigarette from a gold case. She offers you a cigarette.

"I feel like John Garfield," you say.

"Maybe if you dirty up a little," she says. "Take one—see if you can let it fall out of your mouth without using your hands."

"Some trick," you say, taking a cigarette.

"So—you're going to protect me all the way to the coffee shop?" She points out the window, diagonally, across the parking lot. "We can take the long way around and never get wet, although some of us are already wet." She sweeps a hand in front of the stain on her blouse. "And sticky."

"Didn't I apologize for that already?"

Sarah Garner looks at you, then at her cigarette, then at the dense haze of the parking lot. "Yes," she says.

You navigate the covered walk around the rim of the lot in silence, which makes you nervous. She's got a trench coat over her shoulders, like a cape, and as you walk, you measure her—her height, the length of her stride, the impact of her shoulder accidentally hitting yours, the sound of her heels on the slick pavement;

you register this random data too consciously, flicking in imagination from one observation to the next, as if the moment might soon be lost. When she gets a step ahead of you, her gray hair catches the cold fluorescent light of the walkway and turns a startling silver; you begin to imagine yourself in bed with Sarah Garner, making slow and detailed love, touching her hair, and her shoulders, and her skin in response to stern commands.

The coffee shop is a House of Pancakes. A tiny woman with her hair in a wiry bun shows you to a window booth done in turquoise Naugahyde. You order coffee.

Sarah Garner drops her coat from her shoulders, and it sits up against the blue seat-back like a shadow. She plays with her fingers, interlacing their tips, then opening her hands like a kid playing here's the church and here's the steeple; you watch her eyes as she glances around the empty room.

"Do you go to New Orleans?" she finally asks, without looking at you.

"No," you say. "I hate it. I lived there a couple of years, went to school there. It's depressing."

"I love it. But I've only been once or twice."

"I guess it's okay." You're not doing so well. She likes New Orleans. Where is the coffee? "I like the blouse," you say.

She looks down, then raises her eyebrows to look at you. "The wet look. Dangerous and seductive, but not so healthy." She sticks a finger between two buttons and pulls the blouse away from her chest.

"I'm sorry," you say.

The window beside the booth is bubbled with condensation; she starts to draw something on the window, something that looks like a rabbit, then quickly erases the drawing with the butt of her fist. "My husband's in New Orleans now. He's in contract law, oil law." She's still not looking at you—she's looking at the glossy window, at the distorted, flashing reflections of taillights and headlights.

"You always shop at the Safeway?"

"Night and day." She laughs. "I don't come over here very much. I used to live around here, by the park, but I don't now."

"I have an apartment on Richburg Hill," you say. "Forest Royale."

"Oh, yeah, those are nice."

You nod. "I work at the hospital."

"You play doctor?" she says, smiling.

The waitress arrives with two mugs and a steaming glass coffeepot. She grins at you, showing huge gums. She's wearing a black uniform with a slick lavender apron. "Coffee?" she says. "Sorry I'm slow, but Mrs. Kelso forgot to tell me you were in my station, and from the counter you seemed to be in Janet's." She fills the mugs, then slides one to Sarah Garner and one to you. "Cream?"

"Yes, thank you," Sarah says.

The waitress reaches into her apron pocket and produces half a dozen cartons of cream, each the size and shape of a gumdrop. "These be enough?" she asks. "I don't know why they bother with these things. Here, I'll give you a few extras." She deposits another handful on the table, starts to leave, but then stops and returns to the booth. "The thing is that it wouldn't have mattered even if you were in Janet's station, because she's home sick today anyway."

"More work for you," you say. "That's too bad."

"Oh, I can handle it. With this rain, nobody's going to come in."

You and Sarah Garner watch the waitress walk away. "She walks like a man," Sarah says. "Do you think that's attractive in a woman?"

You pull all the cream cartons in front of you and begin arranging them. "Sometimes. I guess. I don't know."

"Peter says I walk like a man."

"Peter's your husband?"

"Yes. He plays racquetball a great deal, but he's not as good-looking as you."

"More distinguished, I imagine."

"Shorter," she says. "But we get along all right."

You look down at the tabletop and see that you have organized the cream cartons like players on a football team.

"He loves to go out of town," Sarah says. "And I don't mind; I like to be alone sometimes, at night, late. It's quiet."

"Sure," you say. "I watch television all the time."

You find a small hole in the turquoise seat and stick your finger in it, then suddenly realize she might be able to see what you're doing. You glance at her sheepishly.

"What do you watch?" she asks. Then quickly adds, "Never mind—I don't want to know."

"Movies. Mostly."

"The tall one wasn't scary," she says, wagging her mug at the window. "He seemed to know what he was doing."

"Do you have any more of these?" you ask, pointing to your team.

She picks two cartons out of the clean ashtray on her side of the booth, spins them onto the tabletop. Then she watches you carefully reseal the foil tops and place the containers with the others.

"I've got to freshen up," she says. She lifts her hair off her forehead, as if to illustrate the remark. "Did you see the restrooms?"

"They're by the door." You point behind her, toward the entrance, over a tray of very green vines that sits on top of a panelled, chest-high room divider. "See that little hallway?"

She slides out of the booth, carefully sidestepping a bubble-topped dolly loaded with pastries. She doesn't walk at all like a man. When she's out of sight, you pull a napkin from the dispenser and wipe the window, then peer out into the parking lot: Roy's truck is there, shining.

You push your mug to one side and move the cream cups around in an approximation of a football play—a sweep around right end, the quarterback pitching out to the tailback. But because you have too few cartons, and because you must move the cartons in sequence, one after another, and because you have no defensive team at all, the play isn't much fun. You start to arrange the players again but decide not to, and start stacking the cups into a kind of tower. You remember the frozen waffles in your grocery sack, which is tucked into the booth on the floor next to your feet, and you pull the sack out and put it on the seat. You look inside: the waffles are wet and limp, and there are spots on the bottom of the grocery sack.

You close the sack, then see Sarah Garner pressed up against the entrance door of the House of Pancakes, looking out, her hands cupped around her eyes. You push the cream cartons aside and pull the coffee back in front of you. You take a sip of coffee and watch Sarah come around the divider.

"I wanted to see if it was still raining," she says, slipping into the booth. "It is." The waitress is moving in your direction.

"Are you long waisted or short waisted?" you ask.

"What?" She is looking at the large, near-round spot where you wiped the window. "Long," she says. "I think. Long waisted. Listen, we'd better go or my stuff will spoil." She reaches under the table, and with one hand pulls up her groceries between the seat and the tabletop.

"My waffles," you say, pointing into the top of your sack.

She waves at the waitress, who is by now almost beside the booth. The waitress rips a green sheet from her pad and places it face down on the table.

"Something wrong with the coffee?" the waitress asks, pointing her pencil at your mug.

"Very good," you say.

Sarah Garner shoves a dollar bill toward you.

"I thought this was my treat," you say.

"Wrong." She starts to put on her coat, and in the bending and pulling you notice that she has opened the neck of her blouse.

On the walkway outside the House of Pancakes you say, "Do you want to follow me? My car's over here."

"You go ahead," she says. "Forest Royale, right? I forgot something at the store. I forgot I'm completely out of facial tissues. Just give me the apartment number." She looks at the truck in the corner of the parking lot.

"One twelve," you say, reading the numbers from a license plate.

"Fine. I'll see you shortly." She reaches for your hand, squeezes it, and smiles. Then she heads for the store, diagonally, through the brittle rain.

It's cold, and the sky has turned inky blue. You stand under the overhang for a minute, watching Sarah Garner walk stiffly away. At the door to the Safeway she turns, sees that you are still watching, and waves. You wave, too, in a quick, jerky movement, then step out into the parking lot, whistling, looking over the tops of the sparkling cars for your black Mazda.

(1983)

PART TWO

TRIP

Harry Lang's company Chevrolet breaks down on the highway fifteen miles outside of Dallas. He gets the car to a small old town
called Cummings, leaves it at the gas station, and calls Fay, a woman
he met at a corporate sensitivity workshop in San Antonio last year
and the reason for his trip. They have spent the last six months having long and wistful and detailed telephone conversations on the
company WATS line, talking about everything that they can think
of, even business, and sometime nothing at all, just sitting on opposite ends of the line, allowing the delicate contact between them a
few extra minutes; finally they agreed that he should come for a visit.

Now, from the garage in Cummings, he tells her that he will not
get into town until the next day, because of his car. Two hours later
he's at the Starlight Motor Hotel watching television when there's a
knock on the door. It's Fay, standing on the other side of the screen,
fidgeting with her shirt cuffs. "May I come in?" she says.

He pushes open the screen and steps back so she can enter the
room, which is small, panelled, dark. It's dusk; the only lights outside
are the star-shaped motel sign and the yellow neon ringing the eaves
of the buildings.

Fay sits on the bed. "It's real clammy in here."

He clicks on the table lamp. The base of the lamp is a bronze
cowgirl on horseback twirling a lariat. "You look wonderful," he
says. "How'd you get away?"

"Easy," she says. "I can't leave you alone. After an hour I decided
I should come to you. You got a Bufferin?" She looks around the
room. "What's that music?"

He listens, but doesn't hear any music. Fay is thirty-five, small and pretty. She's wearing white shorts, a polo dress shirt with a tiny round-tipped collar, and brown-striped espadrilles. She bounces on the bed, testing it.

Harry opens his suitcase, brings out a bottle of Anacin. "Will these do?"

She picks two pills out of his palm and points toward the open bathroom door. "Use your water?"

He tucks in his shirttail and uses the window as a mirror to fix his hair. When she comes out of the bath, she's patting her face with a small coral towel that has "Starlight" stitched into it in awkward brown script. "You want to eat something?" she says.

They go in her car to the Spur station to check on his Chevrolet. The station owner, a mechanic named Gorky, is on his back under the car. "Lucky you don't live out here," he says. "Toss me a five-eighths. Second drawer."

Harry finds the socket the mechanic wants and drops it into his palm.

"Don't get into Dallas much," Gorky says. "I don't mind, though. We got fishing and women. It doesn't matter, really—for an old son like me the fish don't bite and the women don't either. You see a lock washer out there somewhere, about so big?" Again the hand shoots out from under the car, thumb and forefinger spread.

Harry hands him a washer, but the mechanic drops it; when he tries to turn over on his stomach, he can't make it, because the Malibu's not jacked up enough. Finally he says, "Crap," and rolls out from under the car. He sits up, his back against the door, and wipes his hands on a red rag, then rubs the rag around on his puffed, stubble-covered face.

"So, what do you think?" Harry asks. "About the car."

"I'm happy you're spending the night, is what I think." Gorky tells a kid who looks like a young TV actor to watch the gas islands, then motions toward a primered GMC pickup with a bed full of tractor tires. "I can let you borrow this one, but maybe you don't need it, since you got this woman here."

"He hasn't got me yet," Fay says. She loosens her thin leather belt, then refastens it, taking it up a notch and centering the buckle above her fly.

The mechanic stares at her for a minute, then laughs. "Anyway, I'll have yours tomorrow. Maybe one or so, huh?"

"Fine," Harry says.

"Go to Nick's if you want to eat." Gorky scrubs at his palm with the rag. "I mean, if you don't go in town. It's just up here a mile. Good chow. Dottie get you set?"

Dottie is Mrs. Kiwi, the owner of the Starlight, a tiny woman with a barrel chest and a dwarf's face. This afternoon she was wearing a fuchsia muscle shirt.

"I got a nice room," Harry says. "Thanks."

"I told her about you," Gorky says, waving a hand at a circling bug. "Me and her's kinda, you know"—he takes a long time thinking of the word, getting it right—"acquainted."

At Nick's Sandwich Shop Harry orders a Kingburger and Fay has a salad with green goddess dressing. Afterward they go to the Odeon Theatre to see the movie. There's a crowd of a dozen people out front, but there's no one in the box office. Harry stares at Fay's eyes, which are mismatched in a becoming way. Two teenagers in line behind them are talking about a girl named Rose Ann they both seem to be in love with.

"I saw my neighbors making it in the driveway," Fay says, bending to look past him at the teenagers. "I watched out the bedroom window."

Harry sticks his hands in his pants pockets, then brings them out again and folds his arms, admiring the crispness and neatness of Fay's clothes.

"This woman does the dishes in a bikini, you know what I mean? Then she's out in the driveway moaning like a cow. I envied her."

The kids are listening; they've gotten very quiet. Fay points a finger at him. "I wear a fair bikini myself"—she pauses for emphasis, wagging the finger—"but mostly on the beach."

Two teenage couples join the line. Harry says, "Uh-huh."

Fay puts her hand on his side, on his ribs. "Last Christmas I helped Melody—that's her name—last year I helped her build shelves in the downstairs bath, a couple of little four-inch shelves, nothing big. Then, in June, what do you think I found in there?" She pauses and looks at him triumphantly, as if he'll never guess. "It was the saw, the electric saw, tucked in alongside the toilet. If it was me, I'd have had the thing back in its place before it stopped turning."

He folds one hand inside the other and starts to crack the knuckles, but she frowns, anticipating the sound. "Oh, sorry," he says, and puts the hands back into his pockets.

"No," she says. "I want to hear them. Go on."

"I don't think so," he says, shaking his head.

"She plays this music all the time. You're trying to sleep, or read, or sit in the tub—sometimes I spend a whole afternoon in the tub— and here comes Nat King Cole into your life."

The kids have started their conversation again. They're brothers, and they're trying to be sensible about this thing with Rose Ann, but they're having trouble deciding who's going to get her.

"I like music," Fay says. "Don't get me wrong. I even like Nat King Cole, once every forty years or so." She digs in her boxy purse and then turns around holding a Polaroid snapshot of a man in a bathing suit. "This is my husband, Tim. I thought you ought to see him." She pokes the picture at Harry. "Take a look."

The man in the picture is overweight. He doesn't have much hair, and his legs are peculiarly thin for the rest of his body. He's standing alongside a Buick sedan holding a hose with water running out the end. Behind him in the picture there's a two-car garage and, off to the extreme left, the shoulder and leg of another man, also in bathing trunks.

"He looks fine to me," Harry says, handing the snapshot back to her. "He's a good-looking man."

She takes the picture and holds it very close to her face. "You think so?" She moves the picture up and down, examining her husband. "He does have eyes," she says, snapping open the purse and dropping the photograph inside. "I think I married the eyes, really. That's the first thing I noticed about you—eyes."

A kid on a girl's bicycle rides up beside them. "You all on line?" he asks. When Fay says they are, the kid says, "You want to give me a cut? I'm only ten."

Fay nods, so the kid gets off the bike, puts it down on the sidewalk where he's standing, and gets into line.

"I love kids, don't you?" she whispers. "I don't like to think about not having any. I suppose it's my fault. You don't mind me talking, do you?"

"I guess not," Harry says.

In the flickering light of the theatre marquee Fay's face is all white planes and sharp shadows; she looks like somebody vulnerable in a forties movie poster. Her hair is tight to her scalp in dark knots.

"Maybe you should call the police or something," Harry says. "About this woman."

"Not on your life, Buster." She pulls a thread away from one of the belt loops of her shorts. "Melody's one of the highlights of my life. A role model for me." She snaps the thread off her waist. "Besides, she's gorgeous to look at. The husband ain't bad either."

Harry reaches for the thread, which she has rolled into a tiny ball between her fingers.

"He runs the Bonanza out by us. He likes me, but I don't have the guts to sleep with him. I guess I don't want to."

One of the brothers has bumped Harry several times trying to hear Fay's story. He says something to the other one, and the brothers both laugh.

Fay glances at the boy. "He's a handsome kid, isn't he?" she says, loud enough for the boy to hear. "Maybe he needs some attention."

"Excuse me?" the boy says. "Were you talking to me?"

"What?" she says, as if she has been interrupted. "Oh. No, I was talking to Harry—this is Harry."

"Howdy," Harry says.

"Howdy?" the brothers say to each other, exchanging silly looks.

She twists back toward the ticket booth. Looking over her shoulder, she says, "Rose Ann probably loves you both, you're so cute." She pulls Harry forward in line. "Howdy? Oh, never mind. Let's talk about something else—are you hot?"

"No, I'm okay."

"I perspire," she says, opening her arms and glancing at her chest. "I admit it, Harry. And I won't wear those teeny satin tops, those thin ones you see everywhere." She sighs, then smiles and straightens her blouse.

"I don't think we'll ever get in here," Harry says.

"I mean, I could if I wanted to. And plum lips and metallic underpants—you interested?" She laughs and fingers some of the curls over her ear. "It's not that I wasn't trained, you know. I was trained just like everybody else. I can do the business—here, I'll show you." She wraps an arm around his neck, moistens her lips with her tongue, then tightens her grip and pulls his face close to hers, her eyes flashing.

"Hey," Harry says, tugging free. "That's pretty good."

The line is moving. They're halfway to the ticket window. Three boys with big portable radios go by, heading for the box office. The radios are tuned to the same station, and the area in front of the theatre is suddenly full of Mexican polka music. "What are you guys doing?" Fay shouts. "The line's back here."

At the Starlight after the movie Fay gets into Harry's bed. "I'm going to stay all night, okay?" She twists around under the spread for a minute and produces her shorts and sandals, which she deposits on the floor by the telephone. "I think I'll keep this on for now," she says, pinching her shirt and tugging it a couple of times.

"Great," he says.

Harry's up first, at noon. He takes a shower in the metal stall, being as quiet as he can, but when he comes out Fay is gone and Mrs. Kiwi is banging on the screen. "What do you people think I'm running here—a bordello?"

Harry jumps. "Just a minute. I'm coming."

He just gets his pants on before she's in the open door brandishing her passkey. Her muscle shirt is cranberry this time.

She sighs and rolls the key between her fingers. "I've been running the Starlight twenty-two years and I've seen it all. Her creeping out of here like that—you should be ashamed."

He points toward the parking lot. "We're together."

Mrs. Kiwi pockets the key in the stretch trousers she's wearing. "Yes. I see that." She nods gravely, then puts on a grin and pats Harry's arm. "I understand perfectly, Mr. Lang."

"We work together. I mean, she works here in Dallas, and I work in Louisiana, but for the same company."

"Sure," Mrs. Kiwi says, patting more solicitously than before. She makes a sucking noise between her teeth, then laughs. "There's a lot of that around is what I understand. More and more." She shades her eyes and stares through the white dust at her office, then puts her fists on her hips and looks at his bare feet.

Fay pulls the screen door open. "Harry? What's going on?"

"Nothing, darling," Mrs. Kiwi says, shooing Fay with the backs of her hands. "You go on outside before the Baptists see you. Maybe we all ought to go outside." She turns back to Harry. "I was a girl myself—fourteen brothers. You don't get so many families like that anymore, what with the economy and the state of things. All of them died, too. One after another. I had dead brothers all over this country for a while. I would've had a big family if Mr. Kiwi, God rest his soul, hadn't passed on so sudden. That's a long time ago now—forty years." She snorts and does a little twist with her head, then says, "Well, now, that's about enough of that." She reaches into her pocket and gets a folded piece of notepaper. "A. D. called earlier on and said the car's gonna be late. I've got the number here if you want to dial him up."

She shakes the paper at Harry. There's a telephone number in blue ballpoint in one corner, but the rest of the sheet is covered with foreign words and phrases. The words "buena" and "bueno" appear repeatedly in block letters at the center of the sheet. "Maybe I'll give him a call," Harry says.

Mrs. Kiwi wipes at the perspiration stuck in her eyebrows, then looks at her fingers. "I think you kids better come on for some lunch—I mean, once you get straightened away." She points over her shoulder with a thumb.

"Let me check with her," Harry says. "Okay?"

She nods and turns to look at a passing long-haul truck that has huge limes painted on its side. "But you're welcome." She nods several more times, her crinkled gray hair springing in the noon sun, then abruptly starts off toward the office, kicking up dust. "Got biscuits," she says over her shoulder. "Plenty of biscuits."

Fay brings a slimline briefcase when she comes back to the room. She undresses and quickly showers, then puts on a slip and a white shirtwaist dress that clings to her legs when she moves. Walking back and forth at the foot of the bed, she says, "I think I'd better call Tim soon." She looks at the nails on her left hand, holding the hand very close to her face and popping the tips of the fingers out from under her thumb. The nails are the flat orange of flesh-colored stockings. "I don't want him to think I had a wreck and died on the highway. I want him to know where I am." She sits on the bed, keeping the telephone between them. Her hair's wet. "I mean, he still likes me and everything."

"He should," Harry says.

"Damn right," she says. "I like him, don't I?"

Harry goes into the bathroom while she calls Tim. The conversation is quick; Fay's part is full of half-sentences and short silences in which he can hear her flicking her fingers.

When they drive out, Mrs. Kiwi is behind her counter, and Gorky is there, too, playing with some kind of phonograph record, spinning it on a pencil. He waves. His GMC is parked up close to the back of the office, mostly out of sight.

"I feel like going somewhere," Fay says. "Somewhere pretty. I wonder if they have a zoo out here. We could get hot dogs—you like hot dogs? We could feed the seals."

Harry points out the car window at a one-story shack that has a dozen glittery brown vinyl booths piled up on the porch and "Peacock Café" stenciled in silver on the door. "We could go there."

"I don't want to go there, Harry. I want to go somewhere where there are seals, but I guess there aren't any seals out here. I probably should've waited for you in town. You don't seem to be working at this."

He taps on the dashboard and looks at the scenery for a minute; the road is lined with empty lots full of tires—hundreds of automobile tires. "I agree," he finally says.

"What do you agree?" The dress is pulled over her knees, bunched at her thighs, fanned awkwardly around her on the seat.

"Why don't we just get a burger?"

She steers the car into a gas station where a guy in a business suit is looking at a small John Deere tractor. Fay smiles and says, "Excuse me," out the car window to the guy, and he has to step up on the pump island to let her through. "Looks like he sells rats, doesn't he?" she whispers.

They go back to Nick's. She wants to sit at the counter, so they get stools between a huge man wearing bib-style overalls and a kid who's picking his teeth while he waits for food. The big guy takes a look at them when they sit down, then goes back to his smothered chicken.

Nick's is sixty feet deep and twenty feet wide. On one side it's a low counter and a kitchen, on the other a row of wooden booths. In between are a few school-cafeteria tables.

"Well, so tell me about yourself," Fay says after they've ordered hamburgers. "You eat here often?"

"Here come the burgers," he says, pointing at the cook, who's slipping meat patties on two fat buns.

There's a whine from the doorway, and a girl in an electric wheelchair comes in. Everyone seems to know her. She slaps left hands with some of the customers as she steers herself to the back. She has shoulder-length hair, dark skin, puffy lips, big eyes. She's wearing a soft-blue pullover. The waiters, kids in jeans and short-sleeved shirts, dote on her, bring silverware and napkins and water, and stay to talk. She teases them with sexy laughs and white smiles. The waiters stand by her table, straddle the chairs cowboy-style. Harry catches the girl's eyes once, between the turned backs, and she stares at him as if they were old, loving friends.

"Okay," Fay says. "This isn't so marvelous. No more burger for me." She drops her hamburger on the paper plate and shoves it away from her, accidentally knocking it off the counter.

The big guy next to Harry says, "Jesus." He pushes himself up on the counter and peers behind it to see where the hamburger landed. "Hey, Manny. Take a look." He points toward the floor.

The old man doing the cooking shuffles over, picks up the hamburger, and stands right in front of Harry. "What's wrong here? You get a bad one?"

"It's fine," Fay says. "It really is good, but we've got an emergency." She pushes off the stool and opens her purse.

"Look, lady. If it's bad, just say so. We get a bad one now and again."

She puts a five-dollar bill on the counter. "No," she says, smiling. "It's good. You ready, Harry?"

Manny picks up the five and holds it out to Harry. "Take it," he says, waving the hamburger back and forth between Fay and himself. "I can understand this. Take the money."

The guy in the overalls wipes his face on the sleeve of his T-shirt, leaving a strip of coleslaw like a green worm on his shoulder. He and Harry slide off their stools at the same time, and the guy is at least half a foot taller. He looks at Fay, then plucks the bill out of Manny's hand and puts it in hers. "You heard the man," he says.

Outside, Fay goes straight for her car. They drive to the Starlight without talking. She looks determined and lovely steering with one hand, propping her head on the other. Mrs. Kiwi is on her knees in the tiny horseshoe-shaped flower bed by the office; she goes up like a squirrel in the foot-high tulips and waves as Fay and Harry go under the portico. The bed in Harry's room has been made, and there are new towels in the bath; the air-conditioner, which he left running, has been turned off, so the room is stuffy. Fay stands in front of the open door, her legs dark against the light fabric of the skirt; she's fiddling with her pale sunglasses. Harry sits on the edge of the bed and looks at the knees of his pants. She opens her purse, looks inside, closes it again, then comes away from the door and stands in front of him.

"I don't know how to explain this," he says, smoothing the skirt at her hip with his fingers. Mrs. Kiwi is coming across the oyster-shell lot swinging a plastic bag full of biscuits.

Fay slips her glasses into place. "When's your birthday?" she says. "I want to get you something nice for your birthday."

(1983)

COOKER

I tell Lily I'm tired of complaining about things, about my job, about the people I work with, about the way things are at home with her, about the kids and the way the kids don't seem to be coming along, about the country, the things the politicians say on television, on *Nightline* and on *Crossfire* and the other news programs, tired of complaining about everybody lying all the time, or skirting the truth, staying just close enough to get by, tired of having people at the office selectively remember things, or twist things ever so slightly in argument so that they appear to be reasonable, sensible, and thoughtful, tired of making excuses for my subordinates and supervisors alike, tired of rolling and tumbling and being in a more or less constant state of harangue about one thing and another.

Lily, who is sitting on the railing of our deck petting the stray cat that has taken up with us, nods as I talk, and when I stop to think of the next thing I'm tired of complaining about, says to me, "I'm tired, too, Roger."

Our children—Christine, who is eight, and Charles, who is eleven—are in the yard arguing about the hose. Charles has the nozzle tweaked up to maximum thrust, and he's spattering water all around Christine, making her dance to get out of the way.

"Charles," I say, waving at him to tell him to get the hose away from Christine. "Quit screwing around, okay?"

"Ah, Dad. I'm not hurting her. I'm just playing with her. We're just playing."

"We are not," Christine says. "I'm not, anyway. I don't want to play this way." She twists herself into a collection of crossed limbs, a posture that says "pout" in a big way.

"Why don't you water those bushes over there?" Lily says, indicating the bushes that line our back fence. "They look as if they could use the water."

I say, "The thing is, I hate all these people. There's almost nobody I don't hate. Sometimes I see something on TV and I just go into a rage, you know?"

"What things?" she says. "See what things?"

"Somebody says a self-serving thing, I don't know, some guy'll say something about preserving the best interests of something or other, doing the best job he can and all that, upholding standards, and you can look at this guy and tell that what he's thinking is how can he make this sound good, how can he sell this thing he's saying, whatever it is."

"You're talking about the preachers, right?"

"They're all preachers now. They're all holier-than-thou, self-righteous killers. I mean, everybody's a flack these days, they'll say anything just as long as they can keep on making their killings. I see this all the time at work. A guy'll come in and make a big argument for his own promotion, and when he's done I don't even recognize the world he's talking about. Remember that intern we had last fall, kid from Colorado? Then we hired him, right? You know why? Because he made friends with Lumming and what's-his-name, the other guy in production."

"Mossy—isn't that it? Mosely?"

"Something. But when the personnel committee met to talk about this job, Lumming and Mossy didn't say a word about being friendly with this kid. They said he was the greatest thing since sliced bread. It was a clear and simple lie. No question."

"You're complaining about the office," Lily says. "I thought the point of this talk was that you wanted to stop complaining."

"I do, but this stuff is driving me nuts. I don't want to be in a world where this stuff goes on."

"Go to Heaven," Lily says.

"Thanks. That's real interestingly cynical."

"Why not do a little discipline? Ease up." She spins herself off the railing and thumps as her feet hit the deck. "Besides, what would you do if you didn't complain? You wouldn't have anything to talk about."

"You're a charmer," I say. "You're a swell guy. An ace wife and companion."

"Mother of your children," she says, rolling the Weber into place.

"You cooking out here tonight?"

"You are," she says. "Therapy."

I don't mind that. In fact, I'm pleased that she's found something for me to do, something to occupy me, take my mind off the office and the things people are doing wrong. I used to be a lot more easygoing than I am now, and Lily, of course, recognizes that. Watching her mess with the grill, I wonder if she doesn't miss that more than anything else. "What am I cooking?" I ask. I should know the answer to this. I helped bring the groceries in from the car, helped her put them away. I have no idea what groceries they were.

"Lamb chops," she says.

This makes me feel better. Lamb chops, and suddenly the world is new, a place of mystery and possibility. Lily and my mother are the only two women on the planet who believe a lamb chop is a reasonable and appropriate thing to cook for dinner. That she wants them barbecued means I get to look up the recipe in the twenty-four-page no-nonsense Weber Kettle cookbook. I say, "We've got lamb chops?"

"Yep." She's redistributing the coals in the Weber, evening them. She squats beside the cooker and wiggles the bottom vent back and forth to release the ashes into the ash catcher, then dumps the ashes over the side of the deck. "I am serving corn and the lima beans, if you're interested."

"I love the lima beans," I say.

"So get cracking."

I go into the storage closet that opens onto the deck. I'm getting the barbecue tools. As I come out of there, I think: I have no desire to touch Lily. I don't know why, but that's what I think. She's not unattractive—in fact, she's quite lovely—but I don't want to touch her. It's not a desperate thing; I'm not thinking how awful it would be. But at the same time it's a clear thing. There isn't any question. She probably doesn't want to touch me, either. I wouldn't blame her. It's been a while since I've been in any kind of shape; I don't even like to touch me. I try to remember the last time we touched—apart from the usual, casual touches that happen without thinking. It's been weeks, maybe months. Not twelve months, but two, maybe.

I arrange my tools—barbecue tweezers and fork, hickory chips, Gulf lighter fluid—on the redwood table, and I think what brought this stuff about Lily to mind was a TV show I watched last night on CNN: a Los Angeles sex therapist answers all your questions after midnight. What struck me was the assumptions this woman made. She managed, without literally specifying, to predicate everything she said on a version of the ideal relationship which was a joke to me: one man and one woman having happy sex together forever. This was the implicit ideal. Now, we all know that's just plain wrong. It'll never happen. And yet here was this woman taking callers' questions, answering with the kind of dull-witted assurance and authority that characterizes these people: Here are the solutions, follow these three easy steps, put your little foot. I got angry watching this program. Somebody called in from Fairfax, Virginia, said sex wasn't interesting, and asked why this woman didn't get real.

I watched for an hour. This woman wore a lot of eye makeup. Not as much as Cleopatra, but plenty, more than enough. She was good-looking—a dark-skin, dark-hair type, with a handful of freckles—but there was something of the born-again about her, that kind of earnest matter-of-factness that makes you want to run the other way. Almost everybody's born-again these days; if you're not born-again you're out to lunch, yours is a minority view, you lose. Anyway, this woman had an easy rapport with the announcer, who was a newsman, and they traded asides, little jokes between callers' questions—he apologized a lot about his hopeless manhood.

I don't make too much of a mess with the cooking, though I'm pretty angry when I bring the chops in and drip lamb juice on the carpet in the living room. But before I have time to get worse, Lily's got the plate of chops out of my hands and is telling me to remember three weeks ago, when I threw barbecue at the kitchen window.

"That was pork," I say. "And I don't know why you feel you have to remind me about it all the time anyway. I cleaned it up, didn't I?"

"Yes, Roger." She's circling the table, dropping lamb chops on the plates. "It took you two hours, too."

"But it was real cool, Dad," Charles says, making a throwing move. "Splat!"

I say, "No, my little porcupine, it wasn't."

"I agree," Christine says. "It was childish." She's repeating what she heard her mother say immediately after I tossed the pork chops.

"How old is she?" I ask Lily. I kiss the top of Christine's head and then take my chair. "If you're real good," I say to Christine, "we can get a dog later, okay?" She knows, I think, that this is a joke.

"I think maybe you're trying too hard again, Dad," Charles says. He's taken to adding "Dad" to every sentence. It's annoying.

"Yeah, Dad," Lily says. "Take it easy, would you?" She pinches Charles's ear and turns him to face his dinner.

Charles squirms, trying to get away from her. "Jesus, Mom," he says.

"None of that, kid," I say. I wave my fork at him for emphasis, point it at him, wiggle it.

"Who wants a stupid dog, anyway?" Christine says. She's using an overhand grip on her spoon, shoving the food on her plate around to make sure that nothing touches anything else. She's always eaten this way, ever since she was four. She'll eat all of one vegetable, then all of the next, and so on. I've tried to stop it, but Lily says it's okay, so I haven't made much progress. She says Christine will grow out of it. I say I know that, but what will she grow into? Lily says I'm a hard-liner.

"You want a dog," I say to Christine. "What are you talking about? All you've said for the last three weeks is how much you want a dog."

"That was before," she says.

"Before what?" Charles says. He turns to me as if we are coconspirators. "She wants one, Dad. I know she does. She's lying."

"Don't call your sister a liar," Lily says. "Roger, tell him."

"Your mother's right, Charles. Don't call Christy a liar, okay? Not nice." I'm just about finished with my first lamb chop. The mint-flavored apple jelly is glistening on my plate. I feel pretty good.

"It's true," Charles says. "What do you want me to do? Do you want me to lie, too?"

Christine is playing with her food, twirling her chop in the clear space she's left for it on her plate. "I wanted a dog," she says, "but now I don't. Can't anybody understand that?"

"I can't," Charles says.

"Eat your dinner, Charles," Lily says. "You can understand *that*, can't you?"

I know I shouldn't tease the kids the way I do—like telling them we can get a dog. It's a standing joke in our house. They know we're not getting a dog. And they know why: Daddy's bad about dogs, about pets in general. Daddy looks at a dog and what he sees is a travel club for ticks and fleas. Try explaining that to a kid. Lily and I used to have big fights about it, but I won. I outlasted her. I'm not proud of it, but it's okay. I don't mind winning one every now and then. She still thinks I'll come around after a while, but she's wrong about that. I've told the kids they can have fish, but they don't want fish.

So there's a history going on about this dog stuff, in the family, and I tease them about it all the time; it might sound cruel, but it seems to me they ought to understand. You can't always get what you want and all that. It's important that they know what's going on, that once they know no dog's forthcoming, then the dog is fair game. Lily says I'm crazy on this one, that kids don't work the way we do. She says I'm building a horrible distrust. She says it's not smart, that when I'm old and pathetic they'll trick me—tell me they're coming to see me and then not show, or take me out for a drive and slam me into a home or something.

"Okay," I say. "I'm sorry I brought up the dog. The dog remark was a bad idea. No dog. Christine?"

"What?" She's petulant. "I know," she says.

"I shouldn't have said a thing about the dog, okay? I don't know why I did. I'm upset."

"Daddy's upset about the office, sweetheart," Lily says.

"I'm sorry," Christine says.

"He shouldn't take it out on us," Charles says. He turns to me, gives me a real adult look. "You shouldn't, Dad."

I don't think I like the way Charles is turning out. For a time, his early moves toward adulthood, the grave looks and the knowing nods, were charming, even touching. After all, he's a boy, a kid, and it's nice to see him practicing. But it gets old.

"I know that, Charles," I say. "Thank you."

"Well," he says, "I'm just trying to help."

Lily pats his arm. I don't know why mothers always pat their children's arms. It's disgusting. "Yes, Charles," she says. "But Daddy's tired. Let's just be quiet and eat, what do you say? Daddy's had a hard day."

"Another one?"

"That's enough, Charles," she says.

And it is enough. After that, we eat in silence. I watch Christine, who eats her corn first, kernel by kernel, then the beans. She doesn't even touch her lamb chop. When I finish eating, I take my plate to the kitchen, scrape the used food into the brown paper bag we keep under the sink—only now it's out on the kitchen floor in front of the cabinet—and put my plate under the faucet. I turn on the water for a few seconds to rinse, then go back through the dining area, stop behind Lily for a minute, and cross the room toward the back door. "I'm going to straighten up out here," I say. "I may water for a while."

"You're going to water?" Charles says.

"Finish eating," Lily says. "I think your father might want some individual time."

"What's individual time?" Christine says.

"Don't be dumb," Charles says to her.

What I'm thinking about, out there on the deck, is that I'm not living the way I ought to be living, not the way I thought I would be. It's all obvious stuff—women, mostly. I'm not Mr. Imagination on the deal. A woman stands for a connection and another way of living, something like that. So I'm thinking about the woman on *West 57th*, the TV show, and the dewy young girls in the movies—though you don't see them as much as you used to—and thinking of the poor approximations that throng the malls. I'm not thinking anything *about* these women, I'm only thinking *of* them.

I put the charcoal lighter back in the storage closet, finger the hickory chips, think for a minute about sitting down in there. This closet is about six feet square, lined with empty cardboard boxes that our electronics came in; we've kept computer boxes, stereo boxes, TV and VCR boxes, speaker boxes, tape-recorder boxes. Then I decide to do it, to sit down just the way I want to, and I go back to the deck and get one of the white wire chairs and put it in the storage room and sit down, my feet up on the second shelf of the bookcase that I bought from Storehouse so the junk we keep in the storage closet will be more orderly: charcoal, lighter, and chips on the bottom shelf, plant foods and insecticides on the second, plant tools on the third, also on the third electric tools (saw, drill, sander), and accessories on the top. It isn't too bad in there. From where I sit I can see out across the deck to the small lump of forest that borders one side of our lot. She always puts plants out there in the summer, and I look at those—pencil cactus, other euphorbias.

Lily comes out and walks right past the door of the storage closet out to the edge of the deck, looking around for me. "Roger?" she calls. "Roger, where are you?"

"Back here."

She turns and looks at me in the closet. "What are you doing in there, Roger?"

I say, "Thinking about my sins," which is a thing my mother always used to say when I was a kid, that she was thinking about her sins. She didn't have any sins to think about, of course, which is why it was a funny thing to say.

"Why don't you come out of there? Sit out here with me, okay?"

I say, "Fine," and pick up my chair and carry it back out to the spot on the deck where I got it.

She closes the storage door behind me. "Now," she says, sitting down on the deck railing. "You've got this nice family, these two kids and everything, this good job, and things are going great, right?"

"Things are okay."

"Right. And you're complaining all the time about everything."

"Right."

"And you don't want to complain."

"Right."

"So you're like Peter Finch," she says, "In that movie, whatever it was. The one where he went out the window and said he was mad as hell, remember?"

"Sure," I say. "What's the point?"

"Where'd it get him?" Lily says. "He's dead as a doornail. I mean, that's not *why* he's dead, but he is dead. I think there's a lesson in that."

I nod and say, "That lesson would be . . ."

"Take it easy, Greasy," Lily says.

"But everything's wrong now. People'll say anything. Everybody's transparent and nobody minds—like you, for example. Here, now. What you want is for me not to be upset. That's all. You don't care what I'm upset about, you just want me over it."

"Well?"

"In a better world we'd deal with the disease, not the symptom."

"In a better world we wouldn't have the disease," she says.

"Good point."

"Thank you."

Charles comes out of the house carrying a sleeping bag, a yellow ice chest, some magazines, and the spread off his bed. "I'm camping out tonight, okay?" he says as he passes us.

I start to say no, but then Lily catches my eye and gives her head a little sideways shake. This means that she has already signed off on things.

"Watch out for spiders," I say.

"There aren't any spiders," Lily says, shaking her head. She smiles at Charles and holds out her arm to him, and he comes over for a kiss, trailing his equipment.

I nod. "That's right. No spiders. I just said that."

"Your daddy's having a hard time," Lily says.

Charles is hanging around in an annoying way, lingering. It's as if he doesn't really want to camp out in the back yard after all.

"I don't care about them anyway," he says. "I play with spiders at school." He waits a second, then says, "Dad, I'm making a tent. Is it okay if I use the boards behind the garage?"

I say sure.

It's dark, and we've got a pretty good tent in the yard. I'm in there with Charles. He's reading a car magazine and listening to a Bon Jovi tape on the portable we got him for his last birthday. I've already asked him to turn it down twice, and the second time he went inside for his earphones. It must be midnight. I'm lying on my back under the tent, my feet sticking out the back end of it, my head on one of the three pillows he brought out. The floor of our place here is cardboard, but we've got a rug over that, a four-by-seven thing that Lily and I got at Pier I about fifteen years ago. I got it out of the garage, where it's been a couple of years.

The bugs aren't too bad. Both of us rubbed down with Off, so there's this thin, slightly turpentine smell in the air.

I get along well enough with Charles. We're not like some *Father Knows Best* thing, but we do all right. He has his world and I have mine. Looking at him there in the tent, his head hopping with music, his eyes on the magazine, I have an idea what he's about, what it's like for him. I mean, he sees the stuff I see on TV and he believes it, or maybe he believes nothing, or maybe he recognizes that none of it makes any difference to him anyway. I guess that's it. And if that's it, he's right. Let 'em lie. We've got the yard, the bedspread tent, there are crickets around here, and pretty soon a cat will stick its head in the opening at the front of the tent, look us over, maybe even come in and curl up. What goes on out there is entertainment; I'm not saying it won't touch him, but the scale is so big that really it won't. We'll do another Grenada—what a pathetic, disgusting, hollow, ignorant joke that was—but he'll be in school, or doing desk work for some Army rocker, or waiting for his second child. He's just like me, he's out of it. He can get in if he wants to—he can be a TV guy, a reporter, a senator, a staff person. It's America. He can be anything, do anything. I'm stumped.

"What're you doing, Dad?" Charles says.

I keep looking at the top of the tent. "Thinking about you."

"Oh." He waits a minute, then he says, "Well? Is it a mystery or what?"

"It's no mystery," I say, rolling over on my side so I can look at him. He's got the earphones down around his neck. "What're you reading?"

"Bigfoot." He flashes the magazine at me. It's called *Bigfoot*. "The truck, you know?"

"Monster truck," I say.

"Right. It's a whole magazine about Bigfoot—how they got started, what happened, you know. . . ."

"You interested in trucks?" I say. What I'm thinking is, I don't like the way this sounds, this conversation. It sounds like conversations on television, fathers and sons in tortured moments. "Never mind," I say.

"Not really," he says, answering me anyway.

"I don't know why I'm out here, Charles," I say. "Am I bothering you?"

"Not really. I mean, it's strange, but it's not too bad."

"I'm just a little off track today, know what I mean? I think I'm down on my fellow man—talking weenies everywhere, talking cheaters and liars. I mean, normally it doesn't bother me, I just play through. You do what you can. Pick up the junk and paste it back together whatever way you can."

"Dad? Are you drunk?"

"Nope," I say. "I haven't been drunk for ten years, Charles. There's nothing to drink about." I sit up, crossing my legs, facing him. "I never wanted to have a son—any child, for that matter. You and Christine are Lily's doing, what she wanted. I didn't mind, you see. It's not like I hate kids or anything, it's just that having kids wasn't the great driver for me. You're a problem, you know? Kids are. I don't want to treat you like a pet, but you're small—and, of necessity, kind of dumb. I don't mean dumb, but there's stuff you don't know, see what I mean?"

"Sure," he says.

"It's not stuff I can tell you."

"Dad," he says, "are you sure you're okay? You want me to get Mom?" He's up, bent over, already on his way out.

"Well . . . sure. Get Mom."

I lie down again when he's gone. I feel fine, I feel okay. In a minute Lily's crawling into the tent. "Roger?" she says. "What's going on? Do you feel all right?"

"I'm functional."

Charles comes in long enough to get his magazine and his tape recorder. "I think I'll stay inside tonight," he says.

"I talked to him," I say to Lily.

"Uh-huh," She's got an arm across my chest and she's patting me.

"So long, Sport," I say to Charles as he backs out of the tent.

"Night, Dad," he says.

I'm left there in the tent with my wife. I say, "I'm acting up, I guess."

"A little."

"But that's acceptable, right? Now and then?"

"It's fine," she says.

"It's by way of a complaint, huh? So we're back where we started from."

"Yep."

"It's not a vague complaint in my head," I say. "It's just that it covers everything. There are too many things to list. You start listing things that are wrong and you either make them smaller and sort of less wrong, or you go on forever. You got forever?"

"Sure." She waits a few seconds after she says that; I can feel her waiting. Then she says, "But I've got to go to the mall sometime."

"All right."

She gets up on her knees and twists around so she can lie down on her back alongside me. She takes my right hand in her left. "See there? You're not completely gone. You're okay. We've just got to take it one thing at a time. We've got to go binary on this one."

(1987)

LUMBER

The windows of Cherry's station wagon are open, and bits of her furniture—a rolled-up rug, the legs of a chair, a lamp with the light bulb still in it—stick out on three sides. The engine is running, and there's white smoke shooting out the exhaust pipe. She's stopped to talk to me in the parking lot, turning in the seat so she can fold her arms on the car door.

"I never wanted to leave in the first place," she says.

"Sure you did." Then I remember she doesn't like being told what she thinks. "Or maybe you didn't. It's not that far, anyway."

She's moving from Palm Shadows to another, newer apartment group, Courtland, three blocks away, because some kids broke into her apartment a week ago, terrorized her, threatened rape, then took her stereo and TV and a hundred dollars in grocery money.

"You think I should stay?"

"No. I think you're lucky it wasn't worse."

Cherry is forty; she looks like an out-of-date teenager. "Don't be silly," she says. The engine is loping now, faltering and catching up again. She hits the gas pedal once and a fresh pillow of smoke gathers behind the wagon. "You could move too, you know. That might be fun."

I like the way we both stop and wait for the remark to get sexy; in eight months as neighbors, this has become a routine.

"I've got to go now," she says. "But you're going to call me, right?" She straightens up behind the wheel, then reaches into her purse and pulls out a felt-tipped pen. "You got paper? I'll give you my new number."

I don't have paper, so she prints her telephone number on my wrist in big square letters. I crook my hand around, trying to read it. "What's that?" I say, pointing to something she's drawn at the end of the number.

"That's a picture of you and me. Sitting pretty."

Later, in the Handy Andy annex, I'm looking at the half-inch plywood sheets when Cherry comes up behind me and pats my backside. I yelp and jump about two feet. Cherry laughs. "What, you gonna board up the place now that I'm gone?"

"I'm just here being lonely."

"Not me. I'm having a great time. This looks like bad plywood." She fingers the topmost in a stack of precut four-by-four sheets. "What is this, A-D?" She looks at me. "That's plywood talk. Do you want to do something?"

"Yes. Anything."

She moves away toward the full-size plywood and says, over her shoulder, "I could take you to my new place. It's got great locks. We could arrange my furniture." She squints and twists her head like a puzzled dog. "Or we could not arrange my furniture, and eat something instead. I've got peaches."

The guy who works the annex comes up and says, "So you're looking for some first-rate plywood?" He's about forty-five and so thin he looks sick, wearing checked pants, a short-sleeved white shirt, and a purple tie about eight inches long.

"This is the ugliest plywood I ever saw," Cherry says. "What kind is it?"

"Just plywood," he says. "Plywood."

"I guess you're right," Cherry says. "I'm thinking about building a bed—a frame, you know."

"Yeah, well," he says, banging his knuckles on the stack, "this is the stuff, all right. We get a lot of people want to build beds, and this is what they use right here. Fifty cents a cut, but my saw man is gone."

"I'm just shopping, anyway," Cherry says. "I'm not ready to buy."

The salesman frowns and rubs a hand back over his scalp, looking toward the front of the huge store. His tie has a polo player on it.

When he turns back to us, I say, "Maybe we'll come back tomorrow. Your saw man be in tomorrow?"

"Sure will." He shakes his head and starts to walk away. "I don't know why you types come in here."

When he's out of earshot, Cherry whispers, "How rude."

"I don't think you build beds out of plywood, usually."

"No? Well, no wonder."

We go to her new apartment. Courtland is a small complex, only twenty units, and it looks like a Motel 6. I have to park my car behind hers in the parking lot, because all the spaces are assigned. It's a cool night and it smells as if it's going to rain. Cherry stands by my car door as I get out. "You'd better lock it," she says.

It's raining hard when I wake up. Cherry's asleep. The telephone is ringing, but I can barely hear it for the rain. I don't know what time it is. I shake Cherry, but she groans and rolls over. She's not going to wake up in time to get the phone, so I go out into the cluttered living room. It's dark, and I accidentally kick the wooden crate the telephone is on, knocking the receiver off its hook. When I finally get the phone to my ear, a woman's voice is saying hello.

"Hi," I say. "Cherry's asleep. I kicked the phone over."

"Mark?"

"No. I'm Frank. Mark's not here. Who is this?"

There's a pause; then the woman says, "Lois. This is Lois. I've got to talk to Cherry—could you wake her?"

I tell the woman to hold on, and I go back into the bedroom and snap on the desk lamp; Cherry's already up, sitting on the edge of the bed with my shirt on. "That's Lois, I guess," she says. "What time is it?"

I hand her the travel clock from the desk and go over to the window. There's a yellow light on a pole in the alley that runs behind Courtland, and below it the bushes are whipping around in the wind. "Good storm," I say.

Cherry tosses me the clock and heads for the living room. It's four-ten. I put the clock on the desk and follow her.

She's sitting on the floor by the crate, her legs crossed under her, waving a pack of cigarettes at me and pointing across the room.

The only light is from the lamp in the bedroom, so I can't see what she's pointing at. I step over a couple of cardboard boxes full of phonograph records and open the drapes in front of the sliding doors, which gives me enough grayish light to find the matches. Cherry's saying into the phone, "Now, just start over, real slow, okay? Take it easy." I hand her the matches and watch her light a cigarette and push the hair away from her face with her palm.

There's a beach towel on the arm of the couch; I wrap the towel around me and look out across the street, where there's another apartment group, all lit up with thin green light that's distorted by the water on the sliding door. The rain is banging up into spirals where it hits, slapping the glass and blowing off the overhang at forty-five degrees. In the parking lot across the street there are two cars with their lights on; somebody in a yellow rain slicker with a Day-Glo pink stripe across the shoulders is running back and forth between the cars. One of the cars has its emergency lights on, so the taillights blink together; the red-orange flashes are magnified and splintered by the rain. I keep switching my focus between the cars and the glass in the door.

Cherry rocks awkwardly as she talks softly into the phone, coaxing the woman on the other end of the line. I go into the kitchen and open the refrigerator. It looks peculiarly bright and precise inside. I'm trying to decide if I want the half cantaloupe on the top shelf next to the milk when Cherry starts snapping her fingers at me from the other room. When I look, she makes a drinking motion with her hand and then points at me. I pull things to drink out of the refrigerator—beer, orange juice, apple juice, tomato juice, milk, Coke. It turns out she wants apple juice, which was the third thing I showed her; I give her the bottle and a glass. She gives the glass back, then twists the top off the juice and takes a drink.

She's twenty minutes on the phone. I sit on the couch and talk to the cantaloupe, listening to the rain and to her end of the conversation. She's lovely to watch, all folded up on the floor—sloppy but businesslike, deft somehow. I think of the nights I've spent wondering if she was alone in her apartment; even if she had been, she probably wouldn't have been alone in the same way—she'd have had something to do, some project, some work.

"Lois is coming up," Cherry says when she gets off the phone. She hangs her head and fiddles with the juice bottle, which is on the floor between her legs. "I'm real tired. Are you? That's a stupid question, I guess."

Lois comes in wearing a turban and light-blue pin-cord Bermuda shorts. She's got dark skin and a pear-size red birthmark on one side of her mouth and under her chin. She seems cheerful and wide awake. "You must be Frank, right? I'm Lois." We shake hands and I see another birthmark, this one smaller and cloud-shaped, running up the back of her thumb.

"Good morning," I say. I've got my jeans on and the towel draped over my shoulders; Cherry still has my shirt.

"So," Lois says. "What's for breakfast?"

Cherry comes out of the bedroom zipping her pants. "Hiya, baby," she says, opening her arms to hug Lois. I back up a little, trying to get out of the way, trip over one of the record boxes, and then, to avoid falling, do a kind of somersault onto the couch. The women pause in their embrace to look.

"He an acrobat of some kind?" Lois says.

Cherry gives Lois a slap on the rump.

"I could eat a hundred something right about now," Lois says. "First I gotta get rid of this." She hooks her fingers under the turban, pulls it off her head, flips it toward me.

"Frank needs attention," Cherry says. "Why don't you amuse him while I check the food."

Cherry goes into the kitchen, and Lois sits splay-legged on the arm of the couch. "So, Frank," she says, scratching her scalp with her fingernails. "How are you?"

Lois has a burr haircut and pretty eyes, but because of her size and the haircut she looks like a man. I say I'm okay and ask her how she is.

"I'm a mess—oh, maybe you guessed that. I'm having a crisis. I always have my crises at four in the morning, usually. That way they seem more crisis-like, know what I mean? What's that on your stomach?" She points at a crescent-shaped scar on my left side where my sister caught me with the broken neck of a Coke bottle when I was fourteen.

"Scar," I say.

She nods and chews on the side of her lip, "So I'm having this crisis and I call Cherry and here you are answering the phone. It surprised me."

"Me too. What's the crisis? Or is that not my business?"

"Well, no—I'm just having this crisis." She looks at the window. "I mean, I could tell you, but you probably wouldn't understand, because—oh, this is going to sound so stupid."

"What?"

"Oh—because you're a man."

"You're right—it sounds stupid."

"That's clever. Who are you—Sheriff Lobo? What happened was, my boyfriend hit me." She points to her ear. "Here. He smacked me in the head. I didn't like it."

"What did you do?"

"What do you mean what did I do? I didn't do anything—he just hit me because he was mad."

"No, I meant what did you do then, after he hit you."

"Oh. I ran like hell. I don't want people hitting me all the time." She tugs at her crotch. "Doesn't matter. He's just some new thing I picked up. I probably should've known better."

"How many eggs out there?" Cherry calls from the kitchen.

"I wish I'd had some eggs before," Lois says. "I'd have given him a scrambled face." She slaps her palm into her forehead as if she's smacking somebody with an egg. "Take that!"

"Hello?" Cherry says, leaning around the kitchen doorframe and waving a white spatula in her hand.

"Two for me," I say, "Want some help?"

"I don't think I want any," Lois says. She sticks her hands in the pockets of her shorts and leans back, crossing her feet on a box by the couch. "So, you ever hit a woman, Frank? I mean, you know, really hit her?"

"I don't think so."

"What's that mean? Either you did or you didn't. Are you prissy?"

"No."

"Ah." She nods vigorously and loses her balance so that she has to drop her feet to the floor to steady herself. "Yeah, well—some men don't. That's true, I guess. Maybe you're one of those. Anyway, this guy was a jerk, a real bohunk—what's a bohunk?"

"A bad guy, rat."

"Cherry? You got a dictionary around here somewhere? I want to look up 'bohunk.'"

"It's not in the dictionary," Cherry says from the kitchen. "I already looked."

"When did you look?" Lois says.

"So maybe it is," Cherry says. "The dictionary's packed and the eggs are ready."

We eat in the living room. Lois goes over the details of the fight with her boyfriend, Milby. They were in the car, sitting out in front of her apartment downstairs; they were arguing. Milby slugged her when she yelled at him about leaving his junk all over her apartment. Then she got out of the car and ran inside, gathered up everything that belonged to him, and threw it out on the sidewalk. He sat in the car and watched her do this. He looked pretty sitting there in the car in the rain. She stood in the doorway for a long time, staring at him. He was so gorgeous she wanted to get back into the car with him, but was afraid to; as a conciliatory gesture, Lois went out into the rain and got all of his stuff and took it back into the apartment. Then she stood on the doorstep and watched him for another five minutes before he started the car and drove off. He didn't say a word, didn't even wave, just started up and left. This all happened at about two-thirty. She tried to call him, but either he wasn't home or he wasn't answering the phone. She put all his stuff in the bathtub, except the boots; those she put on the top of the stove the way her father used to do with his boots. She tried to call Milby again, then changed her clothes and tried again. No answer. That's when she called Cherry. "And got you," she says, pointing her fork at me. "You guys were probably sleeping, right?"

"Milby's an ape," Cherry says.

"He's a nice ape," Lois says. She looks at me. "Okay, let's have the man's point of view on this."

"Love conquers all?"

"It's the first time he's ever done anything like this."

"Maybe it's a freak thing," Cherry says.

"If you're lucky," I say.

"You're the one who's lucky," Lois says. "You don't get hit in the face if you don't do what we want."

When I wake up on Saturday morning, Cherry's on her back on the bedroom floor, grunting softly as she does stretching exercises for her legs. The bedroom isn't large, so all I can see is her feet—which have thick half socks on them—coming together and separating suddenly. I watch the feet for a few minutes and then say, "Good morning."

"Oh, hi," she says, sitting up beyond the end of the bed. "Did I wake you?"

There's not much light in the room and I have a hard time making out Cherry's features; her face looks bloated and too white. "No. I just woke up. What are you doing?"

"Working on the legs. I probably shouldn't worry about it, but I do."

"They're very pretty—kind of leg-like and pretty."

She turns and talks to the chair that's tipped against the wall. "What does he mean by that? Is he talking to me?"

"Where's Lois? She not here yet?"

"Don't be nasty about Lois," Cherry says. She struggles to her feet and stretches, reaching straight above her head with both hands. I hear things in her back popping. "I suppose you're going to want coffee?"

I roll out of bed and stand there looking around the room for my pants.

We have coffee on the couch. She has on chrome-green running shorts and a white T-shirt with "Spider" stitched in a shallow arc over the small pocket. The shirt is tucked into the waistband of the pants. Outside, the cars I saw last night are still in the parking lot across the street; the hood on one of the cars is raised, and there's somebody bent into the engine compartment. The coffee is bitter.

"This is the part I don't like," Cherry says after we've been silent for a while. "Waiting for the guy to leave." She touches my leg. "I shouldn't have said that, huh? That was a lousy thing to say."

"It's all right. I know what you mean. Maybe I'll go and then call you later."

"We could eat or something." She props up a knee and balances her cup on it. "Maybe we could go to the coast? I just hate this part. It doesn't have anything to do with you." She sighs and gets up quickly, almost losing the coffee, and stands at the glass door. "No, that's worse, isn't it?"

"It's really okay. Just let me get set and I'll move along." Her shorts bag a little in the seat. "The coast sounds like a terrific idea."

"That's the most insincere thing you ever said to me."

"I know. It wasn't very good, was it? But maybe the coast will sound terrific later."

"What a man," she says, picking up my jacket and brushing it with her hand.

Milby is about five-eight, with curly black hair and a drooping mustache that almost covers his mouth. He's wearing a plaid cowboy shirt with pearl snap buttons, and he has spurs on his boots. He's leaning over the railing outside Cherry's door when I open it. "You Frank?" he says, combing the mustache with his forefinger. I nod, and he says, "I'm Milby. We need to have a little meet."

Cherry, standing just inside her apartment, holding on to the edge of the door, says, "You kind of screwed up last night, didn't you?"

"Hello, Cherry," he says. "I didn't want to wake you up, so I waited out here. I figured you'd have to come out sooner or later." He waves to show us where he waited. "Maybe I'd better just talk to Frank here."

"Maybe you'd better talk to Lois," she says.

"I did that already. I've been talking to her since five. I didn't get any sleep." Milby moves a lot when he talks, and the spurs make a noise like a cash register. "She told me I better talk to you all."

"It's you and Lois," I say. "No reason to talk to us."

"I want to talk to you," Milby says. He reaches up, grabs me by the shoulder, and squeezes gently. "I really need to."

"Jesus Christ," Cherry says. "What kind of jerk are you?" She shakes her head. "I'd have your ass in jail."

"I should be in jail," he says. "That's where I should be. I'm really sorry I'm not, but I'm not." He backs up when Cherry steps out of her apartment onto the balcony. "I was thinking maybe I could buy you a steak, Frank. We could talk things over."

I look back at Cherry, and she shrugs and looks away. "I don't care," she says. "He just wants somebody to tell him it's okay."

"It's not," Milby says. "I know that much."

"Then you want somebody to listen to all the reasons, and there aren't any reasons worth talking about."

"No, really," he says. "I just want to talk to Frank a bit. It's nothing like that, Cherry."

"So talk, already. Go get a steak and talk. Be men all over the place. Practice spitting."

He cocks his boot up and kicks at the concrete balcony with the spur, spinning it and holding it up until it stops. Cherry says, "Oh, go on," kisses my cheek, and gives me a push.

When we get downstairs, Milby points at his black Camaro and says, "Let's take mine, okay?"

We go to a place called Western Sizzlin, a franchise with fifteen kinds of beef and a sad-looking salad bar. He tells me to get whatever I want, so I order the eight-dollar rib eye. We take a booth by the window and look at the cars going by in the street. Finally Milby says, "It wasn't that hard. I mean, I know it's stupid, but it wasn't real hard, you know? I just kind of popped her to shut her up."

"Like they used to do in movies."

"Yeah. Hey, there's no bruise. I'm telling you it wasn't that bad." He fiddles with the A.1. Sauce, unscrewing the cap and turning the bottle upside down on his thumb, then sucking the brown sauce off. He sighs. "Yeah, okay I don't know what happened. I knew enough to pull it, though. While it was happening."

"That's a start."

"You damn right it is," he says. "She deserved it, you know what I'm saying? I mean, bitch, bitch, bitch—you got to do something."

He looks tired and short-tempered, and I wonder what I can get away with. "Try a wall."

"You don't think fast enough. The thing is, they take advantage of everything—all the differences—but you can't. You get pissed after a while."

"Everybody gets pissed." I wonder why I don't tell him what I want to tell him, why he scares me. "Who's this 'they,' anyway?"

"The bitches—what are you, some Holy Ghost or something? I don't need catechism lessons, brother. It's jerks like you screw it up for the rest of us. I'm telling you it just happens, and you're telling me Hail Mary, full of grace. That's a big help."

"Yeah, okay," I say, cutting through my steak, "you're probably right."

That does it. He doesn't want to talk about last night anymore, he wants to talk football—what do I think about the Bears? I tell him what I think, something I read in the paper about Payton's legs. When we're finished eating, he pays with a credit card and I thank him for the lunch.

In the car on the way back to the Courtland he tells me there's nothing wrong with Payton's legs, the legs are okay, and then skids into a place in front of Lois's first-floor apartment.

Somehow Cherry has gotten her station wagon out from in front of my car. I thank Milby again and leave him sitting in the flashy black interior of the Camaro, the radio pumping out news. At Palm Shadows I get my mail, say hello to the robust landlord who's digging around in some bushes near my door, and go upstairs. The phone is ringing, so I have to hustle to get through both locks. It's Cherry, calling to tell me she's busy and maybe she'll give me a call tomorrow, I tell her I'm going to take a bath, and she says it's high time.

(1981)

INSTRUCTOR

Southwestern Alabama advertised a one-year, non-tenure-track instructorship in biology, and, more or less routinely, I sent my vita to the chairman of the department. When he called and asked me to interview for the position, I was surprised and pleased. I flew down on Wednesday, rented a Chevette, and signed in at the Tropic Breeze Motel, as he'd suggested. Thursday I spent the morning with him, the search committee, the dean of the college, two vice presidents, and the president, and after lunch I sat in the department lounge talking with whoever happened in. That's when I met Sonia. She was an associate professor from Kansas, three years in rank and ready for promotion because of a book contract with Plinth. She had wavy red hair and a long, almost defiant stride, and she came in late, close to five. She introduced herself, asked who was taking care of me, then invited me to dinner with her and her brother Jack.

We went to a fish place down by the channel, and when we came back into town the rain that had been on and off all day let up. Everything was shiny and bright—the pavement, the stoplights, the violet and green neon from shop windows that lined the street.

"So much for science," she said as we drove past the university. "Let's get some beer—what do you say?"

"Maybe one," I said. "I have my presentation to the faculty at ten tomorrow."

"They shouldn't make you do that for this kind of a job," she said. "Anyway, you'll be perfect, don't worry."

"He's insecure," Jack said, glancing at me in the rearview mirror. Jack was an electrical engineer and apartment developer. He was a small man to start with, and looked smaller because he was driving Sonia's 1955 Buick. His hair was springy, also red, and floated around the sides of his head. We pulled into a 7-Eleven parking lot alongside a police car.

"Yum yum," Sonia said, pointing to the cop who was inside drinking coffee out of a polka-dot cup. He was a young guy with a little-boy haircut and a black leather jacket, and he had his hat cocked back on his head. "Oh," she said. "It's Burt."

Jack lifted up in the seat as he reached into his back pocket for his wallet. "Burt?"

"Ex-student," she said. "Look at him. He's so sweet."

"My sister needs a boyfriend," Jack said, looking at me over his shoulder.

"My brother thinks I'm a one-woman sexual revolution," she said. "But I tell him we all need boyfriends." She went inside and got two six-packs of Coors out of the cooler. Then she said something to Burt. They talked while the skinny girl in the red jumper covered with 7-Eleven patches worked the register and put the beer in a sack.

"I kid her," Jack said. "But she's a good sister. You have a family?"

I slid down on the back seat and stuck my hand out the open car window to feel the rain. "Four brothers," I said.

"Sisters are different," he said. "We have a brother in Kansas, but we never talk to him."

The 7-Eleven overhang was wrapped with white fluorescent tubes, and beyond them the sky was medium gray, the tree limbs black.

"She does need a boyfriend," Jack said. He leaned over the seat back. "What are you doing back here?"

"She shouldn't have any trouble," I said.

"That's what I thought," he said.

Sonia and the policeman came out of the store together, still talking. He walked her to the car and opened the door. The interior light came on, and Sonia said, "Meet Patrolman Burt. This is Jack, and that's David in back. Jack's my brother."

"Howdy," the guy said. He leaned over so that he could see into the car. His jacket creaked.

"He's off duty," Sonia said.

Burt smiled.

Sonia patted him on the back. "So tell them how things are, crime-wise."

"Not much happening," he said. "It's quiet."

"Burt and I are going to drive around awhile," Sonia said. "I love police cars. Are you coming by later?"

"I could take David to Blister's," Jack said.

"That'll be fine," Sonia said, smiling. "Then I'll tell him what Chairman Stibert really thought about him. Okay, David?"

"You don't want to go to Blister's?" I said.

"I hate it," she said. "We'll meet up shortly."

Burt adjusted his gun belt, and while he wasn't looking Jack and Sonia made faces at each other. Then she dropped the sack on the passenger seat.

"An hour?" Jack said. "You figure to get your driving done by then?"

"That'll be superior," Sonia said. She turned to me. "Are you all right, David?"

"Fine," I said, waving.

Sonia rolled her eyes and made a playfully impatient face. "Oh, get up here in front, will you?" She slapped the back of the seat with her palm.

Blister's was full of students and young faculty types. The music was loud. Everyone seemed to be having a good time. Two guys signaled Jack from a table near the bandstand, and when we got to where they were they both started talking right away, completing each other's sentences. The club was dark. The waitresses wore smart yellow tights. I took a seat at one end of the table and said hello to the guy with extraordinary sideburns, glasses, and a black T-shirt that had "COBOL" block-lettered across the chest.

Jack said, "This is David." He pointed at the guy next to him, then at the one next to me. "Mitch, and Hacker. Mitch, you have to do the women."

"I already did the women," Mitch said, and everybody laughed.

There were three women. One of them said, "Mitch is the art department, so you can forget him. I'm Carmen. That's Mamie, and this one"—she patted the head of the woman sitting next to her—"this one with the blue hair is Lucy."

"Hello, Lucy," I said. Lucy had bright eyes to match the hair, which was brushed back and up in a rooster cut.

"Her name's not really Lucy," Carmen said. "Everybody just calls her that."

"Right," Lucy said. "And I don't mind it, either, because my real name's Alma."

"That's not such a bad name," I said, but when everybody started whistling and hooting I held up my hands and said, "Okay, it's horrible."

Mitch leaned across the table and kissed Lucy on the neck, just inside the collar of her shirt.

"A territorial thing," she said, stroking the back of his head.

The waitress brushed her hip against me. I ordered a Stroh's and then listened to two of the women talk about a guy both had had in class. Mitch sat down and put an arm around Jack. Hacker rubbed his nose in tight circles with his knuckle. "I hear you're interviewing. How'd you do?" he said.

"All right, I guess." I wiggled my beer bottle. "The president had some trouble remembering what I was here for, but outside of that it was fine."

"He has trouble remembering what *he's* here for," Hacker said.

"Laughs," Carmen said.

"He's all right," Lucy said. "So what if he likes plaid? That's his job."

Carmen and Hacker both did slow double takes, and I got the idea that this was their routine.

"You're not biology, are you?" I said to Lucy.

"Poetry," she said. "I teach poetry and comp. Mamie's in social work, and Carmen—what do you do, Carmen?"

"I show the little coeds how to tear up men."

"I think she means phys ed," Lucy said. "How come you're with Jack? Where's Sonia?"

"She's probably doing a little biological research," Carmen said. "She does more research than anybody I know."

"Take a hike, Carmen," Mamie said.

"Carmen doesn't know Sonia," Lucy said, bending the edge of a beer coaster. "Carmen thinks Sonia should be a good little girl like the rest of us."

"At least I don't envy her," Carmen said.

The musicians, who had been sitting at the next table, went onstage, and Carmen and Mamie got up to dance, taking Mitch and Hacker with them. Jack came around to my side of the table and sat next to Lucy. We watched the customers trot out onto the tiny dance floor. A willowy blond guy in a tight emerald muscle shirt and baggy white pants started dancing alone, his eyes closed. The other dancers pulled back to allow him room.

"Who's this?" I asked, bumping Lucy's arm.

"That's Paul. He tried to hang himself from the diving board at the pool next to student housing. He used an electrical cord—one of those big orange ones they sell at the grocery stores now. Some swimming coach got him down. Paul's a very intense kid."

"He looks it," I said, watching him do some kind of wobble-knee step.

"Sure he does," Lucy said, glancing at me and then at the Schlitz clock over the bar. "Everybody says that."

On our way to Sonia's, Jack told me Hacker was a computer whiz. "He does all my financial work for half what I'd pay otherwise. He was Sonia's boyfriend when she got back from Rhodesia. She married this black guy and they moved over there, but he got killed, I think. Something like that. Anyway, he didn't come back. He was an exchange student."

Sonia's apartment was at Palm Shadows North, one of Jack's properties. He told me he had apartments in every major architectural style; these were Tudor—brown wood crisscrossing stucco buildings that were bathed in white light. When we got into the central yard, he pointed at a group of buildings partly hidden by a Japanese rain tree. "Her light's on."

The living room looked like a model in a department store. There was a humpbacked sofa with a matching chair, a big red Oriental urn, a rattan basket with tall dried weeds inside.

Sonia and Burt were in the kitchen.

"Still warm," he said, pointing to a pile of French fries on the counter. He was big, thick through the chest and shapeless from the shoulders down, and young. The tail of his blue police shirt was out, and his black belt was slung over the back of one of Sonia's barstools. He stuck out an arm to shake hands. "Burt," he said. "You're David, right?"

"He prefers David," Jack said.

Sonia kept pushing the French fries around in a hat-size pot of cooking oil.

"David," Burt said, repeating himself uncertainly as he shook my hand.

"Either one," I said. I grinned at him. "Doesn't matter."

"We got tired of driving around," Burt said, gripping my shoulder and turning me toward the counter. "We thought we'd make some homemade French fries."

"The first ones burned," Sonia said. "I don't know what I did wrong."

"I told her it was her oil," Burt said. He came up in back of Sonia and patted her rump. She jumped and gave him a look. "Oops," he said. "I think I'd better get the beer. Where's that beer you got?"

I offered to go out to the car, but Burt said he wanted to, and took the keys from Jack. "Which way is it again?" he said from the apartment door. "Out this way?" He pointed off in the wrong direction.

"Straight across the courtyard and make a right past the mailboxes," Jack said. "In the first row about twenty down."

"Back in a flash," Burt said.

Jack leaned against the counter, staring at Sonia, but she ignored him. "Hi, David," she said. "You doing okay?"

"Fine. We went to Blister's. I met the faculty."

"Oh, yeah? Who?"

"The regulars," Jack said. "So what about Burt?"

"Burt's a vet," Sonia said. "Vietnam. He learned a whole lot about human nature over there. He builds model trains. He likes bicycling and he's not good in bed."

"Oh, Jesus," Jack said. "Is he married or what?"

"His wife was Rose Queen in his high school pageant. No kids. He says she's okay."

"Is this peanut oil or regular oil?" I said.

"Crisco," Sonia said. She removed newly browned French fries and rolled them onto paper towels on the counter top. "Salt those, will you?" she said to Jack.

"Just curious," I said.

Sonia patted my arm. "It's a game we play. Actually, I have no idea about his wife, not to mention how he is in bed. My brother, however, likes to think of me as a lady of darkness. So I do the best I can."

"That's cute," Jack said. "Poor kid's probably steaming by now."

"He's doing fine," she said. "Anyway, what about that Puerto Rican girl you liked so much? What was her name—Felicidad?"

Burt opened the front door and shouted, "Beer run." He came into the kitchen carrying the sack with the top rolled over like the top of a lunch bag. His shirt was patterned with coaster-size spots. "I sat in the car a minute waiting for the rain to quit. Then I listened to it on the roof—you know, that old car, the way old cars smell, and here's this rain—thunk, thunk, thunk—you know? It's dark. Nobody's around. So I sit there for a minute, just listening. You know what I'm saying?" He put the bag on the counter and unrolled the top. "Maybe not. Who's thirsty?"

"I'll have one," Jack said, pulling a can out of a six-pack.

"Take off the shirt," Sonia said. "We'll put it in the oven again."

"I'm okay," Burt said. He flapped the tail of his shirt. "It'll dry quick enough."

"Oh, go ahead," Jack said.

Burt shook his head. "Nope." He handed out beer.

Jack took a Kleenex out of the dispenser on top of the refrigerator and wiped off the top of his Coors can, bunching the tissue to clean the can's rim, then put the beer on the counter and wadded the tissue into a ball, rolling it between his palms.

We drank the beer. Jack kept looking at me as if I was supposed to do something. Finally he said, "We still have to get your Budget car out at the school, right?" He pushed off his stool, drained his beer, then flattened the can on the counter. "Right. It's getting late. Time to move."

"It's ten o'clock, Jack," Sonia said. She fluffed his hair. "Although I do have class at eight. I used to like early classes, but I sure don't now."

Burt stuffed his shirttail back into his trousers, wrapped the gun belt around his waist, and put his cap on his head, the visor low over his eyes. "I've got to get on, myself," he said.

We went to the door together, the four of us. Burt was the first outside. "Looks like it's quit again," he said, holding his hands out at his sides.

Sonia followed him out and wrapped her arms around his neck. "Thanks, Burt," she said. "I had fun. Really." She gave Jack a high five as he walked past. "So long, Brother." Then she whispered something else to Burt and let him go. I started to follow them, but Sonia said, "Wait a bit," and tugged my coat. Jack and Burt were fifteen feet away; both turned in our direction.

"You coming, David?" Jack said.

"I don't know," I said.

Burt adjusted his cap, then put his hands on his hips, staring at Sonia, then at me. He was still for a minute, then abruptly turned, waving over his shoulder. "Night," he said.

"Meet you at the car?" Jack said.

"Take yours, Jack," Sonia said. "I'll run him out to school."

Jack caught Burt halfway across the courtyard, and by the time they made the turn to go past the mailboxes they were laughing. The sound echoed in the yard, which was full of lights bouncing off the wide blades of the yuccas, off the wet bushes. Everywhere there was the sound of dripping water. Sonia put an arm around my waist and I put an arm around hers, and we stood there watching Jack and Burt. "I like them," she said. "Isn't that strange?"

My presentation to the faculty the next morning went well enough. When an old guy I hadn't met got nasty in the question period,

Sonia reminded him, gracefully, that a lot of new work was being done in regenerative plant tissue. "We all understand how hard it is to keep up with the literature, Dr. Holdt," she said. He huffed, and then the meeting broke up. I got a polite round of applause.

Sonia had to stop at the bank on our way to lunch. When we got in line for the Auto Teller, she bumped into the back of a Dodge Polara. "How about seafood, Professor?" she said, watching the driver in front look at who'd hit him.

"How about insurance?" I said.

"I'm sorry about that business with Holdt, but I despise the old balloon."

"He doesn't seem to like you much, either," I said.

"They're used to me," she said. "I'm that way in all the faculty meetings. They don't care, or they're scared, or they just think it's funny. I don't know."

We went to a restaurant called Seafood in the Rough, where the drinks came in glasses shaped like telescopes. She looked at the menu and decided on crab claws.

"If they do the chicken and the fish in the same oil, I want fried chicken," I said.

She called the waiter over and asked about the chicken. He was eighteen and looked like John Travolta, with the wet eyes and the jaw. He liked the trout, only they were out of trout. He was mixed on the chicken and didn't know anything about the oil.

I said, "I thought it was traditional in a place like this."

"No kidding?" he said.

Sonia ordered for both of us and asked him to send the cocktail waitress back. "I've heard of it," she said, when he was gone.

My plane wasn't until seven, so after lunch Sonia took me to Jack's apartment. "I wanted you to see it," she said.

Jack had gone out of town for the weekend. His place was two studios converted into one big apartment, and it smelled like cinnamon and had a lot of furniture. Everything was jumbled together. There was a coffee table with a glass top and an Indian sand painting under the glass, and there were oil paintings of horses—horses standing alongside red-jacketed girls, horses staring into the cramped room, horses with blue ribbons pinned to them. At one end of the living room, there were two sliding doors covered with satiny curtains that almost glowed. Two low, shaded lamps provided a grimy light. I made a face by way of appreciation, and Sonia said, "You like it, right?"

"Yes," I said. "It's dark and mysterious."

She tugged on the curtain so she could look outside. There was some thunder and a flash of lightning, and she jumped away from the window. "It's great out there," she said.

I looked at a brass pot stacked with some other pots next to the wall, then settled on the floor and leaned against the couch. "I don't think I slept enough last night," I said.

She sat on the couch and flicked my hair around with her hand. "Yeah, right. You left really late—maybe ten, ten-thirty. You don't like night, you told me."

"Dumb," I said, nodding at her. "I was exhausted."

She nodded back at me.

"Dumb," I said.

She left her purse on the couch, then stood up right in front of me, close, for a minute. I stared at where her knees were under the skirt, then looked at her shoes, which were red with an open toe and a heel shaped like a funnel. The cinnamon smell was strong. I touched her shoe and she took a step closer, then backed away and went into the bedroom. After a few minutes she appeared again wearing a floor-length black silk robe decorated with red piping and a Chinese dragon, antique and stunning. "You want some space candy?" she said, tearing the top of a bag. She flipped her hair out of the collar of the robe. "I'm nuts for the stuff."

"Me too," I said. "What is it?"

She poured some kernels of the candy into my palm. The candy looked like small gray rocks. "Put them on your tongue," she said.

I did that, and the candy seemed to explode inside my head. "Umm," I said.

"Kids used to have this all the time," Sonia said. "I think they took it off the market or something. Jack's got cases and cases."

She went across the room to a lacquered dressing table that was built out from a huge round mirror. She sat with her back perfectly straight and studied her makeup, and when she combed her hair she did it the way women do in shampoo commercials, dreamily, as if the hair were precious. She was watching me watch her in the mirror. Finally, she slid the comb into a drawer, swiveled around, dropped the robe off her shoulders, and made a little flourish with her hands.

I did a short laugh and said, "Yikes!"

"Yikes?" she said. She raised an eyebrow at me and then, when I didn't move, she looked at herself, brushed her fingers across her breasts, and bent down for the robe, which she folded over her hands in her lap.

"Just something that came to mind," I said. "You're real pretty."

"Thanks." She waited another minute, then shook the robe out and started to put it on. "My idea of a friendly gesture," she said, turning to face the dressing table again.

I got off the floor and went over to her and we looked at each other in the mirror, and then she laughed and said, "So you want to go to a movie or something?"

"What a wonderful idea," I said.

She slid to one side of the stool so I could sit down, and then she put her head on my shoulder, then kissed my arm, leaving a pair of shiny red lips on my shirtsleeve.

Sonia dropped me off at the Tropic Breeze. She said she'd come back at six to take me to the airport.

"I can get a cab," I said. "I mean, if you're busy."

"I'm not," she said.

The motel was run by a guy named McCoy, who'd told me that his father built it in the fifties. The wood siding had a fresh coat of aquamarine paint, and the trim was done in coral. My room was floor-to-ceiling wood paneling. I spent the afternoon reading a book called *Guide to Coastal Alabama*, which I'd found on the night-stand.

At four I went for a walk. The motel was on a street lined with fast-food restaurants and gas stations, so I didn't go far. It was cool and there were winds—quick bursts that bent tree limbs and rattled signs. There was a big live oak in among the buildings, next to an abandoned Roy Rogers Roast Beef place, and in it there was a plat-form tree house with three low walls made out of auto hubcaps. The cars going by had their parking lights on, and the tires still hissed on the road. I wondered how I'd done in the interview and if I would get the job. A red pickup went by and the driver honked. I waved, even though I didn't know who it was—it could have been one of the people from the bar, or somebody who thought I was somebody else. I sat down on a concrete bench at the bus stop and watched the cars.

When I got back to the motel, Sonia was leaning on the wood railing outside my room. She was wearing an ice-blue leotard, a leather flight jacket with a fur collar, and a pair of bulky silver pants like some I'd seen in *TV Guide*.

"I'm early," she said, as I crossed the parking lot toward the stairs.

"I'm lucky," I said.

When I got upstairs, she was standing by the door holding a miniature dumbbell in each hand.

"What's this?" I said.

"I've been working out," she said. "I always carry these things in my car." She did a couple of demonstration curls, first one hand and then the other, her breasts popping under the thin fabric. "This place looks like a golf course. I've never been here before." She lifted her head to indicate the colored boards McCoy had around his flower beds.

I nodded and pointed toward the office. "I think the owner likes it here."

She held the dumbbells over her head and then slowly lowered her arms until they were fully extended straight out from her shoulders. "You lift?"

McCoy came out of his glass office wearing caramel-and-white saddle oxfords and high white pants with a thin cordovan belt that seemed to be twisted in the loops. He looked as if he'd just shaved—his skin was smooth and sunburn-red. He had moles that looked like erasers on his left cheek. "What's this?" he said. He looked at me, then licked his finger and tapped it on the burning tip of his cigar.

"This is personal stuff," Sonia said. She dropped the weights onto the balcony. "We're talking about getting you a rocket ship for your place here."

He beamed and looked at the grounds of his motel. "I wanted to bring in some living animals, something like that, but the city wouldn't let me. They got rules."

She nodded, and he wagged a hand, got a newspaper from the orange rack by the door, and went inside.

"He likes you," I said.

She rolled her eyes, then grabbed me by the lapel of my jacket and pulled me inside. "C'mon. I'm a knockout with a motel room."

"Right," I said.

I unlocked the door and we went in. "How come everything's in the middle? Open plan making a comeback?"

I'd moved the bed away from the wall. I always do that when I stay in motels. It hadn't seemed strange to me until she came in and started looking at it.

She walked a circle around the bed. "Maybe you should get some spotlights in here." She sat on the couch that was covered with a Mexican-style rug. "So where were you? Did you call me?"

"I went to see the sights."

"Smooth," she said. "That's the professor in you. Me, I was lonely." She dropped the leather jacket on the seat beside her, then straightened the Danskin over her belly. "I almost hit somebody in a parking lot." She turned to look out the window. "Shut the door, will you? So are you taking the job? You've got it. I talked to Stibert."

I said, "I'll take it." I shoved the door closed and sat on the edge of the bed, facing her.

We grinned at each other for a minute, and then she grabbed a handful of the silver material bunched around her knee and said, "You ever see these things? They make you look so stupid, but they work. I lost two pounds. I had to send away for them." She pressed the fabric into folds that she traced up and down her thighs. "I usually go through pants pretty quick, but these dudes are endless."

(1983)

Export

"Right now you're what I'd call marginal," Mariana Nassar said. We were standing alongside a dumpster she was painting yellow. It was about noon. I had spent the morning cleaning my apartment, and I'd come out with a plastic bag stuffed with garbage. She poked the bag with her brush. "That about a week's worth?"

"Just breakfast," I said, pulling the bag away from her.

Mariana was forty, and looked half of it. She owned a small apartment complex where I'd lived with my first wife, so when the second marriage went I rented an apartment from her. She was wearing khaki shorts and a lime-green tube top, and she was prettier than I remembered.

I angled my bag into the mouth of the dumpster.

"We're painting this thing yellow," she said. "We think that'll make it more attractive to passersby. On this thoroughfare here." She looked up and down the alley, then balanced her brush across the lip of the can. "You ready for our big talk?"

We went into the courtyard and sat down by the pool. She sat on the edge, dangling her legs in the pale-blue water. I took a chair.

"So, Henry," she said, watching her feet distort in the ripples. "You got trouble. Just like old times. Have I got it straight—your first wife stole your second?"

"And my child," I said. "You don't know Rachel, do you?"

"No," Mariana said. She rocked her hips and edged backward a little, then lifted her legs out of the water. "So we're working on tactics right at the moment."

"Right," I said.

The water glittered and shone as breezes got its surface. Mariana sighed and slapped the water with her feet. "What's our worst case?"

"I get a new start."

"Whoopee," she said, turning to look at me over her shoulder.

I grinned. "You busy or anything?"

She laughed and pulled her knees up, putting her feet on the pool ledge. She wiggled her toes. "But what are you doing to these women? How come they like each other better than you? Looks like you need some high-quality advice." She got up, stretched, then slid her hands into her back pockets.

I got up, too. "I remember. You gave me a lot of high-quality advice when Clare left. You told me to go get her."

"My John Wayne period. Doesn't work in the new world." She slapped my stomach with the back of her hand. "First we got to lose a little of this. Then, something about the hair—what is that, a Bruce Dern makeover? And the pants, Henry. It's the eighties, right? We don't have to wear jeans anymore. We can get some regular pants. Maybe a shirt with some kind of color, or pattern, or something. And we can get our things dry-cleaned, you know? Give us a crisp look. There's a lot to do here." She walked in circles around me, pulling at my clothes, poking me with stiff fingers.

"This touching stuff—is this part of the treatment?"

She pinched a section of my shirt. "You're still doing all cotton, right? Right. But—what color is this, anyway?"

"White," I said.

"Just kidding. Just playing around. Actually, you don't look bad at all." She stopped right in front of me and tapped my lips with her fingers. "Spread 'em."

"What?" I started backing away from her.

She came after me, matching my steps, laughing and clicking one of her long, clear fingernails on her front teeth. "Gums," she said. "Open up. Open up."

We drove to the mall, the fish market, then a shop across town that was having a sale on French shoes. As we were leaving the shoe store, a deaf-mute came up selling ballpoint pens. I gave him a dollar and got a red pen with a small flag attached to its clip. Mariana said, "There's your problem right there, Henry. Couldn't be more clear."

"Habit," I said. I watched the guy go down the sidewalk toward the A&P. "You don't want to make too much of it."

"Question of style. You're a born pussycat."

"I'm gonna pussycat you. You want me to get the dollar back?" I turned around and took a couple of steps toward the guy with the pens.

"Eek, eek," she said, putting her hands on her hips. She gave me her bored-to-death look and then spun around and started for the car.

I followed her across the faded blacktop. "I was going to take my dollar back from the pen guy," I said, getting into the car.

"We noticed that. They got you coming and going, don't they?"

"Who?"

"Never mind. Forget it." She reached across and knocked on the dashboard in front of me. "Hand me that pistol out of the glove box, will you?"

"I'll *bet* you've got a gun in here." I released the latch and peered into the compartment. There was a gun in it.

"Just kidding," she said. "It's not loaded. It doesn't even work. Don't worry."

I rolled my eyes, but she wasn't looking, she was backing the car out of its slot, so I waited until she turned around and I rolled my eyes again.

"Saw it the first time," she said. "Why don't you just take it easy here awhile, huh? Kind of ride along, enjoy the scenery—you know, relax. I don't think you're doing so bad. I mean, you could've lost an arm instead of a wife, somebody could've been killed, big shootout over to the One Hour, you know what I mean? You could've been caught with some little Twinkie friend of your daughter's—"

"Never touched her," I said. "I swear."

"There it is again," Mariana said, taking her hands off the wheel and holding them up, palms forward, in front of her. "Maybe you should have jumped her, showed her who's boss. Show the wife. Might be fun."

I found a St. Christopher medal behind the gun in the glove compartment. I brought the medal out to look at. Mariana stopped too close to a traffic light and had to lean forward to see it out of the windshield. "So can we change the subject now?" I said.

She grinned and slapped me on the thigh. "We're just getting started, Bucko. We've got restless nights in the apartment. One after another in a long, endless parade—get that? Long and endless, both of those. We got daytime in the kitchen with four red plastic pebble-finish glasses that you bought because they seemed sensible. We got light in there looks like it's trying to kill you. It's ordinary light, coming in windows and stuff, but it's so dusty and dry it's gonna soak you right up off the face of the planet." She switched lanes very quickly, slipping in in front of a mustard-colored BMW. "So then you put on the radio and what comes out is high school, real soft and sexy. You switch on the lights just to get some red into the room. You get a lot of cupped-up breasts in your mind, from the music, so you put on a record. But the record is old and reminds you of something, or it's new, and hip, and you bought it at Eckerd's drugstore."

"But I've got the light going," I said.

"The light's no better," she said. "You burn up the TV trying to get some color into the place, but nothing works. It's a desert in there. You're a thousand miles away, like the song. You ache. You get a woman in and she smells funny. I mean, she doesn't really smell funny, she just smells funny to you. You tell her that and she gets mad."

I pointed to the speedometer. "We've got a thirty-mile zone here."

She took her foot off the accelerator and let the car coast until the orange pointer got down to forty.

"So this woman packs up and leaves in a hurry. The apartment looks like the inside of a Bake-O-Matic body shop at full tilt and you're in the bedroom with this smell in the sheets and the light look- ing medical, and you got in your head this picture of a sweet-smelling girl you danced with about twenty years ago on the lawn of a rich kid's house. It's a misty night, fall—cold and sparkly, with the patio lights putting tree-trunk shadows across the grass—and this soft girl is up close, her mouth in your neck, and she says something, or you think she says something, so you ask her 'What?' and she rocks her head back and forth, pulling her lips up over the lobe of your ear, and says 'Uh-huh' in a voice that feels like a little bit of warm water going down your legs—"

I put a hand over Mariana's mouth. "I get the picture."

She struggled a little, then playfully slumped forward onto the wheel. The car veered off to one side, narrowly missing a blue mailbox that seemed to come out of nowhere. Mariana spun the wheel, yelled a muffled "Jesus," and sat up, all at once. "Don't mess with the driver," she said when we were going smoothly again.

"Sorry," I said. "I had to stop you."

"Stop me what? I was dramatizing your plight. I was working." She looked at me, and I looked at the car's headliner. "So what are you telling me—that you don't want to go back?"

I rolled down my window and adjusted the outside rearview mirror. "Not a good question," I said, closing my window again.

"Yeah, yeah, yeah. You want to answer anyway?"

Her blouse had come unbuttoned. I could see the curve of the bottom of her breast and the line above it where her tan cut across the pale skin.

She caught me looking. "So what's the answer, Henry?" she said, buttoning the shirt with one hand.

"Don't know," I said.

She nodded and pushed the hair up and away from her forehead. "I thought so. All the men say that. The women don't say that at all, see—that's the thing."

I shook my head.

"Sure it is," she said. "You got girls flying away in droves, caterwauling—going away as if shot from guns is what I mean." She illustrated by wagging her hands in circles and then batting them into each other. "Love doesn't know your name, fella. You've got a serious problem here, and you're thinking levelheaded's gonna get it." She turned to inspect a guy who had pulled up alongside us at the light in a GMC truck. I watched him realize she was looking him over. He was rubbing his neck, and when he saw her he raised his eyebrows a fraction and at the same time dropped his head, acknowledging her attention.

I couldn't see what kind of look she gave the guy, but after he'd done his hello there was a pause, then a smile spread slowly over his face. He looked away, then past her to me, then at her again. His smile turned into a chuckle.

"He's about a two," Mariana said, still looking at the guy.

"You'd better quit or he'll run that truck up on the back of here and start two-ing you," I said. "What are you doing?"

She turned around. "Practicing." She twisted the wheel back and forth. "Where was I?" She started fast after the light changed to get the jump on the guy in the truck. "Oh, yeah. I was helping you. I was being seductive."

I squinted at her. "That's very flattering," I said, but it didn't sound right, so I said, "That's nice."

"You're welcome," she said.

She propped her elbow on the door and her head on her hand and drove more slowly. I looked out the window at the hamburger places, fried-fish places, barbecue places. An old guy with a bicycle decked out like a five-and-dime wheeled by on our right with one of his two overcoats tied up into a cowl over his head and a small TV strapped with duct tape to the handlebars of his bike. I reached over and touched Mariana's shoulder.

She shrugged my hand off and then laughed, a lovely short laugh that flickered over her face and ended in a small, tight smile for me. "Yes," she said. "We have decided to take your case. Our people will be in touch with your people. Not to worry."

We took an eighteen-passenger flight to Brownsville, then rented a car at the airport and drove over to Port Isabel, a coast town in extreme south Texas. We went for the weekend. There were palm trees lining the highway. People pulled carts in the dirt alongside the road. Very quaint. Mexico was about twenty-five minutes away. The rain was thick and blue, falling constantly, relentlessly, as it had done since we left home. I had called Rachel to tell her I was going out of town to think things over. Rachel said, "That's what I'm supposed to tell Mom?"

When we got into Port Isabel, we dropped our bags in the lobby of the Alamo Hotel and went for a drink at a club called the Tim

Tam, which was full of prostitutes. They were dancing together, circling clumsily in dots of light from a fifties beer advertising display. We drank Superior and watched the women dance. Mariana said, "How about this one?" She indicated a woman in a black sheath slit over the hip. "You want us to wrap her for you, Henry?" She fiddled with the thick chips in a gold basket on the table.

"Maybe we should walk around, see the town," I said. I glanced out the yellow saloon-style doors at the rain. "No, I guess we shouldn't."

"We can run to the hotel, if you want."

One of the women we had been staring at, not the one in black, came to the table and leaned on the third chair. She had on elbow-length gloves and a T-shirt with no sleeves. Her nipples were large circles against the shirt. "This your first time?" She glanced around at the little bar, which was dark and used-looking. "Ain't much, is it? Good against rain and not much else. I'm saying we got a perfect roof, though. Tight as a drum." She waved at the ceiling.

"Just taking a look," Mariana said.

"That's what I see. I'm Felice." She winked at me. "I figured you weren't—you know, customers, in the usual sense of that term."

Mariana said, "My name is Mariana. This is Henry. We just got here. For the weekend."

"Uh-huh. And you ain't Texas, are you? I can tell Texas-born. Except Houston. Those folks always sound like they're from LA, or either Michigan. One of the two."

I said, "We're at the hotel a couple of blocks over here." I pointed toward where I thought the hotel was.

"Are you, now?" Felice said. "The Alamo. I've been in there. Seen some of my better days there, matter of fact. You kids having another beer?"

We thanked her and said no, and she thanked us and said to keep her in mind, business-wise. We said that we would, and then all three of us laughed.

The hotel was a six-story brick building on a square that opened on its fourth side to a seedy little dock where people got boat rides.

The trees in the square were tall, but they had thin trunks. The man behind the hotel desk was Hawkins. He had a built-up black shoe on his left foot, and a back about twenty degrees off the vertical. We had used Mariana's card to register, so he called me Mr. Nassar.

Alongside the desk, a sleepy-looking girl about twenty was shaking a clear plastic rain hat. She said, "Sweet Jesus. He's really after me this time."

"Who is?" Hawkins was staring at the wall of slots behind the desk, trying to find our key.

The girl grinned at Mariana, then at me. "Him," she said, pointing up. "Big Guy. It ain't rained like this since I was a kid in love with Rodney Beauchamp. I did naughty things for Rodney Beauchamp in his pickup—he was the football captain at my school. The Big Guy rained on me nearly a month. On that occasion."

Hawkins introduced us. "This is Mr. and Mrs. Nassar. Mariana and—is it Henry? Henry. Meredith Rotel. Meredith does the night work on the desk here. She's a local girl."

"Eighty-per-cent local," Meredith said. "The rest of me's entirely rayon."

I signaled hello, and Mariana stepped around toward the side of the desk to shake the girl's hand.

Hawkins wiggled his head back and forth as if to dismiss Meredith's remark. "She'll run you ragged if you give her a chance. Won't you, Meredith? Don't ask her about hot spots, whatever you do."

"I'm the hottest spot I know," Meredith said. She flapped the collar of her printed shirtwaist. "Only at the moment I ain't so hot. More wet, like."

"Well, I guess we'll be talking to you," Mariana said, grinning at the girl. "I want to hear more about the pickup."

"Me, too," I said.

Mariana slapped my chest. "Settle down there, pard."

We got the key and squeezed into the elevator. The trim was brass and badly stained, and there was some kind of AstroTurf on the walls. We got off on the third floor and found our room, which was large and sour-smelling, with two windows overlooking the square. I took a chair by one of the windows and cocked my feet up on the radiator.

Mariana sat on the bed. "We shouldn't have gone to the bar first thing, right? So I think what I'll do is shower and take it easy for a bit." She unbuttoned the front of her blouse, then its cuffs. She pulled her suitcase onto the bed and popped it open, bringing out a plain leather travel kit. She loosened her belt, then stood by the bathroom door, one hand on the frame. "Well," she said, straightening her blouse with her free hand. "We could just forget it if that's what you want. I think it'll get better, but it's no big deal."

"It's a fair-size deal, isn't it? It's not routine—maybe for you, not me."

"Oh, heck yes," she said, turning away, entering the bathroom. "I come here all the time. I always come here. I was here last week with this guy who plays pro hockey."

"Sorry," I said.

She looked back into the room and waved off the apology, then closed the door.

I sat in the chair and scanned the square, listening to the water sizzling in the bathroom. Somebody knocked at the door. I answered, and a big guy in a khaki uniform introduced himself—C. E. "Fred" Corbett, sheriff of Olympia County. He was six-five, easily. I nodded at his badge and then invited him in, but he stayed in the hall. "You Joseph Butcher?" he said.

I said I wasn't. When he asked for identification I gave him my wallet.

"Vacation?" he said. "Or business?"

"We're having a small vacation. Just a weekend."

He was like a giant William Bendix, with the slablike jaw and the limp mouth. He glanced up and down the corridor. "You met any people here, staying here?"

"We met the desk guy and a girl who works nights—Meredith. That's all."

He handed me my wallet and stuck his hands in his jacket pockets. "Fine. Thanks. Sorry to bust in."

I said, "I wish I could help you," then waited for him to move away from the door before closing it, only he didn't move. "Is there something else?" I asked.

"Nope. You can go ahead and shut her down. We appreciate your coöperation." He smiled but didn't move.

It was awkward closing the door in his face, but there wasn't anything else to do; so I did. When it was shut, I locked it and stood there, listening. For a minute I heard nothing, then I heard his boots shuffle away, and then the sound of his knock next door.

Mariana stuck her head out of the bathroom. "Who was that?"

I was still facing the door, bent forward. "He said he was the sheriff. I sure was glad to see him, too. I'm just glad I'm not Tuesday Weld, or I'd be in real trouble right about now." I went back to my chair. "How did we dig up this place?"

She stepped into the room with a hotel towel pressed against her chest. "Sheriff? I don't believe you."

"He had a badge and everything. I checked it out. I was tough on him, studied the badge. It was a star on something that looked like a horseshoe—it wasn't a horseshoe, but it was shaped like that." I drew the shape in the air. "It had those balls on the star points."

"So he wouldn't hurt himself." She lifted her wet hair, pushed it back above her ear.

"Well," I said, slapping the arm of the chair and then standing. "I'm ready for the big checkout. Find a Holiday Inn or something. Down by the beach—which way is the beach? Over here?" I pointed toward the square.

"Don't be silly. Just because a single sexually potent peace officer knows where we are?" She made a face and came across the room. "Wait a minute. I didn't mean that the way it sounded."

When she was ready, we went out hunting for a restaurant. Meredith suggested Motor Bill's, a seafood house two or three blocks away, along the harbor, "It's my type of a place," she said. "Kind of a more natural atmosphere."

It was a pretty evening. There were people in the street, even though it was still sprinkling. They were walking in twos and threes, enjoying themselves. The sky was a breathtaking silver. We were about half a block from the hotel when the square suddenly filled up with police cars. They slid around corners and out of alleys, without sirens, engines sounding like wind as they accelerated, then stopped hard and diagonal in the street, their top lights flicking the buildings with reds and blues. People started gathering in a circle around the Alamo's entrance canopy. The street lamps were already on, dropping freezing green circles of light on the pavement. Across the small square, pleasure boats pulled dully at their ropes.

We went back and joined the people in front of the hotel. I heard someone say that somebody was the daughter of a Latin who ran the largest rancho in Panama. Two other guys were talking about a business deal; one said, "Hey, the deal is cut, I'm just down here for the signature," and the other said, "Sure you are. And they're talking about sending you to Cairo. That must be swell."

The cops stayed on either side of the hotel, next to their cars, lights still swivelling, flashing. They seemed less concerned with us than with the park and the street. We were in a circle, but there wasn't anything at the center, so I guessed we were waiting for somebody. I said to a small man in a gray chalk-striped suit, "What's the story?"

The guy turned and looked at me, then at Mariana. I put my arm around her. He said, "Out of town?"

"Right," I said. "What's this about?"

"Nothing for you to worry with," he said. His tie had a gold clip in the shape of a musical note about three-quarters of the way down. He fingered the clip as he talked to us. "It's a local situation. You're visiting, so you've got no reason to worry." He took a business card from his vest pocket and handed the card to Mariana. "I am Muhal Richard Cisco. Export. If I can help, please call me. Don't hesitate."

I peeked over Mariana's shoulder at the card, which had on it his name and a ten-digit phone number. Nothing else. Then a tall Mexican guy whispered something to Cisco, who eyed us as he listened, nodding and patting the tall guy's arm. A squinchy kid in high white pants and sparkling red shoes pushed his way out through the hotel's revolving door. He stayed close to the building. Several people from the group pressed forward, closing around him. They talked nervously, several at once, until the tall guy who had been with Cisco handed the kid some folding money, a lot of it, and the kid managed a toothy grin and slipped back into the hotel.

Mariana said, "I'm thinking maybe you were right about this place. Shall we go?"

We crossed the square and walked down along the dock until we found the restaurant Meredith recommended. It was a tiny wood-frame building with a tile floor, bum furniture, and plastic tablecloths decorated with farm animals. We sat in a corner under a hanging jade plant that was on its last leg. Our table butted up against a window that had been painted brown, but a couple of fist-size peepholes had been scratched in the paint. Outside, there was a timber dock that had three white rowboats tied to it. A guy wearing a full-length apron over an undershirt came out of the back of the restaurant and said something to the girl who had seated us, then brought over two bond-paper menus sleeved in plastic.

Mariana ordered fried scallops, and I said I'd try the snapper. The guy took our menus and disappeared back through the swinging doors, each of which had a half circle of dirty glass in it.

There weren't any other customers. On the opposite wall there was a kind of altar—a black sombrero surrounded by photographs, palm leaves, statues, a rosary made of nuggets of red glass, airplane postcards, other stuff. Mariana got up to take a look. I watched the boats through the scratched brown window. Coming back, she said, "So what do you say, Henry?"

"It's sweaty for my taste," I said. "Colorful, but sweaty. We could go out where the rest of the tourists are, wherever that is."

"It's not like I remember it, that's true. That guy was probably just a lottery guy—the kid, I mean."

She slid her jacket off her shoulders onto the spindles of the ladder-back chair. Outside, I saw the man in the apron trot past the boats and around the corner of a rusted steel shed. I waited for him to come back. When he did, he was carrying a stack of white containers like those used for take-out food. Two Mexican kids wearing khaki pants and open shirts ran along-side him, talking and gesturing. I said, "I think Motor Bill just ran out and picked up dinner."

Mariana leaned across the table to see, but the guy was out of sight.

The kids were about thirteen, Rachel's age—maybe a little older. They came in from the kitchen laughing, then saw us and got very quiet as they sat down at a wobbly table. The guy who had taken our order came out and said something in Spanish to the boys, and they screeched their chairs across the floor and followed him into the back.

The food was served on colored plates—mine was peach, Mariana's was lime—and it wasn't bad. She kept telling me to slow down, that I was eating too fast. Out the window I saw the Mexican kids running along the pier away from the restaurant carrying garbage bags twisted down to the size of footballs. The undershirt guy came out to see how things were going.

"Very tangy," Mariana said. "I love the butter sauce."

"Thank you," the guy said. "You would like to have a jar of pulque? I have a pulque that you would never forget in a thousand years."

"He's going to get us on the flies," I said, half muttering.

The guy heard me and didn't think it was funny. He swatted at the next table with the dish towel he carried over his arm, then put on a too-polite smile. "You do not have to drink the pulque, my friend. I have only offered it to the lady who you are with. If she does not want the pulque, then I am sure that she will not have it."

"I think I won't, today," Mariana said, smiling at the guy. She dabbed at the corners of her mouth with her napkin. "But thank you very much. It's kind of you."

"You are welcome," he said, and he bowed at the waist, giving us a view of the top of his head, where a scab the size of a quarter was tucked in under the damp hair.

When he was gone I apologized. "Uncontrollable urge. The flies, I mean. It was stupid. It just leapt out. I'm covered with embarrassment."

"You're gonna be covered with pulque if you don't settle down."

The guy put a guitar record on an old turntable propped up behind the bar, but the music was hard to listen to because a CB radio cut in and out. Mariana turned around and smiled at the guy anyway.

We finished dinner pretty quick and went back out into the drizzle. Mariana had her hair pulled back tight to her scalp. Drops of the mist settled in the wiry hair above her forehead, making her younger and prettier. She took my arm and steered us down a crooked street lined on either side with buildings painted hot, chalky colors. The cars were parked crazily, in the road and up on the sidewalk. At first, we climbed around them, then we gave up and took to the middle of the street. I was watching my feet when the two Mexican kids appeared out of a low doorway and asked us if we wanted to buy vegetables. Very fresh, they assured us.

I was all ready to say no when Mariana said yes. She got out her wallet and gave one kid a five-dollar bill, while the second kid ducked back into the doorway and fetched one of the garbage bags I'd seen them with earlier. The bag was green and a little bit transparent, and through it I could make out carrots and round things that might have been peppers or red onions, Mariana took the bag and peered down into it, then grinned at the kids. "Terrific," she said. "Wonderful. Thank you."

They thanked her in Spanish and vanished through a royal-blue door.

We went on walking, arm in arm, along the curving, sloping road. The rain was so light I could barely feel it, but I was getting cold. "This goes down to the Gulf. That's what we want?"

"I want to play cards in bed tonight," Mariana said. "I love to do that. It slows everything down."

My heel skidded on a badly set paving stone, and I would have fallen on my face if she hadn't held me up with her arm. "I'm ready when you are," I said, freeing myself. "I need to get me a pink suit and duck shoes to walk around down here."

Saturday morning I went down to the lobby and called Rachel. She didn't sound happy to hear from me. I asked about her mother, and about what was happening, and so on, and her answers were terse—single words. Finally, I said, "What's wrong here? What are you mad about?"

"Oh, nothing. Only, where are you? What are you doing down there? Who's with you?"

"Texas, nothing, and for me to know," I said. "I'm just taking some time off." Hawkins was about twenty feet away, behind his desk, stealing glances at me.

"You're taking a ride on the Reading, is what you're taking. I suggest you get your story together. What am I supposed to say to Mom?"

"I told her what I was doing," I said.

"Yes. And she told me, but she's not dumb about it."

I waited a second, then said, "This is great. I feel lousy, so I call you up, and what I get is worse than what I started with. Thanks a lot."

"So jump a plane. I'll set it up for you."

I found a wad of grape-colored gum somebody had stuck to the wooden wing of the telephone enclosure. "I'll be back tomorrow afternoon," I said. "You can take me out to dinner."

"What if I don't want to?" I didn't answer that, and she waited for a few seconds, then said, "Okay. Sorry. Tell me how big a deal this is. I mean, what's the correct level of anxiety for a child like me?"

"You could probably guess. I'm calling you up in the middle of it. Not high."

"Good," she said, her voice softening. "In that case, go ahead and have a really wonderful time."

"Thanks, amigo," I said. We hung up and I sat there for a while, feeling better.

It was still raining when we got the car out of the shedlike garage and drove out to the beach for lunch. Mariana was driving and being quiet. I stared out the window. I liked the desolate, broken-down look of things. The land was empty, and in spite of the rain I could see that it stretched miles in all directions. We passed a big, shallow hill that was a field full of wrecked cars, and around the cars there were black-and-white cows grazing, and birds strutting quickly in the rain. I knotted my hands together and grinned at how lovely that was. We made a turn onto a road that was straight and thin to the horizon. The palms that staked either side were a hundred yards apart and forty feet tall, curved by the wind.

Mariana glanced around, then turned back to the highway. "Feeling better?"

"I called home. Rachel wanted to know about you. I didn't tell her."

"Oh. Not feeling better. I see." She changed her position behind the wheel, then curled her fingers around her hair, dragging it away from her face. "Do you want to go back today?"

I watched a truck in the rearview mirror on my side of the car. "No. I don't think so. We've got cards to play. You think I'm letting you get away with the big winner?"

"No," she said. "I don't."

She turned and smiled at me—a wry, sad smile that made me long for her and for other things. I started to cry and covered it by looking out the window at the stiff trunks of the trees, and the delicate grass, and the helmet-like sky. The tires ran on the highway, and the windshield wipers clacked, and I waited a minute before I faced Mariana again.

"Easy," she said, reaching to circle her hand around my wrist.

(1984)

PUPIL

Each summer I teach a course in BASIC at the junior college. This year Tracy Whitten is my favorite student. She's eighteen—bright, handsome, cheerful all the time. I like her braces. She's self-conscious about them, always remembering a minute too late to keep her lips tightly closed. She comes to class in shorts and a T-shirt, perspiration glinting at her temples, and we talk, and her eyes dart around as if we ought to be more discreet.

By the fourth week of the session I'm so taken with her I'm ready to break the rules. In the hall after class I say, "Maybe you could come for dinner? I'll ask some other people. We can cook out."

"Oh, sure," she says, giving me a look that means maybe I'd better think again. "That'd be real suave."

We walk down the corridor without talking, then go outside and stop near the bike rack. "I'm sorry I mentioned it," I say, making a show of looking for my car in the parking lot. "Well, not really sorry."

She smiles, wires glittering, then turns away and looks out over the baseball practice field. Today she's wearing pale-pink running shorts, the shiny kind, and a thin Jack-in-the-Box T-shirt, and she's tapping her key on the rack, so there's a pinging sound in the air.

Finally, she turns around and gives me a squinty look. "I wouldn't mind coming, if you're serious."

"I am serious." That sounds too serious, so I try for a Chevy Chase joke with some stupid faces, wondering how I could have been silly enough to start this.

"Take it easy, will you? Calm down. Let me think." She watches me and does some faces that look good on her. "We know it's not a great idea. We both know that, right? It's destructive and impossible, and you're too old, and it's bad PR."

"My specialty" I say.

She studies me for a second, then she's all smiles—patting my arm, straightening her hair, ready to walk away. "I like it. I'll come. We'll have a good time. Where is it?"

I have two bedrooms, a large living room with lots of glass, and a small garden—a side-by-side duplex, one of a hundred and ten similar units in a development that has four pools and no cleverly winding paths. I'm used to it. Not so much that it feels like home but enough so that I can overlook, most of the time, the utilitarian way of things. Sometimes I even think it's pretty.

Saturday I go out and buy a barbecue cooker and the tools that go with it—tongs, a giant fork, hot-pad gloves that look like alligators. For dinner I decide to go with chicken, so I spend some time at the A&P figuring out chicken. By late afternoon I'm set up on the deck at my apartment, watching the cooker and waiting for Tracy. There's a lot of smoke around, because I've used too many mesquite chips.

I've only been out a few minutes when the doorbell rings. I go through the house to answer it, and Tracy's there with a guy about forty who has a clean face and pink skin. He's wearing black jeans.

"Hi," she says, moving her hand in a robotlike way between me and her friend. "This is George, and this is Ray. Ray's my brother, but he's really more like a pal, aren't you, Ray?"

"Sure am," he says, and we shake hands. Ray's got a soft, smooth hand and a puttylike grip.

Tracy's hair looks as if it's still wet from washing. She's got on baggy linen pants and a yellow Hawaiian shirt. She comes in first, almost bouncing, and Ray follows, giving my apartment the once-over.

I go into the kitchen to get them drinks—beer for Ray, Tab for Tracy, glasses for both of them—and I cut my finger on the pop top of the Tab can, so I have to excuse myself while I go get a Band-Aid. When I return they're already out on the deck. Ray waves at the yard. "Pretty," he says.

I look at the yard, which is small and brown.

He says, "I didn't know there was so much socializing—you know, teachers and students—out at the college."

"Sure," says Tracy. "All the time."

"There isn't much," I say. "It's frowned on."

"Yeah," he says, nodding. "That's what I thought. I saw this thing on TV about some trouble they've been having out in California. Arrests, you know . . ." He gives Tracy a glance that she, bless her heart, refuses to share. She's smiling, taking in the scenery.

"I like this," she says. "This is a nice apartment." She wipes the bottom of her Tab can down the thigh of her pants.

My neighbors are in the yard working on their bulb garden. They're a young couple with a new baby, and they have a dime-store coat of arms—a painted wood shield with "THE HERNDON'S" across the top, "ESTABLISHED 1977" across the bottom, and a duck in the middle—displayed next to their front door.

"Not much privacy," Tracy says, motioning toward the couple. "What are they doing there, anyway? Looks like they're burying something."

"Bulbs," I say.

They've been working on the garden since midwinter. It's a mound, like a grave—a dog's, or a child's. They roughed up the ground and then dumped a foot of bag dirt on top. That's where they put the bulbs. None of them ever showed up.

Ray says, "Listen, we don't need to be real nervous about me coming over here. It's just a formality. She's a full-grown woman. You're both grown. That's my feeling."

"Oh, Raymond," Tracy says. She turns to me. "Ray's worried about me growing up and all that. He feels bad about it." She looks at her watch, a heavy gold Timex. "How long have these chickens been on here?"

"Well," he says. "You're my sister."

The chickens are reddish brown, I'm ready for Tracy and Ray to leave, to call the whole thing off, so I stare at the chickens and say, "I'm probably out of line." I look at him, asking for some understanding. "I slipped up, okay? Maybe we ought to—"

"Hey!" Ray says. "Hold on. Don't get me wrong. I don't mind. She's a girl, you're a boy—you look okay. Hell, you look like a million to me." He does a broad smile and pats my forearm.

Tracy shakes her head. "Oh, jeez. Raymond? I mean, we're not at home, okay?"

Ray shrugs, waving his hands around. "No more king of the dorks, huh? Well, I can't go anywhere. Helene's picking me up."

"Helene's about twelve," Tracy says.

She wraps her arms around his neck, and he pretends he doesn't like it, picking them off. "How can a person function with you all over him?"

"You wish." She grins and pushes off. "Ray's always ready to do some pretty powerful functioning."

Ray blushes, says, "That's your idea, you and Billy Hunter. He tells everybody he's helping out his secretary, and then he helps her a lot in his office."

"Billy," Tracy says, explaining to me. "One of Ray's close, close friends. He's a happening guy. I hope he catches his rear on a linoleum knife." She rattles the ice in her glass. "Anybody want soda?"

She goes in, leaving us staring at the cooker. "She's touchy," Ray says. He looks over his shoulder, trying to see into the house. "But at least she doesn't think as soon as anything bad happens it's because men run things. I told her it's ideas—all you have to do is have the good ideas. Right?"

"It helps," I say.

"Sure it does," he says. "I mean, if it ain't great, who cares who's running it?"

"Right," I say.

"Take you, for example. You've got something going. I mean, she's pretty, she's young—all that time in front of her, all this stuff to learn. Listen, I understand you college boys. You got women out there in Kmart underpants, guys belong in the zoo—you can't make much of that. I mean—" He waits a second, thinking about it, scratching the back of his head. "I mean, if you're going to have a romance it ought to at least be lovely."

He thinks some more, smoothing his hair where it's standing up from the scratching. "This deal's sweet. It's a little bit stupid, but it's sweet."

I take off the cooker top and wave it back and forth trying to clear the smoke. Flames jump up under the chickens.

"Know what I'm saying?" he says.

I nod at him, then turn back to the cooker. "I'm doing these by the book, the 'indirect' method. Every time I open it I get all this fire."

"So close it," he says, taking a look at the chickens, which are getting black and crusty. "You better get those suckers off before they turn to dirt." He reaches out to wiggle one of the drumsticks and it comes off in his hand. "If I were you I'd submerge 'em for half an hour."

Tracy sticks her head out the door. "Ray? Your wealthy friend is here. This car goes by about three times, checking out the place. You want me to get her?"

"Why don't you work the chickens," Ray says. "George can get her."

Outside, the sky is thunder-gray except in the west, where there's a ribbon of coral at the horizon. There's a fresh breeze, and the street lamps are on, and there's a dampness about the way everything looks. Helene is easy to spot. She's in a brilliant red 318i about half a block down from the apartment. I signal to her and, when she pulls up, introduce myself.

"Ray's inside," I say. "He asked me to come get you."

She's in her twenties, wearing a sleeveless knit cotton top and white shorts, and her arms are tan, muscular. I notice a blue vein that runs over her biceps and down her inner arm. It's prominent, easy to see.

"You must be kidding," she says. "Where's his truck?"

"What truck? He has a truck?"

"Sure does," she says. "A purple eighteen-wheeler. Lots of yellow lights."

I'm standing in the street alongside her car, scanning the parking lots as she describes these lights.

"They're great at night," she says. "He's always leaving the truck going, and you can hear it, even inside, and you look out and all the lights are sparkling—you've got to see it."

I look up and down the road. Nobody's out, but there are cars jammed up behind other cars in the head-in parking spaces. Everybody's having company. I stretch out my arms and say, "I don't know, but Ray *is* inside, with his sister Tracy."

"How do I know you're not woofing me? Maybe you're the kind of a skunk-guy who'd do a thing like that." She gives me a look as if she's sizing me up. "Naw, I guess not. Let me park this job."

I back away and wait for her to pull the car into a slot. She gets out and walks the curb as if it were a tightrope, coming toward me. "We were at the Tubes last night, me and Ray," she says, watching her feet. "You ever been there?" She shakes her head and does a little snort of distaste. "One of the great places. Really."

Out of the car, Helene's a tiny girl, easily under five feet, shaped like a bodybuilder. She says, "Ray's kind of a polecat. I don't meet many men that aren't, know what I mean? All of you got some polecat in you." She smiles at me as if she's pleased about that, then looks up ahead of us. "You live in here?"

"Yes, ma'am," I say.

She flips open the purse she's carrying and pulls out a business card, which she hands to me, holding it between the tips of her first two fingers. "This is me," she says.

The card says SMALL PLEASURES, in chiseled-looking type, and underneath there's a printed signature—"Helene," in red—and a telephone number. I read the card, then hold it close to look at the signature. "This looks real," I say. "The signature part, I mean."

She reaches out and pats my hip. "It's a store, boyo. My own private store. Things for women." She smiles playfully. "Well, so maybe it's not only a store."

I do a little wave with the card as we go up the steps to my apartment.

"I almost called it No Man's Land," she says over her shoulder. She pops the door and it opens, and she turns around and grins at me. "But we gotta be careful."

Tracy has the chickens on top of the stove. "So what do we do with these?" she says as we come in.

"Eat 'em," Ray says. He grabs Helene and lifts her up, high, in the air, then puts her down by the window in the living room. "Hey!" he says, pointing out the window. "A possum just went by out here. Hey! Did anybody see it?"

The dinner is quiet and quick. Helene has to have the single-volume Columbia Encyclopedia to sit on so she can reach the table. Tracy finishes first and moves to the brown recliner across the room, staring at the TV. Ray's watching Helene and, at the same time, talking about a hot-rod Chevrolet he persuaded his father to buy in 1957. He raced this car a lot, made his high-school reputation with it.

"This one kid used to call me Rhinestone Ray," he says. "His mother bought him a Thunderbird. He hated my guts and figured this was his chance, so one night we went out and he did a triple flip into an A&W Root Beer place and I ended up going sideways across a four-lane highway, staring at headlights. Nobody was killed, but he lost a hand in the windshield. I went to see him in the hospital a couple of days later."

"This happened twenty-five years ago," Helene says. "Just to put things into perspective."

"He said he thought maybe I'd jumped the flag," Ray says, softly thumping the table with his forearm. He waits a minute, then says, "I don't know why they bought that Chevy. I mean, it was *fast.*"

Ray fidgets with his glass, then turns to look over his shoulder at Tracy. "What're you up to? You're either out the door like a shot or you're sitting around staring at things."

"I'm rolfing my feet," she says. "I figure it's time to rediscover the seventies."

"Didn't we do that already?" He lifts his glass and wags it at her. "Hand me some ice, okay?"

Tracy gives him a look that means she'll do it but he's a jerk for asking, then comes to get the glass. He watches her go into the kitchen.

"Short legs," he says. "No way around it. Give her another couple of inches and her whole life'd be different. The teeth you fix, but you file the legs."

"You're cute," Tracy says from behind the open freezer-compartment door. She looks at me and says, "He gets this way after dinner."

"I can testify to that," Helene says.

I nod, as if I know it too.

Ray is drawing circles on the wood-veneer tabletop. "Two nights ago, I take Tracy to dinner at this steak place we always go to, and we're sitting there and this guy I knew ten years ago, a guy named Stewart, slips up behind her and starts mouthing her neck. I'm not kidding—the guy's making a mess. You figure she's going to jump or something, right? Not this one. She leans into it."

Tracy is in the kitchen doorway, listening. She's got Ray's ice ready. "I liked him," she says.

"He's greasy," Ray says. "But it's *Miami Vice* grease, so it's okay."

"Ray's afraid of *Miami Vice*," Tracy says, slipping his glass in front of him. "He says it devalues light, whatever that means."

Ray pours beer into the glass. "It means the guys are anchovies, the pictures, the music—it's the Anchovy Show."

"I don't agree," Helene says. "Besides, anchovies have certain desirable aspects."

"Like what?"

"Like they're silver, and if you want to you can slice them up into little tiny pieces," she says.

"I think it's silly to be afraid of a TV show," Tracy says.

"He wants to love it," Helene says. "You like the *Blade Runner* guy, don't you, Ray? He's on there. The gum-wrapper guy?"

"Yes," Ray says. He takes a drink, then fills the glass again. "I hate being on this side of the argument. I'll learn, okay? But first I'm going to finish this story. Please?" He turns to me. "So this guy at the steak place likes Tracy. Guys are always poking at Tracy."

Tracy makes some can-you-stop-this gestures to Helene behind Ray's back, then retakes her seat across the room.

"Poking is central to Ray's world," Helene says.

He gives her a steady look and continues his story. "So I watch and smile at all this kissing, then I wave, trying to get their attention." He demonstrates waving. "Stewart's got the leather jacket, the peach pants. He's probably got perfume going in there—"

"Smelled good to me," Tracy says.

Ray freezes and stares at her. She does a little curtsy, then pulls her foot into her lap and studies her toes, ignoring him.

Ray turns back to the table and pulls both thumbs over his shoulders in her direction. "See?" he says. "Just like that. She shuts me down like a garage door." He points at me. "Are you listening? I'm trying to say something here."

"I'm listening," I say.

Helene sighs. "Speed it up, will you, Butch?"

He gives her an instant smile. "So I'm out there in this restaurant jerking around like I'm dodging a fly. I mean, I might as well be alone."

Helene does some whimpering like a hurt animal, and then Tracy does it, too—there's a chorus of whimpers.

Ray waves both hands, giving up. "Thank you," he says, "I want to personally thank each and every one of you for your kindness and compassion."

"Aw," Helene says. "That's real sweet."

"It's okay," Tracy says to me. "The place is known for flies, fat boys—green, shiny wings and everything. They make this rattling noise when they go by you. They must go a hundred or something, hundred and twenty easy. Scale speed, I mean."

I get up and start for the kitchen. "So what happened?"

"We had dinner with him," Tracy says.

Ray puts his head down on the table. "We had dinner with him," he says. "Way to go, Tracy. Way to hit the long ball out of the park."

"Well? We did."

"Yes. I know. We heard all about his life. We know where he works, we know about his wife and his kids—we saw pictures, I swear to God."

"He's a med tech," Tracy says. "He works at the pathology lab. He sits there in a room the size of a Volvo putting stuff on slides. I didn't believe him until he showed me his badge. He has to wear a badge around, to show that he belongs there."

Helene says, "Is that it?"

Ray looks at her. "See, she doesn't care if this guy crawls on her, but it's painful for me. I mean, I don't want her learning on just anybody."

"You don't want her learning," Helene says.

"That's my pal Helene," Ray says. "Casualty of the sexual revolution."

"Hey," Helene says, "I'm the big winner."

"Yeah. You and Joan of Arc."

She gets up from the table. "Okay. Time for Mr. Ray to say good night."

Tracy comes across the room and puts an arm on Ray's shoulder, standing behind him. She leans over and whispers something, then nuzzles his neck.

He looks up, pressing his head into hers, brushing her hair with his fingers, his jaw set. He gives me a wry smile.

Helene says, "Well, I, for one, had better go out and get me some dessert before I go blind."

I say, "I've got ice cream."

"That," Ray says to me, "is terrifying." He shrugs Tracy off his back and gets out of the dining chair, comes around the table, puts a hand on my shoulder and gives me a squeeze. "A fine boy." He pats my back and follows Helene to the door.

Tracy stays on her side of the table.

"What's this *blind* business?" Ray says. "I like the concept. I like the concept very much."

"Thanks," Helene says, taking a bow. "It's nothing. I do whatever is humanly possible, and if that's not good enough, why—" she pauses midsentence, pretending to have forgotten her thought. "Why, then I just do something else."

"Right," he says, looking in my direction.

I go out with them. It's cool and stars are shining; the light from the full moon is like a veil on the neighbor's Pontiac, which is in my parking place again. Somebody goes by in a bright Ryder truck. There's a faint scent of gas in the air as Ray and Helene move across the lot toward her car. It takes them a minute to get started, then they roll off down the road, taillights burning. I watch until they make a slow left at the stop sign, then go inside.

Tracy's holding a green ceramic bowl, into which she's put the leftover chicken. She says, "We want to save this, right?"

I take the bowl and dump the chicken into the paper bag under the kitchen sink. Then I get a plastic trash bag from the closet and put the paper bag in the plastic bag. I scrape the rest of the plates into the paper bag, and put the dishes in the sink, then turn on the tap full blast and use the built-in spray nozzle to rinse the plates and glasses and the silverware. Tracy's watching me do all this. I get some paper towels and wet them, wipe the countertops and the top of the stove, then the dining table. I shake the placemats over the sink, rinse everything again, then lead her out of the kitchen, hitting the light switch as we go.

"So now we start stuff, right?" she says. She grins after she says it, reaching for one of the buttons on her shirt.

She's so beautiful. Her braces are shining. On one of her front teeth there's a tiny reflection of me and of the living room behind me. I think about touching the white down on her face. I move her hand away from the button.

(1985)

CHROMA

Alicia's taking her weekend with her boyfriend George. It's part of our new deal—she spends every other weekend with him, plus odd nights in between. The rest of the time she's with me. When we started this I thought it'd drive me crazy. One time I actually slugged her. I was sure she was leaving me, but as it turned out she didn't want to leave at all. She wanted to stay. She said meeting George was fate, an accident, that she didn't plan it. I guess I accepted that. Then I started liking the days alone every two weeks. It's quieter, the house is cleaner—things don't get messed up. I don't have to schedule around her. It's as if we have joint custody, George and I.

I'm spending Saturday with a neighbor named Juliet. She's in her twenties, a graduate student recently sold on health—free weights, the gym, night classes in anatomy. She owns the house next door with her girlfriend, Heather, who's thirty-five, tall and angular, and runs boutiques.

Heather's on a shopping trip, which is how Juliet and I happen to be together. It's raining. We're in an old section of town—lots of storefronts turned into eight-table restaurants—looking for a place to get a late breakfast. We hustle from one to the next, deciding each is wrong on decor, grease, or eaters. Finally, we go to this fried-chicken shop on Berry Lane called Bill's. It's been there thirty years, so all the things wrong with it are deeply wrong, which seems to make it okay. There's a lot of big, old rope in the restaurant. Besides, Juliet's been there before.

Juliet thinks I'm depressed. She tells me this and asks several times what it is that's bothering me. I make up the usual stuff, trying to avoid the question, afraid that if I start to tell her, I'll end up saying a lot of junk now that won't be true this afternoon. She gets a chicken-fried steak and I go for the chicken, and we eat watching the plastic tablecloth.

"We aren't very good friends," she says.

"Sure we are," I say. "C'mon."

"Okay," she says. "Okay. Tell you what. When we go back to the house I want to make love to you."

I'm cutting meat off a drumstick right at this point. I've had most of the skin and now I'm looking for what's left. I say, "Oh?"

"I think it's necessary and important," she says.

I get my fork into a piece of meat and whisk it around in the gravy that has slipped out of my mashed potatoes.

"Fair's fair," she says.

That's the last I hear of it until we get home. I park in my driveway and she comes around the car and takes my hand, marching me across the grass toward her house.

All the houses around here are one-story brick jobs, paneled dens, sliding-glass doors looking out to backyards. She puts me on the sofa, which in her place faces the sliding door and the red patio where they barbecue. I notice they don't have a Weber, it's something else, one of the flatter, squarer kinds. Maybe it's from Sears or something. The trees out there are bent and dripping.

I say, "I don't know. We're friends, but we don't have to do this." I have the idea I'm taking the top line on the thing.

Juliet's moving around between me and the window, not really doing a show, but sort of doing a show. "Sex is my guts. It really makes me sting."

"Uh-huh," I say. I get off the couch.

She laughs, the muscles in her neck rippling prettily. She's got a lot of muscles. "I'm sorry. That was dumb. I was just trying to be, you know, seductive." She suddenly droops, going limp on the couch. "So I guess we ought to forget it, huh?"

I come up behind her and rub her hair in this way that's much more awkward than I intend, then I stop that and get down behind the sofa so that our heads are about at the same level. Only our eyes are above the sofa back. I say, "It's real sweet," and put the emphasis on "real," and now I'm doing her hair in a much better way. It's working. "It's a lovely idea, it's very flattering, but . . ."

"My friend Allie?" Juliet says. "She told me about this one time she made love in front of a bank in Paris at two in the morning with this girl she met on one of those boats they have? There was a French dumpster in the street there, and they got in—she said it was crazy. She said she couldn't walk right after. She says when it feels that good you know it's gotta be true."

I look at her real slow, giving her what I imagine is my older-and-wiser look.

"She married the dumpster?" Juliet does a smile that's kind of sad around the edges. "Maybe I'll just put on a record—you think that'll help?"

She does wobble-knees on her way to the stereo and plays something by Nat King Cole, and it's on tape, not record. The music gives me gooseflesh. I haven't heard Nat King Cole since the seventh grade, and I feel like crying about it. I get up and stand behind Juliet, wrap my arms around her and hold her, listening to this awful music, thinking it's crushing the way she loves, that she's such a child.

She says, "Is this okay?"

I say, "Sure," and let her take me back to the couch.

Juliet's nice—we hug some more, kiss a little, mostly sit and stare at the points where our bodies touch. We don't talk. I feel close to her, like I want to protect her from everything.

At four I'm out driving around in the family car, trying to figure out what kind of takeout food I want to take out for my dinner. At a stoplight somebody jiggles a rubber fish out the window of a bus next to me. It's a pale green fish, about ten inches long—shark, or whale. I've seen lots of them, beach toys. I'm a little behind the bus, in the next lane, bent over the steering wheel trying to see who's doing this fish. I think it's a kid, then realize it's Heather, and she's signaling me, so I nose in behind the bus and wait while it discharges people. Then I unsnap the door lock and move up so she can get in.

"Howdy," she says, sliding in alongside me.

"Hi," I say. I reach out and touch her hand, waiting while a carpet truck goes by, then steer into the center lane and say, "Got yourself a belt-fish."

"What's a belt-fish?" She holds the fish up in front of her and carefully looks it over.

"That," I say. "You put the tail under your belt and then walk around just like normal. A guy I know is the father of the belt-fish."

She shakes her head and drops the fish into a shopping bag. "I don't know what you're talking about. This is a present for Juliet, who is fish crazy." She crinkles the bags getting settled. "I was downtown. I used to go down there on the bus to the Majestic Theatre, where I saw *A Fistful of Dollars*, and some Bond movies, the first couple. Today I went to a mall in an office building and bought shirts. Have you looked at shirts? They're nuts. These people think we're fools."

I give her a squint. "Which people?"

"The ones with the shirts. I got four shirts and a bathrobe for three hundred eighty dollars." She reaches over her shoulder for the safety harness. "So how's the perfect Alicia?"

"Okay," I say.

She makes a sorry-I-asked face and nods knowingly. "Oh. Her weekend. That would be . . . George?"

I point at her.

Heather doesn't believe spouses should tell each other too much. We've had this argument before. I say it's easier to handle what you know about than what you imagine, and she says it's better to keep your mouth shut and your eyes closed.

She grins. "You guys still playing Donkey Kong, huh?"

I wait a minute for that to make sense and, when it doesn't, say, "I don't know what that means, Heather."

She shrugs. "Me either. I just said it. I guess it means that it'll never work. You let this go on much longer and she's going to think you don't love her anymore."

"She knows I love her."

"Well, she may know it but not think it."

I lift an eyebrow at her and do some blinky stuff with my eyes. "Logic needs work," I say.

"It's possible," she says. "Tell you what, you and Juliet quit coveting and I'll let her deviate his septum for you—is it a deal?"

"I thought that was my secret."

"You don't believe in secrets," Heather says, flapping her hands like a pair of toe-heavy socks on a line in a wind. "But hey! You guys over there do what you want. It doesn't bother us. We can be savage. We wouldn't be *we* very long . . ."

"She wants something interesting in her life. There's no big harm in it. You can't blame her."

Heather says, "I'm not blaming her, I'm blaming you."

I swerve to miss a broken-up microwave somebody has dumped in the street. When I get going straight again I smile a patient smile.

"I don't know. Whatever works, right? This is the eighties." She makes a flustered, dismissive move with her hand. "Let's forget it. I don't even know what I'm talking about." She's doing flat karate chops in front of her. "I'm having my ongoing struggle with the language," she says.

"Ah, language," I say.

"You touch the doughnut girl, I'll do your teeth in piano wire," Heather says, grabbing her front teeth for emphasis.

Alicia is staking potted plants when we drive up. I don't know why she's home, except that sometimes, on her weekends, she comes back for a couple of hours, to get different clothes, or just to say hello. She waves with something that looks like a car antenna. Heather shakes the fish at her.

Alicia says, "Nice fish."

"We call him Morodor," Heather says.

Alicia taps Heather's arm with the antenna. "Well, who's going to get my cactus? It's by the kitchen door and it weighs three hundred pounds."

"We don't speak power lifting," Heather says.

"She got new shirts," I say. "Very expensive. I found her on the bus."

Alicia looks next door, toward Heather's driveway, at the Volvo parked there. "Something wrong with this car?"

"Nope," Heather says, spreading her purchases on the hood of our car. Alicia and I nod at each shirt. I stop Heather on a black one with a thin silver diagonal stripe, a shirt she says cost a hundred and forty dollars.

"That's mine," I say.

Heather shakes her head, slipping stuff back into bags. "If it's new it's wrong—that's my feeling. You see the pockets on these guys? I don't know. It's a big risk."

Alicia says, "They'll be great. Carry books in there."

"Books?" Heather falls back, holding packages up as if to protect her eyes from a bright light.

Alicia says, "I'm making eight-thousand-jewel rice for dinner and you're invited."

"You're here for dinner?" I say to Alicia.

"Yeah. Sure." She shoves me a couple of times. "What's it to ya?"

When Heather leaves I bring the cactus around, hurting my back in the process. I sit with Alicia while she plays with this plant, trimming parts off, giving it a bath, fertilizing it, putting sticks in the dirt trying to get it to stand up straight.

I'm on the concrete with my head dropped back against the brick window ledge. I say, "She asked about George."

Alicia thinks a minute, but doesn't speak.

I narrow my eyes at her. "That had the look of something there."

"If I thought something I only thought it for a second and I don't remember what it was, so leave me alone."

"Yes, ma'am. Moon rose when you hove into view."

She does a little bow. "Thank you. Why don't we hove on in for a nap? You can hold me. What do you say?"

I put an arm around her and pull her toward the door.

Heather and Juliet arrive at eight on the nose, Heather in jeans and a brown blouse, Juliet in chrome-yellow shorts and one of the new shirts, the black one with the diagonal stripe. It falls open at the slightest deviation from perfect posture.

Alicia brings them into the living room, where I'm fixing the feet on the coffee table. "He's into handy," Alicia says. "Here, he's being handy under the coffee table."

Heather does a polite smile and picks up an audio magazine off the table, easing into the couch.

"Can I turn this on?" Juliet says, stopping in front of the television. "See how the Braves are doing?"

"Sure," I say.

"Keep it low, okay?" Heather says. "We're guests."

Juliet says, "Gee, Mom. If you're sure Mr. Anderson won't mind."

"I'm sure," Heather says.

George calls in the middle of dinner. Alicia answers the living room phone, then moves to the bedroom and has me hang on for her. I listen to him breathe a minute, then hear the click of the other phone and Alicia says, "I've got it."

I go back to the table. Heather and Juliet are looking hard at their plates. Juliet has pushed her food out to the edges of her plate, so it looks like a wreath.

"Just eat it," Heather says to her. "Let's don't attack the poor man with food play."

"Hey," I say. "Who's poor here? I'm licking wounds as fast as she can inflict them."

Juliet gives me a look I like a lot, a sweet look out of the tops of her eyes. We stare at each other for a minute and it's like some force is shooting back and forth between us, like vases are rattling on their tables.

It makes Heather nervous. She stares at Juliet until she gets her attention. "Settle down," she finally says. "Let's don't OD on the compassion thing."

After they leave I watch Alicia fix up the kitchen and, when that's done, make a sandwich and sit on the cabinet eating it. I take a diet Coke out of the refrigerator and sit with her, watching her eat, telling her about Juliet. She listens, eyeing me carefully as if to see what my face might give away that I won't quite be able to say. When I finish she takes a long pause, staring at the part of the sandwich that remains. She has picked off the crust, and pinched the rest into some kind of animal shape.

"I don't like it," she says.

"What?" I say.

"All of it. Any of it. You're supposed to sit here and love me and me alone while I go out and do the rope-a-dope all over the place. Isn't that the deal?"

I look at her.

"So what's this about? I mean, we got melancholy in the mug here." She points the sandwich fragment at my face.

"Mug?" I say.

"Whatever." She downs the sandwich and slides off the cabinet, smacking her hands together. "I guess it's fine if you like tragic longing. Are you going to be okay if I go out?"

"I'm fine," I say.

"You look terrible. Maybe I ought to stay? You look like you're going to hang yourself, or slit your throat, or something. Call your girl."

"I'm okay," I say. We're standing in the middle of the kitchen and we sort of self-consciously lean toward each other, then start hugging, shy at first, then tight. It's nice to feel her against me again, how warm she is, how strong she is. We rock side to side like that for a minute, then pull apart.

I say, "Well, I guess I won't hang myself."

"Cute," she says.

I head for the bathroom. Alicia follows me and watches me brush my teeth. "I think I like her," I say, stopping in the middle of brushing, holding the toothbrush in my mouth.

"You'd like her more if she was on you like bug repellent." She gives me one of those woman looks, the kind that usually comes complete with poised eyeliner brush.

I say, "I'll take some roaches next time."

She's twisting her head back and forth to check her teeth in the mirror. "Take rats," she says.

There's a tiny double beep on a car horn from the driveway. George. He isn't allowed in the house. When he comes for Alicia he pulls up in his Porsche and taps the horn. I've never heard such a discreet beep as George's.

She says, "I feel funny about this. Why am I always leaving? Am I ever staying home anymore?"

I give her a look that means it's the wrong time and the wrong question, and then walk her to the door. I go out on the porch so George gets a good look when I kiss her. "Don't be late," I say.

I'm inside in front of the television before they have a chance to pull away. The TV sound is annoying, and then, when I cut the sound, the things on the screen seem strangely distant, like from another world. That's okay for a minute, but then I feel sad, so I hit the remote button and sit there on the couch, stretched out, looking around the room. Nothing's out of place. It's dark and spotless. I sit there thinking about Juliet, seeing her in disarray, twisted up on the sofa, or relaxed in her bed, or on the floor next to the exercise bike. She's incredibly lovely and sexy in my imagination. Then I think about how fast things fly through your head when you're thinking, about how you see only key parts of stuff. I look at the cover of an issue of *Artforum* that's been on the coffee table for the last two months. It's this painting of an upside-down kangaroo I like pretty much. The only light in the room is from outside, a mercury vapor street lamp that leaves the shadow of the Levolors stretched along one wall, broken by a gladiola on the pedestal where we always put outgoing mail. The shadow has a flicker to it. I get a fresh drink and sit there watching this shadow and feeling like somebody in an Obsession ad, sitting there. I put my feet up on the far arm of the couch and drape my hand over my eyes, staring at this shadow—it's gorgeous. I unbutton my shirt and pull it open. I wish Juliet were with me, on the floor, leaning against the couch, so I could touch the back of her skull, comb her hair with my fingers, watch her cigarette smoke, blue against the perfect gray of the room. I think about tracking my knuckles on her cheek, resting my hand on the freckled skin of her shoulder. I imagine our conversation cut with pauses, her voice always hanging in the dry silence of the room like something lost.

The next thing that happens is I hear the doorbell and don't know what's going on. I think it's tomorrow. I get to the kitchen and look at the clock, see it's eleven-thirty, and wonder why it's so dark at that time of morning. Then I figure out I fell asleep on the couch, and go answer the door.

It's Heather. I say, "Hi. Come in."

"You're a real pony," she says. "With Juliet. I hear she offered the full show this morning." She brushes past me into the house, hitting every light switch she can find. "How long have we been friends?"

I squint at the street. "Pony?" I shut the door and follow her into the living room. It's too bright in there. "Years," I say.

She sits in one of the straight chairs. Her clothes are stuff I've seen in magazines, but that she never wears—balloon pants that get clownish about the calf, a shirt similarly enlarged, skinny purple shoes. "I ought to use an ice pick on her gums," she says, drilling a finger back and forth under her nose.

I say, "It's okay, Heather. We're friends. Nothing happened. It was a sweet gesture. Nobody took it seriously." I look at my hands, backs first, then palms. My neck feels thick. I sit on the forward edge of the couch and crack my knuckles.

"Juliet," she says.

"Yes," I say. "That's why it was sweet."

She watches me do four or five fingers, then starts to fidget with her hands, doing what I'm doing. "I can't do that. It's supposed to be so easy, but I can't even do it."

"Sure you can," I say. I crack my forefinger by looping my thumb over the first joint and pressing hard. "Try it."

She does what I'm doing. There are no pops, so I take her hand and try to do the knuckles myself, but I can't. I say, "No knuckles."

She pulls the hand away and stands up, heads toward the kitchen. "I don't want us in your mess. I can't handle organized infidelity."

I say, "She was being kind, Heather. C'mon. What mess are we in, anyway?"

"Sick-o," she says. "The wife's out with a college kid, doing God knows what, and you're around hitting on the neighborhood girls. Feeling modern."

"I feel lousy," I say. "As a matter of fact."

Alicia's back before midnight. I'm listening to cassettes I've made of a tune off a solo guitar record, comparing three different kinds of chrome tape. They sound the same to me, but I keep listening, trying to find the differences. Alicia says I should come talk to her while she bathes. I finish with the tapes and shut off the recorders, giving her a minute to get settled, then go knock on the bathroom door.

"Hello?" she says.

In the bathroom I sit cross-legged on the bath mat, facing her. She's lying in the tub, hair up, eyes shut. She's having a bubble bath, but her shoulders are out of the water, wet and shining. I look at her for a long time before I say, "I didn't sleep with Juliet."

"I know," she says. She doesn't open her eyes.

"It was okay, though. We touched a lot. I had a great time. She had a terrific time. It changed our entire lives."

"Good work," Alicia says, sitting up in her bath. Her shoulders curve forward into hollows at her collarbone. Her breasts are spotted with bubbles. She starts soaping the sponge and the bubbles sizzle.

I nod. "I was feeling mighty crazy."

"I believe that," she says.

"It wasn't too bad," I say.

I stare at her, thinking how gorgeous she is—cheekbones, the shape of her face, her eyes, the skin. I like her skin because it's rougher than most women's, kind of Texas prairie-looking, toward swarthy. I look at the tiny scar, three-sixteenths of an inch, right of center over her lip, and I remember her telling me how she got it—going over a chain-link fence to a boyfriend's at age eleven. She has three other scars on her face, all imperceptible unless you know where to look, and each with a story. A baseball bat, a fall from her father's shoulder, a car wreck.

I say, "You look great. You look high tone, like you ought to be at some bop club."

That makes her nervous. She starts messing with her hair, dropping nests of bubble bath.

I sigh. "So Heather comes over and says we're in trouble, and she doesn't want trouble like ours, and how come I have to mess with Juliet."

"I was wondering that myself," she says. She's waving the sponge back and forth between us. "Are we in trouble?"

I shrug. "I don't know. You tell me."

She cups some bubbles and looks at them up close. She pokes them with a finger on her free hand. "My guess is we don't have to be if we don't want to be," she says. She shakes her head. "I mean, we're made of steel, right? We're the ones."

"Right," I say.

"We make the rules, we write the songs."

"Right."

"Are you okay?"

"I'm good," I say.

She rinses her legs, then turns to me and holds up both hands as if she really wants to straighten something out. Now. In some big, final way. "Look," she says. "I don't want you to think I'm not a serious person, okay?" She looks at me, waiting.

"What?" I say.

She says, "I mean—could you use some cheese ball right about now? I am *dying* for cheese ball. I've been thinking about it all night long. I'll even make it."

I sit there looking at her, my chin cupped in my hand. I'm wondering about how to react to that, about how I feel about it, about her, trying to figure that out. After a while I reach out and put my hands on the edge of the tub—they're like bird feet, thumbs on my side, fingers on hers—and I pull myself up to my knees so I can kiss her.

She laughs. She's so beautiful.

(1987)

DRIVER

Rita says the living-room lights keep her awake when she goes to bed before I do, which is most of the time. The light comes down the hall and under the bedroom door, she says, and in the dark it's like a laser. So on Sunday, after she'd gone to bed, I started to read *Money* in semidarkness, tilting the pages to get the light from a book lamp clipped onto the magazine. That didn't work, so I gave it up and watched a TV program about lowriders in San Diego. They put special suspensions in their cars so they can bounce them up and down. That's not all they do, but it's sort of the center of things for them. I'd seen the cars before, seen pictures of them jumping—a wonderful thing, just on its own merits. I watched the whole show. It lasted half an hour, and ended with a parade of these wobbling, hopping, jerking cars creeping down a tree-lined California street with a tinkly Mexican love song in the background, and when it was done I had tears in my eyes because I wasn't driving one of the cars. I muted the sound, sat in the dark, and imagined flirting with a pretty Latin girl in a short, tight, shiny dress with a red belt slung waist to hip, her cleavage perfect and brown, on a hot summer night with a breeze, on a glittering street, with the smell of gasoline and Armor All in the air, oak leaves rattling over the thump of the car engine, and me slouched at the wheel of a violet Mercury, ready to pop the front end for a smile.

In the morning I left a note attached to the refrigerator with the tiny TV-dinner magnet, telling Rita what time I'd be home from the office, then got in the Celica and headed for the freeway. I'd been in traffic for half an hour, most of it behind a bald, architect-looking guy in a BMW 2002, when I saw a sign for Kleindienst Highway Auto Sales. This was a hand-painted sign, one-quarter billboard size, in a vacant lot alongside the freeway—a rendering of a customized 1949 Ford. I got off at the next exit and went back up the feeder to get to this place, which was a shell-paved lot with a house trailer at the rear, strings of silver and gold decorations above, and a ten-foot cyclone fence topped with knife wire surrounding it.

A guy jumped out of the trailer the minute I got onto the property. He followed me until I parked, then threw an arm around my shoulders before I had my car door shut. "Howdy," he said. "Phil Kleindienst. Hunting a big beauty, am I right?"

"Just looking," I said.

"We got the classics," he said, making a broad gesture with his free arm. He swung me around toward a Buick four-door. "Mainstream, high-profile, domestic, soon-to-be-sought-after classic road machines for the world of tomorrow."

"That's a big amen," I said.

He liked that. He laughed and walked me around the lot, keeping his hands on me the whole time—on my shoulder, my forearm, my back. He didn't have any cars that weren't huge and American, and he didn't have any custom cars. "Take a gander at this," he said, opening a brown Chrysler sedan. "This baby's autorama clean."

We went up and down the rows together. He was citing virtues, giving me histories, and I was looking for the hot rods. Finally, I said, "What about this sign?"

"What sign?" Phil said.

"Out there on the freeway," I said. I pointed back up to where the sign was. We could just set the back of it.

"Aw, you don't want to mess with that stuff. Lemme show you an Eldorado I got."

He started to move again. I said, "I'm a little late. I guess I'll have to come back another time. Thanks anyway."

"Hold your hanky there," he said. "I got one. I'll show you one. A Lincoln, pretty old."

He took me around beside the trailer to a corner with a banner that said BARGAIN CORRAL strung over the top. There was one car there, and it could have been in the TV show I'd seen. No price was soaped on the windshield, so I asked.

"Oh, hell," he said. "I don't know. Too much. Let's go back up front, lemme show you some sweethearts." He turned me toward the front of the lot. "How about this Caddy? About a '77, a honey-dripper. Purrs like a pistol."

I stopped him. "You don't want to tell me what you're getting for this one? What's the deal?"

"Whew," he said. "You're too tough. You're kidding me, right?" He waited a minute, looking me over to see whether or not I was kidding him. "You don't want that porker, do you?"

The Lincoln was pale blue with black and green pinstripes, front wheels smaller than the rear, and it was low, maybe two inches off the ground. There was an airbrush illustration on the side, between the front and rear wheel wells—a picture of the Blessed Virgin, in aqua-and-white robes, strolling in an orange grove, behind each tree of which was a wolf, lip curled, saliva shining. The glass in the windshield and in the doors was dark green, and the steering wheel was huge and white. A head-bobbing metal Bambi—I think it was supposed to be Bambi—sat on the shelf behind the back seat, staring out the rear window.

I said, "I'm just curious. What's it worth?"

He let go of me for the first time since I'd arrived, backing away, putting a little distance between us as he studied the car. Finally, he slapped his hands together and said, "I don't even want to give you a price on that there. See, that's my boy Pico's car. Was, anyway. Pico got shot up in Nam. He was this kid used to hang around, then worked for me. Built the car himself—did all the custom work, put in the hydraulics, stereo. All that in there's rhino skin. I don't even know where he got that."

"Looks professional," I said.

"Oh yeah, heck yeah. He was good. He's got D. & H. Reds in there. It's real clean. It's about a thousand per cent clean. He's got so much chrome under the hood you could put the hoses in your bathroom, use 'em for mirrors. I don't know why he's got these tiny wheels up front here, I guess that's a cholo thing . . ." Phil gazed at the Lincoln. He was half fat, maybe forty, with prickly blond hair, double-knit pants, a short-sleeved white shirt with a spread collar. "Pico cut her himself—know what I'm saying? Build a car like that today cost a fortune." He grinned and held his hands up as if giving me the bottom line. "I figure we're talking six, in the six area."

"What about the Toyota?" I said.

"Okay. Fine. That's all right," he said. "I can work with you on that." He locked an arm around one of mine and gave me a quick pull toward the office. "Let's boot some numbers around."

His trailer smelled like Pine-Sol. Everything was covered in knubby fabrics, earth tones. There was a dining booth, a tiny kitchen, a living space with a six-foot ceiling and a bubble skylight. He had four TVs, all consoles and all turned off, lined up against one wall. When we sat down, he said, "Let's verify our situation here. What's your line?" He was shuffling around, looking through a wood-grained-cardboard file cabinet.

I said, "I'm in sales. Pools, pool accessories, like that. Above-ground stuff. Is that what you mean?"

"Naw. I mean how come you want this car? Is this a kick-out-the-jams thing for you, or what?" He waited a second, then went on. "Okay, so don't tell me. What's your telephone? I'll check your wife on the deal. You got a wife, don't you?"

"Rita," I said.

"I mean, you tool in Nipponese and want to leave a Flying Burrito Brother, and I don't buy it. What's the better half gonna say? How do I know you got the bucks? How do I know you're in your right mind?"

"I don't know, I do, and I am," I said.

"Ha," he said. "That's good. What's the number? Better gimme the bank, too."

I gave him the numbers. He said, "Great. Get you something in the fridge. I got some Baby Ruths in there, if you got Olympic teeth. Help yourself."

He wiggled out from behind the table, went through a narrow hall to the rear of the trailer, shut a door between that room and the one I was in. There was a Plexiglas panel in the door, so I could see him in there, black telephone receiver to his ear, staring at the ceiling as he talked, swatting his hair with the papers from the file cabinet.

He was only in there a minute. When he came back he said, "The woman's not home, but the bank thinks you're aces." Then he gave me a long look. "Now listen," he said. He reached up under his shirtsleeve to scratch his shoulder. "I'm thinking you don't genuinely want this car. I know I'm supposed to be breaking your leg to sell it, but I figure you got some kind of momentary thing going, some kind of midlife thing—you look like you're about midlife."

I shrugged. "Not yet."

"Yet don't matter," he said. "My brother had his at twenty-seven. By twenty-nine he was putting toast in milk during the local news." Phil brushed something off the table. "Tell you what," he said. "I'll rent it. You take it maybe a day or two, leave yours on a collateral basis, take this guy, drive him a couple of days. Then, you still want it, we come to closure. How's that? I don't want you down my throat next week begging to undo the deal, right?"

I said, "I'll rent it right now."

"Sure you will," he said. "And I don't like it, but now and then, hell—what's it hurt?" He started through the file cabinet again. "I got a form here saves my heinie when you go to Heaven in it."

Phil had to go to his house to get the form. He lived right down the street, and he asked me to mind the store while he went, so I sat on the steps of the trailer and watched the highway.

Traffic had thinned out a lot. He was gone forty minutes. When he got back I took the Lincoln.

I stopped at an Exxon station and filled up with gas, then drove to my office. I had just gotten into my assigned parking space when a young associate of mine, Reiner Gautier, pulled up in the drive behind me.

"What, you went overboard on chimichangas?" he said. "What is that? Where'd you get it?"

"Just trying her out," I said.

"You got a built-in Pez dispenser on there?"

I waved the remark away and pretended to search my briefcase, hoping Reiner would move along. Finally, I had to get out. He'd left his car door open and was giving the Lincoln a careful look.

"That's Mary," he said, pointing to the picture on the side of the car. "She's got wolf trouble there, doesn't she?"

I shrugged. "She'll make out."

He looked at the picture another minute, turning his head back and forth. "That says it all, know what I mean? I like it. I go for this cross-cultural stuff." He walked back toward his car, giving my shoulder a pat on the way.

I let him leave, then got back in the Lincoln and pulled out of my space. I went to the shopping center near the office, stopped in the parking lot, and tried out the lifts. I looked out the door and I was better than eighteen inches off the ground. That got the attention of a black woman who was standing outside the ice-cream store, leaning against one of those phone-on-a-pole phone booths.

She said, "That some kind of trick car?" She was a young woman, in her twenties, and good-looking except that she was snaggletoothed. She was holding a clear plastic shopping bag with yellow rosettes on it.

I said, "Yeah. I guess it is."

She looked at me, then at the car, with a kind of amused curiosity, tilting her head back, squinting her eyes as she sized me up. "Well," she finally said. "What else do it do? Do it dance or anything?"

I grinned at her, shaking my head, then put the car in gear and left. At a bar called Splasher's, which I pass every day on my way back from work, I pulled up and went in for a beer. I'd never been in this bar before. It was one in the afternoon and the place was deserted except for a woman with feathery hair who handed me a wet bottle of Budweiser. She was cleaning up. The ceiling was falling in on this place. The walls were black, and the only illumination came from back of the bar and from the beer signs you always see, the kind that sparkle and throw little dots of light. One sign had a waterfall that light rushed over. I took my beer to a window table so I could watch the car through the stick blinds.

The woman played Country Joe and the Fish on the jukebox. I thought that was amazing. I spun my coaster, listening to this music

I hadn't heard in twenty years. Between tunes I went to get a bag of beer nuts from a metal rack next to the cash register. The woman watched me search my pocket for change, then nodded when I put two quarters on the bar.

Two kids on trail bikes stopped outside to give the car a look. These kids were about fourteen, with dirty T-shirts and minimal hair. They straddled their bikes and stared in the car windows, and I smiled about it until I saw the kid on the driver's side prying off the door mirror. Then I rapped on the glass and went out. "Hey! Get off of that, will you?"

The kid who had been doing the prying gave me an innocent look "Great car," he said. "We're checking it out. Right, Binnie?"

Binnie was already on the move, standing on the pedals of his bike, rolling away. "Pretty good," he said. "For a dork-mobile."

I said, "Sorry you're leaving."

"Whoa . . ." he said.

The first kid started moving, too. Then he stopped his bike and turned to me. "Hey," he said. "You know that mirror on your side? It's real loose. I can probably fix it up. Ten bucks."

I gave him a nasty look and shook my head, then got in the car. I stopped at a drugstore on the way home, went in to get cigarettes. A college-age guy with blue eyes and pretty brown hair was in back, sitting at a folding table, eating his lunch. It didn't look like takeout food—it looked homemade. He had a dinner plate, a salad plate, a jelly glass with red and green swirls on the side. There was milk in the glass. He asked if he could help me.

"I need a pack of cigarettes," I said.

He came across to the cigarette counter wiping his mouth with a yellow paper towel. "What kind?"

I said, "True. Menthol."

He looked at his cigarette rack, one end to the other, then turned around and said, "I don't see 'em. You see 'em out there?" He pointed to the front of the counter, where more cigarettes were displayed.

I'd already checked, but I looked again. "None here."

He came out from behind the counter rewiping his mouth "I don't guess we have 'em. I was sure we did, but I guess I was wrong. I can order you some."

I waited a second or so, looking at the guy, then picked a pack of Kools off the counter. "How about these?"

"We got those," he said.

Rita came to the window when I pulled up in the driveway and honked. It took her a minute, but then she figured out it was me and dropped the curtain. "What's this?" she said, coming out the front door.

I held up a hand and said, "Wait a minute. Stay there. Watch."

She stopped by the gas lamp at the edge of the drive. I jumped the front end of the Lincoln a little, then as far as it would go. Then I raised the rear to full height, then the front. I kept the car up until she was coming for a closer look, then I let it down, left front first, like an elephant getting on its knees in a circus show. That stopped her.

I got out of the car. "How do you like it?"

"Whose is it?" she said.

"Ours." I put an arm around her and did a Phil Kleindienst sweep with my free hand, covering the Lincoln front to back.

"What about the Celica? Where's the Celica?"

I reached in the driver's window and pulled the hood release, so I could show her the chrome on the engine. "Traded it," I said, leading her around to the front. "Guy gave me a whopper deal."

She stopped dead, folding her arms across her chest. "You traded the Toyota?"

"Well, sort of. But this is a killer car. Look at the engine. Everything's chrome. It's worth a zillion."

Rita looked at the sky.

"C'mon," I said. I tugged her arm, leading her to the passenger side, and put her in the car. I went back around, latched the hood, then got in and started the engine. I waited, listening to the idle. "Amazing, isn't it? Can you hear that?"

"The motor? I hear the motor. Is that what you're talking about, that rumbling?"

We toured the neighborhood, then I started to go downtown, but Rita remembered she needed some lemon-pepper marinade, so we stopped at the supermarket. I sat in the car while she went inside. A lot of people walked by wearing shorts, and all of them looked good.

We picked up a family bucket of fried chicken on the way back, ate most of it in the car, then finished up inside. Then we had bananas and ice cream. After that Rita switched on the VCR and put in a tape. "I want you to see this," she said.

It was a PBS documentary about China—about a peasant family. The grandmother ran things and got carried around on the back of a bicycle through this gorgeous countryside of misty, contoured land. Her son didn't know much about Communism but felt things were a lot better now, with the Four Modernizations. His wife cooked, his daughters helped in the fields, and his son wore a leather motorcycle jacket when he went out to help with the harvest. At the end they cut to the father, alone in some room, sitting by a big vase with thin branches in it, dusty light slanting in. He talked about the family, his voice ricocheting around the high registers while out-of-sync white translations popped on the bottom of the screen. When he got to his son, what he said was that the boy had been "stunned by the West."

That was it. Rita stopped the sound and we watched the credits go by, then the network logo, then some previews of WGBH shows. She poked me and pointed to the *TV Guide*, which was on the coffee table on my side of the couch. I gave her the guide and then watched her look up listings.

When she finished, she tossed the magazine back on the table. "Well?" she said.

"It's a rent-purchase thing," I said. I showed her the paper I'd signed for Phil Kleindienst. "I can give it back any time."

She laughed and said, "Hey! Not so fast. I may love it. I may want to go for a spin."

We went out about ten o'clock. It was cool, so we slouched down in the seats and left the windows open. We went by an apartment project we used to live in, and then we went over to the other side of town, where there is a lot of heavy industry—chemical plants and refineries.

Rita said, "It rides pretty good, doesn't it?"

"It's stiff when it's down," I said.

"So pump her up," she said. "I wonder what it'd be like to keep."

"People would stare."

"Great," she said. "It's about time."

She looked terrific in the car. She had on a checked shirt open over a white Danskin, her feet were up on the dash, and her short hair was wet and rippled with wind. Her skin is olive and rough, and it was glowing as if she were in front of a fire. When I missed a light next to Pfeiffer Chemicals, a couple of acres of pipes and ladders and vats and winking green lamps, I leaned over to kiss her cheek, but she turned at the last minute and caught me with her lips.

"Why, thank you," she said when I sat back again.

"Yes," I said.

On the way home we stopped at the mall. The stores were closed, but there were kids roller-skating in the parking lot, and a couple of cars parked nose to nose under one of the tall lights. We pulled up next to a palm tree in a planter about fifty yards away from the kids.

Rita said, "It's amazing out here, isn't it? How can this place be so good-looking?"

"Beats me," I said.

She put her head in her hands. "It's awful, but I have a craving for tamales. Really. I'm not making a joke, okay?"

One of the kids, a girl in shorts, pointed a finger at us and skated over. "How come it stays up like that?" she said.

"Just magic," I said. But then I opened the door and showed her, letting the car down real easy, then jumping the front a little bit for her.

"You got her now," Rita whispered.

The girl stood back with her hands on her waist for a second. "Boy," she said.

She was pretty. Her shorts were satin, with little specks of glitter on them, and she had on a tiny undershirt-style top. Some trucks sailed by on the highway. I offered Rita a Kool. She took it and held it under her nose.

"What's your name?" I said to the girl, rolling my cigarette between my fingers.

"Sherri," she said. "With an 'i.'"

I nodded. "You out here a lot?" I wagged my hand toward the other kids, who were sitting on the hoods of their cars watching us.

"Sure," she said. She rocked back and forth on her skates, rolling a little, then stopping herself with her toe. "Make it go up again, okay?"

I did that, getting it wrong the first try, so that I had one side up while the other was down. Rita was laughing in a lovely way.

The girl watched, then shook her head. "Boy," she said, smiling and skating two small circles before starting back toward her friends. "You guys were weird."

"Howdy," Rita kept saying all the way home. "Howdy, howdy, howdy. Howdy."

She went to bed at one. I couldn't sleep, so I watched a movie we'd rented a couple days earlier. When that was over I rewound it, paged through an issue of *Spin* that she'd picked up at the grocery store, then watched the end of a horror show on HBO. By then it was after four. I tried to sleep but couldn't, so I got up and went outside. It was almost light enough to see out there. I sat in the Lincoln and thought about how nice it was that Rita could just sleep whenever she wanted to. After a while I started the car and went for a drive. I stopped at an off-brand all-night market and bought some liquid refreshment in a sixteen-ounce non-returnable foam-sleeved bottle. I wondered if the glass was less good than glass in regular bottles.

The scent of countryside in the morning was in the air. The rear window was smeared with condensation, and the storefronts were that way, too, and it was hard to focus on the stoplights, because of the way they made rings around themselves.

I went downtown, and it was like one of those end-of-the-world movies down there, with somebody's red hamburger wrapper skittering across a deserted intersection. The sky was graying. I made a loop around the mayor's Vietnam memorial, then took the highway running west, out past the city limits. The mist got thicker. Close to the road the trees looked right, but farther away they just dissolved. In the rearview mirror I could make out the empty four-lane highway, but above that it was like looking through a Kleenex.

Finally, I turned around and drove back by my secretary's apartment, saw her car with its windows solidly fogged, then passed the mall again. Some overnight campers had turned up in the lot, and their generators were chugging away. There were two Holiday Ramblers, cream-colored, squarish things, and an Airstream hitched to a once green Chevrolet. I pulled in and stopped. The air was so wet you could feel it when you rubbed your fingers together. The sky showed bits of pink behind a gray cloud that was big above the eastern horizon. A bird sailed by in front of the car, six feet off the blacktop, and landed next to a light pole.

These two dogs came prancing into the lot, side by side, jumping on each other, playfully biting each other's neck. They were having a great time. They stopped not far away and stared at the bird, which was a bobwhite and was walking circles on the pavement. They stared, crouched for a second, then leaped this way and that, backward or to one side, then stared more. It was wonderful the way they were so serious about this bird. These dogs were identical twins, black-and-white, each with an ear that stood up and one that flopped over. I made a noise and their heads snapped around, and they stared at me for a minute. One of them sat down, forepaws stretched out in front, and the other took a couple of steps in my direction, looked for a sign from me, then twisted his head and checked the bird.

The dash clock said it was eight minutes to six. I wanted to drive home real fast and get Rita and bring her back to see everything—the dogs, the brittle light, the fuzzy air—but I figured by the time we got back it'd all be gone.

The lead dog took two more steps toward me, stopped, then stretched and yawned.

I said, "Well. How are you?"

He wagged his tail.

I said, "So. What do you think of the car?"

I guess he could tell from my voice that I was friendly, because then he did a little spasm thing and came toward me, having trouble keeping his back legs behind his front. I opened the car door and, when he came around, patted the seat. He jumped right in. He was frisky. He scrambled all over the place—into the back seat, back into the front—stuck his head out the passenger window, ducked back in and came over to smell the gearshift knob. The other dog was watching all this. I called him, then put the car in gear and rolled up next to him. He didn't move for a minute, just gave me a stare, kind of over his shoulder. I made that kissing noise you use to call dogs, and he got up and came to the door, sniffing. Finally, he climbed in. I shut the car door and headed home. They were bouncing around, and I was telling them the whole way about the girl in the parking lot and about Rita and me, how weird we had been. "We aren't weird now," I told them. "But we were weird. Once. In olden days."

(1989)

PART THREE

LARROQUETTE

Sheila leaned against her chain-link fence, fingering the decorative scroll bolted onto the top of the gate. She was looking across the street at the Terlinks' garage. The Terlinks were having a Sunday afternoon barbecue. Sheila watched carefully. She hadn't waved. She didn't know the Terlinks—Johnson Terlink and his wife, Emma, their two children, Rita and Herman—had never spoken to them except in passing at the mailbox—Hello, how are you? Nothing more. But somebody else was with them. A fancy rental car nosed into the end of the drive, so she knew they had company. Sheila kicked at Bosco, the dog who kept winding around her legs, in and out, panting, occasionally making little yipping noises.

She liked the neighborhood. It was the best she could afford. The houses were wood-siding things, falling apart, once painted white with colorful trim. The yards were thick grass, tricycles, colorful volleyballs, soccer balls, plastic doodads and whatnots. A kite twirled on the telephone wire behind the Terlinks' house. The kite had been there since Sheila moved in eighteen months before, after her divorce. Eighteen months, Sheila thought, looking at the kite. I should have introduced myself before this.

Sheila worked nights at the hospital, rolling patients over, wedging pillows under them, cleaning bedpans, changing drips and catheter bags. She had six hours before work.

The tall guy on the Terlinks' driveway laughed loudly. He looked familiar, she thought. He looked like John Larroquette.

She went inside to get her son, Tod, who was eighteen, in his room watching MTV. Tod had a job at Don't Nobody Eat Pizza?

He strapped a Don't Nobody Eat Pizza? sign on the top of the car and delivered all night long.

"Come out here and look at this, will you?" Sheila said. "I think we've got John Larroquette across the way."

"What's he doing there?" Tod said.

"Don't know. I'm not sure it's him. There's a guy who looks like him, somebody. Got a fancy rent car."

"So walk across the street," Tod said.

"I don't want to meet him," Sheila said. "I just want to know if it is him."

"I don't care if it is," Tod said.

"I know," Sheila said. "But I do. So come out, look across, see if you can ID him, okay? I don't ask too goddamn much."

"You ask everything," Tod said. He rolled off the bed. She followed him, and Bosco followed her. They were a little parade.

Tod leaned on the fence, squinted hard, said, "I don't know. I give up," and headed back inside.

"Tod," she said.

"I don't know. I can't see. What makes you think it's him, anyway? And why do you care? You never looked at John Larroquette, did you? Wasn't he on *Cheers*?"

"Oh, like you don't know," Sheila said. "*Night Court.* But now he's got his own show. He reminds me of your father."

"Everybody reminds you of my father," Tod said. "Batman reminds you of my father." Tod wore plaid green Bermudas and a soiled T-shirt. He walked around a bush at the corner of the house. "You need a life, Mother. That's what."

"Look who's talking. Come back here." She pointed to the ground in front of her. Tod looked, his hair a tangle of eight-inch spikes. He stood on the back steps.

Bosco tore a limb off the bush and ran around with the limb in his mouth, daring Sheila to chase him. She feinted at the dog, and he dodged away.

"What's wrong with me?" Tod said. He held his T-shirt at the hem, staring down at himself.

"You're eighteen and living at home with your mother," Sheila said.

"So I'll move," he said. He opened the screen door.

"You're just like your father," Sheila said.

Tod shut his eyes and leaned his head back and rubbed his left hand through his hair several times, holding his head. "I'm not just like my father in any way," he said. "I've never been like my father. I don't know why a person would say that. I don't know why you would say that. You know I'm not like my father."

Sheila sat down on the ground, gathering her skirt between her legs.

"Don't sit on the ground, Mother," Tod said. "Come inside. I'll fix you something to eat—a toasted cheese sandwich. Would you like that?"

"Nope," Sheila said. "I want to know if that's John Larroquette."

"It's not," he said.

"I saw him on Leno. He's from Louisiana. He said he visits his cousin in Florida, his only cousin. They have barbecues. In the garage. That's what he told Jay."

"I'm guessing he visits Miami or something. Coral Gables. Not likely his cousin lives in Quantum." Tod came down the steps, into the yard, and reached out to help his mother up, but just at that minute Bosco hopped into her lap.

"I could talk to Mrs. Terlink about her dogs," Sheila said.

"What dogs?" Tod asked.

"She raises Chihuahuas," Sheila said. "That's what Ellen told me. Ellen next door?" She thumbed to her left where Ellen lived. "Said she raises Chihuahuas. She's got maybe twenty-five Chihuahuas over there."

Tod shook his head. "Okay. Here's what I'll do. I'll go out like I'm getting the mail. If it's him, I'll come get you."

"Why would you be getting the mail on Sunday?" Sheila said.

"I wasn't home Saturday?" he said.

"You're always home," she said. "Everybody knows that."

"Oh. Right," Tod said. He finger-combed his hair over his head, one side to the other.

"Why don't you wash it?" Sheila said.

Inside, she sat on an old green stool by the stove. Tod made her a sandwich out of Rainbow bread and wrapper cheese. She took some wrapper cheese to feed Bosco, made him stand up on his hind legs and go around in circles, then dropped cheese strips from shoulder height to see if he could catch them. Most of the time the cheese went right by him.

She walked out through the dining room into the living room and stood at the front window, pulling back the curtain, peering across the street. "I think that's him," she said. "I'm almost certain that's him."

"It's not," Tod said. "Come eat your sandwich."

"Let's go out in the car. We can get really close."

"I thought you wanted a sandwich. I'm making a sandwich. Are you going to eat?"

In the living room, Sheila picked up three copies of *Family Circle* magazine that Ellen had lent her. She gathered up some of Bosco's toys—a pink ball with a pebbled surface, a plastic bone the size of her forearm, a book he liked to chew on. She tossed all three into a basket in the corner of the living room where Bosco's toys were kept. For some reason Bosco wouldn't go near the basket. When he wanted a toy, he would stand about a foot away from the basket and whimper, looking back over his shoulder at her. It would have been easy enough for him to tip the basket over, or reach in and bite whatever toy he wanted. But he would never do that. He just whimpered. Sometimes, if a toy went under a chair or the bench in the entry hall, Bosco would stand there and look, whimpering. He was afraid the furniture was going to jump him.

"Ready," Tod called. She went in the kitchen and ate her cheese sandwich. Tod ate a peanut butter sandwich and stood at the window by the sink, looking at Ellen's house. "There are snakes over there," he said. "Ellen came over last week and told me the yard guy found a snake in the back and chased it under a tree stump, so she had the animal control people come out. But they said they wouldn't touch it. That it was her responsibility. If the snake was out in the open, they'd take it. Otherwise, no dice."

"That's a big help," his mother said.

"She was warning me about Bosco, to keep him out of the yard," he said.

"He can take care of himself," Sheila said.

"Said it was a copperhead," Tod said. "I went and looked, but I couldn't see anything. She wanted me to put gasoline in this tree stump and burn it. I didn't want to do that."

"She's fond of you," Sheila said.

"Oh, please," Tod said.

"Ever since the police came," Sheila said.

"Yeah, big turn-on," Tod said.

Two months before, the police had come to the house to talk to Tod about a case they were working on. Some pizza delivery guy was raping women. They called the guy "the pizza rapist." They didn't think Tod was him, but they thought he might know the guy. Two uniformed policemen and two plainclothes policemen came in and sat in the living room with Tod and Sheila, and, in the middle of things, Ellen had arrived.

"Can I help?" she had asked.

"No, we're just talking to the police," Sheila told her.

"Oh?" Ellen said.

"They're here to talk to Tod," Sheila said.

"Is he in trouble?" Ellen asked.

"Nothing like that," Sheila told her. "They need his help in some case. It's like somebody he may know or something he may have seen. They want a witness."

"Oh," Ellen said.

She stood on the front porch craning her neck, trying to get a look into the living room at the cops and at Tod. Sheila tried to stay in her line of sight.

"Can you come back later?" Sheila asked her.

"Sure," Ellen said. "Later. If you're sure you're all right."

"We're fine," Sheila said to her.

Ellen was twenty-two and an assistant to the pharmacist at the K&B drugstore. She had a junior-college degree and was thinking about finishing a four-year degree at Antonelli College. She wore chrome-rimmed glasses, and Sheila did not think she was unattractive. She wouldn't be a bad match for Tod, was what Sheila thought. But Tod wasn't interested. He had his face fixed for one of the MTV girls, or any girl like an MTV girl. Somebody about sixteen. He had dated a lot of younger girls when he was in high school, but when he dropped out he stopped dating altogether. He hadn't had a date in a year.

•

Sheila opened the front door. "I'm watering the beds out front." She had on a straw hat and sunglasses, and struggled adjusting them.

Tod rolled his head. "Leave the damn beds alone, will you?"

"Just let me water," she said.

"Water the grass," he said. "But don't be staring across the street."

"I'll be careful. I've got these glasses on. They can't tell where I'm staring anyway," she said.

"That will really confuse them. They're not going to have a clue."

"Well, drive me somewhere, then," she said.

"Okay. Fine. Where?"

"I don't care. I just want to go in the car so we can go by the driveway and see if that's him. I'd like to meet him. I'd like to take him dancing."

"Mother—"

"I've earned it," she said. "You're young. Nobody wants to go dancing with you."

"Thanks, Ma," Tod said.

"You know he has a wife. She's very English. That's what he said. He said his wife was 'very English.' Too English. She was upset because they were at this barbecue with his cousin," Sheila said. "Just like these people across the way. He was in the garage just like they are. He said it was cooler in the garage, that's why they were in there. Then his English wife came up and whispered he was a redneck. That's what he said on Leno. He seemed like a real nice guy."

"I'm sure he is. Very well-to-do," Tod said.

"What does that have to do with? Aren't you putting your contacts in?"

"No, I can see with the glasses," he said.

"We might run into Ellen. We might go to the drugstore."

"We're not going to the drugstore. Do you need to go to the drugstore?"

"I need garbage bags," she said. They went out to the car, an Oldsmobile, green, from the eighties. Tod drove. "Now go slow," Sheila said as he backed out.

"I'm going as slow as I can. If I go slower, I'll be going too slow."

"You're going backwards," she said. "How can you go too slow?"

"Mother," he said. He crawled the Olds past the Terlinks' house, past the driveway, and she stared up there and waved at the Terlinks. They all waved back from the deep shadow of the garage.

Two or three houses down the street there was a brown horse standing in somebody's front yard, tied to a tree. It had a bridle, but that was all. Nobody was paying any attention to it. It was just standing there.

"What's with this?" Sheila said, pointing out her window.

"Horse," Tod said. "Somebody got a horse."

"Well, they should wash it. Look at that. It's going to be hot, its feet are caked. They ought to get somebody over here to wash it."

Out by the shopping center on Old Post Road there were two police cars with their blue lights flashing.

"Check the heat," Sheila said.

"That really dates you," Tod said. "Heat."

"Oh, God, I'm so sorry," Sheila said. "Forgive me, really. Can you ever?"

When they got close enough, they saw that somebody had driven a panel van into a ditch. Somebody else had gone in right after and landed on top of the van. That person was still sitting in his car, sort of slumped over to the side. The driver of the panel van was on a board alongside the van, deep in a ditch, surrounded by cops and ambulance people.

"It doesn't look good," Sheila said.

"I've seen that head getup on *ER*," Tod said. "See the way they've got the Styrofoam thing around his head there?"

"That's not Styrofoam," Sheila said.

"You want some yogurt?" he said. "I'm stopping at the yogurt joint."

"That really dates you—'joint,'" she said. "Look at this guy in the Caddy. He's just perched up there. Why don't they get him out? He looks sad."

"You'd be sad, too. I mean, come on," Tod said.

"What if those cars explode?" she said.

Tod changed lanes to get on the side of the street where the yogurt shop was in the strip shopping center. He pulled up to the drive-in window and asked Sheila what she wanted. She said a waffle cone with fat-free chocolate. He got a cup of vanilla and an oatmeal cookie. When the yogurt came, they paid and then drove the car out to the edge of the parking lot and stopped, rolling the windows down. From where they were sitting, they could see the wreck down to their left, the police and the ambulance, the road in front of them, and two shopping centers across the street.

"I don't remind you of my father, do I?" Tod said, after a minute.

"Some ways. What's wrong, you don't like your father?"

"I don't want to be like him. He didn't do well."

"He did fine," she said. "Just ran out of steam."

Tod left the car running and the air-conditioning on even though they had the windows down. "I feel like doing laundry. Dishes, too. I'm doing dishes when we get home."

"Fine. Do dishes all night long," she said. "Your father never did a dish in his life."

"I like my hands in the water," he said. "The way water sounds running. I could do dishes for hours—water's warm and soapy, you know, you've got a good sponge and you get some soap in that and rub it on the plates and the plates get a little slippery and everything gets a little slippery so there's some danger to it."

"Yeah," Sheila said. "That's how I feel about it exactly."

"Don't ruin it," Tod said. "Sometimes when you're gone and I'm there, I wash dishes and clothes at the same time, so I have the washer running and sometimes the washer and the dryer, and then I'm washing dishes, too. God, that's great. I really like that. That does it for me."

"You remind me of your father," she said, shaking her head. She looked out her window at a yellow dog that had its nose stuffed in a Burger King sack. The dog lifted the sack up, throwing its head back so that it could get deeper into the bag. It was walking around on the striped concrete with this bag on its face.

"I hope that guy in the van doesn't die," Tod said.

"Me too," Sheila said, "What do you want for dinner?"

"We had sandwiches," Tod said. "I can't think about dinner yet."

"You want to barbecue?" Sheila said. "We could do that in the driveway, just like the Terlinks. Maybe we could go over there, or they could come over."

"We could have a party," Tod said. "Maybe I'll take up with the Terlink girl. We'll become lovers—tonight, after you leave for work."

"Isn't she a little young for you?" Sheila said.

"Oh, yeah," he said. "She's a babe. She's a babe and a half. She's a twister. Sometimes, I sneak over there and look into her window, crawl around and peep in, see her in her underwear walking around the house. She always wears lace underwear—pink, black, pale blue. She's a real beauty. Sex hound."

"Oh, stop," Sheila said.

"She's probably poking Larroquette," Tod said. "He's grinning that stupid grin of his, revitalizing his . . ."

"Never mind," Sheila said. "Quit."

They were quiet in the car, finishing the yogurt. The only thing she could hear was the smacking of their lips. When he was done, Tod squashed the bag the cookie had come in into the cup, broke the plastic spoon and put it in the cup too, then opened his door and set the cup on the concrete of the parking lot.

"Why do you want to do that?" Sheila said. "Here. Give that to me."

"I'm leaving it here," he said. "It's a gift. I don't have dirty diapers or chicken bones, so this is the best I can do."

"Oh, Jesus," she said. "Tod, open the door and pick that up."

"I'm not," he said. He backed the car in a half circle.

She reached over and struggled with the steering wheel, trying to force him to drive back and pick up the cup, but he turned the wheel the other direction and drove diagonally across the lot.

"I need to get a magazine," he said.

"I need to get home," she said. "We need to solve this problem once and for all."

"Dinner?" he said.

"No," she said. "I've got chicken at home. I stewed some chicken. You can have that. I'm having a salad. I've got to get this cheese off my legs." She grabbed her thighs and wagged them.

Tod drove more cautiously than he needed to. She was struck by it. He drove like his father. There wasn't a bit of difference. If she had shut her eyes, or if she had worn blinders to prevent her from seeing who was in the driver's seat, she could have imagined being with Dan. The ancient Oldsmobile was his car, part of the settlement, the conclusion of their marriage. The car and the house—that was her part of the bargain. She had always liked the car, and the house was comfortable. Sometimes, when she looked at *Better Homes and Gardens*, she wished it was fancier, but most of the time she didn't worry. She kept it clean. It had a nice old-house smell about it, and sometimes, in the summer, when the ceiling fans were going and the attic fan was on and a breeze was being pulled through the house through the open windows, she could close her eyes and imagine she was at her grandparents' house when she was a kid in the fifties. She could remember the way things smelled, the way the air moved. Her grandparents had a house in Bay St. Louis, Mississippi, overlooking the Sound, and it had a certain sweet mustiness she always remembered. That was how her house in Quantum smelled.

She hadn't wanted Dan to leave. She'd spent seventeen years with him, but now she didn't know why she had stayed that long. He'd had different jobs—night watchman, car salesman, menswear sales in a department store. He'd hold on to one for six months or a year, then go crazy after some young girl. Start drinking, staying out all night, shoving her around when he was home. He wasn't much to miss, and he had always ignored Tod. Still, it broke her heart when he left. It did occur to her from time to time that she would like to have another man around, a boyfriend, but Tod was okay for the day-to-day, routine stuff—watching TV movies and renting things from the video store. He was even fun, because he liked things that were strange to her. She worried she was hanging onto him too much, clinging to him, poisoning him. She worried that keeping him at home, making it easy for him to stay, was wrong. But she'd never really lived alone since college, and, even then, she had girlfriends, and she didn't think she wanted to start being alone at forty. She'd brought men to the house before, people she knew at the hospital or at church. There was always tension between the men and Tod. After a while she stopped bringing them. They were just going to sit on the sofa, smoke cigarettes, drink her beer, and watch her television and scratch themselves. Tod could do all that.

•

When they got home, the Terlinks were gone. The fancy rental car was gone and the garage doors were closed. All the windows were covered with miniblinds. There were a few lights on behind them. It was dark when Sheila rolled the barbecue pit out of the garage onto the driveway. She took off its lid, removed the grill, went back into the garage, got some charcoal briquettes, and poured them into the bottom of the grill. She sprayed them with Gulf lighter fluid, then walked around, looking at her flower beds while she waited for the lighter fluid to seep into the briquettes. Tod went inside and came out to tell her there were steaks in the freezer and to ask her if she wanted him to defrost them in the microwave. She said she did.

"Are there vegetables?" she said. "Spinach?" He said he'd look. She opened the aluminum folding chair she'd found in the garage and sat in the driveway with a hose spraying water onto the flower bed between her property and Margie's. A five-dollar nozzle was on the end of the hose. Tod came out of the kitchen door with two packs of frozen vegetables.

"Corn or lima beans?" he asked.

"Both," she said. She released the trigger closing the nozzle and dropped the hose onto the driveway, while she lit the charcoal. Then she put the grill on top and scrubbed it with a wire brush. She sat down again and started spraying. There was a little breeze, and the water from the spray shifted slightly out of its path. Sometimes the mist flew back on her. It felt nice and cool. Refreshing. She swung the nozzle and sprayed the Oldsmobile and then started on the bed on the house side of the driveway. She kept an eye on the Terlinks' garage. She wondered what had made her want it to be John Larroquette. She thought it odd you could want something so bad and never get it. You could spend your whole life wanting something and never even come close.

When she married her husband, Dan, she had been in love with a black man she had met in nursing school. He was beautiful and powerful and very smart. He knew that she loved him, or at least that she had a crush on him. Sometimes he took advantage of it, touching her in ways that he shouldn't have—feeling her waist, letting his hand rest just beneath her breast, testing the strap of her brassiere, casually brushing against her buttocks. It happened too often to be accidental, but that was as far as it went. Later, he became the weatherman for a TV station.

On her wedding night, after she and Dan had made love, she had watched this black man whom she was in love with do the weather forecast on the ten o'clock news. She thought he was so handsome.

•

Tod came out with the steaks on a cookie sheet. He'd put a lot of Worcestershire sauce on them. "How long?" he said, holding the cookie sheet up on five fingers, as if he were a waiter.

"Coals ready any minute," Sheila said. "They're getting gray."

"I've got the vegetables," Tod said. "I did them in the microwave. You want to eat by the TV?"

"Sure," Sheila said. "What's on?"

"Everything," he said. "Probably movies."

"I never watched his show anyway," Sheila said.

"What?"

"Larroquette," she said. "He seemed nice when I saw him on TV. I liked him. He talked like somebody you could like. You know what I mean? He pinched his fingers together and said he was a redneck just about that far under the skin. It didn't seem to bother him. He laughed when he said it. That's such a wonderful thing for a man to do."

Tod looked at her for a few seconds, then brought the cookie sheet down and handed it to her. He pulled a cooking fork out of his back pocket and handed that to her as well. Then he took the hose out of her hand and spritzed the water up in the air so that it drizzled on them, just a little bit—just lightly.

"Sure," she said. "Go on. Rain some more. Rain harder."

(1999)

CLEO

The day before Gretchen goes to visit her family in Albuquerque, we drive over to pick up an old friend of hers, a woman named Cleo Hass. We're going shopping. Cleo has just returned from two years in California, and Gretchen is saying how happy she is that Cleo's back. "I'm talking about friends," she says. "We need to try stuff. We don't want to die in this thing."

"What thing?" I say.

"This," she says, waving her hand between the two of us. "Everything. I'm serious. I'm glad she's back. We need her. You can't just go around losing people all the time."

"We didn't move to California," I say.

"That doesn't matter," Gretchen says.

Gretchen and I have been together three years. We met in a nursery, on a Saturday. Six weeks later she moved in, bringing Cleo with her. Cleo stayed for a year, sleeping on a cot in the dining area of the apartment. Near the end of that first year we were together, Gretchen left and moved to Seattle. Cleo stayed with me in the apartment. Gretchen was gone less than a month. Early one morning she called and said she was coming back. I said that was great. Then, when she got back, Cleo left.

Now the three of us go through a department store at the mall, then split up and agree to meet at the fountain. I head for the mock outdoor café and get in line to order a chocolate-filled croissant, but a young guy with ratty hair and a silver shirt open to the waist comes in singing a torch song and pushes in front of me. He jokes with one of the girls behind the counter. They're in French-maid uniforms. I figure he's a local celebrity, maybe a drummer in some important band. The girl he's talking to likes him, which I think is amazing. I'm wondering about that when Cleo comes up.

"I hate to shop," she says. She orders a spinach croissant, then leads the way to a wire-topped table out in the mall.

I start to say something about not wanting Gretchen to go to Albuquerque, but Cleo interrupts.

"I don't do girl advice anymore. That's the way I am now. You'd better learn to work around it."

"Yes, ma'am," I say.

Cleo came back to open an aerobics franchise called Thigh High. She wears a lot of exercise gear. Today she's got on a peach-and-gray leotard under an open white shirt, a pair of baggy pants, and a yellow sweatshirt tied by the arms around the waist. Red shoes. She's good-looking—long legs, small breasts, radiant skin. Gretchen says she hasn't had a decent boyfriend since she was nineteen.

I tear my croissant in half and break off a small piece with chocolate in it. "So, how's the new-woman business?" I ask, nipping at the chocolate.

"It's all new," Cleo says. "You ought to try it."

A girl of about eighteen comes out of a candle store, leading two children. The kids have fur animals—a red bird and a hippo. They're playing. One kid drops the bird and kicks it six or eight feet in front of her, then the other does the same with the hippo. The mother scolds them, but it doesn't have any effect.

"So, did everybody miss me?" Cleo says. She's waving her croissant around in her hand, not eating it.

"Sure," I say. "We kept bumping into something imaginary in the dining room."

"That's funny," Cleo says. "I was thinking about when Gretchen went to Washington State, you know? You were all over me. You couldn't get enough. Then she shows up and suddenly I'm bad meat. I hated your guts for that, I really did."

"I guess it wasn't my best moment. But it wasn't yours, either—you didn't want to sleep with me."

"Big deal. What is that, a way to measure something? I was a loyal guy." She playfully shoots me the finger, then shakes it for emphasis. "Never forgive, never forget," she says, finally taking a bite of the croissant.

"Don't be mean," I say.

She looks at the skylights. "This time, this time I show you what you missed. Is that nice enough?"

"That's nice," I say. "Did you see this guy inside here?" I point out the kid in the silver shirt as he leaves the serving counter. "What's the deal on him?"

"He works at Slime Land," Cleo says. "I don't know. How am I supposed to know?"

The young mother is disciplining her kids for kicking toys in the mall. She's right alongside us now. She's bent in half and she has the girl by the wrist, whipping her back and forth, shouting in a stage whisper. The girl is crying, trying to get her fists into her eyes, but the mother is jerking her around so much the fists don't seat. "Do you want to be popped?" the mother says. "I can pop you, if that's what you want."

"Probably not what she wants," I say to Cleo.

"Hush," she says, leaning across the table.

"Hell, I think I'll go over there and give her a poke or two myself—what do you think about that?"

"Pick on somebody your own size," Cleo says, tapping her collarbone with a knuckle.

Gretchen wants to go back to Sears after we drop Cleo at her aerobics place, where some workmen are finishing the interior. I don't mind going, but I say, "Why didn't we go when we were there?"

Gretchen says, "I can go in by myself, if it's too much for you. It'll take a minute. You can sit in the car."

It's been raining all day. I take a corner too fast, bump into a curb, then bounce up on the median and rip up a bush. Trying to get out in a hurry, I mash the gas and spin the wheels, so we're kind of lurching down the street, half on and half off the road divider.

Gretchen braces herself against the dash. "This is great. Would you stop and let me drive? Christ."

"Take it easy. I've almost got it." I slow down and let a Jeep with a gray-haired woman in it go by, then I roll off the curb and into a lane. "I'm on track, headed for Sears," I say.

At the mall, I let her out, then park by the curb with the engine running for the air-conditioning, then push in a tape. It's some wet-sounding rock and roll. It fits with the rain and cool-gray sky, and I sit there listening and feeling pretty wistful.

After a while Gretchen comes out of Sears empty-handed, followed by a woman in a short, red-dotted jumpsuit, and a boy who looks like her son, a thin ten-year-old. When Gretchen gets in the car, she folds her hands in her lap and stares out the windshield. "They didn't have any popcorn," she says.

"We came all the way back here for popcorn?"

"So? I like it. It's bright yellow. They soak it in butter. It's good."

"Uh-huh," I say, nodding. "You want to go someplace else for popcorn? Maybe . . ."

"Forget it," she says. "Let's go." She makes a shoveling gesture with her hands and rocks in her seat to illustrate going. Then she hits the direction-reverse button on the tape deck. "I hate this," she says. "What's on the other side?"

"Jason and the Scorchers," I say, but she's already hit the eject button.

"I hate them," she says. "Who are they, anyway? Oh, yeah. The semi-rockabilly revival. I remember." She yanks the tape out and tosses it in back. "Let's just leave it alone, okay? Let's just go."

The jumpsuit woman is eating candy out of a small Sears bag, and the boy is slinking along beside her, one hand on her hip. They stop together on the curb, watching the drizzle. It looks as if that's the rule: whenever they're out together he has to have the hand on her hip. She holds a piece of candy for him, and he takes it with his teeth.

"She's pretty," I say, pointing to the woman. She shakes out a clear plastic rain hat, then curls it over her head, wraps an arm around the kid, and steps into the parking lot. The boy nestles against her, his face pressed into the curve of her waist, and they crab-walk, like a creature with two extra legs, toward a Buick parked in a handicapped zone.

"She's in love with him," Gretchen says. "If that woman ever was in love with someone else, it's over now."

"Leave her alone."

The woman unlocks the front door in the passenger's side. The boy stands off at arm's length, as if waiting for her to reach in and unlock the back door. When she sees what he's doing she leans over and gives him a hug, then steers him into the front seat.

Gretchen says, "My brother says a man doesn't really start to care about a woman until he takes possession."

"Well," I say, whining a little, rocking my head left and right. "Maybe he starts—"

She turns around, chin in hand, and gives me her drollest expression.

I say, "I think your brother's a tough guy."

"Women are the same. Look at this." She points to the kid and his mother. "He's a little monkey-boy and she loves it."

"It's good for him," I say.

"No, it's terrible. It's the same mistake. I don't want to discuss it. Can we go?"

"Sure." I get the car moving and head out of the parking lot. "Maybe I should, like, go with you on this trip. You seem to be upset."

"I thought you were the one," she says.

"I am. I just thought I might go."

"Don't be silly," she says. "Stay here. Do whatever you want. No restrictions, reports—get something going. What about Cleo? You guys have been ripe for years."

"This morning she said she'd show me what I missed last time you left," I say. "When you went West."

"I'll tell you," Gretchen says. "Gorgeous stomach, real white skin, legs shorter than they look. Otherwise, it's a kill."

The evening is uncomfortable. I can't remember the last time there was so much distance between us. I don't know why I'm upset, and I don't know what's bothering her. She watches a show about transsexuals on TV, and I wander around the apartment, making up things to do. Now and then, I look at the screen a minute and guess whether the person talking is a man or a woman.

At eleven, she starts packing. I sit with her on the bed, watching. Finally I say, "I don't want to stay here alone."

She smiles at me.

"I'm serious. I don't want you to do this."

"Take it easy," Gretchen says, "Why don't you watch David Letterman? You like him, don't you?"

"I don't like him very much right this minute," I say.

"I don't think I like him ever," she says.

"Me, too," I say. "Now that I think about it. I used to like him."

"He's all right," she says. She's going in and out of the closet, getting clothes. "Why don't we put on some music?"

I stop looking at her, stop watching her fold the clothes and press them into the open suitcase. I roll onto my back and stare at a spot on the ceiling where the air-conditioning register has stained the sheetrock. Then I stare at the red second hand on the clock on her bedside table. I watch it make two full circles.

"What if I have a heart attack?" I say.

"I'll find you when I get back," she says. "There'll be an investigation. What will you be wearing?" She stops packing a minute and looks at me. "I don't know what's wrong with you. It's not the end of the world—I'm just going to see my family. It's not a big deal."

My shoulders hurt. The bedroom looks like a halfway house for magazine chic—dusty and almost correct. I feel light-headed. I say, "I'm going to end up spending the whole time with Cleo, like before."

"If that's what you want," she says. "Don't tell me about it, though, okay?"

"I'm telling you everything," I say.

She gives me an impatient smile. "If that's what you want," she says, finishing the suitcase.

"What about money? What are you doing for that? Are we spending my money for this trip?"

Gretchen sighs. "No, we are not. The checkbook is yours and yours alone. In perpetuity."

"Sorry. That was stupid." I get up and go into the bathroom, "Take the money, okay?" Before she can say anything, I twist the handle on the hot-water tap. Water splashes all over the place. I forgot about the hot water. It spatters if you open the tap too far. By the time I get the faucet off, my clothes are soaked. I go back into the bedroom, unbuttoning my shirt. "I love you," I say, stepping over her suitcase to get into the closet.

She looks at my chest and says, "Me, too."

The morning is no better. We talk about the plants, and how much water they need, and how much sun they need, and we talk about running the dishwasher, and about the lint filter in the clothes dryer, and that I have to remember to get the slides at the camera place, because she wants them sent to her by overnight mail. Then she has some last-minute errands to run, so she goes off to do that, and I stay at home. She gets back around noon and starts to repack her bag, but then gives that up. At three she's ready and walking around with her coffee, waiting for the cab to take her to the airport. I sit on the couch, staring at the fireplace. When the driver honks, I carry her bags, kiss her, watch her drive away, then stand on the curb, looking around at our neighborhood. The sky is overcast. The parking lots are empty.

A guy in a red truck pulls up and asks if I know where Cheryl Harrison lives. He's hanging out the window of his truck with his chin on his arm.

I tell him I don't know Cheryl Harrison.

"Crap," he says. He pops the steering wheel with the butt of his fist. "Last night I see this chick at the grocery store. You know, the one up here on Pine Tree? So I run my cart into hers and we get to talking. It seems like we're made for each other—you know that feeling? So, finally, she tells me why don't I come for a beer this afternoon, because that's when her boyfriend leaves for work and everything. I mean, she says she doesn't like to do that kind of thing, but they're having rough times and she thinks she's leaving anyway."

I shrug at him, starting to back away toward my apartment.

"She gives me this apartment number," he says. "So I'm cool, and I write it on my arm, just like in the movies. What do you think happens?" He sticks his forearm out the window for me to see. There's some ink there, but it's unreadable.

I do a gasping sound, then say, "That's terrible."

"What it is," he says, "is I read this article about frozen Japanese dinners. You know? So, of course, I had to run out and get some." He shuts his eyes and gives his head a tiny shake. "Last night. I had to have them last night."

I'm about ten feet away from him by now. "I wish I could help," I say. "Why not look her up in the book?" Then I realize that's an invitation, so I say, "I'd let you look in mine, only we lost it in the move. We just moved here."

"Doesn't matter," he says, sitting up behind the wheel. "She isn't in the book. Or, if she is, she's in the guy's name." He shifts the truck into gear and eases it forward. "I must be getting old. I gotta stop." Then he brakes hard and the truck jerks to a halt. "You know what else? I ate one of those dinners, you know? That I bought?" He pauses for emphasis. "Lost it," he says.

I watch him drive off, then go in and freshen Gretchen's coffee and take it into the bedroom. I set the cup on the bedside table, sit on the edge of the bed, pull the curtains, look out at the path between our apartment block and the next one. On the TV screen in the bedroom there's a reflection of me with a quadrant of blue sky out the window behind. The hum of an air-conditioner comes through the walls, sounding internal and basic to life. A couple of birds chirp. I hear bell-like wind chimes repeat a song pattern and wonder how the wind can do the same thing over and over. Then I hear a car horn, then a motorcycle accelerating. There's a pair of ski sunglasses on top of the television set, with the thin black elastic that runs around the neck looped down over the screen.

Some neighbors are walking the path, just below the window. The woman's voice is quick, up-and-down, and the man's is short, slow-sounding—a grunt. The phone rings.

"So, what's the story?" Cleo says. "She go?"

"Yep."

"How do you feel? You all right? You ready for me?"

I put a finger in the coffee to see how warm it is. "I don't know. Maybe."

"Half an hour," she says. "After that, I go for other responsibilities and obligations. You call me, okay?"

"How about five? I'll call at five."

"Don't push me around," she says.

"Right," I say.

"I'm ready to roll. I've been after it since first light, working the equipment. Looks terrific. You're one lucky fella."

"I know that I am," I say. "What if Gretchen changes her mind at the airport?"

Cleo does a big, exasperated sigh. "She's not changing her mind. C'mon. Two weeks is the deal. In two weeks she's back and everything's like it was. I'll be there at five. You want to go to the beach after? I can get us a place."

"Cleo," I say.

"Okay, okay. So long."

She hangs up, leaving me with a dead line. I shake my head at the receiver, then put it away.

We go to a movie, then to dinner at a seafood restaurant on South Main, where I order fried shrimp and Cleo has king crab. It's a place with white tablecloths, heavy silverware, old paneling, waiters in faded red jackets, with huge fish on the walls.

When the food comes it looks great. I ask for some extra lemon, and the waiter zips off to get it.

"I like this place," Cleo says.

"It's good," I say.

"I was in love with you," she says. "You know? Last time." She pinches a claw, digging the white meat out with the tiny two-pronged fork. "I thought I was going to die." She dips the meat in a metal cup of liquid butter, then presses it against the rim.

"Me, too," I say.

She looks at me, making a face.

"I mean I was in love with you, too," I say.

She smiles, shaking her head. "I had fun in California," she says. "Pretty much fun, anyway. I'm a lot different now, though. I don't know if I'll ever be the same as I was."

"That's the way it happens," I say, nodding and thinking about how pretty she is.

"I'm not backing anybody up anymore," she says.

"Why should you?" I say.

"I'm picking my openings," she says.

"Right," I say. "Just like the rest of us."

She does a little take, then says, "I'm going through with this. You know that, don't you? This is the break. I do it. Bang." She narrows her eyes at me. There's a smile in them, but it's not easy.

Cleo loosens up then. We finish dinner, and afterward she drives back to the apartment, staring straight ahead the whole time. When she pulls up in the parking space, she says, "Here we are."

"So, how about some coffee," I say.

She makes coffee, and I sit on the couch in front of the TV, switching the channels. She must know where everything is—she doesn't ask me anything. When the coffee's ready, she sits down for a minute, then takes her cup and heads into the bedroom. I watch her back, then watch the bathroom light come on, throwing a bright trapezoid on the bedroom wall. The light squeezes down to a sliver when she shuts the bathroom door.

I turn off the TV, dump my coffee in the kitchen sink, check the front door, then sit on the couch again. Water is running in the bath. It's almost twelve. For a second I think it smells funny in the apartment, but then can't smell what I thought I smelled. The light flashes across the bedroom wall again and Cleo's shadow passes through it, but she doesn't come out. She's in the closet. Then the bathroom light closes down again, only this time not as far. There's a two-foot strip of light left. The water stops in the bath.

The telephone rings. I answer it, hoping it's Gretchen.

She says, "How are you?"

There's a little cracking sound on the line. I say, "I'm okay," then listen to the sound. "What's that?"

"What?" she says.

"That noise. You hear that?"

"I don't hear it," she says. "So—I'm at the Dallas airport. We missed the connection. I'm here for another hour at least."

"Cleo's in the bathtub," I say.

There's a pause on Gretchen's end. Then she says, "So, was I right?"

It takes a minute to figure out what's she's talking about. Then I say, "I haven't looked."

"Just like old times," she says. "You okay?"

"I guess. We had dinner at Goldsmith's. I'd be better if you were here to protect me."

Gretchen laughs, then tells me she's going to need her recipe for lemon cheesecake, and that I'm going to have to find it in her blue recipe book. "You're going to hate me, because it's a mess. I mean, I'm going to organize it when I get back. I promise."

I take the phone in the kitchen and open the refrigerator. I stand there looking for a minute, then lift the window blinds and stare out at the cars, all the time listening to a story about a woman she met on the plane.

I interrupt her. "So what do I do?" I say, taking a bottle of spring water out of the refrigerator.

Gretchen says, "Rock her socks. It's okay."

"You're a help." I unscrew the cap and take a drink. It doesn't taste like anything special.

She says she has to get a hamburger and a magazine, so she wants to get off the phone. I put the bottle back and tell her I love her, then kick the refrigerator closed, hang up the phone, and go through the living room to the bedroom. It's dark in there. I look at the bathroom door for a minute, then sit on the edge of the bed, just out of the light, and watch Cleo wash.

(1985)

RESET

People at the office assumed that Ann and I had been having an affair for the five years she'd been working for me. We hadn't, though we hung around together all day, every day, and we fought and bickered and made fun of each other the way husbands and wives do, so I guess it's only natural everybody thought we were in some kind of love. We probably were, though we hadn't pushed it. Recently, things had cooled off quite a bit between us. She was rarely around at lunch, and the daily play had turned a little more bitter than it had to be. Still, it was a shock when she came in to quit. She gave me ten minutes' worth of reasons—her recent divorce, from a professional golfer named Carl; that there weren't any good men around; how great it would be to get a new start somewhere; what fabulous job opportunities she'd heard there were in Texas. About halfway through the list I started feeling kind of lost, as if what I had to say, what I wanted, didn't matter at all—she had her mind made up. We'd talked about her leaving now and then, but it hadn't occurred to me that she'd really do it, and now that she was in front of my desk, on one foot, her pale-blue eyes high and bright, the irises clipped by the upper lids, and she was cool, clear, and definite—well, I felt as if the bottom had dropped out.

I said, "I'm real sorry. I thought we'd just stay together. You know, onward and upward."

"Me, too," she said. She was looking down a lot.

I said, "Let me try that again. I don't want you to go. We're a team. We've been together a long time. Why do you have to quit?"

"It's just the way it goes," she said. "I really don't want to do it. I've been sweating this one for a long time. It's much worse, thinking about leaving here, than the thing with Carl. You helped me with that."

"Nope," I said. "I was clean, remember? I stood for patience and reconciliation."

"You wanted him out, didn't you?" she said. "I knew what you wanted."

People kept coming in congratulating her, asking questions about her plans. I didn't like it much, so I asked her to shut the door. She gave me a look, then closed it just enough so that the edge touched the jamb.

"I'm serious," I said. "I want you around all the time. I think about you."

"I think about me, too." She nodded, then took a breath and held it, exploding her cheeks like Dizzy Gillespie.

"Great," I said. Out the window some city workers in orange coveralls were tearing up the street. There were ten guys out there working on a hole the size of a sink. They kept going over to their trucks for water or something.

"I don't like this," Ann said. "Doing this." She made a little wave at me and at the room, then stood there with her hands at her sides. She toyed with her mother's wedding ring on her right hand, rolling it around her finger with her thumb. Her mother had bigger fingers than she did. And then she sat down, folded her hands in her lap, and looked at her knuckles.

She was very still, upright in the blue chair facing my desk, the hands now quiet in her lap. Her skin caught the summer light in this fashion-magazine way, became luminous, delicate, soft. The look she gave me was about the loveliest thing I'd ever seen—fierce, full of determination.

"You're real pretty," I said.

She got up. "Hey! I'm trying," she said. "I'm giving you the A stuff." She opened the window. Our building is old and has windows that open. She crossed her arms over her chest and sniffed the air, watching the guys in the street. I went around the desk and stood beside her, smelling her hair. I always told her how nice she smelled, and she always laughed and said it was Dial.

"Maybe you don't have to do this," I said. "No kidding. It'll kill me if you go."

"That's weak," she said. She put an arm around my waist. "Anyway, you deserve to die." She giggled at this joke and then stared some more at the workers. After a couple of minutes she turned her head a little and said, "Wouldn't it be nice if you could make me stop? I mean, wouldn't that be something?"

Robin Romer, an account rep who worked on the other side of the office, poked open my door and asked Ann if she wanted to go out and celebrate. "You're going to Austin, right? Perfect town, great town." He stared out my window for a minute. "This place reminds me of a place my brother Desmond would like. He's over in Nam working up an import thing."

"He must be the interesting brother," I said.

Romer did a shrug and went right on. "Yeah, you know, the usual crap they bring in from places like that. Grass crap and stuff. Baskets. Those people can do baskets." He did a kind of leer at Ann. "I might go over there and learn the business, but first I've got some stuff to learn around here."

She patted his shoulder. "Mr. Romer has a problem with his chickens."

"Anyway," he said. "No point hanging around, is there?"

"Hey!" Ann said, hooking a thumb at me. "What about him? I have to take care of my boss, don't I?"

"He's cool," Romer said. "Aren't you, Boss?"

He was a small man, always neatly tucked into a little suit, and I didn't like him. She used to make fun of him, but since the divorce she'd been making a lot of new friends, and he was one. A couple of days before, when I'd made some tasteless crack about Romer, she got mad and gave me a lecture on tolerance. I liked him less now that she was defending him.

I scratched two fingernails across my forehead. "I'm cool," I said.

"He can come with us," Romer said. "We'll loosen him up, show him a good time. We're going to Blood's." Blood's was a bar a block away in the basement of a butcher shop. People from the office routinely went there for drinks after work. I'd been a couple of times.

Romer swung out of my office, pivoting on the hand he had on the doorjamb, but no sooner was he out than he was back. "What's he going to do without you?" he said to Ann. "How will he function?"

"Rehire," I said.

She gave me a tight look, then smiled at Romer. "You can go now, okay? We'll be there."

He stayed gone this time, and Ann shut the door again and came around behind me. She traced the hair over my ears with her fingertips.

"I'm sorry," she said.

"You can pick 'em," I said.

"I picked you," she said. "First. Anyway, that's not what I'm talking about. I meant I'm sorry I'm so polite. I think maybe I've got a self-esteem problem. Let's go get the drink."

We went to the bar. Romer must have got lost along the way. We were the only people there from the office. It was dark and cold, and there were pockets of customers around. We got a corner table. While we waited for the woman to bring our drinks, Ann said, "My family used to take these holiday trips. Dad got bored with retirement and decided we needed quality time together. A couple years ago it was Florida—Gorilla World Headquarters, famous for the petting zoo."

"I love those places," I said.

"Me too, me too. They're so seamy. It's like you can barely believe them, know what I mean?"

I looked at the snack menu, which was a hand-done sheet in a plastic sleeve. I was wondering what she'd think of stuffed mushrooms.

"He was a priest," she said. "Episcopal. He really didn't like women very much. He was always putting them down, saying they'd do anything in a thunderstorm." She glanced at me, then checked the rest of the room.

"So," I said, craning toward the bar window. "What's the weather?"

"You're a mop," she said. She studied my face, her eyes doing a tiny box step. It was a way she always looked at me, something I figured was proprietary, something I liked.

"Thank you," I said.

She hunched over the edge of the table, looking earnest and innocent. "Why's somebody so upset? I mean, a girl'd think we were talking major love here, the way you carry on."

"We're talking," I said.

She toyed with the saltshaker, moving it in chess patterns on the checked tablecloth. First the knight, then the rook. Our drinks came. Ann gave me a nice look while the woman was getting the napkins down, then watched her go and spun the ring. When the woman was out of the way she said, "So maybe I'll just stay here with you forever."

I said I thought that was a good idea.

Ann was on the phone when I stopped at her office door the next morning around nine. "Hey," I said.

She held up a finger telling me to wait a minute, then finished on the telephone. When she hung up she said, "You want coffee? I can get us some coffee."

"Not for me," I said. "I want love only."

"Got no love," she said. "You've got a choice of genuine emotion of unspecified type, ordinary friendship, or . . . that other stuff. Any combination. But you're taking a ride on the love."

"Big offer," I said.

"We try," she said.

Her office was drab. She'd brought plants and a Diebenkorn poster, but the effort was halfhearted. The poster was still leaning against the wall, where it had been leaning for over a year. She held the point of her pencil between two fingers while she watched me get into a chair across from her.

"It's personal," I said, reaching to close the door.

"I'm still going," she said.

"I know," I said. I couldn't get the door, and I was all twisted up—legs out in front, one over the other, body turned ninety degrees at the waist, left arm out at full length toward the door. My shoulders were perpendicular to her desk, and my head, which ought to have been facing the wall of her office, was twisted back toward her. "You probably don't recognize this body language," I said. "It's foreign. Dutch, I think it is. Colonial. Celanese, maybe."

"Celanese is a fabric," she said.

"That's what I mean." I shut the door, then sat straight again. "So. This is a great office. I like the poster—what is that?"

"Hard to believe?" she said, examining the mess she was making between her fingers with the pencil. Pretending to be tough was a routine. I played soft, she played hard. It was fun. It had always been fun, from the first day. I thought about that.

I said, "Can you go to Tennessee? I'm going to Tennessee today. Our client—Mr. Romer's client—Starlight, Inc., wants a new head-quarters, and they have, as you know, discovered Knoxville. Or someplace near Knoxville. I leave in an hour. You don't have to go. I just thought it'd be nice to have some company."

She nodded. "Company's nice. Is this, like, a date? I mean, twenty-third-century version?"

"I don't know," I said, drumming my fingers on my knee. I looked at the empty parking lot outside her office. It was empty because the entrance was blocked by the men working out front. "I guess. Maybe it's a bad idea."

"I didn't say no," she said.

"Thank God," I said. Then I held up my hands, smiled, tapped my head. "Sorry. The heart's saying what the brain wants unmentioned. I'm supposed to be playing close to the chest through here, right?"

"You're doing fine."

"Thank you," I said, picking a stick of gum out of the pack on her desk.

"There's a lot of thanking going on this morning," she said. "I don't like it. Makes me nervous." She put her feet on the corner of the desk closest to the window, away from me, and gave me a friendly smile. "Now, how long a trip we talking?"

I put the gum back. "Forty years, tops."

It was noon when we got to Vesco's Motor Lodge & Weekender, in a town called Review, outside of Knoxville. The registration desk was knotty pine, decorated at one end with an inflated heart tied to a straw. The owner was Charlene Vesco, a woman in her fifties, squat and mannish, with rough hands, short fingers, square-cut nails. She was some relation to the notorious Vesco, she told us, and her mother had run the Weekender in the fifties, when it was the Blue Ridge Motor Court. Charlene signed us in, complaining about a couple she'd just signed out. "They were some bozo individuals, I promise you. I hope and pray never to see them again crossing my line of vision." Charlene gave me the eye. "That's a joke, son. But don't you worry about it."

I smiled at her.

"He never worries," Ann said. "He's worry-free."

The motel was eighteen wood-frame bungalows bunched on two acres next to a stream the brochure called "Vesco Falls," though no falling of more than six inches was anywhere in evidence. Up the hill behind this place, stuck up in the trees, there was a plywood flamingo that must once have been painted but was now plain, weathered, streaked with pink at the edges.

Charlene caught me looking out the window at the sign. She said, "I was doing that in '62, when I took over. I figured to go it, you know, tourist art—birds on the ground, the whole thing. So then I started hanging around with the sign guy—he wasn't local—and, well, we did a one-eighty on the plans." She winked at Ann and handed over the keys. "I'm guessing you understand, right?"

"Right," Ann said.

I was in No. 10, surrounded by tall pines. I had two rooms and a kitchen the size of a confessional. Ann was in 7, in a tiny clearing thirty yards away. The bungalows were war-era, white, trimmed brown around the windows and at the eaves.

We put up our stuff and then I called Ketchum, the town-council guy we'd come to see about Starlight. The first thing he wanted to know was if Ann was with me—he'd talked to her a lot on the telephone. I told him she was. "Then I'm buying lunch," he said. "You had lunch? We got motel or drive-in. Or local color, but it's kind of sticky."

I chose the latter and he told me how to get to a place called Raindrop's, and then we hung up.

Ann and I drove into town, following his directions to the letter. At a stoplight we pulled up next to a giant Volvo driven by a guy with hair combed to a point in front. He grinned, then dropped his visor and looked into a mirror on the back.

"Pretty damn thrilling," Ann said, seeing the guy.

We watched him work his teeth. Then his mustache. Then he brought out some tiny scissors. I turned away, but he was hard to ignore. When I looked again he was on the telephone *and* working the scissors. He was laughing into the receiver.

"Maybe you could get a job with him," I said.

"Will you stop?" Ann said.

We followed the Volvo right to Raindrop's. The driver turned out to be Ketchum.

We spent the afternoon with him. I'd hoped to be able to get by on lunch alone, but he was so happy to see Ann, and she was so nice about it, that at five he was still showing us the sights. We got to see the tar pits, the train depot, the rushing brook that sliced the town in half. We saw the land south of downtown that he had a piece of.

"I can get you in on this," he said. He did a slow-motion punch on the top of my arm. "Blind, of course. No problem."

"Looks mighty handsome," I said.

He went back to Ann, slinging an arm over her shoulder. "We're going for the whole 'new town' thing," he said. "Maybe work out a lake over beyond the bank. Wipe all that out, of course." He waved at a two-block stretch of single-story brick buildings. "Nuke those dudes and swing back with the wood-siding thing, you know? Very upscale, West Coast—nothing modern, just nice middle-of-the-road shops, family orientated."

Ann was smiling hard, pointing some.

I took a nap when we got back to the motel, then cleaned up and went to find Ann. She was with Charlene in the office. They were drinking coffee, sitting at one of the three tables in the alcove that was the Weekender restaurant. They were looking at a magazine open to a picture of a model with bruise-colored cheeks, black lips, eye sockets like anodized aluminum. She was wearing a lace top, a zebra skirt with a red belt, burgundy stockings, shoes with silver flames. The jewelry was big wood, and the hair was stiffed up in a wedge.

"Well, she ought to be out tying wieners," Charlene said. She smacked a knuckle on the open magazine. "I'm telling you."

I said, "She's probably real lovely." I had come up behind them and was leaning over Ann's shoulder.

"Well, looky here," Charlene said. She gave me a pat on the shoulder. "You want some eats? Just don't ask for no lobster bisque, hear? I ain't seen lobster in forty years. You want something like that you're gonna roll on down the road."

"I asked for lobster bisque," Ann said.

"That's true," Charlene said. "Now, if you want toast, I can handle toast."

"The toast is great," Ann said.

Charlene, already on her way toward the kitchen, stopped and did a suspicious look.

"Honest," Ann said. "It's incredible toast, really." She started to cross her heart with a finger but stopped halfway through.

The phone was ringing in the next room. Charlene did an eye roll and cut across toward the registration desk. In a minute she was back, dragging the telephone with her. She got about halfway to us before she ran out of cord.

"It's your office," she said, wiggling the receiver at me.

I took the phone. "Hello?" I said.

It was Romer, calling to tell me Starlight had changed its mind. "I guess you'd better forget it," he said.

"Are you sure?"

"Sure I'm sure," he said. "What, I'm making it up? We just got a call ten minutes ago."

"Okay," I said. "Thanks."

"Hang on," he said. "Uh . . ." There was a pause, and that closed sound you get when somebody on the other end of a telephone call puts a palm over the mouthpiece. Then he was back. "Listen," he said. "Is your friend Ann around there?"

I said, "No, she's not around. I think she's at the pool."

"That's all right," Romer said. "I guess I'll catch up with her later. Don't worry about it. You okay?"

"Fine," I said. I hung up and carried the phone through the arched doorway and put it on the desk, then sat down again. I started rubbing my eyes, because the lids were clinging to each other, but then it seemed like I couldn't stop rubbing. Finally, Ann tugged my arm. "Are you okay?" she said. "What's the deal on the phone?"

"Starlight's down the tubes," I said.

"No kidding?"

"That's it," I said. "Romer asked for you." I was working on my eyes again. "You have a change of heart or anything?"

She pulled away, reaching for her coffee mug.

"Sorry," I said. "It's just that I dreamed about you in my nap. We were in a parking lot. There wasn't anything there but this pink asphalt and the blue sky. We were naked, lying out there. You didn't have any legs, and you had one arm. I mean, you had the legs and the other arm, but you'd taken them off or something. I asked why and you said you were saving them."

She sighed and dropped her head into her hands.

"Yeah," I said. "I know. I didn't want to dream it, either. Tonight I'm going to dream about bowling." I looked at her eyes, which were tired and watery.

Charlene came through the kitchen door with a ten-inch stack of toast. She noticed Ann's eyes right away, then mine, and stopped short of the table, pulling the plate back and to one side as if she might withhold it. "What've we got here? We got an outbreak of iritis? We can probably fix that."

"Contact trouble," Ann said. She shut one eye and swiveled around, looking for the ladies' room.

"Mine are fine," I said, and when the toast was on the table I picked a piece off the stack. The toast was as thick as a paperback, crisp at the edge, collapsed in the center.

Charlene pointed Ann toward the front office, then stood in back of me looking out the window, her hands crimping on my shoulders. When the door shut behind us, Charlene said, "Now, you be good to her, hear?"

"Yes'm," I said. "I'm trying."

"No . . . I'm serious," Charlene said, giving me a squeeze. "She's bananas about you. Any fool can see that."

I craned my neck, looking up at her.

She nodded at me. "Sure is," she said. Then she popped my forehead with a finger in a way that was friendly but hurt like hell. "Just be nice. Give her what she deserves."

We went to dinner at a drive-in that was once a Dairy Queen, now a local outfit called Princess Snack. There were hand-painted drawings of snacks all over this place. And princesses. A young girl in red satin took our order and brought the food. We sat in the car and ate. Neither one of us had much to say. I watched the cook and the cashier and the carhop mill around inside the building. They were mechanical, the way they kept repeating the same movements, the same gestures. Watching them, I got angry about Ann leaving.

I said, "I hate it when you're polite."

She raised her eyebrows. "Did I miss something?" she said.

"You were real nice to Ketchum and I hated it."

"I see," she said, drawing it out while she refolded the tissue on her hamburger. "It's going this way, is it?"

I looked out the window.

"My guess is that Ketchum's not the problem," she said.

"Right," I said. "I don't know why you like all these other people better than me. Why you have to leave."

"I explained that," she said.

"Yeah, I know," I said. "But we get along, don't we? We have a good time. It's not so bad."

"Days are good," she said. "Nights aren't."

"They might get better," I said. "Who knows?"

She sighed, and we both watched employees for a while. The cook must have been a basketball fan. He kept doing skyhooks when he was flipping the patties.

Finally, Ann said, "Why don't we just have a nice time, huh?"

I started to say something about how it was hard to have a nice time with her departure looming, but as I was talking I was gesturing with my hamburger and I lost the meat. It slipped out of the bun and fell down around the foot pedals. I had to scrounge for it, and it broke in two when I found it. I got it off the carpet and out onto the tray, and when I turned around Ann was sitting there grinning at her lap.

"What?" I said.

"Nothing," she said.

I smiled at her and pointed at her hamburger. "You finished with that?"

She handed it to me. "You still want it?"

I squinted at her when she said that. A line of pink light reflected from the restaurant sign cut across her forehead, over the bridge of her nose, down her cheek. We sat still for a minute. Then I took a bite of the hamburger she'd given me and I grinned. "Why, sure," I said. "On the something-is-better-than-nothing principle."

She reached over and messed with my shirt collar, then sat back and looked out the car windshield. "That's sort of one of my favorites," she said. "The other one I like pretty much is better late than never."

"Yep," I said. "I'm crazy about that one."

Later, when I couldn't sleep, I got a glass of tap water and stood at the front window of my bungalow peeking at the lit-up grounds. I'd only been there a minute when I saw Charlene Vesco creeping across the grass.

I opened the venetian blinds. Charlene went up on the porch of Ann's bungalow and tested the screen, then stood there moving foot to foot, scanning the property, her back to the door. She patted her hair a couple of times, getting it into place. I checked my watch. It was almost four. When I looked outside again Charlene was gone. Nothing moved for a while, and then Ann's door opened and there was Ann, barely visible through the screen. She had on shorts and some kind of big shirt, and she was wearing her glasses. She hated her glasses. Her arms were crossed over her chest at first, but then she opened them, holding the edge of the door with one hand, rubbing her thigh with the other. She was just looking around. In a minute she pushed the screen and came out onto her porch. She sat on the steps. I watched for a long time. There were shadows all over the place, and there was moonlight. I filled up my glass and pulled a chair to the window, propping my heels on the sill. I stared at the tree trunks, and the flat, nearly iridescent lays of grass. There was something set and fearsome about the scene, like a little tableau at the start of a Hitchcock movie: mist drifting through, water sparkling, lights high up in the pines—and Ann, in the clearing, on her steps. Two cars rolled by almost silently, almost in tandem, on the narrow road in front of the property. My window shone. I studied the scene outside. I tried to see the future.

(1986)

RESTRAINT

So I pass this woman in the hall. I'm leaving my room at the office, entering a corridor—it's a big office, three floors of this sudden building inside the loop, Philip Johnson or something. Architectonica. So here comes this woman—neat, got a nice suit, lemon-colored high heels, the usual—so I'm reading this memo I just got from Harriet Somes, our director of personnel, not really reading it but sort of holding it, and I look up as I pass the woman because that's what I always do, and . . . well, she's the most extraordinary three-dimensional construct I've encountered on the face of the planet in more than forty years without exception. Person—*person* I've encountered. So, anyway, I'm cool. I don't jump her, I just look, but I'm stunned like somebody's hit me with a floor lamp. Maybe I gawk some. I must seem like a goon to her—I mean, she's a young girl, I don't know, maybe twenty-two, twenty-one, seventeen, and she's not used to people looking the way I'm looking, not guys like me, three-piece guys. In the world of high finance we don't do mouth drops at our women in the hall—she has a right to be scared. Me, if I were her, I'd scream. But she's very relaxed. She's five nine, maybe a trace over that, to start with, and a little constellation of freckles perfectly deployed across the bridge of a nose from antiquity—unassailable, impeccable, prototype. It's got this curve to it, a rim at the nostrils—we're talking slight, barely perceptible, so fine it might as well be an optical effect, a passing condor emerging from a gray-green cloud bank casting a shadow that flickers through the mirrored exterior of our building and spins then, distorted and partial, up off the polished corridor floor, up into my eye. And the freckles, sweet and off-center, specks floating before her face, under the

209

eyes, hovering like scout ships in advanced mathematical formation, fractals, ready for some mission into this soiled universe. Ready for Buster music. I don't know—it's like some scene from *Trancers*, full of New Age music, thunder volume, my redundant heart. A big thing. All backed by the eyes, guarded and protected, and yet clear as some glass flute melody lilting from out of nowhere over flat, distant grass-land at last light on a disarticulated winter's afternoon in Montana, Wyoming, or some other state of that persuasion. These eyes are not blue, thank God. These eyes really aren't any color you'd rec-ognize, or be able to name, and they are probably not any color that exists elsewhere in our planetary system, though in the universe, I am certain, the painstaking research assistant might locate a color proximate with respect to hue, holding aside the paradox of texture. Of course, neither color, which in our radically diminished world of prepared things we'd call *brown*, nor texture, which remains elu-sive to verbal signification (i.e., can't be named), adequately suggests these eyes through which this young woman in the hall of our archi-tecturally up-to-date corporate headquarters looks out upon a world that must seem to her a vile parody, the host site for yet another thin-walled condo community wherein lesser beings, cramped hopes whitened by grip, scoot hither and thither in search of niggling sat-isfactions. These eyes swell with hope and anticipation, ambition, crushing vulnerability, quick wit and vivid imagination, large heart, sweet disposition (which I had thought lost to the eighteenth century), all compressed in a two-dimensional array the size of a radio knob, of two thereof. I hasten to add that this is not all they swell with, but the merest sketch still some significance short of beginning to hint at the outline of a rendering of an artist's concept of a TV reporter's version—we got aces on the eyes. We got a fine nose, freckles in the proper number and distribution. We got tall. The hair's good—why, the hair's from the edge of Orion. Shines. Sways back and forth. Got a wispy aspect. Got secrets in it so marvelous as to rewhack the plexus. It's about a thousand colors, each so close to the next that the mordant eye can't tell the difference, only knows up there there's something otherworldly. Soft-looking hair, floats around at the telling moment, otherwise sits there like pure angel grace. It moves slowly, a rocking motion, coming toward you, then dodging away at the instant of maximum extension, in perfect sync with the smile, which gets you to the teeth—white like small wet cliffs, and straight enough to set your watch. No untoward lip-curling either—they retain their exquisite shape through the whole procedure, do these lips, they slide a little, opening into a gesture of welcome as if readying the private whispered report of some lovely indiscretion, something to brace the skin. There is, about this young woman, some quivering possibility I cannot place, a wonder that veils her like the barest morning mist, an interior surprise, a perfect curiosity regarding this time and place that strikes the onlooker more powerfully than icy Oriental scents. One is inclined, against one's will, to follow, to disregard caution and to throw, with all might, the self at the other. And yet I, in the cooling afternoon light of this outer corridor, restrain all still-operative nerve tissue, reduce and control motor behavior, and I do not, I am pleased to report, knock the young woman to the corridor floor, drag her by the gray-veined hair to my dark little post. No. I am an adult. I am a decent man. I grip a potted plant, lean inelegantly against a carpeted wall, gape like a monkey at the biggest banana ever to prowl up out of a tree, but I do not accost, maul, mash, whistle, or deliver myself of some gratuitous oral discharge apropos her stride, her skirt, her slight little ivory-shadowed calves, the taut muscles of which I can already feel swelling into my curled palm. No. I take what is given. As she passes I bathe in the fragrance of thousand-year-old lilacs on a stone path at misty dawn in Shanghai, and, when she turns the corner and leaves my sight, I return to my own boxy place where there is little to agitate the senses, sit in my gray vinyl chair, cock my feet on the round-cornered desk, and, lips pursed, eyes shut like vault doors, I count blessings, first health and family, then friends, and finally appliances, working my way from the large to the small.

(1987)

ARCHITECTURE

It is dark and wet. Holly sticks the credit card in her brother's shirt pocket and takes his arm: "See? I'm still Daddy's little girl."

"Don't get ugly," Park says.

She drives, hits a curb, sends bright bubbles across the hood. He bends forward to find the wipers, then clicks them on. "I'm tired. Let's go home."

"I just got the card," she says.

"I feel sorry for him."

"It isn't his fault we're . . . fond of each other, Park."

"He thinks it is."

She taps Park's shirt where the card is: "All the better for us, my evil friend."

"Cut it out, Holly," he says, drawing a mouse with a corkscrew tail on the windshield. "He's okay."

"What's that? That a mouse? You know he still wants us to see Federman, the psychiatrist."

"Federman," Park says. "Jesus."

Holly is tall, thirty, with hair cut like a man's; she wears big hiking boots and a scarf to her knees, and surplus, *Vogue* style. She hums as she steers the brown car. At a stoplight she puts both arms on the top of the wheel and points her index fingers in opposite directions: "Which way? You want to get Dzubas?"

"Here; Thirty-ninth. The one after the white one."

The stair is beige, the handrail six colors. Raw lumber is stacked neatly on the landing. Holly knocks.

Dzubas opens the door. "All my crazy sick children," he says. "You married yet?"

"Brothers and sisters can't get married," Park says.

"Watch out," she says. "Park's feeling morose."

They go to the Holiday Inn. The rooms have a connecting door, open. Holly bounces on the bed nearest the television: "What do you guys want for dinner?"

"Chicken," Dzubas says.

Park inspects the lamp switch, which is broken. "I think I can fix this with a ballpoint."

"Are french fries really French?" Holly asks, tapping the plastic menu with blue nails while waiting for the restaurant to answer. Then, outlining the drawing of the inn with her finger: "I really like hotel architecture, I mean, I really do, really."

"Steak," Park says.

"I know, I know."

Park turns to Dzubas: "How's Louise?"

"She's going to get married again," he says. He turns the television on. "To some black guy."

"See if they have fish soup," Park says to Holly.

"What kind of fish?"

"Let's go to the pool," Dzubas says.

A person finally answers and Holly recites the order and the room number, then hangs up. "We're going to eat first, remember? And we're going to that mall on the highway to get my coat."

"Is it Thursday?"

"They're open every night now."

"You know him, Dzubas?" Park asks. "The black?"

"What black?" Holly says, changing the selector on the television.

"No. He works for the PBS station here."

"Who does?"

"Louise is getting married again," Park says. "A black guy on television."

"A lot of them are doing that now," she says.

"Getting married?"

"Working on television—see? Here's one." She points at the screen, at a black newsman.

The room service person is a woman, about forty, graying. She puts the aluminum tray on the table by the window and hands the check to Park. Park hands the check to Holly.

"That was quick," Holly says, signing.

She sits down opposite Dzubas and pulls the hubs off the plates. "Why don't we go to Virginia? You want to go, Dzubas?"

He opens the curtains. "Nope." They eat looking at the parking lot.

"I love this," Holly says.

"Sure, sure," Park says.

"We all do," Dzubas says.

At the store Holly buys three nylon suitcases and a man's leather blazer. On the way to the car she says, "I want some pretzels, soft ones."

Park drags a bill out of his pocket and gives it to her, and she gives it to Dzubas: "Please?"

"Pick me up at the entrance," he says, pointing to a portico at the front of the mall.

When Dzubas is gone Holly says: "This isn't any fun, is it?"

Dzubas gets in the back seat and pushes a white sack into the front. "Make you fat, Holly. Park won't love you anymore."

She digs a hand into the sack. "Where to?"

"Get some sleep?" Dzubas says.

"You give up easy, Cowboy."

"It's my art."

"You know what, Park? I think we make him nervous. I think your old friend Dzubas is afraid of us, because of you-know-what."

"Plenty for me, thanks," Dzubas says, cranking his window down.

"Ease up, Holly," Park says.

"Ease up, Holly," she says, mimicking him. "Look, there's a Dairy Queen. Is that a real Dairy Queen or a fake Dairy Queen?"

"Says 'Dairy Queen.' "

"Let's get some, want to?" She twists the wheel and parks alongside a sports car.

"Mother of God," Dzubas says.

"I want a chocolate-dipped," Park says.

On the way to the window Holly slaps her thigh and turns back to the car. "I forgot the money," she says, kissing Park on the cheek.

She stands in line behind a man in green gym shorts and another man in a suit. Dzubas says: "This is real hard, Park."

Park cranes his neck to look at Dzubas and the skin around his eyes wrinkles. "You want to go to Virginia, Dzubas?"

"No, I mean it. She's getting scary."

"Nerves," Park says. "It's because we just started up again. Getting her married wasn't such a good idea."

Holly brings the man in the gym shorts back to the car. "Needs a ride," she says, opening the door for him. "His name's Carl. Carl, meet Park and Dzubas."

"Hi, Park. Hi, Dzubas."

They drive back to the highway and Holly says, looking into the rearview mirror, "Do you work in television, Carl?"

"No, ma'am, I don't. I'm studying to be a dentist."

At a gas station Carl goes to the bathroom and Park says: "Very funny, Holly. Very endearing."

"I like him," she says, signing the charge slip.

Carl comes back wiping a brown paper rag over his face. "Man, that place is full of pinch bugs! Whew!"

Leaning forward, Dzubas taps Park's shoulder. "I think I ought to get home, Park. What are you going to do?"

"Ask Holly."

"We're going to Virginia," Holly says. "Why don't you come with us?"

"Yeah," Carl says, pulling himself forward until he is leaning on the back of the front seat. "What have you got against Virginia?"

"It scares the hell out of me," Dzubas says. Then, to Holly: "You want to let me out here?"

"What, on the highway?"

"Aw, let him out," Carl says.

"Wait a minute," Park says, when she stops the car. "Let me talk to him for a minute."

Park and Dzubas walk to the guardrail together. Dzubas picks up a bottle cap and flips it into the hazy white light of the highway. "I can get home," he says.

"I don't know what to do," Park says.

"Why don't you go home and watch TV together, like everybody else?"

"We're not like everybody else."

"Pretend."

"What do you think we're doing?"

"Pretend better," Dzubas says.

"She feels like a freak. Sometimes I do too."

"I can't help you."

A police car goes by, its siren loud. Park walks to the car and motions for Holly to get out. When she does, Carl jumps into the front seat and drives away.

Park sits on a silver-painted pole. "Way to go, Holly."

"Me? What? You talking to me? How'd I know he'd do that, huh? You told me to get out, Park."

"She's right," Dzubas says.

They walk a little way along the road without talking. A car stops beside them and two women stare out. The car is a Dodge, blue. Dzubas gestures with his hand for them to roll the window down. They look at each other, then drive away.

"Way to go, Dzubas," Holly says.

"Walking is a favorite thing of mine," Park says.

"It's a nice night," Dzubas says.

"Way to think, Dzubas."

They walk until they see a giant Gulf sign, lit over the trees. "Let's see if they have a telephone," Dzubas says.

In the cab, Dzubas gives the driver his address, then turns to Park. "You going back to the hotel?"

"What're we going to do about the car?" Park says.

Holly rests her head on Park's shoulder and looks out the cab window at the falling quarter moon. The driver drives. The tires roll on the concrete, click on the expansion joints in the highway.

She says, "I'm a mess, right? That's what you guys were talking about. 'She's very untidy,' you were saying, correct?"

"Right," Dzubas says.

"You're right, you're right," Holly says. "They'll never let me back into the church. I know. I'm sorry."

"Nice night," the driver says.

(1981)

LAW OF AVERAGES

At the reception after the meeting where my daughter, Karen, got an award for most mathematical third grader, I went for the punch, even though the punch table was surrounded on three sides by earnest-looking parents—clean, bright faces, ready smiles, the knowing and glowing types. I got around behind the table and stepped over a brick planter, but I tripped and hit the woman who was serving. Punch went flying. Most of it hit the floor, but there was some on me, some on her. She patted at her clothes and introduced herself. "I'm Mary Quine, I teach here—fifth grade, civics." Both of us were looking around at the crowd. There were a hundred people there, among the tan folding chairs. "I hate these things, don't you?"

"I don't come very often," I said.

"Take a look at this bean pole over here," she said.

"Uh-huh," I said. I liked it that she called a man a bean pole. I waved to Karen to tell her where I'd be, then handed a guy who'd come for punch a couple of napkins. That became my job, the napkins. I handed them out while Mary ladled. We spent an hour doing that, talking about divorces—mine was more recent. When the reception thinned, I collected Karen and the three of us walked out together.

Mary started to fluff Karen's hair when I introduced them, but thought better of it and stopped mid-gesture. "You don't look like a Karen," she said. "You look like Grace, or Lily."

"What's Grace look like?" Karen said.

We stopped between two lines of cars in the parking lot, and I put my arm around Karen and said, "I think she's more of a Roxy. She's got a Roxy look about her."

"What are you guys talking about?" Karen said.

"Nothing," I said. Ordinarily, Karen would have come with her mother, but her mother had chicken pox, so I got an extra night.

"And sometimes," Karen said, "he calls me Karen." She was towing me toward the car. "Can we go?"

On the way home I pumped her for what she knew about Mary Quine. Karen was uncoöperative. She didn't know a thing. She said, "You want me to ask about her?"

I said no.

"I could go around to all my friends and tell them my dad is interested in Miss Quine and ask them what she's like."

"No, thanks," I said. "Let's change the subject. I'm sorry I brought it up."

We stopped at the light by Popeye's, and Karen said, "Do you like her a lot? I guess she's probably going to be your girlfriend now. You guys'll get married and everything. If that's what's happening, I'm telling Mama."

"Go easy on me, Rox," I said. "I'm a casualty."

"Oh, Daddy," she said, slapping at my leg. "What's that mean? Why do you always say things I don't understand?"

I pulled her over next to me in the seat, sat with my arm around her tiny shoulders as if we were teenagers, years ago. She leaned her head against my chest.

"That's the way it goes," I said. "When you get old like me, you get to be a mystery. It'll happen to you quick enough."

"I don't want to be a mystery," Karen said, "I never want to be a mystery."

I dropped Karen at home and I drove over to the Conestoga Party Club, a remade, windowless ShowBiz Pizza. I never did think Show-Biz would work. I was there once, one of Karen's birthdays; everything was done with aluminum tokens shaped like quarters. These things were as thick as quarters and they cost a quarter. They were just like quarters, only they were these tokens. I guess they figured if you bought ten bucks' worth of tokens, you weren't going to cash in the leftovers; they probably had market research to prove that.

When Show Biz evacuated, the Conestoga people refurbished the cinderblock building into a bar-restaurant combo, but instead of installing windows, which would have been costly, they hired a Junior League realist to do a floor-to-ceiling mural of the great out-doors—white-tail deer, silvery fish leaping out of ponds, geese swimming across the cobalt-blue sky, jackrabbits eyeing the customers. I guess the artist wanted to make a statement: the animals in the painting were all packing guns—rifles, pistols, submachine guns. It was a real animal revolution in there.

When Mary arrived, we took a booth next to a wall on which a couple of bandito squirrels, cartridge belts slung across their bare bellies, stood up on their haunches chewing pecans. We unwrapped our silverware. The napkins were small and thin as tissue. It was awkward at first. We studied the menus and placed our orders with a middle-aged woman in blue stretch, a woman who looked kind of scientific, as if she'd been in the beaker too long. Then Mary and I locked eyes across the tabletop.

For a second I was worried there was nothing to say. I was thinking about picking up women, something I'd done maybe twice in my life—thinking what do you say when there's no reason to be together? Then I decided we'd picked each other up, but that wasn't better, that just made us consenting adults.

Mary was eyeing the mural. "This reminds me of a TV show I saw," she said. "Twenty guys in this trench in a field, all lined up, with shotguns. Some of them had big black paddles, and when the ducks got near enough the guys started waving their paddles, as if they were wings, I guess. The ducks were beautiful—dark against lemon-color streaks. Then the jerks on the ground started flapping, and their friends started blowing birds out of the sky, and what I thought was, you know, that's wrong."

"I've had that feeling," I said.

"I mean, it's just like this," she said, pointing at the mural. "I wanted the ducks to have guns. Make it a fair fight. Ducks coming in plastering these fat guys, you know?" She made a jet fighter with her hand, diving it at the table and doing machine-gun noises. "I'd love to see that. A real bloodbath while these yokels scramble out of the trench, heading for safety, falling over each other, splattering in the mud with the tops of their heads blown to smithereens." She made an explosion sound and popped herself high on the forehead with a flat palm.

"They'd try to shoot back," I said.

"Maybe one," she said. "The rest would be running. We'd cut 'em down. We'd drill 'em."

I noticed that she was looking in my eyes. I hate it when people look in my eyes. I mean, when they stare right at them, when I can see that what they're doing is looking right in there. Because it means they want something. It means they're way off the beam.

I said, "You're real nice and I like you more with each passing day."

"What?"

"Joke," I said. "Kind of an icebreaker."

She got embarrassed, looked at the table. It was one of those tables with real planks encased in once liquid plastic. "I'm sorry," she said, "I guess I missed it. I guess I did too much on the ducks. I don't know what's wrong with me." Then she looked up, showing new resolve. "So, you want to just zip through dinner and go back to my apartment and be careful? No . . . that's wrong. I also saw this show about the Peace of Mind club. It's a safety club. You know, for sex. You're not a member, are you? I hate it." She traced an outline around a squirrel in the painting. "This is wrong, too, isn't it? Aggressive? I don't care about sex, really."

"Well," I said. "I don't know."

She sat up, straightened her place setting. "Okay. Great. Can we just start again?" She tapped the wall. "Good squirrel," she said. "I don't know what we're doing. Let's talk about you or something, okay? I always get myself in a mess when I talk."

I said, "Okay. Me."

"I am *so* sorry," she said. She was going into the tabletop again. "I always do this. I get out here and I don't know what to do. I don't fit."

I said, "You're fine. Really. Where don't you fit?"

"School," she said.

"What's wrong with school?"

"I don't like it." She turned to look toward the cash register, drumming her fingers. "I used to love school, but now—I don't know why you'd want to hear this, do you?"

"Sure," I said. "I'm interested."

"We've got teachers you wouldn't let near your kid," she said. "Lots of them. But in our evaluations we all grade out superior. It's a joke. I mean, to hear us tell it we're all one in a million." She shrugged, shook her head. "I'm going to stop," she said. "I promise."

"It's okay," I said.

"So today I had a fight with the guy in the room next to mine. He had the TV on all day. I asked him to quit it."

"TV?" I said. "You have TVs?"

"What're you, a guy who's been asleep for a hundred and twenty-five years or something? You never heard of that? They're supposed to be for PBS stuff, but we use 'em to shut the kids up, because we're so good."

I watched her. When the food came she quit talking and started eating. She held her knife wrong, like a pencil.

We took both cars to her apartment at Château Belvedere, an eighty-unit cedar-shake project buried in tall pines back off the highway feeder. It was near two when we pulled into the parking lot and walked up the hill to her block of apartments. I watched the wet sidewalk as we walked, listened to the wind chimes—lots of people out there had wind chimes. Two guys and a girl were in the laundry building drinking beer and sitting on tables. Mary's apartment was upstairs, a two-bedroom with fur-brown shag and a low, mottled plasterboard ceiling. There was a crummy light fixture in the center of the ceiling in each room. She went to get drinks out of the icebox, and I sat down in front of the television.

I thought it was going pretty well. I hadn't been out much since the divorce. When I had been, mostly what I wanted to do was go home. Sometimes I thought I didn't want to "get over"' my divorce. I knew I was supposed to, but I wasn't sure I wanted to. There's something seductive about it, something safe and easy—like you've done your duty and you don't have to do what you're supposed to do anymore, you can go home and watch TV and do some scraggly cooking and not feel bad about it. You're not missing anything. I'd been so close to my wife that now when I was around somebody else I felt like I wasn't where I was supposed to be.

Mary came back with beer for herself, Coke for me. She sat at the end of the couch, her legs crossed under her, skirt punched down between her knees. I didn't look at her. I was staring at the channel changer that was on the coffee table. I was thinking I might pick it up.

"Why don't you tell me about your wife?" Mary said.

"Who?"

"That's great," she said.

"Sorry."

"Don't worry about it."

"Fine. I won't." I looked from her to the blank TV, then back. I was thinking about what I could say about my wife, and looking at the coffee table trying to figure out if it was an acceptable coffee table or if it was junk, and then I decided to go ahead and tell her. "The good stuff that happened, every nice memory I've got, came from her. I don't know why, but it's all hers."

Mary didn't say anything.

"I probably should have said that some other way."

She went back to her bottle. "It's okay," she said. "It's interesting."

"No," I said, shaking my head. "It's not. It's not good. It's like I feel like I'm going to be small and mean for the rest of my life."

"Well, I guess it's better to be small and mean than too sensitive," she said. "You know, we're all earnest, right? We don't have to be unctuous."

I thought about "unctuous," about what a good word it was. "I don't seem like a child anymore. I can't live like a child, feel that way. I could only do that with her."

Mary nodded, waited a minute as if she were thinking, then said, "I've got a fire engine."

I looked to see whether that was friendly or hostile; she wasn't smiling, so I figured friendly. I traced a knuckle on one of her hands. "What color?"

It was a nice night after that. We made love and it wasn't a disaster, and then we went for a walk through the project. It was cool out there, damp, there were quiet stars in the sky. We stuck to the sidewalks and didn't say much; but after we'd gone through the place once, we were holding hands. I was comfortable. I hadn't been in an apartment project for a while, and I had forgotten the odd comforts of them—being close to people in your economic bracket with whom you have almost nothing else in common, the community feeling even though you never talk to these people and only rarely see them. I had forgotten what it felt like to look down a five-hundred-yard line of apartments, cars parked in front, yellow street lamps dousing the asphalt with little slicks of light; forgotten the pleasure of somebody pulling up across the street at two-thirty in the morning, some couple coming in from a party or a club, their too bright, too loud voices suddenly hushed when they see you. As we walked, heavy trucks soared by on the highway I could just make out through the trees. This wasn't a fancy project, but under the cover of night it was gently transformed into a place of small mysteries—elegant shadows cast by young trees on badly painted wood siding, the reassuring clicks and whines of air-conditioning compressors snapping on and cutting off, the almost inaudible thump of somebody's giant woofer. I could make out the music, I could picture the people, a young couple, turning up the wick any way they could.

Somebody screamed somewhere. It sounded to me as if it had come out of the woods, but Mary thought it had come from the other direction, from one of the apartments toward the front of the project, toward the highway. We stopped and stood perfectly still, listening.

In a minute she whispered, "The beast—"

We started walking again. The grass alongside the walk glittered as we passed. Things were getting kind of smoky. Mary and I went from hand. in hand to arm in arm. She leaned her head against my shoulder. We stopped in front of a chip-filled garden to watch a gray cat box with a twig, flip it up into the air and then catch it and roll over on its side and do Ray Leonard with its back feet. Even the fire plug out there was pretty good-looking—pale yellow with a lime-green top. We walked a little more and ended up sitting on somebody's doorstep, facing the central courtyard of the project, watching the shining blue water in the pool through a chain-link fence. After a time Mary asked me if I was ready for sleep. I said I was, and as we walked back toward her apartment I pointed out somebody's pretty, violet-lit bug zapper.

Mary was apologetic about breakfast. "I didn't mean to force you into anything," she said, pointing at the dishes on the table. "Eating and stuff."

She'd made breakfast while I was showering, and she was self-conscious about it, about what it suggested or what it might suggest.

I said, "It was delicious," but I realized that sounded wrong, too formal. "I didn't mean that. I mean, I meant it was delicious, but I didn't mean the other part—you know what I'm talking about?"

"The repellent part?" she said.

That's when I started thinking I really liked her. I thought maybe we fit together. The real way, like people you can't imagine passionate, or passionate together, or who look as if they were passionate once and were done with it. I'd always wondered how those people got together in the first place.

Mary was clearing away the breakfast dishes. I watched the way she stacked. I liked it; she took the stuff out from between the dishes—the utensils. I imagined her driving Karen to school, and then later, in the evening, the three of us in the car picking up Popeye's. I looked around the apartment, and it looked a lot better in the daytime. There was plenty of sun in there—white Formica and light-colored wood, plants in the windows. The TV was on, tuned to one of the morning shows, the sound low. Even the carpet looked okay.

I figured if we were together we'd be like ugly people, or old people. We weren't either of those—I don't mean we were young and beautiful, but we were only half old, and we weren't so much uglier than everybody else that you'd run and scream if you saw us. If I had to say, I'd say regular. Mary had brown hair that was kind of wiry and specked with white, a slightly troubled nose, good skin, eyes that brought the beach to mind, and a fair body for thirty-five. Maybe I was a little on the short side—under six feet, although well over the average height for American males—and I guess I didn't help myself much with the khakis and the short-sleeved shirts, but my face was all right. People sometimes said I was "ruggedly attractive," if that's possible for somebody of my height. I had all my hair, even if it wasn't trained. Brown hair. Washed nightly. I wasn't the best judge of what I looked like, but I was attentive, and I'd spent some time studying other men—in the movies, in the magazines, on the street. I figured I had a kind of look. We both did.

(1987)

STORYTELLERS

—Who you calling Archfiend?

—Tell me a story, Archfiend.

—I could tell you a story, yes I could, tell you a sandblastin' story, all about my employer, maybe a postcard I have in mind—I could tell you a thousand things.

—Two monkeys you saw scratching once.

—In an interesting way, yes. Or what is important and how it came to be, don't you know.

—How the wind blows.

—Exactly. And why. These things are mine to tell.

—Ours.

—Technically, yes.

—The old man told us what was right and what was wrong.

—Do I deny it?

—I didn't say that you did, no.

—The old man was a peach, a lobster.

—Attacked our mother with jewels and ornaments as I recall, broke our mother's heart as I recall.

—Yup.

—Then Mother called us from the porch and said These are *my* jewels, and struck the bitch dead, remember?

—Yup.

—Remember the reflections in the night glass, each and every one more lovely than the one preceding?

—And my fondness for small animals, kept in the home.

—*Your* fondness?

—Well . . . ours.

—Now I know about the business world, the world without end, and I know something about the bass clarinet and the other clarinets, and the saxophones and fiddles.

—I have heard the piano played.

—That cowboy who fell in the mud.

—Broke his daughter's leg.

—Yup.

—There are many stories.

—The comic blew his wife away, that's a funny story.

—He laughed forty years.

—I have a postcard called *International Solvay Conference, Brussels, 1927.*

—I could describe a rounded protuberance at the edge of a surface of a thing, sticking out.

—A small bird-like creature which cannot fly.

—The business world is thick with stories.

—Metaphors are available for discussion.

—I knew an employer who complained that his employees were all wishing for crazy things.

—They say it all comes down to metaphor anyway.

—Told me one wanted the Fourth Crusade for Christmas, one wanted to marry the four dwarfs, one wanted to design four buildings so beautiful.

—The process whereby we are made to feel bad for wanting what we want.

—The fourth wanted to dance with snakes.

—We all want to dance with snakes, snakes is our great love.

—What I told him.

—And how, feeling bad, we change what we want so we won't feel bad anymore.

—He was an interesting man.

—Using perhaps the example of the potato and the big black horse.

—Yup.

—A person, call him Jack, wants a potato. For reasons unknown another person, call him the Potato Association, does not want Jack to have his potato.

—Potatoes.

—Yes. Now in his wealth and wisdom the Potato Association gives to Jack a big black horse.

—Call it Ingemar.

—Now this horse Ingemar is pretty damn big and black, and Jack is crippled with bigness and blackness and starts feeling stupid and greedy for wanting the potato too.

—Potato Association is smiling.

—Stinging with guilt, Jack allows the potato to slip from mind, replacing it there with the inedible horse Ingemar by name, a wonder in its own right.

—Amen. A classic.

—Very effective if you happen to have a lot of big black horses and not so many potatoes all of which you'd like to keep for yourself.

—The birthday cake we put in the street.

—Who put in the street?

—Well, you.

—Go on, elaborate. Embellish. Do the scrollwork and walk the dog.

—It's only interesting because nobody'd eat the cake.

—Yup. Yup.

—There's the painting I'm working on in fire and which remains incomplete as of this writing.

—Forever incomplete—there's an idea in that.

—The flames are going to be difficult, I'm aware of that.

—When I made the pies that Christmas and how hard it was to make the pies and how you all laughed when the pies were brought to table and how it hurt to have my pies a laughingstock.

—We apologized for that.

—Not enough.

—We were sorry.

—Not enough.

—I know how bricks got their name.

—To hear a nose blown in the room adjacent to the room you're sitting in and to know, hearing that nose, that is not the nose you love, not even the nose on the face that you love, and that you must leave, sooner or later.

—I became an operative and put a sign in a tree and the neighbor tore it down because he didn't know what Umfa Umfa Investigations meant.

—And because it was his tree.

—Because it was his tree, yes.

—And you repaired the sign.

—Repaired the sign and sold it to an art dealer for a few hundred thousand stotinki.

—Launched headfirst into the washtub that is art.

—In these ticklish times.

—How we manage to live in days gone by and in the shape of things to come, most of us, most of the time.

—You could reveal the true purpose of the night.

—Or why smoke always follows you when you walk around the fire.

—You know, you know.

—What the firemen say when they speak to the smoke, the words they use.

—The old man loved red leather, didn't he? Built a whole damn house out of it, right down to the crockery.

—He showed me the scars night after night and night after night I looked, searching for some magic in the skin.

—Didn't show me no scars.

—There's a story in that, Brother.

—My wife dreamed about great philosophers discussing great and ancient philosophies in a language composed entirely of brightly colored pairs of pants.

—Wife? Wife?

—Dead now.

—Sorry.

—She was a good wife.

—A man with something interesting in his mouth, walking around on the streets of a city wishing he could sing.

—A curious numbfish or a forty-pound note.

—Yup.

—Then there's video art. There are lots of stories about video art.

—Or are we more inclined to determine whether Mother was a good mother or not, and if she should be punished.

—For making all those chocolate chip cookies when we were young.

—And yesterday.

—I could tell a good old-fashioned story that'd make your hair stick up on end, but I'm tired and you already know the story, I suspect.

—If Father's scars of which we were once so frightened and so proud do not now cripple our arms, our chests.

—Yours.

—Or what a good green looks like, or why I love a choir.

—I have some feelings about the chair I'd be pleased to share with you.

—I knew a man once who was always drawing on his body with a knife.

—Heard tell.

—Drew a biplane on his cheek one day.

—Beautiful day.

—Maybe a short little story about feeling good and feeling bad.

—Or my new song *You And Capablanca, He Said,* which is a new start for me.

—Just enough to make you feel a bit of something, don't matter what.

—A story you'd never forget.

—And one you couldn't remember no matter how hard you tried.

—What was that you say?

—Matter of faith, Brother.

—We could do the one where the hat falls off the cat, or the one about the rat, or the one that ends For we are like children.

—For we are.

—Amen in a foreign language.

—That at least.

—Yup.

—Yup.

(1980)

Sis

My sister's husband Byron called and asked how I would like it if he stayed a couple days at our place. It was late afternoon and raining again. We'd had rain for days—winter rain, with fine, whitish drops. There was some flooding, trees were down, the power had gone off a couple times. My wife Emily had phoned ten minutes earlier to tell me the oil light in the car was blinking and she was at a Star station getting it checked. I was home walking around in red cotton socks and thinking about starting a fire when he called.

"How about it?" Byron said. He sounded uncertain, I guess because I'd waited too long to say yes.

I said, "Sure, it's fine. Is Janie okay?" I was listening to the traffic in the background, trying to figure where he was.

He said Janie was great, and nothing in the world was going on, nothing to worry about, and he was standing in front of a Jr. Mart and thought he'd be over right away and fill me in on the whole deal. Then he hung up before I could say I'd be looking for him, which is what I'd planned to say.

My sister picked Byron out in a Dallas bar ten years ago, then she married him. From my point of view it was reasons unknown, but she didn't ask me. He's a furry type, if you know what I mean—furry hair, furry beard, furry back you see when you go swimming with him, which I did once, a couple of years ago. He's beady too, around the eyes, which is bad if you're furry. It's a bad combo. I don't know why he doesn't get some kind of treatment. By now he doesn't have a steady job and he watches a lot of old movies on TV, and, to hear Janie tell it, which I do in our weekly phone calls, he's not a lot of fun for her.

It took him twenty minutes to my back door, and he was happy to see me, which made me feel guilty for what I'd thought about him in the interim.

"How-dee," he said when I opened the door. He slapped me on the shoulder, then held his hand there, pushing a little so I'd get out of the way and let him and his bag, which was like a small futon, into my kitchen.

I got out of the way. "Come on in." I slapped his back a couple of times. "Hey! You're a wet boy, aren't you?"

He grinned. "I'm Mr. Wet—where's Em?"

He called my wife Em. It was his invention, nobody else ever called her Em. I said, "She's at a gas station on East Bilbo—car trouble."

"God damn!" he said, making a face like you'd make if thirty people just died in the crash of a light plane at O'Hare, and you were watching it on CNN. You'd watch the live coverage with this face.

He was squishing around the kitchen in soaked running shoes, gray with purple decorations, some brand I didn't recognize, and he was already at the cabinets. "So," he said, yanking a Ziploc bag of candy—M&Ms, Tootsie Roll Pops, orange play peanuts—out of the bread cabinet. "Hey! Jackpot!" He laughed and tested the bag to see if the Ziploc was working. It wasn't, so we got candy on the counter, some on the floor. He bent to get the stuff on the floor and stepped on a Tootsie Roll Pop that splintered and shot out from under his shoe. "Oops!" he said.

"Hold on," I said. "Freeze. Don't move."

"No. Hell, I got it," he said, lifting the foot, spraying brown candy crystals around. Right then the phone rang. He pointed at it. "Incoming," he said. "That's a pretty phone, too. That a decorator model?"

It was a yellow telephone. It came with the house, or something. Or Emily wanted it. I don't really remember.

Emily was calling to tell me the car was okay. "It was low on oil, a quart low. There wasn't any on the stick when he pulled it out the first time, so I figured I'd torched it, but the guy says the new ones are all that way, I mean a quart low and they show nothing between those two little creases—you know what I'm talking about?"

"Byron is here," I said.

"Byron who?" she said. "You mean Byron Byron?"

"Yes," I said.

By this time Byron himself had made it across the kitchen and captured the receiver. "Byron to tower, Byron to tower," he said. "Come in with a friend. What's shaking, Em?"

He gave me a grin and a black-eye wink, then unwrapped a Tootsie Roll Pop he'd saved, a red one, and plopped it into his mouth as he talked. After a minute he put his hand over the mouthpiece and said, "I'm sorry about this mess here, Billy. Just lemme say hello to my sweet Em and I'll clean her right up." Then he screwed up his face as if thinking about that, jabbed a forefinger into the telephone mouthpiece, and said, "The mess, I mean. Not her."

I nodded my understanding and went for paper towels, listening to Byron's end of the conversation.

"You're too worried all the time, Em. You're off the beam, here. You got to stay low, flop around with the rest of us. Huh? Hey—but it's great to be here! I mean, I'm looking forward to sitting down with you, you know"—he gave me good front teeth, laughing at the joke he was making—"at the dinner table. Maybe you can cook me up that chicken thing you do, know the one I'm talking? Oranges and everything. Brown sugar? Boy, I've been missing brown sugar."

He took off wet clothes while he talked. The coat, then the shirt. He got the shoes off and was unbuckling his belt when he started doing kisses into the phone and pointed at it with his free hand to ask if I wanted to talk some more. I said I did and took the phone back from him while he got down to his shorts.

"Hi, Emily," I said. "It's me again."

"What's he doing?" she said. "What's he there for?"

"He looks great," I said. "Wet right now, and naked, but good. He has some kind of hair attitude, but I can't really tell. It's wet—he looks like a pop star."

"Pop star?" Byron said. He pulled the sucker out of his mouth and yelled, "We got designer hair. We got seventy-five bucks into the game right now." He pointed the red ball on the stick at his head. "The latest," he yelled, leaning so close to the phone that I could smell his breath. "The hair's hot!"

"It's hot," I said to Emily.

"It weeps for chicken!" he yelled.

When Emily got back an hour later Byron was on the couch in a pair of tennis shorts and a red polo shirt reading our movies-on-TV book. He was smoking a thin cigar with a wooden mouthpiece and talking to nobody in particular. *"Mr. Arkadin,"* he said. "A must-see— you ever seen that one, Em?"

She went right by him into the kitchen and started unpacking groceries. "Saw it," she said. "Starts with an unmanned aircraft circling a foreign capital, right? There's a lot of stucco in it."

Byron dropped the book, swiveled off the sofa, and trailed her into the kitchen. "You get me a surprise?" he said.

"Chicken," she said.

He did a quick circle, jamming both fists into the air one after the other, then danced around in a touchdown-style frenzy—kind of Mark Gastineau out of Martha Graham via Bob Marley. "Killer chicken," he said. "I eat the wings, I break the back, ya ya!"

Emily wasn't moved. She had on her career-woman outfit—tightly creased clothes, full-face makeup, jewelry—all slightly debloomed by the weather.

"And . . . that's not all," she said, pulling a package of Mallomars out of a sack. She did a little flourish with the cookies, then spun them onto the countertop next to Byron. "For the Mallomar man. You ate a hundred of these in one night, didn't you?" She turned to me. "Didn't Janie tell us he ate a hundred of these one time? They were fighting or something? Remember?"

I shrugged, although I did remember and I don't know why I didn't just say yes.

Byron groaned and rubbed his stomach. "God, I was crazy then. I must've been nuts. She was killing me about something or other, and then did the dinner thing, you know—" He did a mincing imitation of my sister that made her look like a bad TV homosexual. "Like what did I want for dinner right in the middle of this huge brawl we were having, and I said I wanted Mallomars and went out to the store and bought about forty packages and brought 'em back and dumped 'em all out on the table and sat there eating all night while she punched around on a salad with a tiny fork. Next day she told me I had the stink of Mallomars about me."

"You were looking for trouble," Emily said.

He grinned at her, something that was supposed to be conspiratorial, I guess, and said, "Still am." He must've thought the look I gave him was disapproving or something, because then he laughed and said, "Not really, Billy. I just said that to be interesting. Em understands, don't you, Em?"

She was busy working on the chicken, her back to us. "Sure," she said. "You're just talking, right?"

"Right," Byron said. "I'm a big talker."

"That's what we hear," Emily said. She has a way of saying things like that and making them seem, if not friendly, at least not terribly hostile.

I smiled at Byron, and he smiled back, the same smile as before, untouched. "Well," he said to me. "I suppose we're wondering what I'm doing in these parts." He took out a new cigar and lit up, rolling the thing between his fingers while he mouthed the smoke. In a minute he let it out and said, "That's a good question. I'm glad you asked me that, Billy. Honest."

He didn't get a chance to tell us then because the doorbell rang. I went to get it and it was Janie, my sister, standing on the stoop looking like she'd walked over from their place. She had on this huge coat, one of those thick, tan, winter jobs, good around Christmas time, and it was soaked, and her hair looked as if they'd just finished skull surgery on her and were trying to obscure the evidence. I hugged her, but then we got in the middle of this hug and she wouldn't let go, so I stood there looking at the rain falling off the edge of the roof and thinking that I'd probably like to hug her more if she weren't soaking wet. I felt guilty for thinking that, and for wishing she and Byron would just stay over at their house and have their fights alone, like everybody else, and then she said, "I love you, Billy. I really love you."

"Me too," I said, thinking how uncomfortable it was when somebody says they love you when you're not expecting it, or when you kind of take it for granted and wish they would too, and I wondered how many times in a life you say "Me too" to somebody who has just said they love you and then think that it isn't what you mean, that you love yourself too, that what you mean is that you love *her* too, or him, but that there isn't any quick way to say that, not in two words, anyway. That's the kind of thing I think about all the time—that, and wondering what the other person is thinking about, if the other person is thinking the same thing. "Byron is here," I said. I was trying to wedge my way out of the hug, but she was having none of it.

"Oh, Christ," Janie said, and she started crying. It was a very quiet kind of crying, she wasn't bawling, just kind of standing there with her arms locked around me and jerking like some kind of mechanical device having taken leave of its senses. I was trying to figure how to play the thing. Nobody'd told me anything—I mean, I knew we had a fight going on, but that's all I knew—so I was wondering what I should do next when Emily came out of the kitchen with her fist inside of a clean-plucked three-pound chicken.

She said, "Who is it, Billy?"

"It's Janie," I said. "My sister Janie."

Byron stuck his head out of the kitchen. "Why, how-dee, little flower. How you doing? You following me around the country or something?" He moved across the foyer toward us as if to kiss her, but she was still hugging me and he pulled up short. "Oh," he said. "I forgot. We're having a tiff, right?"

Janie nodded at him, splashing her hair around. "We were. That was a couple of days ago. Before you left without telling anybody in the world where you were going or anything."

"I slipped down to Tampa," he said. "I was looking around. Checking it out. I was down there with Bruce Weitz."

She looked at him, a steady look, then rolled her eyes toward the ceiling. "Okay. I give up. Who's that?" she said.

"Belker," Emily said. "On TV. The ratty little guy on *Hill Street.*"

"Only he ain't ratty," Byron said. "He looks like about a zillion. He had shoes on I'd be happy to drive around in. Had this jacket must've dropped him two thousand. Genuine chrome thread in there. Really."

"Byron hungers for the high life," Janie said. She'd finally let me go and had started hugging Emily, who could only hug back one-handed because of the chicken. You could tell it was bothering her. First she tried keeping it behind her back, then she tried a two-handed hug using just the arm of her chicken hand, but that didn't work, either, so the chicken was kind of dangling out there at the end of her arm, there at her side, as she hugged Janie.

"That ain't it," Byron said. He was scratching his stomach again. "The guy looks like a Swiss, know what I'm saying? Like they scrub him with white bricks every morning. I asked the desk girl what he was doing there and she said she didn't know, but that she didn't think he was *shooting*, like I'm some kind of rube's gonna get in the way if the man's there *shooting*, know what I mean?"

"He didn't like the desk clerk," Janie said.

I was worried about Emily and the chicken, so I put an arm around Janie and gave her a little tug, trying to break up the thing, and I said, "Well, it's like old home week around here. No clerks." I did another tug, this time toward the kitchen, figuring that even if I couldn't get them apart, at least in the kitchen Emily would have a chance on the bird. There were a couple of little spots of watery blood on the tile there in the foyer, but it wasn't too bad.

Janie took this opportunity to start hugging me again. She got me around the neck with one arm so she wouldn't have to let go of Emily.

"Hell," Byron said. "This girl was main line, only she was main line Tampa, which is like a gum-wrapper town out of Reno. I mean, Fitzgerald would've done stuff on her. Anyway—" he was keeping his distance, looking at the molding around the opening between the den and foyer "—there ain't anything there over four feet tall, know what I mean?"

"No, Byron," Janie said. "We don't know what you mean. Nobody ever knows what you mean." She finally gave up on Emily, though she still had me, and she pulled me over to the front door so we could get her shiny black duffel bag in off the stoop. This bag said PLAYERS, like the cigarette, on the side. "Cars are taller than four feet, right?" she said when we got the door shut. "Don't they have cars in Tampa?"

"Sure," he said. "They got one. But it's this truck George Barris worked over in the fifties. Three foot eight."

She gave him an impatient smile.

"What I mean is—" Byron started to say, but as soon as he'd started she waved him off, which gave me a chance to get free, so I did.

"We don't care," she said, looking at me. "I don't care, anyway." She pointed to Emily and me. "Maybe they care, but I don't care what you mean. You could mean anything in the world and I wouldn't care." She shouldered the wet Players bag. "I had to wear this coat because I don't have the right kind of coat to wear at this time of the year in the rain because my husband's not such a knockout provider, if you know what I mean."

"I bought the coat," Byron said, talking to me and Emily, who had backed up all the way to the kitchen door.

"Yeah," Janie said. "My wedding present."

"There she goes," he said. "She's starting."

"Let me get this chicken put away," Emily said, waving the chicken hand at me. "Why don't you get Janie settled and then we'll all meet in the kitchen for a drink."

"She doesn't drink anymore," Byron said. "She's into health. If it doesn't have spinach in it she won't touch it."

"I know this great spinach drink," I said.

All three of them shook heads at me. I shrugged and grabbed Janie's bag. "Let's go, sis," I said. "We'll put you in the bedroom."

"Hang on," Byron said. "That's not my bedroom, is it?"

"You can have the office," I said. We'd made the third bedroom into an office that Emily used at home. We put the old couch in there.

"So what about my stuff?" he said. "I got it in the bedroom already. You gonna put her stuff in there with my stuff?"

Emily, who had gone around the corner into the kitchen and who had the water running in the sink, came back out drying her hands on three feet of paper towel and said, "So what's the deal? The luggage doesn't get along either?"

After dinner we stayed at the linoleum-topped table Emily had insisted we buy when those things were popular a couple of years ago. We sat around this table, the four of us, and stared at things. Everybody was staring in a different direction, like people in one of

those realistic sculpture setups that you always see in *Time* magazine stories on modern art. Byron was watching something out the
window over the sink. Janie was playing with blueberries in a bowl
in front of her. Emily was reading the ads in the back of a boat
magazine, and I was staring at the three of them, each in turn. We'd
finished and we were just sitting there.

Janie said, "Where do these things come from, blueberries?
I mean, where do they grow?"

"What are you talking about?" Byron said. "They grow on trees.
Blueberry trees."

"Bushes," Emily said without looking up.

"You mean what state?" I said.

"No," Janie said. "I meant how. I mean, I've never seen a blueberry grow."

"Oh, that's great," Byron said. "Spent all your time watching
watermelons, did you?"

"I've got it," Emily said. She circled a spot on the magazine page
with a Day-Glo pink marker. "This is it—twenty-eight-foot Bayliner.
Cheap."

"That's your Kmart, Em," Byron said. "You'll be wanting a Bertram, be my guess. You can really hump a Bertram."

Janie said, "I'm sure that's just what she wants to do."

"La la la," Byron said.

"Why don't you leave her alone," Janie said. "If that's what she
wants, that's what she wants."

"Oh, sure," Byron said. "Listen to Miss Genuine Fur-Lined
Downy-Soft They-Said-So-on-TV the Third." He was checking
the skin on his arms, twisting his arms forward and pulling the skin
around his biceps. "Do people get warts at my age? I've been finding splotches." He turned around to show me what he was talking
about. "See that?" he said. "That look a wart in embryo?"

There wasn't anything there—a little sun dot or something.
I said, "Doesn't look bad to me."

"May this house be safe from warts," Janie said, making an
ugly face at Byron. "He's worried about his age. He's going to be
forty-one this year and he's getting all these tiny age spots. They're
everywhere, they're all over him."

"She's happy about it," he said.

"I don't know what's wrong with it," Janie said. "Your life's half over. So what?"

He dropped his face into one hand, covering his closed eyes with fingers and shaking his head. "I was forced to marry her, wasn't I?" He jerked up and smiled at me. "No offense, Billy. She's a wonderful woman. It's a personality thing. She wants me to be a ninja."

Janie did a real sour look. "That's a joke about me watching karate movies on TV."

"What the hell is a ninja, anyway?" Emily said. "I've been hearing ninja-this and ninja-that for five years and I've got no clue. They wear a lot of black, right?"

"At least my brother doesn't whimper all the damn time because he's not Dan Pastorini or somebody. And he can keep a job," Janie said. "He has a career. He has a house—you know they've been in this house for eight years? And he's only thirty-something." She turned to me. "What are you now, Billy? Thirty-six?"

"Eight," I said.

"He's steady," Janie said. "That's what it's about."

Byron got up, adjusting the shorts again. "I know that it is," he said. "You're right. And it's a real nice house, too. I wish it was my house. I wish I'd been living here the last nine years."

An hour later I was lying in bed twitching the way I do when sleep won't come and my legs go numb—circulation stops and I jerk around like a kid getting electrocuted, or what we thought electrocuted would look like before we really saw it on TV. It drives Emily crazy when I do it, so I got out of bed and went to the kitchen and had Rice Chex. I was sitting there thinking about Byron and my sister and how much trouble they were having and I started thinking about me and Emily, and how we got along pretty well. I mean, I started wondering if we were from another planet or something.

Then Janie and Byron came in wearing matching purple terry-cloth robes. They were holding hands.

I looked at the clock on the stove but couldn't read it, which is something I hate. It happens all the time. Even in broad daylight the thing is hard to read. I said, "What time is it there?" and motioned toward the stove.

Janie bent over. "How do you read this thing?" she said. "Looks like it's four in the morning."

"It doesn't look like morning," Byron said. "Where does it say morning?"

She gave him a playful little shove. "He's a detail guy," she said to me. "You know what I mean, right?"

"Twelve-twenty," I said.

Janie came over to the table and rubbed my shoulder. "We just want to apologize, okay? We're sorry to be messes, aren't we, Byron?"

"Yep," he said. He got a hand on my shoulder too.

They were both standing there beside me with hands on my shoulder, and I was sitting there wishing I'd stayed in the bedroom with Emily, thinking I should have been smart enough to stay out of the kitchen. "Nothing to worry about," I said, and I made as if to get up, thinking that'd get rid of the hands, at least.

It didn't work. Byron came with me to the refrigerator, kneading my shoulder on the way. "You know how these things go," he said.

Well, I did know, but what I was thinking was how much I hate it when people that have no business touching you go around touching you all the time. But I figured I couldn't say that without hurting his feelings, so I let it go and opened the refrigerator, thinking the sight of leftovers might encourage him to forget me and go for the food.

"We got it all worked out in the bedroom," Janie said, coming up behind us. "We're going back to our place now."

"Tonight? You don't want to just sleep over?" I hated that. I felt like a bad guy, like no kind of brother at all. I reached into the refrigerator and got the black banana I'd been meaning to take out of there for a couple of weeks and handed it to Byron. "Toss this, will you?" I said. "It's Emily's, but she'll never get rid of it. She loves that banana like a son."

"What's wrong with it?" Byron said. He held up the banana, twisting it back and forth as if trying to find the flaw.

"Hell, it's perfect," Janie said, slapping his back.

I said, "There's steak here if you want steak."

Byron said, "Steak?"

"No thanks," Janie said, poking his shoulder. "We'd better go. It's just that we wanted to come in and apologize for hanging you up with our troubles. We always do it, don't we?" She'd backed up to the counter opposite the refrigerator and hoisted herself up on the countertop. "I didn't want you to worry about me."

"She thinks you spend all your time worrying about her," Byron said. He had the banana stripped down and half-eaten.

"I'm his little sister," Janie said. "Of course he worries, don't you, Billy?"

"I guess so," I said, but what I was really doing was looking on the bottom shelf in the refrigerator at a Ziploc bag of black beans, trying to remember when we'd last had black beans, and it seemed to me that it had been a while.

(1987)

PART FOUR

PERFECT THINGS

Jerry Jordan was upset the morning he found out his wife, Ellen, had a lover. The first thing he did was refuse to carry the army-green garbage sack to the edge of their driveway for the men to pick up, thinking that if he did not carry it, it would not be carried, and that this would be a clear natural consequence of her action not lost on Ellen. As it turned out, Ellen, in a bit of drama Jerry characterized as "endearingly small," took the garbage herself, making a great show of it, banging the overstuffed sack into walls and doorjambs, groaning under its weight, pausing to rest and catch her breath more often than conceivably necessary—it put him in mind of some biblical story, something with Moses and a number of huge, sand-colored rocks. Jerry watched and listened, his feet propped on the butcher-block coffee table just where they had been when, moments before, Ellen had told him about Toby. Toby was a friend of a friend—she'd started with that. Somebody familiar, even close, but somehow obscured. Not a friend of a friend of his, but a friend of a friend of hers, meaning not only did *she* have friends that were not also his, but *they* had friends she took as lovers.

Jerry did not know his next move. He waited for her to return from the long march to the end of the drive, then sat on the couch and watched as she fetched her breakfast to the table, trip after trip for coffee, toast, utensils, newspapers. She seemed to be ignoring him.

"So what do you think you're doing?" he said, crossing the room to the table.

"Eating," she said. "Toast?" She waved a slice of toast at him.

"Marbles?" he said, mimicking her wave. "What I want to know is what you think you're doing slipping over to some kid's house at three in the afternoon for a little hanky-panky." "Hanky-panky" had just come out. He hadn't thought about it, and it didn't describe what he saw in his head when he thought about Ellen and her lover, and it gave the impression, he thought, of a man hopelessly out of touch—it was his mother's expression, something from another era. He was so self-conscious about this unfortunate choice of words that he could not even look up from the tabletop, from a point just alongside his peach placemat where a triangular bit of jelly caught the light and shined. "Or whatever you people call it now," he said, thinking the effort to separate himself from her and from such behavior might salvage his ground—making the behavior so foreign to him that he could not even call it by an appropriate and timely name, thus cutting her off from their life together, isolating her in a sea of her own bad faith. He was immediately aware, however, that the isolation cut both ways, reminding him of the distance she'd strayed from what he had theretofore taken as their mutually satisfying marriage.

Ellen said, "I don't know what I'm doing, if anybody cares." She had her cup in two hands, poised before her chin, precisely square, he noticed, as if some internal gyroscope maintained for her limbs at all times a perfect equilibrium, a perfect relation with the horizon.

Jerry nodded. A minimal nod. Two short up-and-downs of the head, total movement perhaps half an inch. Just enough to register her reply, to say that he heard, and to suggest he was thinking about it. What he in fact thought was how pretty she was, and how surprising that after eleven years of marriage he still thought that. "You don't know," Jerry said, repeating it to buy some time. It was his turn, and he had spent the moment thinking about how attractive she was and he needed to come up with his next line, so he repeated that she didn't know, again hoping the repetition would put her on defense, suggest that her answer was so inadequate that it taxed imagination. Of course, it was a rhetorically ordinary move that he knew would have little effect other than holding his right of next remark. Still, if she felt just a touch guilty, if she felt she weren't operating in good faith in the conversation, she might attempt to revise and extend her answer. That was a possibility.

He decided to try and improve his position. "You always know," he said. "Cut me some line, will you?"

"I'm tired," Ellen said. "I'm old. I'm lonely most of the time. I don't have any fun. I despise all of your friends and I'm never comfortable with them. I'm almost forty, can you believe that?"

He nodded again, picked up the jelly with the tip of his forefinger, and wiped it onto the edge of his plate. He had two thoughts. The first was that she was changing the turf, expanding it, and he wasn't sure what to make of that. They'd gone from confrontation to revelation—they were going to play Tell the Truth, which, of course, obligated him. The second thought was, he imagined, somehow extrapolated from the tone of her remark. It was, What if she begins to wear a muumuu around the house?

"Me too," he finally said, thinking that it was not only true, but also safe. He was nearer forty than she was.

Ellen took a minute, then went on. "I get up every day and do stuff I don't want to do," she said. "I grind coffee beans, for example. I don't know why I do that. Why can't I just have regular coffee, Maxwell House or something? But, no. I get up and I come in here"—she pointed toward the kitchen—"I get the coffee out of the freezer, I put the beans in the grinder, I grind 'em." She made a helpless gesture with her hands. "I hate it. I hate the way it sounds. Every morning. It's awful."

"I know what you mean," Jerry said. "For me it's getting the paper. I walk out there on the pea-gravel concrete there and it hurts my feet, and I always wonder who's watching, if anybody is, and I'm out there in this sick-looking robe I've had since Nixon—I don't know why I don't just get another robe, you know what I mean? How hard can it be?"

He took the coffee bean story as a signal that she wanted to turn down the wick, to diminish the gravity of the complaint—her complaint, and his by association—by facing it with this silly example, and he wondered if, after the broad charges she opened with—the business about friends and loneliness—she had not already softened some, cooled off, decided in the short space of the minute or so he'd taken to reply that things weren't so bad.

"I'll get you a robe," she said. "What color?"

That had to be read, he thought, as conciliatory. He decided to go the opposite way, take a hard line. "I don't want a robe. That's the point. Why do I have to have a robe? I hate robes. They're so stupid. I don't even want to see another robe."

"White," she said. "You'll feel like Macho Camacho."

Clever. She'd set him up for the macho joke, of which he was, unmistakably, the butt, inasmuch as she had hours before seen fit to seek sexual gratification elsewhere, with a young man, a student, and, at that, a Latin. Jerry watched the slits in the Levolors brighten as the sun finally rose above the roof next door and came down their own east-facing kitchen wall. He noticed that the blinds were cranked the wrong way, with the lower edges of the slats toward the inside rather than the outside, and he got up to fix that. It was something that Ellen did every night, turn the blinds that way, because she liked the way they looked better when the concave part of the slat was facing out. This in spite of the fact that she was always first in the kitchen in the morning and had to face first the harshness of the light that penetrated the blinds when they were closed that way. The morning did not seem to bother her at all. Jerry was the opposite. He agreed that the blinds looked better at night when they were closed downside in, but he thought they ought to be downside out at bedtime, so that in the morning there wasn't this ugly smear of light when the sun hit.

"I hate it that you leave the blinds this way," he said, going into the kitchen.

"I know," she said. "You told me. But I hate the blinds. I hate curtains too. As a matter of fact, I don't like windows all that much. I wish we could just put chunks of plywood up there, know what I mean?"

"That's a great idea," he said.

"It's what I feel," she said.

"So—you really like sleeping with this guy or what?" He was disappointed with "sleeping with"—why hadn't he gone for sleaze? He'd been thinking sleaze—details, fleshy stuff—why had he backed away? He decided he was afraid to show himself, show that he cared not about the depression, the malaise she might be suffering, not about the reasons for her choice, or the motivation, or the vulnerability that led her to it, not about fear, or need, or any genuine or humane aspect of her situation, but about the nickel-and-dime stuff. He was back in high school. He wanted it to sting. "You like it, huh?" he said.

Ellen gave him a steady look, her features unmoved, at rest, the flatness of the gaze telling him she thought he was dull, cheap, disgusting, and pathetic. Then she moved her mouth into a nasty-looking small smile, small enough so that it could not be mistaken for a real smile, and she said, "He's very good."

This reminded him that he did not want to hear the truth about his wife and her twenty-four-year-old boyfriend.

Instantly, he hated her. Dim-witted, wedded to sensation, a masseuse's dream. Why wasn't she lame, like him? Immune to the physical, bound instead to talk and fantasy, stuff that could turn pigs-in-blankets into hot tamales—lightning cracking between two unexpected parts of two unsuspecting bodies? He was vulnerable here. Felt weak and defensive. But—Toby? His aggression had backfired on him and now he looked at Ellen, who was sitting across the table feeling sorry for him, for his . . . limitations. It made him want to tear his skin off, but he resisted the temptation to say something about dogs, which he knew would be inflammatory, out of line, which might terminate the conversation, shut her up semipermanently, and instead nodded again, taking his medicine, accepting his failure, or, at least, appearing to accept his failure, or appearing to accept her idea of his failure.

He said, with only slight bitterness, "I'll bet he is," and he was proud of it, of the way it had come out. The tone—the content was hot, but the presentation lacked affect—disdain paired with disinterest. She would know, of course, which was meant and which was camouflage, but the disentangling might slow her down, might even seed some doubt.

Jerry was picturing Ellen in the heat of a video version of lovemaking, or trying to picture her, for they had grown so comfortable together, so matched, and so far from lust, that the image of her in passionate embrace, perspiration rolling off her shining cheeks, eyes glazed, lips ballooned into pillowy sexual membrane—this wouldn't quite come to him. The problem, he imagined, in a nutshell.

"So what do you want to know?" Ellen said. She had repositioned herself in the chair, and she was pouting. "You want to know why? Why is because it came up. Maybe because we could be doing better, you and me. We used to do better. I don't know why we don't anymore. I feel left out. Of everything. You name it, I feel left out of it. The war in Vietnam, for example. The Me Generation. Farm Aid. The New German cinema. The BMW crowd. I mean, where's *my* 505? Hawaiian shirts—I wanted to wear one of those, a couple of 'em. The sexual revolution. Making ends meet—remember that? You get a dump and clean it up and everything? I can't do that. I get to choose between a hundred-and-fifty-thousand-dollar house and a hundred-and-eighty-thousand-dollar house—what fun is that? Or I can be postmodern, read *Metropolis*, pay five grand for a chair, eight hundred for dinner. It's all under control, right? I hate it. I hate the lawn, Jerry, know what I mean?"

Jerry studied her face and decided that this remark was a sincere expression of disenchantment with the success they had shared.

"I don't like the lawn either," he said.

This was true. He had, on more than one occasion, thought exactly that he hated the lawn. He remembered staring out the window at the lawn, particularly the back lawn, and thinking how much he hated it. So now he tried to remember how he had gotten over that. But he couldn't remember a thing, he could barely remember what the lawn looked like, and he felt she had twisted the talk around to be about something it wasn't really about. That made him angry, so he said, "But I don't go out picking up college kids for amusement just because the lawn disgusts me."

"Why not?" she said.

He thought she ought to be feeling guilty, but, watching her, he could see that she didn't feel the slightest bit guilty, or, if she did, she wasn't letting him see it, which wasn't fair. Not only was it not fair, it wasn't kind, or compassionate, or good-hearted. In fact, her question was so perfectly weightless that it was like some terrible explosive accidentally swallowed.

"We don't do that because that's the definition of rabbits," he said, and immediately wished he hadn't. There were so many things wrong with it. It was clumsy, didn't quite fit as an answer—and why hadn't he put some lower life-form in for rabbits? Rabbits were so cute, inescapably furry and flop-eared—how could rabbits be bad? But he couldn't think of another, lesser animal with the same kind of reputation, and he realized the point wouldn't be made at all without them, so he let it go and tried to think of some other way to say to Ellen that the release suggested by "why not?" was, in a way, the problem, for if you had no more restraint than that implicit in the question, if you were already leaning in the direction of doing whatever it was, so that the burden of argument was placed on the dissuasion side of things, then you had not much restraint at all, about as much as a hot monkey—he liked that "hot monkey" part, and wondered if it was too soon after the rabbits to throw it in.

She, meanwhile, had begun to clear away her place at the table— the plate with the orange peel on it, the plate that had held her toast, the plate with the husk of her honeydew melon, her small glass of milk and larger glass of water, the three crumpled napkins she had accumulated during the meal, the butter-encrusted knife, and the four bottles containing the various pills she took every morning at breakfast, the pills themselves remaining on the tablecloth in a tight, multicolored group.

"You're kind of a complex molecule, here," Jerry said, circling a finger toward her mat and the debris she was clearing away.

She stopped at the kitchen door and turned to stare at him, her eyes narrowed, a bemused expression on her face. She didn't say a word, just looked.

He wondered why things seemed to accumulate around her wherever she lit for more than a moment—in order to watch TV she had to have a glass of bottled water, the bottle of cold water itself for possible refills (not the bottle the water actually came in, since that was a one-gallon plastic jug which wouldn't fit in the refrigerator, and thus couldn't be chilled, but an intermediate container, a two-liter ripple-plastic French spa-water bottle, which would fit in the lowest door tray of the refrigerator and was constantly refilled from the larger container kept under the sink), a diet Coke, her cigarettes, lighter, and ashtray, two newspapers (yesterday's and today's), and at least one magazine to flip through during commercials, Kleenex, a sweater in case things got chilly, one each package of gum and package of breath mints, and miscellaneous other equipment from sewing stuff to ankle weights, depending on the secondary pursuits being pursued right at the moment of the show she was setting out to watch. He hadn't, heretofore, been bothered by it the way he was this morning.

"What about it?" she said. She was out of sight, in the kitchen.

"What about Toby?" Jerry said.

"Toby's a nice boy," she said. "Toby's external to our relationship. In fact, I think you'd like him."

"I don't like him. I never would like him. He could cure spinal meningitis and I wouldn't like him."

"They already cured spinal meningitis," she said.

"I knew that," he said.

"You'd like him."

This was typical of his conversations with Ellen. She had her ideas, inhabited utterly, which for practical purposes could not be addressed. He saw these ideas as at the mercy of dark forces, which is to say that he didn't know what forces there were that would lead to her ideas. He had, of course, tried reason, as he would try again shortly, sure of its failure, confident that she would not alter her thought on the matter at all, but bound nevertheless to make the effort, to point out to her that it was unlikely that he, the wronged party, would, under the present circumstances, or any other circumstances subsequent to those present ones, *like* Toby. Toby was her lover. Toby was to her what he was not. Toby was an intruder in their otherwise satisfactory, or thought-to-be-satisfactory, marriage, the intruder whose appearance suggested that the marriage was not satisfactory at all, that it was, in fact, stupid and empty.

"I hate his guts," Jerry said.

He didn't feel this, he felt nothing like it; in fact, he didn't have much feeling about Toby one way or the other. What he did feel was much in love with Ellen, more in love than he had been in a long time. He thought about the way she smiled, the huskiness in her voice sometimes, the goofy way she had of laughing when she was really amused, the peculiar rituals upon which she insisted, the trouble she had dressing from time to time and the way she got angry if he tried to help, tried to suggest that the yellow flats were probably never going to walk comfortably beneath the purple-and-black shirt. He was flooded with images of his wife at her most lovely, which was not necessarily coincident with her most beautiful, although it often was, but a separate thing entirely, a capacity she had for breaking his heart at moments when the tide of things seemed to run against her and she, recognizing this, gave up, shaking her head and reminding herself of the foolishness of attempting to impose order on a thing so disorderly as ordinary life. Those were the times he liked her most, and, since the idea she now championed—that he would like her newly taken lover—was so dumb, and since she had some sense left, and since she was standing there and he could see the recognition of the silliness of her position closing over her like the shadow of a rain cloud sliding over a sun-dappled pond, her face beginning to register the wrongness of the idea, expanding with it into a smile and then a wide, self-mocking grin, Jerry Jordan realized that this was one of those times that he loved her most.

"I guess you're right," Ellen said.

"Still," Jerry said. "There he is."

She came to the kitchen door and leaned against the jamb, nodding. She was eating lemon yogurt out of a paper tub. "Yep," she said. "Like a hatchet buried deep in the soft flesh of our relationship."

"Yes," he said.

"I see that," she said.

He watched her carefully as she cleared the remaining breakfast dishes and prepared for her morning workout. She was splendidly young and sexy in yellow nylon shorts and a mint-green T-shirt, minicassette strung dangerously at her waist, earphones in place, blue-leather ankle weights belted like huge, stylish watches to her wrists. He went out with her, stood on the ten-by-fifteen-foot white pine deck as she strode purposefully away, arms already pumping, embarked on what his father would have called her constitutional.

He was staring at a redbird when she made the block for the first time and waved in that bothered way people who are preoccupied wave when they feel it is their duty.

(1987)

Pool Lights

There are things that cannot be understood—things said at school, at the supermarket, or in this case by the pool of the Santa Rosa Apartments on a hazy afternoon in midsummer. A young woman wearing pleated white shorts and a thin gauze shirt open over her bikini top introduces herself as Dolores Prince and says, "You have a pretty face." Automatically, you smile and say, "Thank you," but, looking up at her, wonder why she selected that particular word, that adjective.

She is small, already tan, delicate but not frail. Her dark hair is in a braid tight against her scalp. "I mean it," she says, dropping her canvas tote on the pea-gravel concrete apron of the pool. "It's all soft and pink." She steps out of the shorts and snaps the elastic around the leg openings of her swimsuit.

"It's the shirt." You pluck at the collar of the faded red alligator pullover, then point at the sky. "Bounces off the shirt."

"You're at the school, aren't you?" she says. "You're the swimming teacher?"

"Two years, yes. How did you know?"

"Mrs. Scree told me. She tells me everything."

Alongside the edge of the pool, ten feet away, Dolores spreads a black towel laced with salmon, peach, and gray-green flowers, then pulls things out of the tote—a tall red plastic glass and a can of Sprite, a pack of cigarettes in a leather case with a lighter pouch, a rolled copy of *Cosmopolitan*, a ribbed brown squeeze-bottle of suntan cream, a thin silver radio the size of a wallet, a pair of square-lensed sunglasses with clear frames; she arranges these items around her towel, on the perimeter of her new territory, at the ready.

"It isn't the shirt," she says after she's in position, on her back on the towel, her knees up, facing the open pagoda next to the pool. "I know enough about color to know that the shirt would turn you brown, not pink."

"Oh." The sureness in her voice is startling. "Then maybe it's the clouds?"

"Clouds are white," she says without opening her eyes.

She's probably not right about the shirt, and she's wrong about the clouds—they're undefined and sulphur yellow.

"You new at Santa Rosa?" she asks, wiping the backs of her lotion-slick hands on her belly.

"I'm in 281 over here." You gesture sideways across the court-yard in the direction of your apartment. "Two months, but I don't come out much—out here, I mean."

She pushes up on an elbow and twists to look. "That's too bad. I'm out here all the time."

"You like it."

"Who doesn't?" she says. She sits up and spins around on her rump, wrapping her long dark arms around her knees. Her finger-nails are pointed and chocolaty.

Your sprung metal chair rocks a little. "I imagine all these people looking out their windows at me. It makes me nervous."

"Oh, you can't think about that," Dolores says. She scans the buildings surrounding the pool. "If they look, they look—who gets hurt?" She says this with a coy smile, as if she suspects you watch pool-side parties from the apartment window. She wipes more lotion on her thighs. "Some Saturday afternoons in summer the sunbathers are irresistible, I guess, especially through a narrow slit in the curtains."

"I look. Sometimes I start to watch a ballgame on TV and then end up watching people out here all afternoon. Don't you do that?"

She adjusts the thick braid at the back of her head. "Not really. I just come out."

"I like watching them talk to each other. The way they move around, gesturing, making faces—it's interesting."

"I know what you mean. And the women aren't bad either."

"No. Some of you are quite lovely."

•

Because the floral brocade furniture the landlady had to offer was unacceptable, the apartment looks almost vacant—as if someone is moving out. Buying a round card table at Wilson's seemed dumb, but now that it's in place in the bedroom, it seems right. It's sturdy and large enough to hold the twelve-inch Sony, with room left to eat or work. The two pinkish-brown steel folding chairs that came with the table are uncomfortable but serviceable. The only other furniture in the bedroom is a queen-size bed pulled out into the room on the diagonal so it floats, like a great lozenge, on the harvest-gold carpet,

At midnight Friday you go into the small living-dining room and click on the overhead light. There, in neat low stacks along three walls, is the summer project: piles of *Time, Rolling Stone, Sports Illustrated, Money, Road & Track, Stereo Review, American Photographer, Skin Diver,* and *Vogue.* All from American Educational Services at a terrific discount. When they started piling up unread, they became a collection. After better than a year, the subscriptions got canceled. And after two moves—one across country, one across town—the project was born: look through the collection, maybe save an article or two, a peculiar picture, a curious headline, and toss the rest. Reading every word seemed at first a possibility, but finally the idea was exhausting.

The project isn't far along. The first thing was to strip the covers off all the issues of *Time* and put them together with Acco fasteners. Then the same for the other magazines. These "books" of covers are on the floor between two natural-wood deck chairs bought at an import store. The chairs and the covers and the magazines are all that's in the living room except for a huge pencil cactus, easily six feet high, which stands just inside the sliding door to a three-by-eight-foot balcony.

Picking up copies of *American Photographer* and the latest *Vogue* in the stack, dated January, 1981, you take these into the bedroom, put them on top of the telephone book next to the TV, then go back and water the pencil cactus, straighten the pile of *Road & Track*—looking at the contents of the topmost issue to see what cars were road-tested that month—and switch off the light on the way to the kitchen for cornflakes to take into the bedroom. The first issue of *American*

Photographer has lots of small ads. The featured pictures seem to be of the edges of things—buildings, cars, furniture, streets; another portfolio, in color, is of women's backs, taken from down low so that the backgrounds are all blue sky. Some of the pictures are attractive, but fooling with them seems like too much trouble, so you push the magazine back onto the stack and take the cereal to the kitchen, put it in the sink, and run the faucet until the bowl is full of gray water.

Undressing in the bathroom, you watch the small mirror above the lavatory, then drop the clothes in a tall plastic basket kept in the hall closet for outgoing laundry. You floss, thinking of the dentist. His assistants wear matching Cheryl Tiegs jeans and T-shirts; he pipes Willie Nelson's "Stardust" into the cubicle; he makes jokes about the color of teeth, and he talks to the mouth when he's working on it: "How's Mr. Mouth doing today?" or "Would Mr. Mouth like a club sandwich?" All this and he tries not to punish. Still, you avoid him.

At one-thirty a movie called *Berlin Correspondent*, starring Dana Andrews, starts on Channel 17.

•

At noon on Saturday, Dolores is already arranged flat on her stomach at the deep end of the pool, almost directly below your window.

She waves. The phone rings. Your brother in Taos wants to know what has been said to so seriously alienate your father. You tell him you love your father. He says he knows that, but what was said? You just woke up and don't remember. He urges that the family try to understand the father. "He wants to be loved," he says, making it sound stupid. "He wants us to think he's wonderful."

"He is."

"He's sad. I'm trying to help."

The glistening sliver of Dolores is visible through the curtains. She's wearing a dark Danskin. "I didn't want to upset him. I tried to talk to him. I tried to tell him to take it easy."

"Just be sensible about it. We've got to stop jumping all over him."

This view of the situation is not as correct as he assumes it to be, but when told this, he does not back away from his assertion. You promise to think about it, and ask what is going on in Taos, to which he replies, "Nothing." You agree to call him later, after breakfast.

"Talk to you," he says, and hangs up.

In the kitchen you turn on the coffee, then fill a pan with water to poach eggs, and put the pan on the stove.

Later, when the eggs are ready, shaking gently on crisp muffin halves, you carry plate, flatware, coffee, and napkin back into the bedroom. Getting the one-bedroom apartment overlooking the pool was lucky—so Mrs. Scree said when she agreed to show the less expensive one-bedroom, which overlooked the Santa Rosa parking lot and the laundromat. "The drain backs up sometimes," she said. "I gotta tell you so when it happens you won't go yelling at me." It is hard to imagine—yelling at Mrs. Scree: after twenty-four years, by her account, managing apartments, she knows how to handle dissatisfied tenants.

By one o'clock Dolores has been joined by several other tenants: a balloonish young husband and his skinny wife, a single girl named Beverly, who works at Sears, a plump woman in an emerald terry-cloth slit-to-the-thigh bandeau-top sundress, an older man named Wilkins, whose chest is covered with bright silver hair, and on the fringe of the group, standing near the corner of the pool in conversation with a young couple who are obviously apartment hunting, Mrs. Scree, dressed in her usual dark-blue slacks and sleeveless flowered blouse.

You stand at the window for a few minutes, watching the party. When Mrs. Scree finishes with the apartment hunters, she pulls a long aluminum pole from behind the redwood pagoda and starts to scoop multicolored miniature plastic bowling pins out of the pool. She is not very good at this, and after she makes several passes at a bright-red pin painted with an Air Force insignia, Wilkins pushes himself out of his lawn chair and, with flourish, wrests the pole from her. The others are immediately drawn into the action, giving directions, cracking jokes, pointing and laughing as Wilkins tries to capture the bowling pin. He walks to the long side of the pool and eases the pole into the water so its small net dips just under the pin. When he tries to lift the pole, the bowling pin topples off the frame of the net and slides away on the surface of the clear water. Everybody laughs. Even Mrs. Scree, who ordinarily laughs only at her own jokes, punches her tenant playfully on the arm, points at the floating pin, and laughs heartily. Dolores, who sat up when Wilkins took the pole, turns away from the pool, shades her eyes with her hand, and with the forefinger of her other hand beckons you downstairs.

You jerk the two edges of the curtains together, lapping one over the other, certain that she couldn't actually see, that she was just guessing. Getting back into bed, head wrapped in a towel because of wet hair from the shower, you pull the sheet up, lie there, and leaf through the magazines.

•

Later Dolores catches you by the mailboxes, says she wants to go for a drive, and hustles off to her apartment to change. The afternoon is hot.

"You hid earlier," she says, getting into the car. "I'm ashamed of you."

"I almost came out when Mr. Wilkins was going for the pin."

"I signaled you."

"It was hard to resist."

The interstate takes you fifty miles to a small coast town, Conklin, population 8,528. It's almost five o'clock.

"Let's buy something," Dolores says. "There's a market. Let's get shrimp to take back."

"What's special about shrimp?"

"Nothing." She's got a wraparound skirt over her thin plum suit and she looks sexy.

The butcher is busy with a customer who looks as if she never had anything but shrimp in her life—crisp clothes and crisper hair. The butcher holds a half-dozen lamb chops up on a piece of white paper for her, and at the same time nods at Dolores to indicate that she's next. Dolores squats in front of his case to get a closer look at the shrimp, which are half buried in ice. The woman wants to inspect the chops; she tells the butcher to put them on top of the counter for a minute. The clock says it's five of five. The butcher drops the paper onto the case and the chops teeter for a second, then tip over the edge and slip one by one down the sloped front, piling up at the lower edge of the glass.

The woman isn't upset. She bends over and sticks her face very close to the meat. Abruptly she straightens and says to the butcher, who is standing behind the case with his hands on his hips, staring at the ceiling fan, "I don't know, Carl. What do you think? They don't smell too good."

"Lady," the butcher says, moving toward the end of the case and wiping his hands on his apron. "They ain't supposed to be gardenias."

The woman turns. "Sir?" she says. "Would you help me with these chops? Would you take a look?"

"I will," Dolores says, popping up from her crouch in front of the shrimp. She takes a close look at the lamb chops, picks up one and squeezes it, then pokes it against her nose. The butcher comes out in front, pulls the paper off the top of the case, and stacks the other chops on his hand again.

"What do you think?" the woman says.

"Yeah," the butcher says. "What do you think?"

"I think they're fine," Dolores says, placing her chop on top of the others. Then she whispers, "Let's get out. It's dog food."

After a wrong turn trying to get back to the interstate, you end up on the old highway, a two-lane job, but it's got signs pointing toward home and Dolores says she wants to stick with it. An hour later the terrain begins to look familiar.

"See. That wasn't so bad."

She's right. With twilight the temperature goes down fast, and the old highway is more interesting to drive, because of the towns, roadside signs, and animals.

"Better than trees," she says.

At the crossroad that goes back to town she sees a motel, one of those old places with two-room brick bungalows back off the road in a cluster of pines. Its neon sign says "Golden Gables Motor Lodge" in purple, "Vacancy" in pink, and "Bass Pond" in lime green.

Dolores points at the sign. "You game?" she says. "I've never been in one of these. Let's try it."

"I don't think so." But you brake and pull over next to the entrance anyway, in case Dolores is dead set on seeing the inside.

She is. The office is an Airstream trailer jacked up on cement blocks. The registration desk is a freestanding paneled bar with a thick black pillow of padding around the edge. A man shorter than a ten-year-old boy pushes through a beaded curtain and walks across the small room as if he had a spring on his right foot.

"Can we see a room?" Dolores says.

Only his shoulders and head stick up over the bar. He looks at Dolores, then pokes a knobby forefinger into the collar of his starched white shirt. He tilts his head when he talks. "You staying long? A night? A week?" His voice is high, nasal.

"We don't know," Dolores says, grinning. "First we want to look at the room."

"How come you don't try in town? They got everything in town. Television, food, Magic Fingers—the works." He crawls up onto a barstool with a swivel seat.

"No bass pond."

"Right," Dolores says. "No bass pond—where is it, anyway?"

"You drove over it coming in. Sucker dried up on us last summer."

"How much per night?" Dolores asks.

"You going to use the kitchen?"

"Not tonight."

At this the little man catapults himself off the swivel stool and limps to the front of the trailer, where he steps up on a wooden box draped with a yellow rubber car mat. He looks out the small round window. "This your car?" he says. "Registered in the country?"

"We live in town," Dolores says. "We just want to see what the rooms are like."

He hops off the box and looks hard at Dolores. Sweat as thick as Vaseline is collecting on his neck just above the tight collar. "You bring your tiger-skin drawers?"

"Let's go, Dolores. I don't think the man wants to rent a room."

"Oh, I want to rent one, all right." He's cleaning the fingernails on one hand with the thumbnail of the other. "Sure I do. I want to rent twenty. Just don't much want to show one, see what I mean?"

•

On Sunday at half past ten in the morning, going down to pick up the paper—which the delivery-woman has gotten in the habit of placing, unrolled, on the third step up from the bottom of the stairs—just out of bed, wearing jeans and a terry-cloth bathrobe, hair sticking out in all directions, you meet Dolores. She's coming around the corner of the building carrying a beige plastic garbage bag full of sharp-edged objects—boxes, it looks like—that give the bag a set of curiously geometric surfaces.

"That was fun last night," she says. "That guy was really short, wasn't he?"

The morning light in the apartment courtyard is strangely cheerful. The palms around the pagoda shift a little with the wind.

"Sure was." The newspaper slips down two steps.

She laughs and props her bag against the side of the stairs. "House keeping," she says, pointing to the bag. "Maybe we can get together later?"

"Sure."

Mrs. Scree follows her dog out of her apartment and, seeing tenants in conversation, rumbles across the courtyard. "Dolores, I forgot to tell you yesterday that they're coming to do your carpet tomorrow."

"Finally. That's great."

"And what's he dressed up for? That your samurai outfit?" She laughs.

"We're discussing cocktails by the pool this evening," Dolores says, smiling lavishly.

"A new romance right here in the complex," Mrs. Scree says. She acts as if she knew it all along. "Well, I'll keep Raymond inside if that'll help—he's such an old gossip." Raymond is her husband.

Then Wilkins backs out of his apartment in tennis shorts and flip-flops. He's got a thick purple towel bunched around his neck, and his sunglasses are balanced on top of his head. In one hand he has a tall glass of tomato juice and in the other a portable radio.

"There you are," Mrs. Scree shouts. "With weather like this I expected you out at dawn. Now, where's that dog got to? Here Spinner, here boy." She crouches down to look across the court for her dog.

Wilkins waves his tomato juice and then points at one of the squat palms around the pagoda. "I think he's in there," Wilkins says. "I see his tail."

"So do you want breakfast or not?" Dolores says.

"Don't go too far, honey," Mrs. Scree says without turning around. She falls forward on her hands and knees, trying to look under the sagging fronds of the palms; she's wearing something like boxer shorts under her black knit slacks. "Making breakfast is serious."

"I had breakfast already, thanks."

Mrs. Scree is crawling about on the grass at the foot of the stairs, occasionally dropping her head to the ground to check another opening in the foliage. Wilkins drags a recently painted steel lounger out into the morning sun, aligning it for balanced distribution of the tanning rays.

"Just let me get set up here, Peggy," he says, "then I'll go in there after him."

"Don't be silly, Fred," Mrs. Scree says. She pushes herself upright on her knees and, with some effort, gets to her feet. "He'll be out on there the instant I go back inside."

An older woman who lives in the apartment directly beneath yours comes out dressed as if for church.

"Good morning, Mrs. Talbot," Mrs. Scree says, brushing at the whitish stains on her pants. "How's the knee these days?"

"Much better, thank you," Mrs. Talbot says. "The hot-water bottle you gave me helps a good deal."

"Your neighbor here been behaving himself?" Mrs. Scree says.

The older woman nods and says, "I'm Irene Talbot." She switches her purse and gloves around, then extends her hand. "I'm very pleased to finally meet you; after all the times we've said hello, I feel as if I already know you." She turns to the landlady. "He's quiet as a mouse, although with my hearing I'm not sure I'd know if he wasn't. Anyway, it's very reassuring to know that there's a man nearby, in case something should happen."

"And a man with such a fine face," Dolores says.

"Now that you mention it," Mrs. Talbot says, eyeing Dolores. "The face and skull *are* very good." She smiles faintly and toys with her gloves.

"A new romance," Mrs. Scree says, winking broadly, making her face a parody of collusion.

"Morning, Mrs. Talbot," Wilkins shouts from his place by the pool. "You look mighty handsome today."

"Thank you," Mrs. Talbot says. Then, when Wilkins turns away, she grins at Mrs. Scree.

Backing up the stairs, you say, "I think I'll go on up and read this," then flap the newspaper a couple of times at no one in particular. "A pleasure meeting you, Mrs. Talbot."

Mrs. Talbot nods, gives a short wave of her gloves to Mrs. Scree and Dolores, and walks off toward the parking lot.

"Well, I'll leave you two alone," Mrs. Scree says. "Raymond's going to need breakfast soon and I just wanted to get Spinner done." She calls the dog again, and Spinner, so named because he likes to chase his tail, pops his head out from under the edge of the pagoda. "There he is," Mrs. Scree shouts. "Come here, Spinner. Right now."

The dog wipes his nose on his paws, but does not budge from the spot under the building.

"Don't forget tonight," Dolores says. She hoists the milky plastic bag onto her shoulder. "He's so pretty," she says to the landlady. "It's embarrassing."

"What's tonight?" Mr. Wilkins says, propping his chin on the carefully folded towel at the end of the lounger.

"Never you mind, Fred," Mrs. Scree says. "You weren't invited. This is a private affair."

Wilkins frowns, and Dolores says, "Oh, sure you are, Mr. Wilkins. We're having cocktails by the pool at six."

"Cocktails?" he says, blinking furiously.

Mrs. Scree pads across the concrete and playfully pushes his face back into the towel. "Fred doesn't need any cocktails today," she says. She reaches behind her, under the tail of her blouse, to scratch her back.

"We could even have a barbecue," Dolores says, following Mrs. Scree. "If we had anything to barbecue."

"I'm going to barbecue that dog if he doesn't come over here right now," Mrs. Scree says. "And tell your young man not to come dressed that way—he looks like Karl Wallenda."

Inside, you drop the newspaper on the kitchen cabinet, go into the bedroom, take off the jeans and the bathrobe, and get back into bed.

●

The telephone wakes you. "Look," your brother says, "I want to clarify something. I'm not accusing you of being stupid and insensitive about Father, I'm just reporting what it was like there last week. How he sees things. It seems to me at his age we've got to think about that—I mean, how *he* sees things. You know what I'm saying?"

"Yes." Your arm is numb and tingling.

"I'm not saying you're not right. He can be a butt sometimes."

"Uh-huh."

"But that's not even the point. The point is, you have a tendency to jump on him whether he's being a butt or not. I mean, if he wants to play Lord High Executioner, where's the harm?"

"I don't want to humor him." With all the curtains, it's dark in the apartment. "Listen, what time is it?"

"Three," he says. "About." He shouts to his wife for the time, then says, "Three-thirty. I didn't mean humor him. It's just that he isn't always wrong."

"Sure."

"Talk to you," he says.

You toss the receiver at its cradle, miss, shove it into place, reach across the table to switch on the television, and then, when the picture appears, twist quickly through the channels until there's a movie. When the sound is fixed so the actors can just barely be heard, you hunch forward in the metal folding chair, naked, elbows on knees, flexing the left hand and watching. At the commercial you make toast and pour orange juice into a large glass of ice, then go back to the bedroom.

There are shouts from the courtyard. Dolores and the others from yesterday, along with a few more tenants, are gathered in a loose group at one end of the pool. You shut the curtains, sit down at the card table, and eat breakfast.

●

By five, most of the tenants have returned to their apartments. Mr. Wilkins and Mrs. Scree are the last ones by the pool. They sit at a round green table under the pagoda, sipping drinks from mismatched glasses. You straighten the bedroom, then bathe and shave; at five-thirty the courtyard is empty. In fresh Levi's, a checked shirt, and a black corduroy jacket, you pour a small glass of milk and watch the end of the local news.

At six the court is still empty. The lights in the pagoda have come on early, as have the yellow lights at the front doors of many apartments facing the pool. The sun is almost gone except for a reddish glow reflected from low clouds, which are gray in the eastern sky and shiny scarlet in the west.

Dolores hasn't come out. Mike Wallace interviews a California man who stuffs pet animals for their owners. Harry Reasoner reports on the Florida drug trade. It's not clear whether Dolores intends to come out or was just playing. To be sure, and because talking to Dolores outside in the courtyard might be pleasant, you turn off the television and go down to the pagoda. All the chairs and tables are painted the color of the lighted water in the pool. For the hundredth time, water seems beautiful. The palms around three sides of the pagoda make it feel secluded, even though it isn't really. The apartment windows where there are lights have drawn curtains; the dark windows could hide people. Still, it's comfortable outside, and if Dolores doesn't show, it's not a total loss.

Two young girls go by carrying two plastic baskets of clothes. The overweight young husband and his skinny wife come in from the parking lot—from an early dinner perhaps—and say hello before entering their apartment, switching on the lights, and hastily shutting the curtains. Someone passes between the pagoda and the pool and says, "Aren't summer nights incredible and amazing?" A large tree roach runs along a floorboard. In the distance several dogs howl. Mr. Wilkins, whose front door is almost on a center line with the pool, opens his door and stands on the threshold. There's enough light to see him, even though his porch lamp isn't on. He's wearing shorts and a square-tailed shirt.

"Hey," he says, shading his eyes with a hand. "That you? How's it going out here?"

"Fine, I guess."

"How's that?" he says, moving the hand from over his eyes to cup his ear. "Where's the party?"

"It's a slow starter."

"Well," he says, waving. "Sometimes that happens." He goes back into his apartment. His porch light snaps on.

Upstairs, you toss the coat on one of the deck chairs in the living room, then take a Coke out of the refrigerator, go into the bedroom, and drink the Coke, thumbing through an issue of *Stereo Review* devoted mini-components.

•

At nine you pull the slim telephone book out from under the stack of magazines and look up Dolores Prince, writing her number on the inside back cover of the book. There is a knock at the door.

Two kids, a boy and a girl, neither older than ten or twelve, are on the landing. Below, on the sidewalk, a man is silhouetted against the pool.

"We're working for Jesus," the kids say in imperfect unison. The boy wears a blue suit and the girl a lilac dress, black pumps, and taut white socks.

"Aren't we all."

"We have Jesus in our hearts," they say. "We have subscriptions to *Spirituality, Aspire,* and *The Beacon,* and we're trying to win a trip."

"Thank you, but no." You hold up your hand like a crosswalk guard in after-school traffic.

They continue, though the young girl, as she speaks, turns and looks toward the foot of the stairs. "Wouldn't you like to have His message come into your home each month? Only twenty-six dollars for twelve issues." Then the girl adds, "Please? Two more and our whole family gets a chance for a trip to Six Flags."

"Yeah," the boy says. "Dad has a chance at a boat, too."

Apart from their clothes, the children are quite ordinary-looking, like kids at the school, or at the shopping center, or on bicycles going down Park Street in the afternoon.

"No, thank you." The man below moves forward slightly to consult a piece of white letter-size paper in his hand, and you call to him, "No, thank you."

The kids turn uncertainly and look down into the dark courtyard. The boy grabs the frame around the door as if he's lost his balance.

"Okay," says the man downstairs.

The children turn around, obviously disappointed, and say, "Thank you, sir. May the Lord Jesus come into your heart." Then the girl goes down the steps, her heels clacking on the metal, and the boy, much more cautiously, follows her, his hand a tight fist around the railing.

When the door is closed and the kids and the man have stopped talking outside, and the kids are knocking on Mrs. Talbot's door, the telephone rings.

"Hi," Dolores says. "I tried to call earlier, but you're unlisted. I have to apologize about tonight."

"How'd you get the number?"

"Mrs. Scree. Listen, I got into something I couldn't get out of—you know how it is. Sundays are bad for me."

"We'll do it another day."

"Sure," she says. "I'm out there all the time. Just come on out whenever you're ready."

"Whenever I'm ready I'll just come on out." The telephone book is still creased flat on the table in front of the television.

"Did the kids get to you?" she asks. "They must've thought I was Mary Magdalene, the way I was dressed when I opened the door. But look, are you busy? Why not come for a nightcap?"

The TV is making a curious high whine, even though the sound is off. Outside there are people talking, and there is the sound of a chair being pulled across the pebbly concrete, then Mrs. Scree's loud, sudden laugh, like the bark of a monkey, "I don't think so. Not tonight."

There's another pause, and then Dolores says, "Well, suit yourself. If you want me you know where to find me."

"You're in the book."

"Right."

She hangs up. You hold the telephone to your ear until the dial tone returns, then replace the receiver. Some people are running back and forth across the television screen. The voices are coming up from poolside. After a few minutes you go into the living room, put on the black coat, take a Löwenbräu out of the refrigerator, and go outside. You sit sideways on the diving board and talk to Mrs. Scree and her husband, Raymond, and another tenant—the plump woman from Saturday. The subscription kids go out the front gate. Mrs. Scree wags her arms like an explorer in jungle and introduces you as the king of the crawl.

(1981)

GILA FLAMBÉ

The woman with the menus stops me by the cash register, because the restaurant is crowded and she doesn't think she has a table for one. I'm soaked after running across the jammed parking lot in the hot rain, so I'm not sympathetic when the woman, whose lips are a juicy red, shakes her head and gazes forlornly around the room. "Nobody ever comes in alone," she says.

I point to a small man sitting by himself in a corner.

"Oh," she says, straightening the menus on her arm. "That's Mr. Pelham. I forgot about him."

"Well, maybe he'd like company?" I don't want to sit there, but it's better than nothing.

"No. He always eats alone."

Mr. Pelham occupies a small table near the kitchen doors—not a good table at all, but it has two chairs, one of them empty, and there isn't another unoccupied chair in the room. The restaurant used to be a hardware store; now it's all done up in cheesy LA late-thirties gear, the hardboiled version—palms, ratty paintings, neon, ersatz columns, colored lights, pale-salmon walls in bad plaster, black tile floor. The waitresses slink around in period evening dress; the blondes make an effort at Veronica Lake. There's a lot of smoke-colored taffeta and lamé in evidence. This is my first trip.

"Why don't you ask him," I say. "He looks like he could use a friend."

The woman with the menus doesn't want to do this, but after another look around she agrees, and slides across the room toward his table, narrowly missing a waitress in a shiny dress who's carrying a tray of squat cocktails.

There's a commotion in the corner; abruptly Mr. Pelham gets up and pushes the menu woman aside. He's short. He stands awkwardly, bent forward, his fists planted on the table, his black raincoat still tight around him, and he stares across the room at me. I point at him, then at myself, then back at him; he says something to the woman, then sits down. She flaps her hand at me, telling me it's all right, I should come over.

Pelham looks fifty. At the neck of his raincoat—only the topmost button is undone—the bright, starched, tightly buttoned collar of a white dress shirt is visible. He isn't wearing a tie. On the table, half covering the chrome wire rack of sugar packets, there's a black hat with a ribbed band. I remove my raincoat and drop it onto the floor next to the second chair. "Thanks," I say. "I didn't want to bother you, but"—I turn and look quickly around the room—"there's no place left to sit. My name's Harold. Sometimes I'm called Zoot." I stick out my hand, but Pelham doesn't look up from his soup. He's bent over the shallow dish, blowing on the soup, pulling away occasionally to whisk his spoon around the rim. "I'll move if something opens up, okay?"

Pelham's hair is thin and sticking to his scalp. "I'm waiting for somebody," he says. "You'll have to move when she comes."

A woman who can't be twenty hands me a glossy scarlet menu. She's wearing a black dress with thin straps and a feather motif in sequins up under the bodice. She looks good. I ask her to keep an eye out for a vacant table, but she doesn't seem to understand.

"Mr. Pelham has been kind enough to let me join him until another table becomes available."

"Oh," the waitress says, reaching for the menu she's just given me.

"I'll keep it." We have a little tug-of-war over the menu, very quick, which she gracefully allows me to win. She's not sure about the water glass she's holding, but finally decides to leave it.

Pelham says, "Don't stain the table," so I open the menu and slide the glass onto one corner of it. There's an eight-foot-high potted palm behind him, and every time the kitchen doors swing open, one of the largest fronds sways, brushing the back of his head, and he jerks out of the way.

"I'm not alone all the time," he says. "I've got people come to see me night and day." He's looking very carefully through his soup, picking up spoonfuls, twisting them to catch the light, then dripping the soup back into the dish. "Don't get the idea that I'm bad off."

"Okay," I say, and drink my water. There's a dark, irregular stain on the corner of the menu; I try to put the glass back exactly where it was. "You come often? Here, I mean?"

"What're you, an accountant? You run a small store or something? You're not from the Board of Health, are you?"

"No." I wish I'd waited at the door. "No, I just came to try the food."

He laughs and drops the spoon into the saucer. "Yeah, and I love yams," he says. "Slinky's food is nothing. She goes off to Vassar or someplace and suddenly everybody's stiff for her."

"The desserts—somebody said they were good."

"Her aunt. Slinky's idea of dessert is a weekend with wet hair in a station wagon." He presses a hand to his forehead, then slides the fingers back over his scalp, gluing new points of dark hair to the skin. He rolls his eyes. "Look at these people—why the hell don't they go home? Go to Bonanza, for Christ's sake."

Looking around the room, I wonder the same thing. Bonanza's not so bad, and you can usually get a table.

Pelham looks at me for the first time since I sat down. "What're you doing here, Mac? You're out of town and it's raining and you're here alone—don't that beat all. Where's your beautiful wife? Where's your beautiful house?"

I grin and shrug stupidly, aiming for camaraderie. "No wife, no house. My beautiful car's in the lot outside, only it's a Chevrolet."

Pelham shreds four crackers into his soup, which must be room temperature by now. "Zoot? What kind of name is that? That's a stupid name."

I nod and study the menu, trying to decide whether I want to stay. I've been called Zoot since I was a kid—my father played lousy saxophone and loved Zoot Sims. "It's all tongue, boy," he used to say while we listened together to a Sims record so loud it rattled the figurines in my mother's china cabinet. "Tongue and breath." And we sat, listening, my father's open saxophone case on the sofa, the horn a light, glistening gold, until late into the weekend nights. As nicknames go, Zoot isn't so bad. "My dad was a musician. He gave me the name."

"I know a guy named Stick," Pelham says. "And I used to know a guy named Nipple, but he got his throat cut on a rig in the Gulf. Stick's a bowling champion somewhere—Little Rock, maybe. He's got himself set up with a bar called the 7–10 Club, something like that." Pelham flakes more crackers into the dish. His soup is beginning to look like day-old cereal.

"Stick," I repeat.

Two couples come in together and are seated at a table against the far wall. I catch the eye of the woman with the menus, and she tosses her head a little to indicate that she gets the message.

"Yeah. Stick. And you're Zoot. And I'm Blink, because I never do. Ain't that wonderful."

•

I eat a small steak while Pelham watches, still nursing his soup. The steak isn't bad. The waitress with the sequins says she's sorry ten or fifteen times, talking, it seems, more to Pelham than to me. She suggests a dessert that turns out to be a circle of fresh pineapple embedded in a square of white chocolate and topped with curled almond shavings.

"I need a ride," Pelham says while I add the tip on the Visa slip. "Hot young thing like you can afford to give me a ride, can't you?"

"Sure. Where're you headed?" It's reflex; I don't know why I'm agreeing. Maybe it's the way Pelham looks—the eyebrows and the sallow skin and the disdain. Maybe I want to prove I'm not such a rotten fellow.

"It ain't far," he says. "I'll buy gas if you want to be pissy about it. I've got to meet somebody, and my Lamborghini's in the shop."

"Fine, okay."

"Course if you're too busy I'll just crawl." He pushes his chair back from the table, deposits the hat on his head, then falls to his knees and crawls toward the entrance. For a minute I think he's crippled, but at the door he gets up and gives the menu woman a hug, then brushes his knees. He signals for me to hurry up. I'm still seated at the table, trying to figure out what's going on, when he shouts, "Let's move it, kid," as if we were marines in a movie.

The first thing I do when I get the car started is look at the gas gauge; half a tank, plenty. Then I turn on the windshield wipers and turn off the radio. Pelham jams his hands in his raincoat pockets and says, "That way," jerking his head to the right. "How old are you, thirty? Thirty-five?"

"Two," I say, wheeling out of the parking lot. "Where're we going?"

"I'll tell you where to turn." He stares straight out the windshield. "I'm fifty today. When you're fifty, it goes very fast. You people don't know that."

We drive through town, which is eight blocks of two- and three-story buildings, then go out a winding road past the industrial section, past some kind of all-lit-up oil refinery, and out onto an old highway that used to be the truck route; it's raining heavily, so I can't see much except the occasional brights of a passing tanker truck.

"I'm going to help you out, kid," Pelham says after we've been driving a few minutes in silence. "I'm going to introduce you to Melba."

Oncoming lights make the rain on the windshield look alive, the way the water pops off the glass and flies into midair. I wait for Pelham to tell me about Melba. Suddenly he says, "Here. Turn here."

I spin the Chevrolet onto a red clay road full of potholes and brown standing water. We buck and heave in the front seat of the car, and there's nothing to see but the hood, the rain, the almost pumpkin-colored road. We go a little way, and I start to say something but Pelham pulls his hand out of his raincoat pocket and grabs my arm. "Okay," he says. "Here. Stop. Cut the lights and sit tight." Then he yanks the hat down over his forehead, opens the door, and pushes out into the rain.

I do what he says. With the lights off I can't see anything at all; at first I can't even see the steering wheel in my lap. I know where we are, how far we are from town, but when lightning cracks somewhere in the distance to the left, I'm too slow to catch it, and see only empty space, a field—no trees or buildings—before the blackness closes in again. Pelham's only been gone a minute or two, but it seems longer. I pull the knob that turns on the instrument lights so I can read the clock: nine-eighteen. It's ridiculous—I can't leave the poor bastard in the rain in the middle of nowhere. There's no place to turn the car around anyway; I'd have to back up the three-quarters of a mile to the highway. I feel stupid for getting into this. I start the car, snap on the lights, and punch the horn button a couple of times; he doesn't show, so I lock all four doors, then turn the engine and lights off and listen to the chatter of the rain.

Pelham knocks on my window, and I roll it down. "Come on out, kid. It's okay." He's got an umbrella—one of those oversize golf umbrellas with alternating wedges of color, red and white. "Got to get you inside, get you into some dry clothes."

"Inside what?" I say. "There isn't a place for miles. I'm leaving."

I begin to close my window, starting the car at the same time. He shouts, "Wait a minute, kid. Hold on."

"You want a ride back to town, Pelham?" He's got on different clothes—a red checked shirt under the raincoat. "I'm going."

"Sure, kid. Sure. Hold on a minute. Let me get Melba." He goes off again, and I sit there with the motor running. It's nine-thirty-seven.

Melba's a dog—coal black and the size of a small pony. When we get her into the back seat, she shakes herself off, throwing water all over the inside of the car. Pelham hammers on the passenger window; that door's still locked. "Fifty yards up, there's a drive," he says, getting into the car. "You can turn there."

I go out a lot faster than I came in, the car bouncing and sliding through the holes and the slop; when I make the highway, we head for town, driving fast. Pelham is talking to the dog, which has vanished from the rearview mirror. "I knew right where you'd be, Melba," Pelham says. "Came for you just like I said I would, didn't I?" He talks all the way. When I take the turn into the parking lot outside the restaurant too fast and slide the rear end into the back fender of somebody's white Mercedes, Pelham says, "Attaboy."

"Okay," I say, pushing the shift lever into park and turning off the engine. "Get the dog out." I go around to the back of the car to see how bad the damage is. Pelham eases the dog out of the rear seat, holds her on a tight chain, and heads for the restaurant, twirling the bright umbrella. People are lining up at the windows of the building, rubbing the glass and peering out. It looks as if my bumper is caught in the Mercedes' rear wheel well, and the tire there is flattening fast. I jump on the trunk of my car, trying to free the bumper, but the jumping doesn't do any good; the cars are hooked tight.

At the cash register inside I tell the woman what's happened and give her the Mercedes's license number.

"That's Miss Landson's car," the woman says. "You sure know how to pick 'em. Wait here and I'll get her."

I look around the restaurant. There are lots of empty tables now. Back toward the corner where I ate dinner, Pelham comes out of the kitchen carrying what must be a new bowl of soup, the huge dog right behind him.

•

Miss Landson looks twenty-five and calm, like a hippie girl who suddenly got rich. Her hair is long, straight, thin, and brown. She comes out through the swinging doors of the kitchen talking to the cashier; she's wearing Levi's and lime-yellow running shoes—Nikes, from the look of the decoration—and a denim jacket. As she passes Pelham, who's sitting at the same table playing with the soup, she taps him on the back. She extends her hand when she's still ten feet away from me. "Ericka Landson," she says. "We had a wreck?"

"Only a small wreck, but you lost a tire. I'm sure there's no problem—I mean, Allstate will take care of it."

"Maybe we ought to have a look." She smiles at me and walks toward the door. "It's still raining, I guess." The tail of the jacket is curled at the bottom in back; she doesn't seem to have a shirt on underneath. "Betsy," she says, turning to the cashier, "bring a couple of umbrellas, will you?"

"I'm sorry about this. I was going too fast coming in. It got away from me."

Ericka stands with the door slightly open, looking out into the parking lot. "I heard that. My husband tells me you were mad at him for making you go get Melba."

"Excuse me?" I heard what she said; I just need a minute to get used to the idea. "Oh, yes. Pretty dog. Big."

She laughs. "Dumb. She's afraid of the rain. That's why Warren wanted to go get her, although I don't know why he didn't drive himself." She lets the door close, then looks at her watch, which is black and digital, like an underwater watch. The cuffs of her jacket are rolled twice; she has small, masculine hands, long fingers, clear nails, no wedding ring.

"I sat with him at dinner. Your husband, I mean. Only I didn't know he was your husband."

Ericka looks across the room at Pelham. "He likes soup," she says. "Today's his birthday."

Betsy comes out of the kitchen with Pelham's red-and-white umbrella and a second, tan one. Pelham looks up as she passes him, then looks at the two of us standing inside the front door. He seems to chuckle to himself, a vague grin creeping up on one side of his face. "This is all I could find, Miss Landson. This brown one is busted. Carlos has a good umbrella, but he couldn't find it."

"Take one," Ericka says, pointing to the umbrellas. I take the tan and follow her out into the rain. Her shoulders are broad; she's a big woman but not heavy—like an athlete, a runner.

Our cars are awkwardly banged together at the edge of the now almost empty lot. A street light hanging off a telephone pole just beyond the entrance to the lot throws a ghoulish green-white light on the wet cars, and they glisten. The Mercedes is covered with thousands of mirrorlike bubbles. Ericka squats between the cars to assess the damage; the tire on her Mercedes is spread out like a pool of tar under the chromed wheel. She fingers the lug nuts as she surveys the situation.

"I tried jumping on mine, but it didn't help."

"No. It wouldn't," she says, standing. "It'll come out when we jack this one up to replace the tire. The fender's torn a little." She comes out from between the cars, fishing in a breast pocket, from which she pulls a ring of keys. "Let me check the spare. I don't want to get somebody out here if the spare's no good."

She opens the trunk of the Mercedes, then bends under the lid and flips up the carpet to get at the spare. When she closes the trunk, she looks at my car and says, "You didn't do so badly, outside of the taillight. It's Warren's fault, really—he likes intrigue."

We go back inside. She suggests I sit down at a round table near the cash register while she takes care of the cars. "I'll bring coffee in a minute," she says, heading for the kitchen. Pelham watches me strip off the raincoat, shake it lightly, and drape it over the back of a chair. When I sit down to inspect my shoes, Betsy arrives with two cups of coffee. "Miss Landson'll be out in a minute," she says. "Did you want something else? A nice dessert?"

"I don't know." I look past her at Pelham; he's working on the soup. "No. I guess I'm fine."

Betsy turns to look at Pelham too, then whispers to me, "It's his birthday today. He's a nice man—he really is. I don't think it makes any difference that he's so much older than she is."

"No," I say, nodding. "I agree with you. Thanks, Betsy."

The last diners are leaving, pushing arms into raincoats, picking up purses, straightening clothes. A small fellow in a navy chalk-stripe suit, coral shirt, and regimental tie stops alongside my table and hands Betsy a ten-dollar bill. She says, "Thank you," and folds the bill twice, then slips it under her wide patent-leather belt.

The guy turns to me. "What, you staying all night?"

I look at Betsy; she raises her eyebrows and rolls her eyes in a quick half circle. The guy looks at me as if he expects an answer.

"What's that mean? Who're you?"

Ericka slips up behind him before he has a chance to answer. "Hello, Bill," she says. "Did you enjoy dinner?"

Bill grins uncomfortably and catches up with a weak-faced woman who is waiting for him in the aisle.

Three Chicano busboys are noisily stacking dishes in spattered gray rubber trays. Betsy and two waitresses cluster around the cash register, smoking and counting the evening's receipts. Pelham has put his soup on the floor for the dog, which laps hungrily at the dish while Pelham watches, expressionless.

"You dance?" Ericka says, holding her coffee to her lips with both hands. Her eyes seem very bright.

"Not much. You?"

"Sometimes I go to this cowboy bar out on the bypass—Boots, it's called—and dance all night. I love it. It's going to take a while for the Triple A people to get here—maybe we should go out?"

"I don't think so, thanks," I say, watching Pelham and the dog. "We've got no cars."

"Oh, I've got a truck in back. Warren can stay here and take care of the accident."

"He'll love that."

"It's okay." She turns and looks over her shoulder, her elbows still planted on the table. "Hey, Warren. We're going out to Boots; you come out when the wreckers get finished, okay?"

Pelham looks up from the dog, then closes his eyes and drops his head maybe a quarter of an inch. He reaches into his coat pocket and pulls out two car keys on a thick yellow string.

"Toss it," Ericka says. He does, and she shoves her chair back, leaping off the floor to make a one-handed catch. "Come on, buzzard," she says, grabbing my arm. "I'll teach you every dance I know. Let me have your keys for Warren, so he can bring your car out."

I give her my keys, and she takes them across the room and hands them to Pelham, then squats down and cups the dog's ears. The dog stops eating long enough to look up and lick her lips, soup dropping off its black jaw. Ericka says something to Pelham, then pats his calf, and they both laugh.

I put my raincoat on. For a minute I leave the collar of the coat turned up, but then decide it looks too stupid that way, and fold it neatly down.

"Let's go, youngster," Ericka calls. "Don't be shy, now."

The truck is parked in a narrow alley in back of the restaurant; the passenger side is so close to the brick wall that I can't even squeeze between the fender and the wall, much less get into the truck. The rain has let up.

"I'm already having a good time," Ericka says. "You want to drive?"

"I don't want to go."

"Listen to the man, will you? The man's got 'Born to Bop' tattooed on his neck and he's talking about retirement. Try this side over here, Slick." She does a little two-step, opening the door for me.

•

Ericka Landson did a year at Sarah Lawrence, hated it, and went to Georgia Tech, where she took bachelor's and master's degrees in chemical engineering. She delivered the diplomas to her father on a Thursday and bought the building for her restaurant the next day. That was almost a year ago; since then her father died and left her half a million dollars in cash and three times that in land.

"So I married Warren," she says while we're sitting in the cab of the Ford Ranchero waiting for the attendant at the Sinclair station to return with her credit card. "I'd been in love with him since I was a kid. He had a lot more money than I did, so I figured I was safe."

The attendant, a boy with wet blond shoulder-length hair and giant lips, stops in back of the car to write the license number on a charge slip, then pushes the green plastic clipboard in Ericka's window. "I like this weather," he says. "Brings out the bugs. Get me plenty of food for my Gila monsters."

"I want those lizards," Ericka says. "I need them for my menu. The palates of the customers demand monster."

The boy grins messily; the grin distorts his face, drawing the lips tight over a row of brown teeth. "I believe you'd try it, too, Mrs. Landson," he says. "But they gonna come dear."

"And go dearer," Ericka says, passing the clipboard back out the window. "We'll call them Bobby Murtaugh's Gila Flambé—how's that sound?"

"Put a little spinach around the edges too, huh? I love spinach." He tears her carbon of the slip from between his copy and the company's copy and hands her the tissuey sheet. "And some melon balls, all different colors."

"We'll leave the heads on. Let the customers see what they eat."

"They gonna have to pay, though," Bobby Murtaugh says. "Gilas ain't easy to copulate, know what I mean?"

Ericka starts the engine, then holds up her hand in a stiff salute. "Amen. Things is tough all over. Thanks, Bobby."

The kid takes a step back and watches us pull out; when we get to the edge of his station, I turn around and see him crawling around the pump island, hunting for bugs.

The highway heading out of town is the same one Pelham had me on earlier, but the thunderstorms have moved off to the east, where they sit like huge colored cliffs, made visible by the diffused lightning. The rain is so spare we drive with the Ranchero windows open. "I don't feel like dancing," she says after we've listened to the tires on the wet road for a while. "I dance all the time. Dancing makes me sick to my stomach." She turns to look at me in the headlights of a passing truck. "This isn't routine. I made it sound routine, but it isn't."

I shrug, then put my right arm out the window parallel to the ground, palm flat, and play that kid's game of flying the hand as if it were the wing of an airplane.

"Sometimes I hate it out here," Ericka says. "Living out here away from everything." She puts her hand out the window and does the same thing I'm doing, makes the hand swoop and dip in the air by slight twists of her wrist. "Warren helps."

One headlight of the Ranchero is out of whack, aimed upward and off to the side, and as we slip down the highway the light glitters on the telephone wires.

"He reads everything," she says. "He gets papers from all over the country and reads them; he reads books all the time; he subscribes to forty-seven magazines. When he goes to Houston, we have to buy new luggage to bring back all the stuff he buys. He's got three computers at the house—three. You'd think one would be enough."

"More than I've got."

"Ask him for one, he'll give it to you. They're a lot of fun at first." She slows the truck and points out the window at a clay road cutting out into the field on my side of the highway. "That's where you were earlier, when you came to get Melba. Warren has a trailer out there in the woods. We live back toward town."

"How long will it take to untangle the cars? I mean, maybe we should turn around here somewhere?"

"I don't know your name—what's your name?"

"Harold Ohls."

"What are you, French?" There's a Union 76 station ahead, and Ericka slows as we get near. The place is a diner too—white wood siding and a big horizontal window like a lozenge. One of the rounded pieces of glass is badly cracked; struts of two-inch tape have been stuck on to hold it together. "Let's get something inside before we go back, okay?"

Ericka orders chicken-fried steak, cream gravy, mashed potatoes, green peas, toast, and iced tea, then looks up from the greasy vinyl-sleeved menu. "What about you?" I order Coke and lemon pie, then nod agreeably when she says, "I always eat late. Want me to put something on the jukebox?"

The waitress, a pudgy woman wearing a purple satin-look bowling shirt with "GlueSlingers" in gold script across the back, gives Ericka a handful of quarters in exchange for some bills and disappears through the swinging door into the kitchen. Ericka pushes the coins into the jukebox, then hovers over the selections, pressing big colored buttons. By the time she gets back to the table, the room is filled with rock and roll. "The original Doctor Funkenstein," she says. "You like it?"

The diner is no bigger than a single-car garage; all three tables have red linoleum tops with rippled-chrome strips wrapped around the edges. The chairs don't match the tables or each other, except that everything in the room seems to have pitted tubular-chrome legs.

"What's Pelham going to do when he gets to that place and we're missing?" I ask, leaning back so the waitress can deposit my pie, which is perched on thick restaurant china with cordovan triangles in a circle around the rim.

"Warren won't go to Boots—he never does. He'll just go to the house and wait. He's long-suffering—remember that word? He didn't want to marry me, but he'll kill you if you hurt me."

My fork is wrapped tight in a paper napkin. "That's funny. Is he going to kill you if you hurt me?"

"Eat your pie, why don't you?"

"Happily," I say, pulling the fork out the end of the rolled napkin. One of the tines is missing. I show this to Ericka and then start on the pie. "We're not doing so well, are we?"

"We're not supposed to," she says. "How is it?"

"Pretty good. You want some?"

"Dessert is later." She grabs my free hand and yanks it across the table, then pins it to the red linoleum and bends over to inspect the fingernails. "These are a mess. I can clean them up if you want me to."

"Maybe later."

Her food arrives on a brown oval plate with portion dividers; the dirty-whitish gravy has been liberally applied so that it seeps from one section to the next in an uninterrupted flow. Ericka starts with the toast, plunging the corner of the first piece into the thick pool on top of the potatoes. I finish the pie and then watch her eat. She asks a couple of questions—what do I do, where was I born?—but then she loses interest and concentrates on the food. We go through the rest of the dinner in silence. I'm tired.

"Now," she says, when she's finished. "Now we dance." She tears a couple of napkins trying to get a whole one out of the chrome-faced dispenser screwed to the table just under the window.

"Please—no dancing tonight, okay? Tonight let's go home."

She unbuttons one of the pockets of her denim jacket and brings out a five-dollar bill. She puts the money on the table and gets up. "No dancing?" she says, affecting a hurt expression. "You seem like kind of a drip, Harold."

"Thanks."

In the car she says, "We'll have cake with Warren and then you can go, okay?"

•

The house is modern, white as ice and lit up like a circus. My car is parked in the U-shaped drive next to the Mercedes. Warren is inside watching a bank of three Sonys; he's wearing a black silk robe with scarlet piping, and under that he's got on green pajamas. Melba is asleep beside his chair. "You have fun?" he asks his wife.

"We decided to have cake," she says. "You need cake."

"What's on?" I ask, motioning toward the televisions.

"A movie, Tom Snyder, and *Love Boat*."

"I got the truck filled up," Ericka says. "Harold didn't have such a great time. We went out to the diner. I don't think he knows what's going on." She sits on the arm of Pelham's chair, facing the televisions. She rubs the back of the dog's neck.

"We don't have any problems," he says. "That's easy enough. Slinky's looking for a companion because I wear out fast."

"Me too," I say. "Sorry."

"I'll get the cake," Ericka says, heading for the kitchen. "I made it myself, Harold. It's really good."

"Her aunt made it. I've had it before," Pelham says when Ericka's out of the room. "It's pitiful-looking."

I laugh sympathetically. "What about the cars? How're we going to work that out?"

"Don't worry about the cars."

"I won't if you'll send me something I can give the insurance guy."

"Yeah, well," Pelham says, waving at the sofa, "it just isn't necessary. What you're supposed to do is distract Slinky, but I don't guess you're going to."

I drop my raincoat over a ladder-back chair near the door, then take a seat at one end of the sofa. We sit there in silence watching the televisions. All three of them have the sound on, so that what we hear is a garbled, random mix of talk and music. Pelham pets the dog and looks from one screen to the next, his eyes shifting from left to right with habitual precision. Then all three stations start commercials at the same time—a Pepsi ad, a car ad, and an ad for perfume—and all three look the same: dramatic silvery colors, surreal spaces, glittering sexy women. "Look at that," I say, pointing.

"I know," Pelham says, without turning around. "Good."

Ericka comes back into the room carrying a tray on which is a large flat cake stuck full of lighted candles. The icing is sherbety orange. She puts the tray on the coffee table and starts to sing "Happy Birthday," gesturing for me to join in. I'm embarrassed, but I sing along. Pelham hangs on to his composure for a minute, then grins and starts singing. When we finish the chorus, Ericka starts it again, and everybody sings loud this time, complete with conductor's gestures, vibrato, and three-part homemade harmony. The singing wakes Melba, who yawns and shakes, then steps up to the coffee table waving her big tail and rips a four-inch hole in the cake's fruity icing.

(1981)

TORCH STREET

Vicky and Roswell were in his stepfather's living room in the house on Torch Street in Bay St. Louis, Mississippi, three blocks from the water. If they went out into the street and leaned over and looked real hard, they could see a little thumbnail of Gulf under the heavy arch of the trees. Vicky had just come in. Roswell was stretched out on the shiny green velour sofa.

"What are you watching?" she said.

"I'm not watching anything," he said.

"You appear to be watching this television over here," she said.

"Be that as it may," he said. He had on jeans, rubber sandals, a white T-shirt, and was on his stomach on the couch. She had come home on her motorbike and looked a little windblown. She wore a seersucker shirt and carried a comically big crash helmet covered with gaudy purple graphics. She stood inside the front door, the helmet dangling from her hand, and stared at the television which was showing a picture of some airplanes, some old passenger airplanes, with an inset picture of some furry animal crawling around the rocks near a stream. Roswell was clicking up still pictures from the other channels on two sides of the screen.

"How many eyes you got?" she asked.

"Forty," he said. His voice was muffled—he was talking into the pillow.

"Where's Jack, anyway?" she said. She took a couple of steps and sat down on the arm of the sofa. Roswell jerked his feet out of her way.

"Went for chicken," Roswell said.

"Great," Vicky said. "It's going to rain."

It was dark in the living room. The blinds were three-quarters closed and the skies outside were overcast, so there wasn't much light. The TV color looked aggravated by having all the stills frozen on the screen. There were pictures of police, weather maps, people hunting for something in a field, an irate short man with bristly hair, a senator from somewhere. The window air conditioner rattled and hummed, stuffing the bungalow with damp, cool air.

Jack was the stepfather. The three of them had lived in the house on Torch Street for six months. Before that, Jack was there alone. Roswell had an apartment in a scummy complex down by the fishery where everything smelled of bad shrimp. He'd run out of money and asked if he could stay at the house. Jack agreed—he was happy to have the company. Then Jack met Vicky and brought her home from the casino where they both worked. It was a date for them, a little barbecue, but it went wrong right away. Roswell and Vicky hit it off, and Jack *was* older, was dreaming, and he knew it.

"You're a void," Vicky said, spinning the helmet into the air as if it were a football. She caught it heading for the kitchen.

"Throw me some chips or something," Roswell said. He was flicking the picture-in-picture back and forth, so he was picking up sound from different shows. On the mammal show he caught somebody saying, "Beaver lodge, my home . . . not only my home, but the home of my beaver people . . ."

He repeated that a couple times.

"What?" Vicky said from the kitchen. "No chips."

"What've you got?" he said.

She stood in front of the cabinet, one hand on each of the cabinet door knobs. "Oreos, gum, animal crackers—*the endangered collection*—Crazy Dough, Twizzlers."

"Oreos," he said. The air conditioner, a fat old brown Fedders with a dusty grille in the dining room window, did a triple clunk and cut off with a hissing sound. Vicky half shut one of the doors and looked into the dining room at the air conditioner.

"Is that thing okay?" she said.

"It's older than you are," Roswell said.

"Got gas," she said. She grabbed the crackly bag of Oreos, stripped off the rubber band, took a cookie out and ate it as she carried the bag back to Roswell. "I think we ought to get married maybe. Move out of here."

"Too young," he said.

"Who?" she said.

"All of us," he said.

The room was dark and cluttered. Big furniture and heavy drapes, green to match the couch. Heavy chairs and a big sideboard and a couple of dark mahogany dining chairs put in the corner to keep them out of the way. The carpet was thick and musty and old. When you walked on it, you could hear the aching floor underneath. A thin stream of light cut in between the blinds of one of the windows, suddenly brightening the room. Gritty little dust circled in the light that cut the room.

"This room is glowing," Vicky said. "Like those paintings where the guy has the candle, you know? Like the picture is glowing from inside?"

"It's me," Roswell said.

"Give me another cookie," she said, reaching down to get one out of the bag. "I'm going to be twenty-two pretty soon."

"Yeah, and I'm going to be a hair technician for Al Sharpton," he said.

"Isn't he dead yet?" she said. She swiveled toward the television set, sat down on the floor with her back against the sofa.

"In the way," he said.

"You weren't watching," she said.

"I started watching after you came," he said.

"Did not," she said.

He shoved her aside by the shoulder. Her hair was red, short, kind of hacked off on one side. The neck was pale and thin. She wore glasses with black rims.

"Is Jack going to support us forever?" she said. She was gnawing the icing off half an Oreo.

"If we're lucky," Roswell said.

"He loves me more than life itself," she said.

"Mean," Roswell said. "You're a fresh young thing. You've got the natural charm. Everybody loves you. I don't know who doesn't love you."

"We could find somebody if we looked hard," she said. "Darrin." Darrin was her last boyfriend.

"He doesn't count," Roswell said. "He's the one before the present one, if you know what I mean."

"Lies," Vicky said.

Jack came in with a fifteen-piece box of Popeye's, a quart of mashed potatoes, a quart of coleslaw, a pint of gravy, and nine biscuits. He was a chunky guy, an ex-beat cop from Chicago who had moved to the coast years before when he had married Roswell's mother. The mother had inherited a gas station on the beach highway. She and Jack worked it day and night, made plenty. When the marriage blew up, she got everything. He had to start a new career, so he started dealing blackjack at the Bubble Casino in Gulfport, for $6 an hour and tips. He'd worked the graveyard shift for a year and a half, but now he was working swing. Usually eight to four. He was used to eating dinner early. Roswell's mother had moved to Arizona.

"How you doing, Vicky?" Jack said, dusting his fingers over her hair as he went into the dining room and put the food on the table.

"Never better," she said. She got up and followed him and started unpacking the dinner, setting the table with paper towels for place mats and other paper towels folded into napkins.

"How's young Lochinvar over there?" Jack said.

"He's great," Roswell said.

"He watching the beaver show," Vicky said. "And fifteen others."

Roswell said, "Not only my home, but the home of my beaver people . . ."

"Beavers," his stepfather said. "Check."

He was already half in casino uniform—black slacks, black shoes, white tux shirt. He didn't have the suspenders or his red tie—he kept those in the car. Dealing wasn't bad, especially in Mississippi, where things didn't cost much. He'd bought the house after the divorce for under a hundred grand, complete with furniture, and he hadn't touched a hair on its head. An old woman had died in the house. At first Jack acted as if that scared him, but he gave it up. He was a decent-looking guy, a little haggard maybe, with black hair that stayed combed whether he liked it or not, ruddy complexion, rough skin, the smell of cologne. And good-looking hands–he had his hands done once a week at a salon. It wasn't required, but when he was in blackjack school, they'd given him a list of places.

He brought two bottles of beer out of the kitchen and put them alongside the paper-towel place mat Vicky had made for him at the head of the table.

"Well, come on," he said. "I'm not waiting all day."

She brought the strawberry preserves and sat down with him. Roswell didn't move much.

"I like it cold," Roswell said.

"He would, wouldn't he?" Jack said to Vicky.

"He loves you a lot," she said, patting Jack's forearm. She had one leg folded under her and she sat up a little bit and leaned over the table so she could see into the box of chicken. "You want breast or thigh?"

"One each," Jack said.

She fished chicken parts out of the box and dropped them on Jack's plate. They used high quality paper plates—Chinet brand.

"He's never getting off the couch, is he?" Jack said.

"Not since I got here," Vicky said.

"At least it's not MTV," Jack said.

"Lost to the pan," Roswell said. He groaned and rolled off the couch, landing on his knees by the coffee table. Then he came in and took a drumstick out of the box and began eating it as he stood by the table, looking at the big Fedders. "We may be getting married."

"Uh huh," Jack said.

"I'm sort of serious," Roswell said.

"You are?" Vicky asked.

"Yeah, kind of," he said.

"We've been thinking about it," she said to Jack.

"Fine with me," he said. "Where you all gonna live?"

"Here, if it's okay," she said. She looked at Jack, then Roswell. "I don't think anything has to change. Do you, Roswell?"

"Don't know," Roswell said.

"I'm worried about change," Jack said. "I don't like it. And I like you here anyway. I want you to stay."

"It'll be fine," Roswell said.

"Are you going to have a baby?" Jack said.

She laughed and snapped his cuff down over his wrist. "Nope. No babies," she said. "Never a baby. There are enough already."

"Too many," Roswell said. "People buy and sell 'em."

"Oh, hush," Vicky said.

"It's in the papers all the time," he said.

"How would you know? You never read," she said.

"So maybe it's on television. I've *seen* it. Rich people want babies but they only buy this certain kind and they go black market in Atlanta or someplace."

"Lots of babies in orphanages," Vicky said.

"We could become big suppliers," Roswell said.

"Well, keep it down in there," Jack said. He had a little hooked piece of fried chicken skin caught on the side of his lip.

"I might want to get a dog," Vicky said.

"Oh yeah?" Jack said.

"Sure," she said. "A big dog, something you could play with and walk around with and do stuff. Labrador. Yellow."

"Cost you ten hundred to get a good one," Roswell said.

After Jack left for work, Vicky and Roswell got on her scooter and rode out Menge Avenue to Lake Forgetful, a couple miles inland. It was a tiny pond, really, maybe three, four acres, with a trailer park built around one end. There was a visitors' parking area with room enough for six cars on the road leading up to the trailer park. That's where Roswell put the scooter. There were ducks on the water, and a few lights in the tall pine trees that surrounded the lake which, in the dark, looked bigger than it really was. They walked arm-in-arm around the water in one direction, then turned and walked around in the other direction. They were kids, young lovers, just happy to be touching each other, to have their bodies colliding, to have their hips bumping into each other. She flattened her hand into the back pocket of his jeans. He felt the curve of her waist beneath the thin seersucker shirt. She was wearing a burgundy bra underneath.

"Why do that? That shirt that bra?" he asked.

"I'm not trying to hide anything," she said.

"I'll say," he said. "You don't think it's a little—obvious?"

"I'd have to wear it on my forehead," she said. "In the world today." She swung around in front of him, walked backward, matching her steps to his. She held her arms out as if to showcase the bra, then said, "You know, sometimes I just want to kiss you for ages. We could be joined at the mouth. Wouldn't that be great?"

"We'd get a workout," he said.

She stopped and waited for him to catch her, then put a finger on his chin. "Make your lips soft," she said. "I want to kiss you."

"They're already soft," he said.

A moon was sliding up behind the pines. It filled the clearing over the lake with vanilla light. Cars fizzed by on the highway. There was some dinky music coming from the trailer park. Pine needles everywhere.

"What if we lived up here?" Vicky said. "We could have a place of our own. I bet these things cost next to nothing."

"They cost plenty," he said.

"I wouldn't mind having a baby," she said. "It would be like having a talking dog."

"Not as sturdy," Roswell said. "Two legs. And they got brains. Say the wrong thing it drives 'em crazy. They grow up maniacs."

An owl hooted in a tree somewhere. Leaves rustled. The water lapped uncertainly at the edge of the lake. Lights winked on and off in the trailer park. Somebody came out and a screen door slammed. People were laughing, coming toward them.

"Babies don't have much hair," Vicky said. "Wrong kind, too. There's somebody coming here." She pointed behind them, toward the trailer park. They stopped and turned around and looked toward the sounds. They were almost directly across the water from the trailers. Two figures came out of the pines, out of the darkness, and stood at the lake's edge, laughing.

One of them said, "Why is heroin better than a woman?"

The other one said, "Huh?"

"Why is heroin better than a woman?" the first one said.

The second one laughed. Then with a rush, they heard one of the men pissing into the water, then the other one started.

"So that's how they do it," Vicky said in a whisper.

"Shh," Roswell said.

"What's the answer?" the first guy said.

"I don't know. I give up," the second guy said.

They both laughed some more and finished up and started back for the trailers.

"Ah, you guys," Vicky whispered. "C'mon. What is it? What's the answer?"

When the men were gone, Vicky and Roswell skirted the end of the lake, crunching through the noisy grass. When they got to the parking spot, Vicky made an elaborate business of getting into her helmet—she smacked herself a couple of times in the head, readjusted the chin strap, grabbed the helmet with both hands and wiggled it until she was comfortable. She looked ready for space travel.

"I'm driving," she said, swinging a leg over the seat.

"Fine for me," Roswell said.

She kicked the scooter's engine to life and twisted the thing around, settling on the seat and bouncing. He got on the back and they shot out from under the high pines, away from Lake Forgetful. They went back into town and rode the beach highway toward home, Roswell with his arms around her tiny waist. She was singing as she drove. There was a lot of wind. Sleek and mysterious cars zoomed by them. Lights sparkled out over the Gulf. He kissed the back of her flashy helmet, sure that she would never know.

(1996)

EXOTIC NILE

The water was running in the tub and I had Theo on the telephone when Dewey Nassar appeared outside my door waving a plastic bag with a four-inch goldfish in it. This was a blue goldfish. Nassar was my landlord at the Nile, a thin fellow with no black hair on top of his head but plenty around the sides. I told Theo I'd call her back and turned off the water in the bath.

"Let's get him into something where he can breathe," Nassar said, jiggling the fish at me. We dug through the boxes of kitchen equipment. "How about this?" He peeled newspaper off a white mixing bowl. "This is Theo's, right?"

Nassar liked her because she used to clip Egypt stories out of newspapers and magazines for him. He was crazy about Egypt. When she and I separated, he was upset, and he never missed a chance to remind me that his life too had been impoverished by her departure.

The day after she left, she sent some people to take the furniture. All of it. Left me with a studio apartment, the crockery, and four table legs that belonged to my father. They were wonderful legs— Aalto, I think—but that hadn't been our arrangement. I liked Theo and I didn't care much about furniture, so I bought a bed and two lawn chairs, and a tripod lamp, and made do.

"No more cakes, huh?" Nassar flattened his hand and swam it around inside the bowl. "Plenty of room."

"Keep looking," I said.

We finally settled on a quart orange-juice bottle, but the fish didn't quite fit. It had to swim at a sixty-degree angle to keep from hitting the glass. "Looks a little cramped in there," Nassar said. "I'll get you an aquarium tomorrow." He tilted the bottle so the fish could straighten out. "Make this a happy fish."

The fish was gulping and staring at us through the bottle.

The Nile was thirty apartments bunched around a small courtyard. Nassar had built the complex in 1953 after a trip to Cairo with his mother—designed it all himself, right down to the camels in the peach stucco and the carnival-striped awnings. The courtyard featured rock flower beds, a kidney-style pool, three pyramid doghouses, one each in red, blue, and yellow, and palms—skinny, wretched looking things nine feet tall, with bits of growth at their tops. At one end he'd put a fountain shaped like a crescent moon. The water shot out of a green boat that was supposed to look as if it was flying out of this fountain. He'd put a life-size papier-mâché steer next to the pool and hand-lettered O-F-F-I-C-E on its side, with an arrow pointing toward his door. And at night, every night, colored floodlamps lit the buildings of the Nile.

He stood at one of my two sliding glass doors, looking out into the court. "I wanted a real cow," he said. "Wouldn't that have been something? Theo would've loved that."

"Thanks for the fish," I said.

The next afternoon I went to the university library and got the new Dick Francis book. I'd been reading more since Theo left. On the steps outside the library I bumped into Nassar's wife, Mariana. She was using the pay telephone. She was wearing a short-sleeved shirt with pink and blue triangles all over it—the kind of shirt young girls find in thrift shops—and it looked good on her.

"My fault," I said. "Pardon me."

She put her palm over the mouthpiece. "Thanks for the rubdown, Buster."

"Absolutely an accident," I said.

"I believe you," she said. She was smiling, laughing a little. "Really. So get lost, okay?"

Nassar was parked three cars down from mine, sitting in his Toyota truck with his windows up. He had on clear-rimmed dark glasses, and he was toying with his newly grown pencil mustache. He too was talking on a telephone, a white one with a curled cord stretching toward his dashboard.

I started my car and then sat for a minute watching his wife. I didn't know her well at all. She and Theo had gone running a few times, and when they finished they'd come into the apartment for water. Sometimes in summer they sat by the pool together. I'd gotten the impression that Mariana thought I was silly, but there wasn't any evidence that that's what she thought.

Nassar rapped on my passenger-side window. He did it with his ring, so the noise was annoyingly sharp. "Hey," he said, twirling his forefinger next to his ear and then pointing toward his wife. "She's nuts. She made her hair red."

"It's very pretty," I said, turning the window crank.

He wore a yellow-and-black plaid shirt, and his face was an almost perfect oval, the wrong shape for the mustache. He tucked his head in the window and glanced around at my car. "Clean," he said. His wife had hung up and was walking toward the library entrance.

"Thanks."

"You busy? Want to take a ride?" He popped up my door lock with a thick finger. "I gotta get back before dark, though."

"I don't know," I said. I let the car roll back a little, but he opened the door, so I braked.

"Sure you do," he said. He grinned and stepped into the front seat. His boots were too big, laced up in front almost to the knee, with his pants legs pushed inside. He drummed on the glove-compartment door with the nails of his fingers. "You looking for Theo?"

"Hunting a book," I said. Theo worked at the university, but I hadn't seen her, hadn't gone looking for her. She was living with her new boyfriend at another of Nassar's properties. I'd been to her apartment a couple of times, but I hadn't met the boyfriend. In fact, I'd seen Theo only a few times, maybe half a dozen, since we split.

At the highway intersection we stopped behind a Cadillac. "A book," Nassar said. "A book. That's what I figured. I just got this new phone in my truck. I was trying it out."

"So I saw," I said. "You were talking to Mariana."

"Right. But she didn't say anything. She said you bumped into her." We got caught at the light again and then watched a fire engine go by. He said, "How about that? Must be a fire. Let's take a look, huh?" He banged me on the arm with the back of his hand, then pointed after the truck.

"Chase the truck," I said. I swung into the turn lane.

"Might be headed for one of mine," he said. "Blue Gardens, out beyond the loop."

I made the turn and then got sandwiched between a rental van and a four-door Mercury on the highway.

"Hit this dude with your horn," he said.

I poked the horn stalk a couple of times and watched the Mercury's turn signal come on, blinking slowly as if the car had some electrical problem. The fire truck was gone when we got past.

"Doesn't matter," he said. "Let's go to Howard Johnson's. Unless you've got a major date."

The road was new, smooth blacktop. A bright-green gully separated the in and out lanes, and the amber lights must have just come on. Damp air swirled through the car, tossing some papers around in the back. I let up on the accelerator. Nassar twisted around and reached over the seat.

"I'll handle it. You drive," he said. "Past the light and make a U." He sat up and hit me on the shoulder. "Get you a waffle. You've got waffle written all over you. How's my fish doing?"

"Great," I said.

The motel was on top of a small cliff overlooking the freeway. Nassar pointed to a blue-lined handicapped-parking zone by the front door. "Take that one."

The lobby smelled bad. A kid in a white short-sleeved shirt and a solid-black tie asked us if we had reservations.

"This is Ramone," Nassar said, pointing to the kid. "Ramone, this is my favorite tenant, Mr. Leaf."

"Sure," the kid said, tipping an imaginary hat.

The restaurant was large and empty. The chairs were studded with big black-headed furniture tacks. Nassar took a booth by the window, but a pretty teenager came out of the kitchen and told him to move because she wasn't serving that station. The girl had rough skin, blue eyes, and freckles. Her hair, which fell to her waist in back, was the color of boot leather. "Didn't you see the sign?" she said.

Then she realized there wasn't any sign. "There's supposed to be a sign over here." She walked toward the table. "Says 'Section Closed' or something. You know the sign I'm talking about?"

"We missed it," Nassar said. He got out of the booth. "Which section's open?"

"Depends what you want," the girl said. "I mean, you want a meal, you're out of luck. Coffee, maybe a piece of pie. I guess you could sit anywhere. Except here—this is closed." She stuck a knee on the seat of a booth two down from ours and leaned close to the window for a look outside. "This must be the winter," she said.

"My wife's baby sister Lorraine," he said, gesturing toward the waitress. She turned around and smiled, and he said, "Two coffees, and a waffle for Mr. Leaf."

"Got no waffles," she said, smiling at me.

I smiled back at her. She looked a lot like Mariana, only younger, fresher. "Hi," I said. "How about pie?"

Nassar pointed across the room. "We're going to sit over here at the counter."

"Takeouts," she said. She wiped at the tabletop with a brown rag she was carrying, and then straightened and came back toward our booth. "Hey," she said. "What the heck. Go on in the booth. Just don't make a mess."

"Okay," Nassar said, sitting again.

She did our table with the rag, bumping the sugar bowl and the salt and pepper shakers out of the way. "Now, on the pie"— she turned to look at the glass-fronted cooler behind the takeout counter—"I know I've got lemon, and there's a new thing, raisin delight or something. Does that make sense?"

"Well, pie's pretty messy," Nassar said.

"Naw, pie's fine. But these two aren't real good. Even the show-boats won't eat 'em." She sighed and slapped the rag at the back of my seat. "We get these guys, you know? Black hair and all that, pointy shoes in ice-cream colors, and they're real polite for about ten minutes, and then bang, they're on you like some kind of squid." She started for the kitchen but stopped halfway across the room to get a ketchup packet off the floor. "See what I mean?" she said, waving the packet at us.

Outside, the motel's sign was blinking, and the sky behind it was the color of pewter. Lorraine's radio was playing "Hotel California," and through the slit into the kitchen I saw her dancing. A fat fellow in red checkered pants peered into the restaurant. He was bald, with a black beard trimmed very close to his skin.

"I sure don't like the look of that moose," Nassar said.

Lorraine brought the coffee. "Ardith's late," she said. "I guess that's why you came, huh? She may not even be on tonight. I'll have to check the schedule. Actually, I'm not on, either. I was on this afternoon."

"She thinks I'm in love with her friend Ardith," Nassar said. He got out of the booth and took Lorraine's arm, and they went across the room. I heard them talking, but I couldn't make out what was being said. Then Lorraine disappeared into the kitchen, and he came back to the table grinning. "Well, Mr. Leaf, we're going to the bay."

"We are?"

"Yeah. The Wet Club—you know that place?"

When I shook my head, he said, "It's terrific, really. Lorraine wants to eat. It's only twenty minutes." He smacked me on the biceps and wagged his head toward the kitchen. "She's driving. Don't worry. We can get your car on the way back. She's got a convertible."

"I don't think so," I said. I yawned and stretched. Then I yawned again. "I think I'll go home, take a rest. Thanks anyway."

"Aw, come on. You've got to eat, don't you?" He raised an eyebrow and pointed toward the kitchen with his head. "She's young, but she's not that young. And she likes you."

"She does?" I said. I punched him in the arm. "That makes all the difference in the world, doesn't it? Tell me how you manage to be a sicko and be charming at the same time."

"Breeding," he said.

Lorraine came through the kitchen doors smoothing the skirt of her black uniform. She stopped for a minute at the cash register, then came across the room and dropped a set of car keys into Nassar's hand. "You get him?"

"Hard to say," Nassar said. "I think he wants to go home."

"Oh, don't be such a bozo," she said, linking her arm through mine. "It isn't that far. I want you to come."

"Tell him please," Nassar said.

We went back through town in Lorraine's convertible with the radio too loud and the top down. We had to shout to talk. "Dewey says I look like a hippie," Lorraine said. "Do you think so?"

"You aren't old enough," I said.

"I know. I've seen pictures, you know—magazine articles."

I nodded and tried to keep her hair out of my face.

"He just says it because I wear a lot of tank tops in the summer."

Nassar was low behind the wheel, playing with his mustache. He caught me looking and winked. Lorraine turned around and yelled something into his ear, and he grinned and gave her a hard squeeze on the thigh. Then she was back at me, her breath warm on my ear. She made me nervous, and I think she knew it. I liked that about her, the way she played.

Nassar was doing seventy-five and Lorraine's hair kept slapping around. Finally she pulled both hands back over her forehead and twisted the hair into a roll that she brought over her shoulder and held up in front of her to look at. "I probably ought to get rid of this," she yelled.

We went through a little town with shiny dark bushes and soft-looking lawns. Even the buildings looked good, because of the copper light. Then we were back on the highway, which was lined with billboards, property-sale signs, barbed-wire fences. No trees. At intervals along the road there were brick houses that looked as if they ought to be in subdivisions. I wondered how it would feel to live out there, with the highway and the big electrical towers.

"I love it," Lorraine yelled into my ear. She pointed her hair toward the scenery. "Makes me feel romantic." She put an arm around my shoulder and pulled me toward her. "Are you married?"

"I was. Not anymore."

"You probably liked it."

I smiled at her and at Nassar, who was just then looking in our direction. "I'm afraid so," I said.

We passed a shopping plaza—a mall and a dozen smaller buildings scattered across acres of new black parking lot. A theatre marquee in one corner of the lot read "BRING 'EM BACK ALIVE FILM FESTIVAL."

"That's really wonderful," she said. "To say that. About being married, I mean." She looked toward the shopping center and at me again, then wiped a thin curve of hair off the side of her face and started playing with the radio.

By the time we reached the bay exit, the sun was gone and the juke joints had their signs on—the Hi Hat Club, the Green Parrot, Topper's, Redfish & Candy's, the Surf Café. The oyster-shell parking lots were jammed with trucks. The air was salty. There was the smell of rotting fish around. As we got closer to the bay, there were more joints, bars, fish camps. The gas stations were selling live bait and cane poles. Horns honked and cars whistled by with riders sticking out windows waving beer cans and shouting obscenities at people in front and back. There was radio music all around us—a couple of the cars had loudspeakers mounted in their grilles. A place called the Heron had a covey of white neon birds flapping across its roof.

We were moving very slowly, stopping and starting in the traffic. "So, do you like me?" Lorraine said.

Nassar bent forward over the steering wheel and nodded at me. In the open bed of the truck in front of us a huge spotted dog licked at some kind of bone between its crossed paws.

"I do," I said.

We followed the truck over a wood-planked bridge, then turned onto a gravel road. For two or three blocks we plowed through gravel that felt a foot deep. There was thunder off in the distance. The sides of the narrow road were lined with boxy houses built on telephone-pole pilings. It was very dark. Behind us the hump of the bridge was silhouetted by tavern lights. In front, the car lights hit chrome bumpers, bike reflectors, and the gold eyes of a cat that looked and then vanished.

Nassar put up the top. It made a whirring noise. The car's engine barely idled as we crunched forward. He latched the top and then pushed buttons on the armest to raise the windows, and we were sealed in.

"I'm real glad you like me," Lorraine said.

I combed my hair with my fingers and then pressed my palms over my ears. "I can't hear anything."

"Don't be silly," she said.

"You're dead, pal," Nassar said.

Lorraine frowned at him. "Be quiet, Dewey." She rubbed my shoulder where she'd stuck her finger earlier, when she was telling me about the tank tops. "We're almost there." There was a line of what looked like Christmas decorations a couple of hundred yards ahead. We crossed a narrow bridge with no railing.

"What's over here?" I asked, waving to our left where it was pitch black except for one blue bulb dangling under a corrugated-tin shed.

"Inlet," Nassar said.

Lorraine looked. "You can't even see it." She tried the radio buttons one after the other and got static and an ad for True Value Hardware. She clicked off the radio. "I love new guys. I mean, look at how nice you're being."

"I am being nice," I said. I looked out my window at a man in leather shorts who was washing his under-arms using a spigot next to the road. "But I'm having a good time. You're really strange."

"Me?" she said.

The Christmas lights were Japanese lanterns hung over a makeshift walk running from a building down to a pier. There were a lot of bugs.

Nassar twirled the steering wheel, and the car bucked up an embankment that served as a parking lot for the restaurant. We got out. There was a wind coming off the Gulf, and there were metal things banging, a boat motor, the sound of ropes straining.

From the boardwalk the restaurant looked like a milk plant or some other factory built in the forties. It had a fresh coat of white-wash. The walls facing the bay were clear glass block.

"Are you hungry yet?" Lorraine said. She wrapped both arms around my waist and steered me toward the building.

"Not a bad joint," Nassar said.

"Lemme take a look at you," she said, squeezing my waist. She stopped on the boardwalk, then stepped in front of me, fingering my shirt but talking to Nassar. "You know, Mariana's crazy," she said. "He's just a regular guy." She started walking again, bouncing down the boardwalk toward the restaurant. The paper lanterns were jerking in the wind, making a rattling noise. I held the door and Lorraine ducked under my arm.

Nassar said, "There's this piece of furniture in here I want to show you. A highboy. Red lacquer, and paws for drawer handles, animal paws, bells all over it. Has a hydraulic system, so if you even touch it the thing floats away, tinkling."

"Sounds terrific," I said.

We got a round table next to the window, and Lorraine started reading the menu out loud.

"It's a fantastic deal," Nassar said. He looked toward the rear of the restaurant. "Used to be right back there." He shook out his white cotton napkin and tucked it into the neck of his lumberjack shirt.

I looked over my shoulder. "I don't see it. Is this the Wet Club?"

"The what club?" Lorraine said. "This is Red Head Boars." She flapped her menu at me so I could read the name.

"There ain't no Wet Club," Nassar said. "I made that up."

"That's the kind of guy he is," Lorraine said. She didn't look out from behind her menu. "Just makes up stuff all the time. What's a wet club?"

"Boy, what a low-brain," Nassar said, pointing at her. "Where'd we get this low-brain, anyway?"

"Mariana's got school tonight is where you got me," she said. "That's how come we can do all this."

Nassar stretched across the table and clapped a hand over my wrist. "We're taking you out to dinner, okay? Because we honestly like you. Mariana would be with us but she's at school, she's not here. You following this? The only people here are the three of us. You and me and Lorraine."

"I've got it," I said.

"See," Nassar said. He opened his hand toward Lorraine as if introducing her. "Angel of mercy."

"Pleased to meet you," I said. I swept my menu off the table, opening it with a flourish that rocked my empty wineglass. Lorraine caught the glass before it hit the table. "Thank you," I said.

"We'll just get the girl a snack," Nassar said. "Then speed by the blimp ruins on the way home. You know about the blimp ruins? Out past the Air Force base? It's crazy out there at night."

(1983)

SHOPGIRLS

You watch the pretty salesgirl slide a box of Halston soap onto a low shelf, watch her braid slip off her shoulder, watch like an adolescent as the vent at the neck of her blouse opens slightly—she is twenty, maybe twenty-two, tan, and greatly freckled. She wears a dark blue V-neck blouse without a collar, and her skirt is white cotton, calf length, slit up the right side to a point just beneath her thigh. Her hair, a soft blonde, is pulled straight and close to the scalp, woven at the back into a single thick strand. In the fluorescent light of the display cabinet her eye shadow shines.

She catches you staring and gives you a perfunctory but knowing smile, and you turn quickly to study the purses on the chrome rack next to where you stand. You are embarrassed. You open a large red purse from the rack and stick your hand inside, pretending to inspect the lining. Then you lift the purse to your face as if the smell of it will help you determine the quality of the leather. The truth is that having sniffed the skin of the purse, you don't know what material it is, and, for just an instant, that troubles you. You look more closely at the purse, twisting the lip a little so you can see the label, on which, in very small print, it says: MAN-MADE MATERIALS.

After what seems like a long time, you glance again at the perfume counter: the girl is not there. You drop the red purse back onto its hook and stand on your toes looking for the girl. Then you start toward the center of the purse department for a clearer view.

"Can we help you with something?"

It's the salesgirl in Purses. She's thin, a brunette, with stylized makeup that seems to carve her face. She's wearing a thin black silk-like dress—a sundress, and her shoulders are bare. She has caught

305

you off guard and presses her advantage by putting a smooth hand with perfect red nails on your forearm.

"Sir?"

"Well," you begin, "I was looking for a gift."

"Of course you were," the girl says. The tone is patronizing. She has seen you staring at the blonde girl in Perfumes.

"For my wife," you say.

"Something in the way of a purse," she says. "Or perhaps a nice perfume?"

"I'd better go," you say, but she tightens her grip on your arm and glances over a lightly rouged shoulder at a middle-aged woman who is standing impatiently at the far end of the purse department.

"I have a customer," the salesgirl says. "But why don't you wait a minute and talk to me? Jenny says you're very handsome but painfully shy—are you shy? Will you wait?"

You laugh self-consciously.

"I'll get rid of her," the girl says. "Be right back." As she turns away she draws her nails down on your arm, leaving thin white trace lines.

You watch her show the woman a purse, watch her arms move as she selects a second purse off a treelike stand, watch the way she cocks one foot up on its toe behind the other as she sells. The soft black skirt ripples and clings gently to the backs of her thighs as she moves, and when she goes behind the cash register to ring the sale, one of the straps falls off her shoulder, and she pulls it back into place routinely, smiling past her customer at you.

•

"Jenny says you followed her everywhere for weeks, is that so? All around here?" Finished with the middle-aged woman, the salesgirl has come back to you.

"I don't know Jenny," you say. But when the girl tugs at your arm and points over the tops of the displays toward the shoe section, you don't need to look. You know the girl she's talking about, the tall girl with the very short hair who works in Shoes. You trailed her around the store and around the mall for a few weeks, watching her shop, watching her eat, watching her sit by the garishly painted fountain in the center of the mall—you trailed her until you got worried. Then you stayed out of the mall for nearly two weeks, and when you returned you carefully avoided Shoes. That's not entirely true. Once you spent half the morning going up and down the escalator so that you could see her over the thickly forested juniors' casual wear.

"She likes you," the brunette says. "I think when you started in on Sally it hurt her feelings, Jenny's, I mean."

You nod to indicate that you have understood, then realize you shouldn't understand, so you say, "Sally?"

"Sally?" the salesgirl says, mimicking you, exaggerating your delivery until it is a high prissy whine. "Sally's the blonde you've been staring at all morning while playing with my purses."

"Oh," you say. You think you should have left when you had the chance, but the salesgirl has her hand on you again, her nails biting your skin, and to leave you'd have to jerk yourself out of her grip.

"Half the day," the girl says deliberately, "and that's a conservative estimate. That's this morning only. Then there's yesterday, and Saturday—you're quite a regular around here, aren't you? At first Sally thought you were the store dick, but she checked with Mr. Bo— he's our manager for this floor—and found out you weren't. My name's Andrea, what's yours?"

You don't want to tell her that. "Wiley Pitts," you say. It's a football player's name you saw in the morning paper. "I'm thirty-six years old." Instinctively you reach out to shake hands, then abruptly withdraw your hand and lift it to your forehead where a thin string of sweat has broken out along your hairline.

"Are you nervous?" she asks. "You shouldn't be nervous. Come sit with me." She guides you by the arm to a small round-topped stool in front of her sales counter. "I have to stick pretty close to this," she says, tapping the cash register with one bright fingernail.

You take the seat. You are inexplicably docile, obedient. You feel suddenly faint, as if moving about for the first time after a prolonged illness. Andrea is pretty, she smells pretty, she is being kind and gentle with you, and you are enjoying her attention. The sheen of her dress reflects the store light as she moves.

"The others think you're crazy," she says, twirling her finger near her temple and smiling. "I said you were just lonely."

"I suppose I am," you say. You cross your legs clumsily, then uncross them when you find it difficult to maintain your balance on the stool.

"We're all lonely sometimes," Andrea says. "I'll tell you what—I'll get the others and we can go to lunch together, would you like that? That way you can get a really close look at Sally."

"You're very pretty, too," you say. But as soon as you've said it you feel you shouldn't have, and you say, "I'm sorry. I don't know why I said that."

"Of course I'm pretty," Andrea says, laughing, obviously pleased. "We're all pretty. That's why they hire us. Do you think they want ugly girls out here trying to sell this stuff? We have to be pretty because that way the customers buy more so they can be pretty just like us." She tucks and smooths her dress for a minute, for your benefit, then says, "Well? What about it?"

Before you can reply, she's on the telephone. You realize she is talking to Jenny, the girl in Shoes. "Yes," Andrea says, fingering the curled cord and looking at you, "I'm sure he's the same one—you pointed him out, didn't you? No, not at all. Very nice. Yes. No, no—the first thing, yes. Right. Morrison's. You tell Sally—huh? Yes, she will."

You watch a young woman customer in very tight shorts and a lavender tank top glide up the escalator, which is directly across the aisle from Purses. Then Andrea is off the phone.

"Jenny's very excited," she says. "She didn't believe me at first."

You nod again, now staring at the empty escalator.

"Listen," Andrea says, "are you all right? You look very depressed." She tosses her hair over her shoulder and twists around on one leg to look at the store clock mounted on the wall above and behind her. "It'll just be a few minutes," she says. "You won't mind waiting, will you? Is your name really Pitts?"

"Robert," you say sheepishly. "Robert Caul. I'm sorry about the other." But Robert Caul is not your name, either.

"Oh, don't worry about it, and don't look so forlorn, Robert Caul," she says. "You're going to have a great time, really you are. It'll be a dream come true."

"Yes," you say. Then you look away, around the store, seeing only colors and shapes and reflections in columns that've been turned into mirrors. Andrea moves off to chat with a customer, a young man in jeans who explains that his wife is pregnant and needs a new purse for when the baby comes. Finally, accidentally, you look toward Perfumes, and the blonde girl is back, sitting primly on a tall stool inside her glass enclosure, talking on a black telephone and toying with the braid in her hair. She is looking at you.

•

At the cafeteria with Andrea, Jenny, and Sally, you take a thin slice of roast beef, three round white potatoes, a salad, and a shallow cup of peas. The women talk to one another as the four of you slide your trays over the polished aluminum rails attached to the serving counter. They are talking about you, whispering, being a little impolite, but you don't mind. You laugh, too, and smile to yourself as if you are in on the joke.

When everyone is seated at the table by the window, Jenny says, "Why are you doing this?" The window is the size of a bathroom window, small and heavily curtained. It looks out into the center of the mall.

"Never mind that," Andrea says. "He sure is handsome, isn't he?"

"Within certain well-known guidelines," Sally says.

"Posh," Andrea says, smiling at you.

"You really scared me at first," Jenny says. "Following me like that. I didn't know *what* you wanted. But then I got used to it, and I wasn't scared anymore."

"You were going out of your skull," Sally says. "Admit it."

"Sure, at first," Jenny says. "After he'd followed me for a week, I almost went up and introduced myself one day."

"He wishes you had," Andrea says. "Don't you, Robert?"

"I don't know," you say. "Not exactly—maybe." You try to smile, but your lip catches on your teeth somehow, hooks itself there, and your smile feels horrible.

"I like a man who knows his mind," Sally says.

"Oh, leave him alone, Sally," Andrea says. "Can't you see he's nervous?"

"What's he nervous about?"

"You," Jenny says. "He thinks you're beautiful."

"He's right," Sally says. "But that doesn't mean I don't like him. I do like you, Robert. Really."

"Listen to her," Jenny says. "It takes her two hours every day to look like that, and she's so blasé."

"It's worth it," Sally says, wiping a small cone of mayonnaise off her dark lower lip with the tip of her third finger. "It makes me a more sensual person."

"If you were any more sensual," Jenny says, "you'd be an open sore."

"We had to go to school to learn how to look, Robert," Andrea says. "Would you believe that?"

"Some of us did," Sally says.

Jenny bobs her head and mouths some words to make fun of Sally, then turns to you: "We're professionals, like models. We make the women envious and we make the men feel cheated, and that's not as easy as it sounds."

"He doesn't talk much, does he?" Sally says, waving her fork in your direction. "What are we going to do with him?"

"*We're* not doing anything," Andrea says. "I'm taking him home with me." She drops her fingers over your wrist and pats you twice. "We all live in the same complex, Casa del Sol—ever hear of it?"

"I don't," you say. "I mean, I never heard of it, no. Sorry, Andrea."

"It's got a hot tub," Sally says proudly. "More than one, in fact."

"Six," Jenny says, smiling. "By actual count. Of course, some are hotter than others."

The three women laugh at this joke, then Sally says to you, "Jenny would know, she's a real hot-tub artist."

"Thanks, Sally," Jenny says.

"You know who he reminds me of?" Sally says. "He reminds me of one of the Dead Boys—I can't remember which one, though. I think it's the one they call Johnny."

"Jeff," Jenny says. "I saw them last week at the Palace, but he doesn't look much like Jeff, anyway."

You look down at your plate and see that you have cut your roast beef into tiny squares less than an inch on a side, and you have stacked the squares one on top of the other in three small piles. You begin to play with your peas, lifting them onto your plate with the fork and then pushing them across the open center of the plate, encircling the stacks of beef.

Sally says, "You're not going to eat your salad, Robert? I'll eat it if you don't want it." She pulls your salad across the table, then turns to Jenny. "I wish somebody would tell me what we're going to do with him."

"Andrea's going to marry him," Jenny says. "The dear girl."

"Why don't we ask Robert what *he* wants us to do with him?" Sally says.

"We know what he wants," Jenny says, pushing a large square of lettuce from your stolen salad into her mouth. "He wants to lurk around the store watching you bend over."

"Or you," Sally says. "Or you, Andrea."

"We're just friends," Andrea says. "He can watch me at home."

"Well," Sally says, suddenly pushing back her chair and standing up, "I think it's me he really wants to look at. Isn't that right, Robert?" She comes around to your side of the table and leans over you and wraps her bare arm around your head, then pulls back and with her other hand opens her blouse slightly. "See, Robert? Isn't it pretty? Tell the girls I'm the one you really like."

"You're the one I really like," you say, but you don't think Andrea and Jenny hear you because you can hear them laughing, although you can't see them because Sally has your head in an awkward position, her upper arm almost covering your eyes.

"That's nice," Sally says, and she kisses you lightly on the top of your head.

"Doesn't prove anything," Jenny says, dragging a napkin over her lips. "If I showed him mine, he'd swear he'd marry me ten times."

"He'd swear you'd *been* married ten times," Sally says, "if memory serves. You're a little lank through the chest, darling."

"Why, you cat," Jenny says. "You bitch."

Laughing, Sally says, "You guys ready to go?"

"Come on, Andrea," Jenny says, pushing her chair away from the table. "And bring your friend."

"You two go on ahead," Andrea says. "We'll be there in a minute."

Jenny and Sally walk out of the cafeteria together, and you watch them go, you watch the way each careful step causes a particular swing in the hips—they strut, their sleek clothes snapping precisely.

"That was fun," you say.

"Well, I'm sorry," Andrea says, looking at you over the rim of her coffee cup. "I didn't know."

·

In the living room of Andrea's Casa del Sol two-bedroom apartment identical white rented sofas face each other. You sit on one of these sofas. Andrea is not home. Her television is small, white, balanced on top of a tall straw basket in front of the window. There is a white Princess telephone on the back of the sofa opposite you. The late afternoon sun slants into the room, cutting across the twin sofas and casting dense, hard-looking shadows. You have the feeling that you are the only one home at Casa del Sol.

When Andrea arrives she has two whole barbecued chickens she bought at the grocery store. The chickens are in aluminum foil pans, wrapped in clear plastic. You watch her unwrap the chickens and listen to her talk.

"My father," she says, picking at the skin on the breast of one of the chickens, "was a speedboat racer. Not for a living, but that's what he was really. I have home movies of him on Lake Livingston, if you want to see. I've got lots of movies, in fact, of the whole family—Dad worked real hard editing the movies, putting them all in order by year, you know the kind of thing I mean. He even shot titles and put them in. He wanted so much for everything to make sense."

You notice that the legs of each chicken are twisted together so tightly that the bones have bent around each other.

"He wanted to know how things worked, even the simplest things—the air-conditioning, the movie projector. The first thing he did when he got a new movie projector was take it apart. Then he tried to improve on it, gluing little sticks of foam to the lens mount to cut down on the vibration and, when that didn't work, hooking rubber bands around the lens itself. It was terrible the way all his improvements didn't work. But he didn't notice that, or, if he did, he didn't talk about it. And he always did it, no matter what. He busted the television trying to make a better antenna, and he busted the stereo when he decided he could make a spindle that would drop fifteen records instead of the five the factory suggested. And the older he got, the worse it was. I mean, he just kept busting things and busting things until there was nothing to do but laugh, we all laughed, he even laughed, it was so horrible."

You listen and nod, but she's finished. You don't know why she's telling you about her father anyway. It has gotten dark outside, and the only light in the apartment is a tiny night-light pushed into a socket on the kitchen wall. Andrea is crying.

You ask where Sally and Jenny live, thinking this will help, and Andrea leads you to her front window and points across an open courtyard, empty except for the brilliant green island of the pool, at some apartments in another building. "They don't know you're here," Andrea says. "Do you want to go surprise them?"

"No," you say. "Not tonight."

"My grandmother is ninety-one," she says. "She lives in Palestine, Texas. She runs every day, she was running before everybody else started running, she was ahead. I don't know, around here everybody runs now. You go out at six o'clock, and it looks like one of those sports shows on TV. There isn't any reason to run, but they do it anyway. Bunch of goons. They think just because it's an apartment complex suddenly they're in California. I bought the shoes, but that's as far as it went. Are you getting hungry? If we don't eat I'm going to scalp this chicken."

She serves you a quarter of a chicken neatly severed between breast and thigh and two slabs of white bread on a bare plate. This makes you very happy. For the first time you stop wondering if you should have taken her key after lunch. Andrea sits on one sofa and you sit on the other, and both of you eat with your fingers, occasionally stopping to tear away a bite-sized square of bread. You smile at each other as you eat. The chicken is tender and spicy, the perfect meal. When you finish, you carry your plate into the small kitchen and drop the bones into the garbage sack under the sink. Then you rinse the plate and turn it upside down on the flecked Formica counter, then you wash your hands with her Ivory soap. As you run the water over your hands, you splash a little first on your lips, then over your entire face. You pull two paper towels off the roll alongside the sink and dry your face and hands. You throw the crumpled towels at the garbage sack, miss it by a full yard. When you return to the living room, Andrea is sitting in the semidarkness, licking her fingers.

•

"Once, when there was a hurricane coming," she says, not talking directly to you but rather into the room and to herself, "my father required that we make all the preparations, and we checked the flashlights, counted the candles, drew clean water in the tubs and sinks, bought bottled water to drink, taped the huge bay windows in our house with gray duct tape, and nailed plywood over the smaller windows. He carefully plotted the storm's course on a chart he cut out of the newspaper. The storm moved very slowly. My father called the weather service often, cursing and slamming the phone down when he got a busy signal. When the storm finally reached the Gulf it stopped dead in its tracks for twenty hours, whirling itself into a two-hundred-mile-an-hour frenzy, and as the storm got larger and more powerful my father spent his time sitting silently by the radio, his head slightly bent, a coffee cup balanced on the arm of his chair. He wouldn't talk to any of us. He hushed us angrily when we tried to talk to one another. He was intent on the storm, and he sat up all night listening for news bulletins, marking and calculating on the crumpled chart in his lap. The radio spewed instructions about what to do in case of fire, what to do in case of flood, and also history—the great and dangerous hurricanes of the century. We were prepared, and, as far as I knew, the real danger to us was minimal. Nevertheless a silence spread over our house like nothing I'd ever felt before. The kids kept watch at the windows, but the weather outside looked fine and breezy. At eight in the morning the radio announcer read a bulletin from the weather service: Elise had started to move again, but she had reversed her course and was now headed south-west, straight for Mexico. This news did not deter my father from his vigil, and, seven hours later, when the storm made landfall well below Brownsville, my father came to the door of his study and told us the news. He was a big man, a powerful man physically, and I remember him filling that doorway between his study and the living room of our house, I remember the way his voice sounded and how his eyes looked when he told us, and I remember watching him retreat into his study and close the door. He shot himself in the temple with a twenty-two-caliber pistol."

"Killed himself?" you ask, sure that you shouldn't, sure that you already know the answer.

"No," Andrea says. "Crippled himself. In a wheelchair the rest of his life."

"I'm sorry," you say.

"Me too," she says, staring at her red nails.

•

You notice for the first time that one of Andrea's eyebrows is plucked too much, and that the brows are not symmetrical with respect to the bridge of her nose. Her left brow, the one that is far too thin, also starts well over her left eye. Once you have seen this tiny imbalance, you cannot stop seeing it. Every time you look at Andrea's face you see this odd-shaped patch of skin there above her nose. You stare at it. Her face looks wrong suddenly, almost deformed. You try to think of something to say about her father, but you can't think of anything. You wonder if you should ask Andrea about Sally and Jenny, but decide that that might hurt Andrea's feelings, so you say nothing. You sit with her until well past midnight—hours of occasional sound, occasional movement.

When she decides to go to bed you make no move to follow her into the bedroom, and she makes no special invitation. You sleep on the sofa, fully dressed, without even a sheet to cover you. You imagine yourself leaving the apartment on a sunny day in the middle of the week. Three beautiful women in tiny white bikinis lift their sunglasses as you pass them in the courtyard. They smile at you.

You drive to the mall in a new car and spend two hours in Housewares on the second floor. You do not remember ever having been on the second floor before. You buy a wood-handled spatula from a lovely girl with clean short hair. Kitchen equipment is exquisite, you believe.

(1981)

FEEDERS

Iris shares a two-bedroom town house in Meadowdale with Polly, a nursing student. Iris hates it way out there, so when I mention on the telephone that Mrs. Jaymar has moved out of my duplex, Iris says she wants it. It's the second floor of my house, and since we used to live together, I say I'm not sure this is a great idea. She says maybe we could meet at Coleman's, a restaurant we used to go to, and discuss it.

"Her son got a condominium in Lakeland," I say. "The last day, she asked if she could leave her plastic bird feeders, which are all over the trees like party lights, and I said okay, so she gave me a bag of seed."

"She's wonderful," Iris says. "I remember. So how about six-thirty?" When I don't answer, she says, "I know, I know. You aren't promising anything."

Coleman's is a storefront in a thirty-year-old strip shopping center not far from my house. When the neighborhood was revitalized, Coleman's was revitalized too—now it's all palm trees and captain's chairs and Varathaned tabletops. At first I don't recognize Iris, who's sitting off in the corner of the porchlike front of the restaurant with her back to me. Then she waves, and I squint and wave back. It's the first time I've met Polly, and it's a little awkward; she doesn't say anything, just looks at me and gives me a short nod. At the next table there's an almost bald man in a short-sleeved shirt, who's bent backward over his chair, telling her what to do about ordering. "This steak-and-seafood might be good. But it depends what kind of steak it is. If it's some junk cut, round or even porterhouse, you shouldn't get it."

"Right," Polly says. "Okay."

"We know him," Iris whispers.

Except for the hair—Iris's is black, Polly's red—the women look surprisingly alike. Both have dark circles under the eyes, chiseled faces, pale hands. Iris is older and more delicate, but her eyes are hard, like colored rocks. Polly is wearing a scoop-neck black pullover and worn khakis, Iris a pinstripe dress shirt I think I remember, and a thin silver tie knotted off the neck.

The guy at the next table is staring at Polly's back. "But if it's a petite filet, then it might be good."

"A what?" Polly says, craning to look at him.

"Petite filet. Like this up here, only smaller." He reaches over and bops on her menu with his knuckle. "Sometimes they try to nick you on the platters."

"Oh. Thanks," Polly says.

Iris leans close to me. "We don't want any trouble, Eddie."

"Who is this guy?" I say.

"Never mind," she says. "Don't worry about it." She gives Polly a stern look, and Polly shrugs helplessly.

I make a joke about inviting the guy to join us, and Iris smiles dryly and says, "It's a little late for that, don't you think?" She writes a check for the rent.

"Shouldn't we discuss this?" I say.

"Don't be silly, Eddie," Iris says. "That's all over. It's okay. I mean, unless you feel funny about it." She presses the kinky hair back off her forehead and then tears the check out of a red checkbook. "Polly's at the university, and I'm still with the telephone company. Putting 'em in, I mean." She waves a hand toward Polly, who brightens theatrically as if she's been hit with a spotlight. "She's going to be a nurse, maybe. Or a doctor."

Polly shakes her head, then looks out the large window at the street in front of Coleman's. There's a Quik Stop drive-in grocery across the street, and in the parking lot two police cars are parked side by side, nose to tail, the drivers talking to each other out the windows. "I think you two ought to discuss it," she says.

"We're quiet, no pets, regular hours," Iris says. "Ideal tenants." She pushes her check across the glossy wood tabletop. "Well, is it a deal or what?"

Iris was always too direct, too demanding. Now it's as if she's challenging me to take her on as a tenant. But even though I haven't seen her very often in the last eight months, when I have seen her we've gotten along all right; the separation was a success. "I guess I can stand it if you can," I say. "When do you want to move?"

"Soon," Polly says, glancing over her shoulder at the guy at the next table. She turns to Iris. "Are we going to eat?"

"No. We're going to finish and go. Take it easy."

"It's four seventy-five—can you afford that? I pay water."

"I remember. See? It's here." She picks up the check and waves it casually. I take it and she stands up. "That's a deal. We'll be coming tomorrow. I'll knock for the key, all right?"

"I don't want to be squeamish, Iris, but you're sure this is what you want to do?"

She smiles and says, "You look good, Eddie." She pats my cheek in an unpleasant way—three short, light slaps—and then she and Polly leave. The guy at the next table waves and watches them go. When they're out the door, he turns to look at me. I nod and glance over my shoulder, as if to be sure he's not looking at something behind me, but the only thing there is a wall covered with snowy paper and pink flocked birds—cranes or flamingos. When I turn back, he's pushing his chair out. He almost knocks over his tea glass. He comes straight to my table and points to Iris's chair. "Do you mind?"

"Excuse me?"

He sits, pulling up close to the table. "I didn't want to barge in like this. My name's Putnam, Cecil Putnam. I'm over here waiting for my daughter." He jerks his head toward his table. "She didn't show yet, so I thought I'd come over a minute." He reaches across the table to shake my hand.

"How are you?" His hand is small and covered with soft black hair.

He frowns, then bends closer and whispers, "You know these women?" He points at the chairs. "I don't want to pry. You can tell me to go to hell."

"They're renting an apartment from me. Why?"

"Oh," He nods gravely, "Tenants. I thought you might know them more personally."

"No."

"See, I know the one with the red hair, that's all. She's a body builder, right? She has arms, you know what I'm saying? This one does." He points at Polly's chair again. "I mean, is she Portuguese or something? The arms are real good."

"Student. That's what she told me. She didn't say anything about weight lifting."

"It's not weight lifting."

"She told me student."

"She'd look swell with that oil they slop on, you know? Glistening, wearing one of those tiny pouch bikinis—you know the kind I'm talking about? You ever watch 'em?"

He's hunched over my table, drawing greasy circles with his finger on the tabletop. Because he's bent forward, I'm staring at the top of his head, where the hair is brushed forward in queer spikes that stand out from his scalp. He looks as if he might be fifty years old. "I think you've got the wrong girl," I say.

He seems displeased, but he doesn't want to leave. He glances over his shoulder at his table, then back to me. "My girl's a body-builder, that's how come I know about this stuff. I watch 'em on television. This girl here is a pal of my girl's, I think. I wanted to check it out. They kill me," he says. "The oily business kills me every time. I'm a sucker for it."

The waiter has come up and is giving me signals with his pad and pencil, asking if I'm ready to order.

"Excuse me," I say, pointing over Putnam's shoulder to the waiter.

"Oh, hell yes," he says. "Lemme get out of your way here." He pushes his chair back and stands, then steps around the waiter. "Sorry to bust in. Listen, you try that combo platter, hear? But check the meat."

•

Iris and Polly show up on bicycles at nine the next morning. I answer the door in my checked robe. Iris is in jeans and a plaid flannel shirt; she has a tool holster slung low off a leather belt around her hips. She keeps pushing the holster back as she shifts from foot to foot on the front step. "Welcome home," I say.

"We'll go around to the upstairs entrance," Iris says. "Okay? You bring the key?"

I show them the apartment, and Polly thinks it's perfect except for the ochre carpet.

"I hate it too," I say.

"It's good and thick," Polly says. "Anyway, we won't see it when we get the pads down." She drops cross-legged to the floor and rocks back and forth a few times.

"Pads?" I say.

Iris pats my shoulder. "Don't get worried. No furniture, so we put quilts on the floor. Kind of Japanese, you know?"

"Yeah," Polly says, "We've got different colors for each room. And plants, of course. How many rooms are there, anyway?"

I try to imagine the apartment with wall-to-wall quilts. "What about the kitchen? What do you do in there?"

"She makes a key lime pie that'll rip skin off your tongue," Polly says, getting off the floor and going to the window. "But you probably know that." She bends to look at the control panel of the air-conditioning unit. "This old or something?"

"Of course it is," Iris says. She tugs on Polly's work shirt.

I point out the windows at the trees in the front yard. "The feeders disappear when the leaves come."

"We like it," Iris says. "You give me the seed and I'll take care of the birds."

"It's a deal," Polly says.

That afternoon they bring clothes and some boxes in the back of a dark-blue Volvo station wagon. I prop open the screen door of the upstairs entrance with half of a concrete block and then offer to help with the boxes, but Iris says it isn't necessary, so I go back to my apartment and put on a Bob Marley record. Then I remember it's a record Iris sometimes put on when we made love, so I take it off the turntable and put on something else, a New Wave band that I don't like at all. I stay up late, sitting in my dark living room listening to Iris and Polly walk around upstairs.

•

Cecil Putnam knocks on my door at six in the morning. He hasn't shaved, and he looks as if he's been beaten up. There are small abrasions all over his face and hands. "Remember me?" he says. "I met you at Coleman's. I asked about the girls."

It's barely light outside; the grass is shining. I'm cold. "It's early, isn't it?" I rub my eyes and squint at him in what I hope is a discouraging way.

He sticks a boot in the door. "Let me talk to you a minute, Ed."

I look at him and he looks back, and that tells me he's not going to leave, so I lead him into the kitchen.

"Ed," he says when we're sitting at the table, "I'm an educator. Been an educator twenty years and I never did anything like this before. But there's a good reason, and it's not what you think. Bear with me a minute here, will you?"

"I don't think a thing. You want coffee?"

"I'll do it. You took tired."

"Up late."

He's a small man with a too-large upper body; when he goes across the kitchen, he moves in fits and starts, like a gorilla going around a cage. "Me too. All night in the van." He points at the ceiling. "I'm in radio, TV, and film," he says, opening and closing a couple of my cabinets. He's wearing an olive-green cardigan sweater, khaki pants, big work shoes with rawhide laces. "Where's the coffee, anyway?" He picks up a can of Final Net from the counter and points the nozzle at me. "What's this about?"

"Roaches. The coffee's there with the red top."

He puts the Final Net back where he found it. "I guess that slows 'em down pretty good, huh?" He spoons coffee into the percolator and plugs it in. "I know you got a clean place, Ed, but just let me help you out here." He wets a paper towel and comes across the room to wipe the table. When he finishes one pass, he leans on the table with his elbows, looks straight at me, and says, "That's my baby girl you got upstairs, Ed. I know it's peculiar, me coming in here like this and everything, but I'm checking to be sure you're okay, you see what I mean? That's the way I have to do things."

He stands alongside the table and pours me a shallow cup of coffee. I look at his free hand, which is opening and closing very fast. Then it straightens out and the fingers wiggle jerkily.

When both coffees are poured, he takes the chair opposite me, pulls the thick-lipped mug to his mouth, blows on his coffee.

There's a yellow fleck that looks like a pencil shaving floating on the surface of my coffee, so I stick the tip of my finger into the mug.

Cecil watches me for a minute, then relaxes and surveys the kitchen. "How long you had this place, Ed? You got a pretty good mortgage on her?"

We chat for half an hour, and at quarter of seven he abruptly has to go. "Let me rinse these first." He sweeps our mugs off the table and takes them to the sink. "I hope you understand, Ed. I'm an educator and I know what I have to do—you follow me? It's not my first choice. I got to look after these women, see what I mean?"

"Sure," I say. "Gotcha."

Then I follow him to the front door and watch through the mini-blinds as he cuts across the front lawn toward a bronze van with a couple of bubble sunroofs, parked next door.

•

Iris comes out about two that afternoon, wearing an aqua leotard, leg warmers, a down-filled flight vest, and French canvas hiking shoes. I'm on the porch painting the doorframe blue. She walks like a clown, rubbing the small of her back with both hands. "Good morning," she says vaguely. She crosses the small yard to the Japanese rain tree and studies the bark on the trunk.

"Your friend Putnam came for breakfast," I say, balancing the brush on the lip of the paint can. Her back is to me, about ten feet away. I wipe my hands, then jump the two steps off the porch and come up behind her.

"I'm sorry," she says, picking at the tree trunk with her nails.

I look up and down the street. No van. There are birds on the telephone wires but none in the trees. There's a dull, even light everywhere—it reminds me of the "cloudy-bright" on Kodak film directions. "What's the story on the guy, anyway? I mean, Jesus, Iris."

She turns to face me. Her hair is pulled straight away from her face and there's a washed-out red in her cheeks from the cold. Her eyes are a little bit blue. "I can't stop him." She shuts her eyes, then opens them and looks past me at the house. "I don't know why he can't just leave us alone."

She looks beaten and pretty, so I smile and say, "None of us can," reaching to brush a bit of hair away from her forehead.

She ducks and jerks her hand to her face, knocking my fingers aside. "That's not what it's about, Eddie." She looks down at her hands and rubs the fleshy part of one thumb over the other's nail. "I can't take care of everything. Polly works for him, and he's around. If you can't handle it, we can go somewhere else."

She's thin—thinner than I remember, in spite of the thick jacket and the leg wraps, or because of them—and she looks frail.

I pull some blackened berries off a branch. "What about the college? He said he was at the college."

"He says whatever he wants to say. I thought since you're a man, he'd back off."

I follow her to the Volvo parked at the curb and watch as she writes her name in the dirt on the fender. "I don't want to deal with him, Iris. It's your business, not mine. But what is it? He going to be around all the time or what?"

"I don't know. Probably. He won't hurt you or anything."

"That's terrific."

"He's not a terrible guy, Eddie. He's friendly."

"So I see. But he's your friend, Iris. I mean, I'm just renting an apartment here, right?"

She starts to write something else on the fender, then quits and faces me. "So what—you'd rather I was alone?" She pushes past me and walks off, following the line down the middle of the street.

•

Two nights later Iris calls. "We're ready for the dinner," she says. "Can you come tonight?" I haven't talked to her or Polly since the day Putnam came, although I've seen them carrying things up the drive, and I've heard them at night, arranging things, padding around on my ceiling.

"Sure. Want me to bring the wine?"

"Wine? Nobody up here likes wine. Just bring yourself. Eight o'clock."

She hangs up without saying goodbye. I look across the kitchen at the clock on the stove, but I can't read it from where I'm sitting, so I have to get up and go across the room. It's five-fifteen. I wrap the rest of my sandwich in aluminum foil and put it on the top shelf in the refrigerator. Then I see some brown stains on the wall of the refrigerator, so I get the sponge from the sink and wipe them off. While I'm doing that, I notice a hair stuck to the bottom of the milk carton. The refrigerator is a mess. I start to clean it, taking everything off one shelf at a time, then removing the shelves and washing down the inside walls. I throw away a sack of carrots I find in the crisper, but the three apples look okay, so I save those. The lettuce is bad, so I toss it, and I toss the mushrooms, celery, and peppers, and the soft black banana. By the time I get everything back together, the refrigerator looks clean and empty. It's almost seven. I take the bag of old food out to the cans by the garage.

At eight Iris calls and tells me Polly needs a lemon, so I get one I saved, rinse it in cold water, and go around the house to their entrance.

The apartment doesn't have any furniture in it, just the way they said. There's a square white Formica coffee table in the center of the living room. The ochre carpet has been covered with bright solid-red quilts. In the corners and along the wall where the windows are, they have plants, and a large Monet garden poster is pushpinned to one wall. The coffee table is set for four.

"This is the only room we've finished," Iris says. She points to a pile of cardboard boxes covered with a clear plastic drop cloth in the next room. "We like to do one at a time. That's all our stuff there."

I follow her through the apartment. There's a mattress on the floor in one of the bedrooms, but otherwise the place looks the way it did after Mrs. Jaymar left. Polly is in the kitchen staring into the glass plate in the oven door.

"Oh, hi. You bring my lemon?" When I give it to her, she says, "I don't know how I could have forgotten this."

Iris takes me back into the living room and points to the coffee table. "You want a Coke?"

"Fine." I sit clumsily on the floor, facing one of the placemats. In the center of the table there are two square red plastic flashlights and a small box wrapped in burlap, made to look like a cotton bale. "What's this?" I ask, pointing at the box.

"Music." Iris slides to her knees and tips open the top of the cotton bale, and a soft tinkling version of "Dixie" comes out.

The dinner is chicken wings and rice. The wings are served with a brown sauce, and the rice is full of vegetables and nuts. Polly tells a story about finding the wing recipe in the *New York Times*. "I always liked wings, but nobody would believe me. So it was great finding this recipe."

"They're very good," I say.

"Try the sauce on the rice," she says, passing a coffee creamer with about an inch of sauce in it. "Not too much."

My back starts hurting after I've been on the floor twenty minutes. Both women are careful not to disturb the fourth place at the table, and when the setting gets cleared with the rest of the dinner dishes, Iris says, "We were expecting somebody else."

"We invited Cecil," Polly says. "Iris saw him at the Spa." Polly pours two-thirds of a cup of coffee for me, then offers a creamer just like the one used at dinner; I wonder if they have two or if she quickly washed it after the meal. "She's trying to get herself back into shape."

"You don't seem out of shape to me. Maybe thin."

Polly looks at Iris. "You think she's too thin?"

"I've got small bones. Take a look at these wrists." Iris pulls up her sweatshirt sleeves and thrusts both arms out over the table. "Didn't you like the sauce? It's Cecil's. He copied it from somewhere."

"According to Iris," Polly says, "everything is copied from somewhere. Do you believe that? I think it takes something away."

"I guess he made part of it up," Iris says.

"Cecil's a caution," Polly says, folding her napkin into a flower shape and pressing it down on the table.

"So, Polly, how's the nursing business?" I say.

"I'm looking for something else in my field."

"Gore," Iris says. "She's in gore, primarily. The stuff she knows about would curl your hair. Tell him about that printer at the hospital."

Polly looks at me out of the corners of her eyes. "It wasn't anything. They put these hands on the wrong guys one night. Sewed 'em on."

"One was a printer's hand," Iris says. "This guy had an accident."

"A mixup," Polly says. "They had to act fast. So they switched these hands. The printer got another guy's hand, one the surgeon had to take off. The other guy got the printer's hand, because when the surgeon found the printer's hand it looked okay and he thought he'd made a mistake. Neither hand worked. Cosmetically it worked, though."

"Cosmetically it was great," Iris says. "The printer was Italian and very dark, and the other guy was a poet or something."

"After a while they looked okay," Polly says. "The hospital did follow-up—color photographs and stuff. After a while you could hardly tell. Iris went out with the poet."

"Just twice, and he wasn't a poet. He was something else. But he could type real fast one-handed."

"Cecil was going to do this documentary about it," Polly says. "That's how we met him. But he was so messed up he couldn't carry it off. Then he got in on this Spa deal with some AA guys."

"He didn't want to do it anyway," Iris says. "That was just an excuse."

Polly rolls her eyes. "After the poet, it was Cecil. She's hittin' 'em hard, this one, since you guys quit."

"That's crap and you know it," Iris says. "Besides, we never really saw each other, not that way."

"Picking 'em up and putting 'em down." Polly grins at me. "He's like a father to her."

"Oh, Polly." Iris takes her coffee into the kitchen, leaving me and Polly staring at each other.

After a couple of minutes I point at the flashlights. "What's with these?" I say, taking one of them off the table.

"Lanterns," Polly says. "They were great when Hurricane Monica came through last year—or was that the year before?"

"Before, I think."

"They float. I took one of them—that one, not the one you've got—to the bathtub to test it. They really do."

I snap on the light and shine it around the room, making twisty shadows out of the plants.

"Sometimes we have wars," Polly says. "In the dark. It's pretty much fun." She takes the second lantern and clicks it on and off several times, hitting me in the face with its beam. "I shouldn't tease her, should I?" She holds the lantern with both hands and shines the light up into her face. She looks very sexy and mysterious with the light on her that way. "I really shouldn't nag her," Polly says. "But it's so easy." She turns off the light and puts it back in the middle of the table, then struggles to her feet and goes into the kitchen.

I hear her talking to Iris, whispering, but I can't make out what's being said. I wonder if I should just go ahead and leave without saying goodbye, but I decide that would be worse than staying, so I sit and drink my coffee. I shoot the lantern beam around the room, then out the window, where it hits one of Mrs. Jaymar's feeders. I play the light out there for a few minutes, thinking about Iris and me, how we used to roughhouse together and how we used to do certain things—like wear heavy coats inside in the winter. That's when I spot Putnam, wrapped up in a lime-green parka, hugging the trunk of the willow, about eight feet up.

(1983)

Retreat

The English department's first annual retreat was held at the Carlsbad Motel on the Gulf Coast of Alabama in late October. When Mac and Cam arrived they met Mac's brother Rudy and his assistant, Mimi, for dinner. It was the first time they'd seen Mimi, who was also Rudy's new girlfriend. Rudy had just taken over as chairman of the department and was having a bad time trying to be one of the guys. He wore a beaded buckskin jacket that didn't fit right, jeans, and motorcycle boots. He invited Cam and Mac for an early dinner Friday in the motel restaurant, the Schipperke.

After they'd ordered drinks Rudy said, "What is that?" He was tapping the name on the restaurant menu.

Mimi said, "Who cares what it is? I'm so excited about this retreat—I'm dying to see all these professors in action. The Personal Makeover people say when you get people out of the office you see what they're made of."

"I don't know about that," Rudy said.

"It's a dog," Cam said. "On the menu."

"People *need* a chance to open up," Mimi said. "Show themselves. The PMI manual says they'll strip down for you, uncover their scars."

Mac pretended to wave for a cab. "Cab!" he said.

"They send you all this stuff," Rudy said. "They have great graphs, really killer graphs in their brochures."

"Killer," Mimi said. She was young and looked like she was about to sizzle.

The waiter brought drinks, and after they'd been delivered around the table, Rudy said, "I'm glad Cam could come." He reached for Cam's hand. "I heard you were thinking of not coming—why was that?"

"Mammogram," she said. "I was scheduled for this afternoon. I moved it."

"You going to eat these crab claws, Rudy?" Mac said, snapping four or five of the fried claws off Rudy's plate.

"PMI reps gross sixty to eighty thousand the first year," Mimi said. "I may moonlight for them."

"No kidding?" Mac said.

"Even if it's stupid, there are worse ways to spend a weekend," Rudy said. "You see Pokey Willis brought that graduate student of his?"

"See, that's exactly what I'm talking about," Mimi said, her face brightening as she pointed a crab claw at Rudy. "People need a chance to go public with their stuff."

·

The Carlsbad Motel was six stories, as clean as beach places ever get, given the traffic. The staff was used to dealing with the small-bore conference trade, so Mac's job turned out easy—he did the setup, then stood around outside the meeting rooms taking care of people who couldn't find the public restrooms or the bar.

Friday, after dinner, he made sure the correct conference rooms were going to be available when they were supposed to be available, unpacked some handouts Rudy and Mimi had prepared, and went over the luau plan with the motel's Director of Conferences & Workshops. Then he set up the projection video system in the Matrix Room for the nine o'clock showing of a taped program Rudy had gotten off C-SPAN, a panel on the film *JFK*, which was back in the news for some reason. That was followed by a discussion period moderated by a regional assassination buff who had slides, and who went through the evidence again, including some of the new material released the previous year from Dallas police files, details about the detention of the "three tramps," and some CIA materials recently leaked to the press. He had a lot of slides of car crashes, too. Snap-shots taken right after the crashes, with body parts strewn around, splashes of blood dripping down windshields, ripped-up faces.

It was hard to know, since Mac was in and out of the conference room, whether these deaths were related to the assassination or a separate interest of the speaker.

Finally there was the two a.m. Late Sky Seminar. An astronomy guy took everybody to the beach. They stood in a circle holding hands and staring up, while this guy told them what they were look-ing at. Cam stayed in the room, but Mac was out there, squeezed between Mimi and some hefty woman. Mimi's hair was wolf-like.

Most of Saturday was free—the faculty went into town, sat on the beach, or slept. There was a late-afternoon roundtable discus-sion of departmental priorities. Mac made sure there was coffee and the correct number of Style Three snack trays, but that was it. Sat-urday night was the luau.

●

All afternoon a pig had been roasting in one of the two fishponds in the courtyard. The pond, which was twice the size of a Jacuzzi, had been filled in with dirt, then dug out again to make a pit to cook the pig. Mimi had xeroxed "Pig Hawaiian" handouts that explained the long Hawaiian tradition of cooking a pig this particular way, buried in dirt, covered in palm leaves and pineapples. She had encountered this style years before in her travels for the Geiger Foundation, the handout said. The pig was her baby.

The luau was scheduled for the courtyard, but as soon as peo-ple got their first drinks it started storming, and everybody had to trail inside. At first they all stood there staring out the huge glass. Mimi had gone overboard on the decorations—dime-size glitter disks, Christmas lights, tiny white paper flowers, sagging used-car-lot boas of twisted mirror-finish plastic. It was third-worldish when the rain hit.

The pig was hustled out of the courtyard strung between two six-foot Pier 1 bamboo poles carried on the shoulders of Ken and David Whitcomb, twin homosexuals who team-taught a class in rock video, baseball, and Madonna, and taken to the motel kitchen where it was cut up into oven-sized portions and rushed to completion.

Cam had dodged a lot of the weekend, so she had agreed to attend the luau, but when the rain hit she caught Mac in the lobby and said, "I'm going to the room. I'm bringing you bad luck."

He said, "I'll be there in a minute. Just as soon as I get these pig eaters squared up."

"I'll wait for you," she said.

Mac moved everybody to ballroom two, the Blue Conquistador Room, which he had arranged to have available against just such a contingency. When he got it set up, he went and sat out in the courtyard for a minute. The rain was spotty by then—unnaturally large spurts of water that looked like there was somebody on the roof shooting a hose.

He sat on the lip of the still-working pond and stared at fat goldfish circling in the alarming blue water. There were hidden lights in the pond, and when fish swam through them it was as if the fish themselves were strangely shaped bulbs. One fish was almost as big as one of Mac's new cross-training shoes. The shoes seemed much bigger and brighter than they'd seemed in the store—he'd been thinking about that all afternoon, wondering if he'd made another shoe mistake. He stared from fish to shoes, then back to fish. The fish was much smaller, he decided, about the size of a believe-it-or-not potato.

•

When Mac got back to the room Cam said, "Thank God they roped it off." Cam was on the bed in her ribbed underpants and a kid's T-shirt. "I thought for a minute we'd be staring into the burning eyes of that thing as it was yanked out of the dirt. I thought we'd have to watch them burst."

"They take the eyes out," Mac said.

"In Hawaii they probably suck them out," she said. "Like they do out of chickens in France."

"They're too big," Mac said. He stood at the mirror pushing the tip of his nose to make it a pig nose.

"Your brother's new gal said it was the most beautiful pig she ever saw," Cam said.

"Let's go home," Mac said. "Or leave here, anyway. I'm ready."

"What, tonight?"

"Let's tell them we're going home and then move to another motel—what about that? Just you and me on a high floor. Romance. Wind. Pounding rain."

"Sounds good," Cam said.

They were sprawled together on the satiny comforter that spread over the bed like simulated icing on a microwave cake. "I hoped it would," he said.

"But we're probably not going anywhere," she said. "Are we?"

She'd spent Saturday rooting through a few stories from the local newspaper, then she linked up her little Toshiba with Compuserve for a quick scan of the AP and UPI wires. She told Mac she found a piece about a woman who was out of work and beheaded her three children while they slept, then told her neighbors she was offering them as a sacrifice for the Darlington 500, a stock car race. The woman's name was Lolita Portugesa. She had gotten up at midnight in her trailer in a quiet fishing village north of Tampa, grabbed a Chicago Cutlery carving knife that had been a Christmas present from her ex-husband, Fernand, and slashed off the heads of her children Miniboy, 8, Squat, 6, and Junior, 3. All this was from the police report, Cam said. The woman then hacked at her own wrists in an unsuccessful suicide attempt. The Florida authorities said she would be given a psychiatric evaluation to determine if she was sane. A note Portugesa left in the kitchen for her ex-husband read, "I am leaving to you the heads of our children. This is what you have deserved."

There was a knock at the door as Cam finished telling him this story. "Jesus," she said, getting out of the bed and pulling on jeans. "What, now they catch us?"

Mac put his hand over his eyes as if to hide.

Mimi was at the door. "Rudy wonders if you will join him in the garden," she said. She was wearing a swimsuit, one-piece, way low in the front, with a long but open wraparound skirt and backless heels.

"What's the Big Rudy want?" Cam said.

"He wants to thank you," she said. "Both. He's proud of the way things are turning out."

Mac said, "I guess he's deaf, dumb, and blind?"

Cam frowned at him and said, "It hasn't been so bad."

"You haven't been out of the room, how would you know?" Mac said.

Mimi said, "Everybody downstairs loved the pig."

"Well, I didn't *love* the pig," Cam said.

"So I guess you're not in the preponderance, huh? You guys want to come down now?" Mimi said. "Or later? Like in a minute or two, when you have time to get straightened away?"

"You go," Cam said. "There's one other story I want to download. It's a guy who caught a fish with a human thumb in it. Six people disappeared in this lake recently, so they don't know whose thumb it is. It's a detective thing."

"Yeeech," Mimi said. "We have to talk, Cam."

"What other kind of thumb is there?" Mac said.

Cam tapped Mac's shoulder. "Go on. I'll find this, and then I'll change, get my makeup all straightened away, and then I'll be right down. Show Mimi your elevator moves."

"She likes me in elevators," Mac said.

"I do not," Cam said, ushering them out the door. "I just said it was possible."

The elevator was lined in seat-cover vinyl, dusty-rose colored, with a thick, padded handrail all around the interior to prevent kids from hurting themselves when they bashed their heads against it while rampaging up and down in the building—as the designers apparently knew they would. Mimi leaned against the rail on the far side of the car, her head turned to stare at the clicking numbers over the door. Mac studied her calf.

"I need to get away for a while," she said, not taking her eyes off the numbers. "Maybe I should go back early. Maybe tonight."

"Ah," Mac said. He smiled and nodded, but felt that it was too much, too phony. "We were talking about leaving, too. Everything's done, really."

"Yeah. Maybe we'll go together," she said. "Why not?" She hit the Emergency Stop button.

"What's this?" Mac said, pointing to the control panel. "What're you doing?"

"Let's rest a minute," she said. "Okay? Let me just rest a minute here, Mac. I don't ever get to just rest, you know? Since Rudy took this job I'm all over the place, and I don't say a thing. I argue, smile and nod and wave and make my eyes twinkle and draw my lips back and do my nostrils—but I never rest. I'm not like most women."

"Mimi," he said.

"Have we ever talked, just you and me?"

"No," Mac said. "But we will, we'll talk all the time."

"I like you, Mac. From the moment I met you. I love Rudy, but that's not the same thing. I suppose you know what I'm talking about, don't you? One of those suddenly-out-of-whack things?"

"We did that, didn't we? Back when we were thirty?"

"Yeah, that was fun. Two years ago. Longer for you, huh? I miss it already."

Mac caught himself nodding again in a silly way. He stopped.

"I used to want children," Mimi said. "I always figured I'd be good at that. I always think of the kinds of things I'd say to them. I'd tell them not to let anybody kid them, that people will say anything, they'll say they love you, but they really don't. They try, but no matter what they're after, they're not after what you're after. Not usually."

"That's kind of depressing, Mimi. I don't think we're supposed to tell kids that kind of thing," Mac said. "It's OK to get depressed, and maybe it seems like it's that bad, sometimes, maybe it even is, but we're supposed to keep it to ourselves, I think." Mac had his arm around her. They were slumped against the back wall of the elevator. The call bell was ringing.

"That's why I don't have any. I keep pointing to Rudy, talking to him about little Rudys," she said. "But he isn't buying."

"Well, say good-bye to projectile vomiting."

She gave him a look, and there wasn't any laughing in it. "I'm pretty forlorn tonight," she said. "Sorry."

"Never mind. It was stupid," he said, gently finger-combing her hair.

"Once, I was at the store, and this guy who looked like Rudy came in," Mimi said. "He held a stun gun on this checker. I'm standing right there. I couldn't get over it—Rudy's double. After all the TV shows, the cop shows, the movies, the mystery books, here was this guy in Pass Christian. Anyway, so I talked him down. Just like TV. We had a talk about stun guns. I told him the way he was holding his he was going to take big electricity."

"When was this?"

"Couple months ago."

"He was holding it wrong?"

"How do I know?" she said. "A guy talked somebody down on *Cops,* so I tried it. I said he was going to burn his ass if he zapped her. He was thin, sick-thin like cancer, so I asked him if he'd been checked up recently. I pointed at this spot on his neck with my fingernail and asked him if anybody had looked at that. There wasn't anything there, a smudge, but I made it sound like there was something, trying to give him a little doubt. He said he thought he was holding the gun right. He'd read the instructions and shot it off on a dog that way. I asked what happened to the dog. He said it spit up and then bit him, and I just shook my head. 'There you go,' I told him."

She was threading her fingers in and out between the buttons on Mac's shirt.

"Rudy likes gun magazines. You don't, do you? He gets dozens of them, but he never reads them. *Soldier of Fortune,* stuff like that. He's always decoding the mercenary ads in the backs of those magazines. Like, when it says 'rotunda OK,' that means the guy does kidnapping. 'Wet work' used to be one. Stuff like that. And *Paintball*—have you seen that one? Rudy's dying to play paintball. The magazine's full of masks and paintball guns, crossbreeds of forties futurism and nineties street weaponry. Full-head dressings, choice of ball colors. I look, too, but I'm afraid of guns. Aren't you?"

Mac caught her hand, slowed it down, then held it for a minute. "Let's see, I shot a squirrel once, a long time ago. I felt bad afterwards—it was worse than after really ugly sex. Once I shot a bird out of a tree, one off a wire, and I killed a groundhog at my uncle's farm when I was ten. I think that's the complete catalog."

"I guess killing's not about manhood after all," Mimi said. "I'd be afraid to have a gun, though. How would you avoid it? How would you stop playing with it, pointing it out the window at passersby and stuff? Going over the line?"

"That'd be a problem," Mac said. He eyed the panel with the floor numbers on it. "Bell's ringing," Mac said.

"At least there'd be the risk," she said. "Don't we all go a little nuts and slam the hammer through the bathroom wall sometime? Crack up one of those hollow-core apartment doors? Wouldn't we use a gun then, if we had it? Or like when Rudy started to jump up and down on the mini-satellite dish because it wouldn't find G2-A? What we do in private is scary sometimes. Maybe that's a good reason not to have a gun."

Mac started to slide out from behind her but didn't make it. She had him pinned. She had a bittersweet aroma, a new scent, dark and slightly overdone in a nasty way.

"I figure we can do anything we want, Mac," she said. "Whenever we want to do it. Anytime. Anywhere. Just get right down and do what we want, and nobody ever knows the difference, nobody ever knows what goes on."

"Rudy's waiting, isn't he?" Mac said.

"I guess, but he's way down there and we're way up here."

"We're not that far," he said, sliding sideways on the rail, pressing out from behind her.

She backed away, holding up her hands the way TV wrestlers do when they want to persuade the ref they're making a clean break. "Hey, if that's what you want," Mimi said. "I was thinking you might want to open up some, like PMI says, you know, show yourself, but if that's not the way you feel, okay. It's up to you, I'm just following the keys here—that's what these things are for, right? These retreats? To let you guys catch up?"

"You are lovely, Mimi," he said. "Really."

Then she stalked him playfully around the edge of the little elevator, and when she caught him they held each other for a few long seconds, then separated. Mimi smiled at him, tracing his cheek with the backs of her nails. "I'm fine," she said. "I'm a lot better than I appear." She fingered the red Emergency Stop button for a minute, eyeing him, then shoved that button in, and hit the one that said Lobby.

•

Rudy was on the edge of the goldfish pond staring into the lighted water at the big things circling in the thickened sea grass. "I love these," he said to Mac, pointing into the water. "If I had it to do over again, I'd be a fish, I swear to God. See how they move? Look at that, look at the white one there."

"Mimi said you wanted to talk?"

"Yes, sir." Rudy leaned to one side to look around him. "Where's your partner?"

"She's resting. Too much Hawaii, I think."

"Ah." Rudy shook his head and stared at the fish more. "I tell you, that Cam. She looks a little like Mimi, you know? She's just real nice and young. And so on."

"Thank you," Mac said. "I'll pass along your compliments."

"How'd you like the weekend? No problems?" Rudy asked. "You and Mimi get along okay? She's peculiar, like she seems one way at the college and completely different when she's not there."

Mac took a minute, then shook his head. "I don't know what you mean."

Rudy reached out to shake his brother's hand. "Doesn't matter. I just wondered. We're going over to the beach. You and Cam can leave if you want to. Tomorrow's nothing."

"Probably not," Mac said. "We'll probably stay."

"Up to you," Rudy said, noticing Mimi in the lobby. She was waving.

"I guess I *do* know what you mean," Mac said. "About Mimi. She's so calm. We came down in the elevator. It was the only time we had to talk, you know—"

"Yeah," Rudy said, rocking his head back. He dropped a fingertip into the water, and the potato-size fish swam up for a look.

Mimi came out the doors into the courtyard and strode toward them, her heels clicking on the paving stones.

"I gotta run," Mac said, getting up.

Mimi did a little circle right next to him and brushed a hand across his shoulder. "You ready?" she said to Rudy.

"About," Rudy said.

"Boy, I like it out here," she said. "I used to be out all the time, at clubs and parties, I used to see people, I used to do stuff. I remember what it's like, what night smells like when you're out here on your own. Sometimes I watch MTV, those dance shows where the kids jerk at each other every way they can, so hard, and it just carries me away, you know? I feel every move they make."

(1993)

PART FIVE

Bag Boy

We were in Dallas because Jen's father was an assassination buff. It was his hobby, something to do when there was nothing else to do. He wasn't new to it, but he wasn't a freak about it, either. Some people go overboard on everything, but that wasn't Mike. He was just interested in the assassination, the research, the testing, the theories—he perked up whenever anything about the assassination came across his line of sight. Mike was fifty-three and already retired from an Aetna Casualty job, so he had plenty of time on his hands to study the books, the videos, the gray-market paperwork he'd ordered from tombstone ads in magazines, the geek view he downloaded from assassination BBSs and the internet, and the half-dozen assassination CD-ROMs he owned, including one he'd shown me called *A Practical Guide to the Autopsy,* and others on the Warren Report, conspiracies in general, and great assassinations in history.

Mike had never been to Dallas. Jen and I hadn't been there, either, and we weren't particularly interested, but Jen and I had been living together for two years and Mike and I hadn't been introduced except by phone, so one Sunday in the weekly call we decided to go see Dealey Plaza, just the three of us. The next day Jen added an old college friend of hers, Penny Mars, to the mix, because she thought Penny would be good company for Mike, who was long divorced and a confirmed bachelor and twice Penny's age. We were sensitive to age because I was twenty years older than Jen, nearer Mike's age than hers, and we thought there might be some talk about that. So Penny had her uses.

After the drive from Baton Rouge the four of us were going up in the carpet-and-glass elevator of the Dallas Ramada with a young guy who had "Rhumbo" stenciled on his name tag. He was handling the bags. He was disease-thin, gangly, burr-cut, tattooed, and properly earringed. A man of his time. For the job he wore a too-big maroon uniform with bad gold piping.

"Where'd you get the name tag?" Jen asked the bag guy.

"The name or the tag?" He was naturally unpleasant, impatient, lots of attitude. "Which?"

"Name," Jen said.

I couldn't figure out why she was bothering—maybe it was highway-blindness. She was wearing cutoffs and a washed-out T-shirt and looked younger than the twenty-seven she was. Penny looked younger than that. Mike and I looked rumpled and tired, like we were on the wrong side of middle age.

"I was in prison in Minnesota," the kid said. "B and E. They called me 'Rhumbo.'"

"Oh," Jen said.

The guy was too tall and he stooped to look at her as he explained things, pointing with one finger at the palm of the other hand, as if he needed that for emphasis. "See, some dead man there had this kid's book about an elephant named Rhumbo, it was the only thing he could read, and he figured I favored this elephant, so that's what he called me all the time. I was, like, his pet."

"Cool name," Jen said, giving a little nod and digging into her purse searching for something.

He gave her a look. His skin was blotchy and sore red, patches the size of fists ran around his neck, and his eyebrows were furry and queer-looking on his shaved head. He had some kind of vinegary smell coming off the costume. "You want the tag?" he asked. "I can tell these Ramada dorks I lost it, I can tell them anything. That's something you get inside—how to take what you need, just rip it out of somebody's hands if you have to. These dips, what're they going to do? They're not going to fire me. They need a guy like me around here at night." He unhooked the name tag from his jacket and held it out to Jen. She hung back a minute, then took the tag.

"What about the Rhumbo-Dumbo thing?" Penny said, dodging her head back and forth in a way that meant she meant the question in a friendly way. "That a problem or anything?"

The guy rolled his eyes big, leaning his head off to one side. I watched his reflection careen around the elevator glass.

"Look," he said, like he was explaining something to a ten-year-old. "The Rhumbo book is *fact*. Elephants sleep on their stomachs. An elephant's height is calculated by measuring twice around the largest part of its foot. Real stuff. Dumbo was just some Disney slop."

Jen snapped the tag over the pocket of her T-shirt. "Hi, my name's Rhumbo," she said, shaking hands with an imaginary elevator-rider, practicing her introduction. Then she poked some high-floor numbers on the elevator panel. "Rhumbo, up!" she said.

The bag boy led us to our rooms on the ninth floor. He went in and did a lot of curtain-swishing and bed-patting in each room, then stood there at attention waiting for his reward. Mike gave him a twenty, and the guy went away grinning. We were still in the hall talking when the guy reached the corner by the elevators, did an elephant-trunk wave, and then disappeared.

•

In our room, Jen stripped to the waist, went straight into the bathroom, and came out wiping herself down with a damp washcloth. "I'm calling Penny and taking her for drinks," she said. "You want to come with?"

I was on my back on one of the beds. "I think I'm staying in," I said.

"You're getting along all right, aren't you? With Dad?"

"Sure. Everything's fine. He's not so bad—I don't know why we were worried. He doesn't seem to care how old I am."

"Well, he was prepared," Jen said. "He was talked to. You think he likes Penny?"

"I think he thinks Penny is a great big apple on a stick."

We'd been driving for so long that I was still swaying like we were out on the highway. It was nine and the city was lit up, and all I wanted to do was stay still and let things stop moving. The downtown buildings were all outlined with lights. One place had twin spires and these circular towers and looked like it came from Buildings R Us. Downtown wasn't that big. One building had green wiggly lights all over it, reflected in its glass. I couldn't tell whether the lights were strange or it was fabulous architecture.

The room was cheesy in that motel way—silly-looking dressers, veneered night tables, a nondescript table-and-chairs set by the window. If somebody you knew owned the stuff, it would be horrifying, but at the Ramada, it was comforting. You knew where you were. No mistakes.

Jen called Penny and arranged to go out for drinks, then knocked on the connecting door to her father's room. Mike opened up wearing a royal blue satin smoking jacket.

"Check it out," he said.

"Where'd you get that?" she said.

"Found it," he said. "On a hanger in here." He thumbed back toward his room.

"Looks mighty suave," I said, getting out of the bed. It didn't feel right being in bed with Mike in the room, like I shouldn't be that relaxed. When I sat on the edge of the bed I saw some kind of food crumbs on the floor right by the night table. "There're crumbs here," I said to Jen, pointing to the floor where the crumbs were.

She came over for a look, then swept her shoe back and forth a couple of times over the spot. "There. All gone," she said. She invited Mike to go out and have a drink with her and Penny, but he asked what I was going to do, and when I told him, he said he thought he'd just hang out with me, if that was okay.

She said, "Sure. Fine. You guys can give each other lectures or something."

"No lectures," Mike said, raising his eyebrows at me as if he hadn't a clue what she meant. I didn't either, so I shrugged.

"This traveling together isn't so bad, is it?" Jen said, sliding past him, headed for the door.

"No, it's great," Mike said. "I mean, it's okay for me. I'm doing fine." He sat down in one of the chairs by the window.

"You guys stay out of trouble," Jen said.

We both waved at her, the same kind of wave. It was odd happening the way it did. Mike had a Coke can he'd gotten somewhere, and he was flipping the tab making thumb piano sounds.

"So, Mike," I said, climbing into the second chair by the window. "You okay?"

"Pretty much," he said. "I guess I feel a little awkward. It's hard to be the father, us being the same age. I guess I never was a father to Jen all that much. With the first two I wasn't so tolerant, I didn't give them a lot of leeway, but by the time Jen came along I'd just given up, I mean, I knew whatever happened would be okay."

He was alternating between thumping the tab on the can and rubbing his thumb on the wood-grained Formica table between us, making a squeaking sound, like he was trying to rub some spot off the tabletop, some sticky spot that wasn't giving up without a fight.

"Uh-huh," I said.

"I'm sorry, Del," he said, putting the can down and rubbing his forehead instead of the table. "I didn't mean to bother you with that. It's just I've been thinking about things all day. You know—Jen, the other kids, the family. I haven't seen her in a long time."

"Yeah, I know. And it didn't bother me. I just didn't know what to say. I don't have any opinions about parenting, families, all that. Well, I mean I have ideas about *my* family, but not about the parent side of it, or any general sort of ideas about parents, just about my parents, you know, like from the point of view of the kid. Me, I mean."

"Sure," he said. "You live one way and I live another. All my life I'm a little tucked-in fella, sitting in my neat house, paying those bills right on time. Looking into problems and acting like I knew what I was looking at. I guess I had more order than I really needed."

"Actually, that sounds great to me," I said. "No kidding. Mine's been a mess, first to last."

He laughed. "Yeah, I gathered that from Jen. What I don't get is how come you're not worried. Fifty, aren't you? Close to it? You've got a good job, but it's not paying you a fortune, is it? And I'll bet the retirement program's not going to turn out the way the brochure described it. It takes a lot of nerve to be in your shoes."

I glanced at him, trying to see if this was criticism, an aggression, but it wasn't there in his face, so I said, "I guess I am kind of worried. I mean, I never was before, I was always too busy being this or that, disdaining this or that—you know how that goes. But now I'm a little nervous."

"Maybe I could help out," Mike said. "I mean, setting things up, some plans so you're sure you're okay when you retire."

"You think you could do that? That'd be very nice. I could use help."

"Sure," he said. He got up and leaned against the window, looking down to the freeway below us, first left, then right, scratching his cheek. He had a heavy beard, so there was a loud sandpapery sound. "You think we ought to go over to Dealey Plaza tonight?" he asked, tapping the glass.

"We can if you want to." I was watching a helicopter flying on the other side of downtown. It reminded me of some movie. I couldn't hear it, but it was moving lazily around the buildings over there, doing that spotlight thing.

"I was playing golf," Mike said. "When he was shot. Somebody came by in a cart and yelled at us, and we headed back for the Pro Shop where there was a TV. I watched there for a while, then went home and stayed there for days. Saw Ruby shooting Oswald—all of that. I liked the music at the funeral, the cortege, the boots backward in the stirrups—that's what got me, that riderless horse. Walter Cronkite talking about the riderless horse—he must've said those words hundreds of times. 'And now the riderless horse—' That got me. The drums, the music. The procession. All that walking. The backwards boots—damn. That was something. That was new as hell."

I got up and skirted the table, then picked up my wallet and keys from the dresser where I'd put them earlier. "So why don't we go over there now? Take a look."

"Should we eat first?" he said. "We can eat. You want to eat?"

The light coming up from the freeway caught his face in an odd way, and suddenly I saw him as a much younger man. This had happened to me before—in some odd second you see what somebody was like when he was twenty years younger. Most of the time it wasn't particularly attractive, but with Mike it was nice, it made me like him more than I already did.

"Chicken-fried steak, mashed potatoes, brown gravy," Mike said. "Let's hit a One's A Meal. Open-face roast beef with mashed potatoes. Either one."

"Hey now," I said, doing the guy on *The Larry Sanders Show.*

"I've got that mashed potatoes thing going." He grinned and caught my shoulder.

"I'm right there," I said, touched by our sudden camaraderie.

We started down the hall for the elevator, but Mike had to go back and get something in his room. I waited in the hall remembering a scene with Eddie Constantine in some early Godard movie I couldn't even remember the name of—*Alphaville,* it suddenly came to me. That's what the Ramada hallway looked like—desolate, frighteningly utilitarian.

"The art of the chicken-fried is a lost art," Mike said, coming out of his room and raising both hands as if to forestall any argument. "Now, I know that mostly what happens in life is that stuff gets lost, all kinds of stuff, and that food's the least of it, but you'd think they'd be able to hang onto chicken-fried steak, wouldn't you? The rest I don't care so much about. These days it's all rude people and their rude hair, anyway. That Elephant Boy in the elevator. You and me, Del, we're the old cars out there in the way." He soft-popped my shoulder with his fist. "But sometimes, don't you just want to bump the little creeps, you know? Just nudge them with the front end—bam! Sixty miles an hour, that kind of thing. I'll bet you know that feeling."

"Yes, sir," I said.

"See," Mike said. "Yet another reason to like you."

●

Rhumbo was backwards on a plastic chair at Jen and Penny's table in the Twin Sisters, the Ramada's house bar. We stopped there to see if they wanted to eat.

"You taking a break?" I asked him.

"I was just asking how come these girls were with you guys," he said. "What, you can't find women your own age?" He switched to a too-intense expression. "Just kidding. Jen told me she's"—he hesitated, ready to point at one of us, not sure which one until Jen nodded toward Mike—"your daughter, right? And you," he said, wagging a finger at me, "are the boyfriend."

"Good work," I said, then turned to Jen. "We were thinking of eating something."

"I can tell you where I'd go," Rhumbo said, swinging his leg over the back of the chair, getting up. "I'd hit that IHOP. Right around the corner here. Get me a batch of German pancakes. Real good." Something wet shined on his teeth when he smiled. He smelled sour. His little maroon suit was wide open over a white T.

"I don't play that pancake game," Mike said. "We're looking for chicken-fried."

"California Cafe, off eleventh," the kid said. "Go there all the time."

"I wouldn't hate pancakes," Penny said. She was fooling with her long and auburn hair, finger-combing it.

"We're going to see Dealey Plaza afterward," I said to Jen.

"He wasn't in prison," Penny said, patting the bag boy's head. "That's just something he made up. He's in grad school here. His name's Roy."

"Hey," the kid said, holding his hands out. "Caught me. But I can't believe you're going over to Dealey. I've been here eight years and I've never been there."

"Hello, Roy," Mike said, shaking the kid's hand.

"How about Roy shows us the Cafe and then we all go to the plaza," Penny said.

"What about work?" I asked. "Don't you have to work, Roy?"

"Fuck 'em," he said. "I'm on my break."

The California Cafe was greasy and small, just right, and chicken-fried steak was there. No brown gravy, only white gravy. It was nearly midnight when we got to Dealey Plaza, which was just a couple of highway feeders, half a city block with nothing on it, and a concrete train overpass. All the streetlights were orange.

"What a joke," Roy said, looking around from the sidewalk across from the Texas Schoolbook Depository. "Oswald's up here, and the limo goes there, and blam! Even I could have made that shot. Do it in my sleep."

"Oh, settle down," Penny said. "You couldn't make the shot."

"On TV shows, Dealey Plaza does always seem bigger," Mike said.

"What is it—a hundred yards from there to there?" Roy said. "It's tiny. Why'd they make a big stew about this? Anybody could make it. Glenn Ford could make it. It's a groundhog deal."

"Six FBI marksmen," Mike said. "They tried it with pumpkins and missed. I mean, using pumpkins for Kennedy's head. Did it here and did it in a field in Iowa or Wisconsin."

He looked a little shell-shocked. I grabbed his arm, and we walked across the street to see the Texas Schoolbook Depository close up. Then we came back and walked the route Kennedy's car had taken, then climbed up the grassy knoll and went around behind the fence into the vacant lot where the other shots were supposed to have come from. We watched a train go by on the overpass. "This is where the three tramps were," Mike said. "Maybe they were getting into a boxcar over there"—he pointed toward the tracks—"but some reports say they were over behind the Depository building there, that back corner there. This lot was full of cars."

Jen, Penny, and Roy were sticking close to the terraced part of the plaza where there was a reflecting pool and a commemorative plaque explaining everything. There was a spotlighted American flag in the middle of it, looking like red and white vinyl flapping up there. "I'm going to go see what Jen's doing," I said. "You okay here?"

He nodded, and I went back around the fence and crossed the street, climbing the little rise to the terrace. Jen drifted away from Penny and Roy.

"How're you doing?" she asked.

"Fine," I said. "But what's the deal with Penny?"

"She thinks he's interesting."

"Roy? She must be starved to death," I said.

"He's right about how small this joint is," Jen said. "Where's Dad?"

"Over here," I said, looking back toward where I'd left Mike. "He's behind the fence, above the grassy knoll. He's being the second gunman. He seems kind of forlorn."

Across the street I could see Mike's head poking out above the wood fence that separated the grassy knoll from the parking lot. The train going by behind the parking lot was squeaking and squealing, rocking on the tracks.

"Places are always letdowns," Jen said. "I wish it was scary, at least. You know, an eerie feeling like going back in time, or time could switch around and you'd be caught there that day, running to the limo, but it'd be snaking off toward the underpass. You know what I mean? *X-Files*. That'd be cool."

The big flag was snapping overhead, the wind was driving it so hard. Mike came out and stood for a minute in the colonnade on the other side of the grassy knoll. Then he headed our way. When he got to us he looked like somebody who'd gotten real depressed.

"You feel all right?" I asked him.

"Fine," he said.

"The Depository isn't open," Jen said. "It's open days but not nights."

Penny and Roy came up behind us. "Everything okay?" Penny said.

"I don't want to go there anyway," Mike said.

"This is cheap shit," Roy said. "It's a toy, like a scale model where a toy president was killed. Toy people scattering. Toy shots. What a shank."

Jen was trying to bring Mike around. "We can come back tomorrow, and you can get right up there to the window where Oswald did the shooting," she said.

"Unless he was hanging upside down from one foot with a squirrel in his teeth it ain't worth it," Roy said.

"I think I'll go back to the Ramada for now," Mike said.

Jen looped her arm through his. "Aw, c'mon, Dad. Let's sit here and just soak it up. Maybe it gets better if you hang out a while."

"History's always so small when you see it in person," Mike said.

"Yeah, this is Buck-A-Day," Roy said. "Who cares, anyway? It's like about as important as John Wilkes Booth, or whatever."

A busload of tourists came in behind us, maybe twenty Hawaiians in Hawaiian shirts carrying cameras and wearing funny hats. The tour guide gathered them on the terrace alongside the reflecting pool in front of the Dealey Plaza plaque and started explaining stuff. Mike went for the street and hailed a cab that was going by.

"I'm going to the motel," Mike said. "Anybody want to go with?"

"We're ready," Penny said, yanking Roy with her.

"Are you okay, Dad?" Jen said. She looked at me as if I was supposed to stop him. I started toward the cab, but her father waved me off.

"Forget it. I'm fine. I'll get some rest."

Then the three of them climbed into the backseat of the Yellow and rode off. The car squatted as it accelerated.

•

Jen and I went back to the grassy knoll and sat down, watching the traffic dip left to right into the underpass. There were plenty of sightseers, not a crowd, but fifty or so, circling and pointing out the highlights, the Schoolbook Depository, the spot below us where the president was shot, the knoll, the fence. There was a big road sign in front of us, and I couldn't figure out if it was the one the president's car disappeared behind in the Zapruder film or if it was some new sign. It seemed as if it was the same sign but it was in the wrong place, as if it had been secretly moved, as if they didn't want anybody to notice.

"This is a big deal, isn't it?" Jen said. "I'm supposed to get the weight of history here. Great events upon which our future turned."

"Jen?" I said.

"It's not really working," she said.

"Maybe you have to believe things would've been different if he wasn't shot. You know, like coherence and history and all that," I said. The train had been squealing nonstop for twenty minutes. "I like this train pretty much."

"You would," she said.

"I like the way it's shimmering, and that steely noise the wheels make, and the way the cars shift back and forth into each other, kind of lurching," I said. "It's like a car-crash audio slowed way down."

"I wasn't even born," she said. "I think that's why for me. It's textbooks—You're supposed to think about it, feel stuff, maybe that's it. You're supposed to, so you don't, blah, blah. Pretty quick you resent it."

"Yeah?"

"I really don't feel shit, except I'm kind of pissed because it disappointed my dad."

I put an arm around her, then leaned against her, dropping my nearly fifty-year-old head on her shoulder. "Still, you don't want Kennedy killed, there's that. He got his skull exploded right down here in front of us. Think of that. We're ringside."

"People get that everywhere," Jen said. "Plus, who cares? Why's the president getting it worse than somebody else? He's just one more goofball going down."

"He had big ideas," I said.

"He was just another guy with a sore dick," Jen said.

She got up, and I followed. We went behind the fence where Mike had been earlier and toured the parking lot, then I leaned up against the fence. It was kind of broken down at the corner. I wondered if it was the real fence. Then I wondered if I cared if it was the real fence. We walked through the colonnade Mike had been through and back up alongside the Texas Schoolbook Depository, went and looked at the entrance to the museum part, and came back to where we'd started.

"I think things were different back then," I said. "There was a whole different deal, I vaguely remember. The idea is things changed because he was shot—that wised us up, made us all callous."

"That's junior, Del," she said.

"Hey, it hadn't happened before. Nobody thought it *could* happen. It was like something in those fifties movies with Henry Fonda or somebody, you know, the black-and-white ones?"

"Oh, please. If there's a change it was you and your buds cheating each other, stretching truth, pushing at the edges of things, getting that little extra. Everybody got used to it. You all held hands and evolved into us."

"My generation."

"That's it," she said. "Do the crime, do the time." She waved toward the Depository, then the rest of the Dealey setup. "This whole show looks like it's lit with bug lamps. It's yellow. Isn't everything kind of yellowish, or is that my imagination?"

"It has a parchment-colored thing," I said.

"Part of the plan, I guess," she said. "It's shitty to charge for the Oswald window. That's like, Kill a President so your town can make six bucks a pop on the yahoos. How many you figure they get a year? They even charge for kids."

"Do not," I said.

"Yes, sir. It's on the sign."

"So," I said, brushing off my jeans. "Let me see—you want to go back to the Ramada and get in bed and see what's on TV?"

"Exactly right," she said, smacking my arm. "Maybe that *JFK* movie. That'd be cool. Or some real rainy movie like that Kurt Russell Florida thing where he's the blown-out reporter and that Hemingway woman is his girl—that's really great rain in there." She kissed my shoulder. "I tell you, you older guys are slow but you're okay. You get there."

"Thanks," I said. "Now all we've got to do is refocus Penny, get her back on track."

"I'm getting her some new heels," Jen said. "Saw them in a catalog—chrome toe, six-inch stilettos, the works. They moan when you walk."

"She'll use 'em on Roy," I said.

"Well, then I'll keep them just for us," she said. "How about lemon yellow?"

We walked back to where we'd parked the car, which was next to some architect's idea of a Kennedy memorial—thick slabs of concrete making a sort of room that stood up off the ground in an open half-block space. You were supposed to stand inside it and feel the gravity of events. Somebody had posted a clown-show sign on its side. We got in the car and headed for the hotel.

The streets of downtown Dallas were almost empty, so it looked like one of those end-of-the-world movies, where all the people have been killed, and we get long shots of the empty downtown streets, and there's a wind blowing coffee cups across the pavement and pieces of paper are flapping in the breeze. But nobody moves. It was nice, so we ran the windows down on Mike's car and floated through the streets for a while—going six or eight blocks in one direction and then turning, coming up the next street going the other direction, the wind whipping into the car, twisting our hair. It smelled that strange way empty cities smell at night, clean and metallic. Jen switched on the radio, and we turned it up and let it thump as we rode through the streets.

•

Roy met us in the corridor outside our rooms. He looked worse for wear, like he was loaded. "So?" he said. "How're you guys? The big man turned right on in. You want to come down to Penny's and get trashed? We've got some shit."

"I don't think so," I said.

"Why not? What're you doing? Don't go getting all historical, okay?" he said, his hairless little face twisted into a smirk.

"Don't know much about history," I said.

We tried to get past him, but he followed us.

"Where's Penny?" Jen asked.

He grinned way too big. "She's freshening up. Just, you know—freshening up." Then he laughed a kind of snort-laugh.

"Great," Jen said.

"See, what I figure," he said, "I mean Kennedy and all that, is there's no difference—Starkweather, 'Nam, this cute Oklahoma trick—it's all settled. It's going down. That's what's out there. You gotta have the hard stuff or you got nothing. The government does it best. Blowing hands and feet off Iraqis on that road out of Kuwait or whatever—you see that? Real time-morphing. Big trade in corpse and body-part snaps. Big profits."

"Slow it up, pal, will you?" Jen said.

"And great TV, too," he said. "Sometimes I like that militia thing, that time-to-clean thing that we're doing now—flush the bad, act with maximum efficiency, scrape out evil's eye. Know what I'm saying? That appeals."

"You're a moron," I said, giving him some phony thumbs-up that I didn't quite have control of.

"Maybe history is calling," he said, grinning.

"Yeah, and maybe it's not," Jen said.

•

In the room Mike's connecting door to our room was closed. Ours was still open. I started to shut it as quietly as I could, fearing the latch. "I guess I'll just leave this alone," I said to Jen. "He's probably asleep."

"He's got a model of the plaza," Jen said. "It's wonderful. Made it himself, took years. Perfect scale, perfect grass, lampposts, signs, cars, and the different people who were there that day, all reconstructed from video and photos." She was hooking her notebook computer up to the telephone.

"I want to see that when we get back," I said.

"I'm sure he'll show it to you," she said.

I flipped on the television and went through a few stations until I got to the Weather Channel and stopped there and watched a new hurricane named Camellia messing around with Hawaii. A lot of the video of Hawaii was quite beautiful, so I watched that for a while. Buildings were falling down. A Holiday Inn fell down, or part of it did—the sign and the portico over the drive-in entrance. The trees were all bending vigorously, and the whole picture looked wet. It was lovely and relaxing.

In a minute I heard Jen's modem screech as she made her connection. She turned around and caught the tail end of the Hawaii video and asked me what it was.

"Hawaii," I said. "They're having a hurricane."

"Cool," she said.

There was a light knock on the door. I eyed Jen, then got up to answer. It was Penny. She was done up in a short black dress and lots of makeup. I let her in.

"Look out in the hall and see if jerk-boy is still hanging around, will you?" Jen said.

"Oh, don't be that way," Penny said. "He harmless, he's okay. Besides, he's down in my room."

"Here's what he is," Jen said, clicking some computer keys. Then she read something off the screen. "'With skillful manipulation of the Japanese rope harnesses you first find the middle of the rope and make a sizable overhand knot so you have a loop big enough to fit your partner's head. Employ a rope of appropriate dimension and surface. Consider the path of the rope from the breasts, just above the vagina, taking care to border the labia with

the length running then to her head and neck, and have her hold
her hands behind her back—'"

"Okay," Penny said. "I get it. But he's doing the best he can."

"Like us," I said.

"Exactly. He's trying to be somebody."

"Why couldn't he try to be Alf?" Jen said.

Penny smoothed her skirt, what there was of it. "He wants to
impress us. He's just trying to make himself more interesting. Anyway, we're going out for beers."

"Everybody always wants to be so interesting," I said.

"Yeah," Jen said. "That's our generation."

"I thought I'd tell you so you wouldn't worry," Penny said.
"I don't think we'll be out too long."

"Okay. We won't worry," I said. "You look mighty, uh, breezy."

"Let me be, will you?" Penny said, looking at Jen. "What's
with him?"

"He is just a rat," Jen said, walking Penny to the door. "Go. Have
fun. Be lucky."

When Penny was out of the room Jen tossed herself onto my
bed. "Oh, baby, you're so right it just gives me chills. I just want to
watch some TV with you. Watch those news gooks, potatoes with
olive eyes, talking as if it mattered. I wish we had that Saturday
night one with the guy from the *Wall Street Journal,* Novak, and the
woman with the prissy little mouth and the mole. Everybody sits up
so straight on those shows."

"You're a true postmodernist," I said.

"No alternative," Jen said.

They were doing local stuff on the Weather Channel—chance
of rain. Jen shut down the computer, unplugged the phone cord and
stuck it back into the phone.

"I thought Penny hated men," I said.

Jen shook her head and rolled her eyes and did a little puppet
jerk, as if she were being controlled on strings from above. I took this
to mean I was being stupid.

I clicked through the channels, stopped again at CNN. There
was something about Whitewater, new revelations, more unending
true drivel.

"Now *that* is pissing in the wind," Jen said, looking over my shoulder.

"You guys are supposed to be less cynical than us," I said.

"That's another generation," Jen said. "The one before us, I think. They were less cynical than you. We're more. Our cynicism takes paint off warships, knocks planes out of the sky—this is a problem for you old guys when you get three or four generations out of touch."

The O. J. backdrop came up on the screen along with the theme song. Jen lunged for the remote.

•

I was the last one down for breakfast. The motel restaurant was all light wood and light Formica and plastic flowers in fifty shades of green. It was almost empty. Mike and Penny and Roy were sitting together at a small table near a window that looked out toward the freeway. I saw Jen in the lobby as I came out of the elevator. She waved me into the restaurant. She was getting a newspaper. Mike had scrambled eggs and toast. Roy was slicing his fork through a tall stack of pancakes covered with pretty syrup. Penny was eating a piece of bacon off his plate. I said good morning.

"Morning," Mike said. "Long time no see."

"I slept," I said. "What time is it?"

"Eleven," he said.

Penny was patting Roy's arm. She picked up her fork and got a one-inch square of pancake off his plate. She had coffee and a roll in front of her, but she was more interested in Roy's pancakes.

"Dealey wasn't too great, I guess," I said.

"It's putz country," Roy said, waving his fork off toward town. "That's the real deal."

"It's deadly," Penny said. "That's what we decided."

"Maybe if we go over today that would help," I said. "You know—it was night, we were tired, we'd been driving."

"I don't think so," Mike said. "I've seen enough."

"It's fucking pathetic over there," Roy said. "So what are you anyway, some kind of investigator? You trying to figure how many gunmen there were and all that?"

"Yeah. That's it," Mike said, smiling at the kid.

I thought about some things Mike had told me, stuff about the videos, the autopsy photographs, the little girl running—was she really looking back up at the Depository, or had she been called?—about Badgeman, Umbrella Man, Dark-Complexioned Man, and the skin flap on Kennedy's head, the fence people, the tramps, the boxcar deal, the woman on the Louisiana highway, the bar deal with the CIA, the Moorman Polaroid. I figured he was smart to keep it in his head where he could work on it in peace, let it show him new angles, where the questions were still viable and the pleasure was getting close to something that always disappeared when you tried to look at it. He could do that forever.

Jen came back to the table with a *USA Today* and a Dallas paper. I ordered eggs like Mike's. Penny went on picking off Roy's plate. Jen scanned the Dallas paper. I tried to figure the quickest way to get the four of us back in Mike's big Lincoln.

(2000)

SOCORRO

Socorro was a ratty little town that dangled off the highway the way a broken leg hangs off a dog that's been hit by a car. It was mostly dirt, sand, red grass, and squat cactus, peppered with little brown houses that might as well have been ovens. Jen and I had planned a driving trip to see some places where there'd been UFO sightings in New Mexico, but we'd picked up her father, Mike, and a college friend named Penny along the way, so it wasn't quite the trip we'd planned. Mike was short and bristly and Penny was lanky, long-haired, and angry about men. Fortunately, both Mike and I were near fifty, him on the top side, me on the other, so we weren't quite men in Penny's sense of the word.

We'd been through Roswell and Corona, and the next place to see was Socorro, because of the alien craft that landed there in 1964. Jen was keeping a trip diary on her notebook computer, a tiny Compaq she used to link up to email services when we stopped overnight, and she had been writing notes to herself about Socorro all afternoon.

"First we find the site," she said, "then we go after Lonnie Zamora and Sergeant Chavez. Everybody okay with that?"

"They sound like a couple of real dweebers," Penny said. "What's their deal, anyway?"

"Zamora saw the spaceship and Chavez came in later and saw the traces—burning bushes and all that," Jen said. "It's a big deal because the Air Force didn't write it off."

"Typical," Penny said.

We found the spot out of town where the deputy had seen the UFO. That was pretty easy. The UFO had supposedly landed there in this gully, and these little men were standing around it, and then when Zamora got out of his car or something the men got back in the ship and blasted off. The town had the spot marked with a big sign. But when we tried to find the Zamora himself, that wasn't so easy. Everybody we talked to had a different idea of where he lived. In fact, some people had different ideas of who he was, which made tracking him difficult. What we did was cruise up and down the dusty, chuck-hole-filled roads, sliding in and out of stringy subdivisions. We knocked on a few doors and finally ran into some people having a chicken picnic in the dirty sand that was their front yard. They invited us to join them, but we declined, though it looked to me like Penny was interested.

"We're trying to find the guy who saw the UFO," Jen said to an older, skinny man with a rubber-like complexion and a bum leg that seemed to point toward the other leg whenever he tried to walk. The Charlton Heston thing.

"Everybody's seen them," the guy said. "They're all over the place. You only have to turn around and you see one."

"Have you seen any?" Jen said.

"Well, I haven't," he said. "Not me, personally. But everybody else I know has."

"I hear that," Penny said. "Lot of young bright men seeing UFOs every day."

"We're looking for Lonnie Zamora," Jen said. "Or Chavez, the state cop. You know them?"

"There's a cop lives around the corner there," the guy said waving off to one side. "But he's new, just got here in town last year. He's from Anchorage, I think. May be an Eskimo, or have some Eskimo blood. That's what I heard, anyway."

The guy was standing knock-kneed in his front yard holding a quarter chicken by the end of the drumstick. One bite of chicken about halfway down the leg was already gone. He was sort of shaking this chicken at us as a kind of invitation. His wife and their kids, all of whom seemed extraordinarily tiny, much tinier than they ought to have been, almost like circus tiny—the wife was maybe four and a half feet tall, the kids were smaller—were back by the folding table on top of which was a fat pitcher of blue Hawaiian Punch. I figured it had to be Hawaiian Punch or Kool-Aid because it was blue, but these folks looked like the Hawaiian Punch crowd. The kids were slurping this stuff out of giant lock-top plastic glasses that had elaborate roller-coaster straws coming out of them.

On the card table there was a boom box that plugged into an orange extension cord that slid back across the dirt, up over the porch rail, and into the front door that was cocked open a little. They had old-fashioned ballroom music swinging out of the boom box, dance music, and both the elders—him tall and skinny and her small as a medium-size dog up on its hind legs—were swaying a little in time with the tunes, threatening to dance in the driveway. We waved as Mike dropped the car back into gear and let us roll away.

"That poor woman got stuck and stuck hard," Penny said, shaking her head.

Apparently the town council had tried to set up a tourist deal in Socorro like the one in Roswell, but it hadn't worked out. They had a Spaceship Cleaners, a Fourth Dimension Cafe, and, on the way out of town, a homemade fast-food place called Out of This World, but that was about it for UFO-marketing. O-O-T-W, as its neon said, looked like a Dairy Queen that'd been caught between a couple of giant pieplates and then rolled in car aerials and whip antennas covered with SuperStik. The parking lot was spray painted a remarkable golf-grass green. We stopped in the drive-through and Penny got their specialty, a Littlegreenmanburger. She told Jen she didn't know whether to eat it or smack it so hard it blistered.

It was turning chilly when we pulled out of the lot. Mike was ready to pack it in, find a local motel, but Jen wanted to visit the UFO Museum, so we drove two blocks and parked nose-in at the storefront museum.

Inside, a retired postal worker from Cleveland did his best to explain the Philadelphia Experiment—those cables wrapped around that ship, the space in the water where the ship had been, anti-matter machines, all of that. He had wiry hair and wore his jeans nipple-high, and he was eager to please—a volunteer, he explained, at the museum. He was reluctant to let us browse without instruction. The place was the size of a shoe shop, three rooms, the largest arranged around a long folding display board with photos, texts, crummy sketches of flying saucers pinned to it. In a side chamber there was a four-foot-high wooden alien with teardrop eyes and several coats of Tester's Alien Lumina Silver. We listened to the retiree tell us about the rash of sightings in 1947 and about how the Army Air Corps had clammed up about the Roswell incident. He was quick to put the kibosh on the Air Force's new bonehead spy balloon explanation of the original cover-up, too. There were snapshots of the Brazel ranch where the Corona UFO crashed, but the property looked like nothing special, just dirt, like the rest of New Mexico.

"You see," the guy said. "In 1947 there were sightings all over this country—way up in Washington and Oregon, all the way down here, over to Alabama, up toward Minnesota, in New York State— they were everywhere. Strange lights, abductions, interactions, exchanges of fluids—I mean priests, nurses, even military officers reported stuff. For several weeks in the summer of 1947 this went on and then it suddenly stopped."

At that, the retiree did a deliberate pause, a long pause, nodding, watching us with a shrewd smile.

"It *stopped*," he repeated. "What does that tell you? What does that say? Think about it. It says they came for a *reason*. It says they got what they wanted and they left." He slapped his hands together for emphasis. "Bam!" he said. "You have to keep up with these deals, or you miss everything. You have to think back to what happened in 1947. Who was born that year? What world historical events were precipitated by incidents that occurred then? What was invented in the year 1947? These kinds of things are the kinds of things you have to think about when you're trying to keep an eye on the big picture. Where there's smoke, there's fire—that's all we are saying."

"Amen," Jen said. "But what about that magic aluminum foil, you know? And where are the tiny purple I-beams?"

"Oh, a TV watcher, huh?" he said, shaking his head. "Well, they weren't purple, they were magenta, and where do you think? Government's got all that. Maybe Groom Lake, Area 51—you know Area 51?"

"Where some aliens were held captive, right?" she said. "But somebody discovered there really wasn't any Area 51, it was all a hoax."

He smiled and took a look at his black shoes. "Oh, there's an Area 51, all right. And a Hangar 9. There wasn't any Hangar 54, maybe that's what you're thinking about, that's more TV stuff, but there were Rainbow, Phoenix, and Montauk projects. And there's S4, MJ-12, Zeta-Reticula, and there are underground hangars at Kelly—there's a lot out here. If you're interested, check into Groom Lake, check out the Vegas airport sometime, the white jets without markings that go into the desert at night." He thumped his temple. "Don't let 'em confuse you."

Penny's eyebrows were doing Groucho moves. She pointed out toward the lobby and mouthed that she'd be waiting for us. Mike slipped off with her, leaving me and Jen to listen to the Socorro story, how the deputy had been driving along, minding his own business, kind of a pleasant evening, enjoying himself after work when he'd seen this craft in a ravine just outside of town—the full story. While he was talking I read the actual front page of the Roswell newspaper the day the Army put out the story that it had recovered a saucer. I knew the story, but seeing the paper, yellowed and brittle and hiding under glass, gave me a new sense of that time, made it seem as if the world was a toy world back then. The way the story sounded, the people it talked about and quoted, what they said, how they said it, even the people you could imagine reading the paper—they must've been like kids in adult bodies running things. That was a little eerie.

The museum was strange in the same way. It was childish; it looked like a sixth-grade science show. But there was something edgy and nagging about the pencil drawings and the snapshots with their rippled edges and the Xeroxes of typewritten accounts, something that made you uneasy—why was this enterprise still so ragtag after all these years? I stared at sketches supposedly done by the medical examiner during the autopsies of the Corona aliens, at a photo of the supposed Socorro deputy pointing at the place where he'd seen the aliens—there was a dotted marker line showing the path of the departing spacecraft—and I began to think that in spite of, or maybe because of, the farfetched and unconvincing displays, the UFO Museum was entirely disturbing.

About then the retiree rubbed his hands together and looked around, as if scanning for something else to tell us. "I guess that gives you a start on it, huh?" he said. "Why not kind of meander around and get your own sense of the place now that I've introduced you? That be okay?"

"That's great, thanks," Jen said.

When he was gone I said, "I envy him—living here, volunteering here, explaining everything to the tourists."

"Yeah," she said. "Cool job."

"Like the details of Corona, or the Philadelphia Experiment, or Groom Lake. Wouldn't it be great to go home every night and read new stories, watch bad video copies, go through new evidence compiled and distributed by the Society for Recognition of the Adaptations of Alien Life Forms?"

"S-R-A-A-L-F," she said.

"Yeah," I said. "Or just sit out on a dusty porch in the middle of nowhere and stare at the saucer-filled sky."

"You're a wonderful person, Del," Jen said.

"Well, he's like those guys who spend twenty years building railroads in their basements, who really don't do anything but play with their trains. They live perfect lives, devoted to love."

"Oh, baby," Jen said, doing a fifties deal. "Come to me, baby." She gave me a playful and sexy hug.

I watched as the little guy stood at the front window for a minute talking to another volunteer, then he cornered three new tourists— husband and wife with child. The retiree took them on, brought them into the main room and then to one of the side spaces where he'd originally taken us. I heard him start his speech about the anti-matter machine, how even he didn't quite understand it, but he would try to explain it to them if they could picture this massive World War II battleship wrapped in miles of thick steel cable—cable as thick as your arm!—the ship tossing in the stormy ocean waves on a bleak, wintry night, rain coming in visible sheets, and then, suddenly, without warning, in a wash of lightning the ship vanishes, leaving an indentation in the water, a footprint in the shape of its great hull.

"I can drive," Penny said. We'd finished the museum and were climbing back into the car. It was beginning to get dark.

"If we stay here we can try to find Zamora tomorrow," Mike said. "I mean, get the story firsthand."

"He's another guy who ain't ready for us," Penny said.

"You figure he ought to be standing out here on the highway?" Mike said.

"That'd be a start," Penny said.

"Dad," Jen said. "We're hitting the road."

So Penny took the driver's seat and we headed back down Highway 25 to the place where we could catch a state road to Arizona. In the dusk we could still see the mountains on either side of us, tall solid hulks criss-crossing the road up ahead. There was a big stream running down one side of the highway, silver, reflecting lights from the little cabins alongside it. Pretty soon we were higher into the mountains, and the cutoffs were smaller and the stream was gone and there weren't any houses, just a big, black hump squeezing the highway. We hadn't done much night driving and I was thinking that was too bad, because things seemed more comfortable in the car at night. The inside seemed a lot bigger. There was territory there between the riders, and the car was cooler and quieter. The road wasn't making so much noise, and the noise it did make was more soothing in darkness than daytime. Looking out the front window at the white lines edging the road and the yellow lines in its center, I had a vivid sense of riding on a seam, an edge between two voids, a track pointed somewhere, coming from somewhere, lit only by headlights. The big Lincoln seemed to shoot itself forward into that night. The few lights in the hills were glittering on the windshield. Headlights jiggled as they came toward us, and the reflectors embedded in the highway threw our brights back in our eyes.

The road was two-lane blacktop interrupted now and then by brand-new sections of divided highway. These sections didn't make any sense, there wasn't a pattern to their appearance or disappearance. We'd drive a while and then suddenly there'd be a mile of divided highway, then back to blacktop. We passed a hut on the side of the road renting trailers, and our lights caught the taillights of all the trailers at once, making them look like a herd of small animals cowering there in the ditch alongside the highway.

Jen pulled out the Compaq and said, "I'm going to read your tarot. I got this program off the Net."

"I'd rather watch TV," I said. We'd been carrying Jen's handheld TV, a Casio the size of a Walkman with a two-and-a-half-inch color LCD, but I hadn't seen it for a while. "Where is that TV, anyway? I want to check what's on."

"Maybe you could tune in some aliens," Penny said. "You know how those spaceships always gray out the screen?" She and Mike, in the front seat, giggled about that.

"It's in the trunk, probably," Jen said, cranking up the computer. "But wait'll you see this—Celtic cross, a couple other spreads, and it explains everything, so when you get the Death card, I can explain the hell out of it."

"Death is just another word for nothing left to lose," Penny said. "Death is never having to say you're sorry."

"Oh, Penny," Jen said. "You're always so negative." She ran the program and asked me to shuffle the cards by punching a couple of keys. "You can stop whenever you want to," she said.

"How do I know the cards are shuffling under there?" I said.

"You trust me," she said.

So I stopped and then she said, "Okay. Now you have to pick out your cards." The notebook had a trackball, which made picking out the cards difficult, but I got it done.

"Are you ready?" She moved the cursor to a button that said "Reveal" and clicked. The first card in the center of the cross rolled over. Death. I shook my head.

"That's great," Jen said. "Death's a really great card to get in that position. It's all about starting a new part of your life, putting the things of your past behind you and going forward, reaching out to conquer new challenges, stepping out of old, bad habits, leaving your worn clothes behind. It's a wonderful sign, really. It's about the best card you could possibly ever get in that position."

"Short of a letter bomb," Penny said.

"Okay," Jen said. "I won't kid you. There is a downside. But it could be a lot worse. See, position is important. If it were up in the fourth house that would be a problem. I'd tell you that, too, I'd just come right out and tell you, but here, at the center of everything, it's a very, very good sign." She clicked on a button to bring up the explanation of the Death card. "See here," she said, pointing at the screen. "It says right here that 'the Death card represents the clearing of the old to usher in the new and, therefore, should be welcomed as a positive, cleansing, transformative force in our lives.'"

"Let's do it again," I said.

"What do you mean, do it again? You can't just do it again," she said.

"Give him another chance," Penny said.

"Let's shuffle and do it again," I said.

"Are you sure?" she said. "We'll lose this whole spread."

"That's the ticket," Penny said. She was watching us in the rearview, bobbing her head around to see me, then to see Jen.

So Jen clicked on the "Shuffle" button, and we went through the whole process again, dealing another set of ten cards. This time when she clicked on "Reveal" the first card that came up was the Devil.

"What is it?" Penny said.

"Progress," I said. "Satan."

Jen clicked the "Interpret" button and read parts of it out loud. "'The Devil represents hidden forces of negativity that constrain us and deceive us into thinking we're imprisoned by external forces,'" she said. "'There's a devil in each of us. He's like an inner force. He's an embodiment of our fears, addictions, and harmful impulses.'" She pointed to the screen picture of the card. "It says these two people chained at The Devil's feet are 'entranced with the paralyzing fear of his illusory power and therefore stand there and look numb.'"

"Dumb?" Penny said.

"Hush," Jen said. "But see, the chains hang loosely so they can break free of their hypnotic attachment if they really want to, if they have the will. That means you can, too."

"This is worse than last time," I said.

"Well, maybe," she said. "But there's a way it's better—a cleaner beginning, a solid ground against which to work."

"Why don't you go ahead and turn over the next card?" Penny said. "Take it one card at a time."

Jen clicked on the button to turn over the second card and the second card was Death.

"One of the most fruitful and positive cards in the deck," I said.

"Death?" Penny said, looking over her shoulder into the back seat. "Sorry, Del. I was rooting for you. Honest."

"Watch the road, will you?" I said.

"This is not good," Jen said. "I think maybe we want to move away from this spread."

The third card was the Hierophant. Jen said, "Let's just take a peek at what's here, not really taking this one seriously any more, but just to see—" She clicked through the rest of the cards. I had the Emperor in the recent past, the Moon and the Crown, the Wheel of Fortune in the future, and the other four cards were the Chariot, the Hanged Man, Judgment, and the Magician. "Now, this isn't really so bad," Jen said. "It looked a little iffy there at the beginning, but as it plays out, it's not so bad. I've seen worse than this."

"Yeah, I did one for Gary Gilmore that was worse," Penny said.

"I'll save it and we can look again later, okay?" Jen said. "You don't believe in this stuff anyway."

"I believe in everything," I said. "A little bit in everything."

Jen shut the computer down and slipped it back into the bag she had in the footwell on her side of the car.

"Penny," she said. "Where are we?"

"Thirty-one miles from Pie Town," Penny said.

"Is that all?" Jen said. "What are you doing? Eighty?"

"Something like that," Penny said.

Mike stirred and I realized he'd been asleep with his head pressed against the window glass. Penny waved a hand to hush us and Jen turned sideways in the seat, resting against the door on her side and running her feet across my lap into the door on my side.

"We stop there, okay?" she said.

Penny waved again.

Jen said, "I want to wake up in Pie Town. Just the idea is great. Maybe the idea is greater than actually doing it even. But I want to do it. I'm beginning to like this traveling stuff, this touring around and seeing stuff." She gave me a little kick. "Don't you like it?"

"Yes, I like it. I told you I liked it," I said.

"Could you guys whisper?" Penny said from the front. "The oldster is napping."

"I think it's worthy," Jen whispered.

Up in the front Penny sneezed a couple times and then looked up into the rearview to see if we were watching her.

Mike sighed, his head still against the window. "Why is everybody making so much noise?" he said.

"Maybe we should call ahead to Pie Town and see if we can get reservations," Jen said, tapping his shoulder.

"Why don't you?" Mike said. He slipped the cellular phone over the back of the seat.

"I guess we can't," Jen said. "We'd have to call information and get somebody and ask about motels—they're not having a Holiday Inn in Pie Town."

"So why are you asking me?" he said. He was still bent against the car door.

"Wake you up," Jen said.

"We'll just get something when we get there," Penny said. "It's not going to hurt if we don't call."

"Let me have the phone," I said. "I'm calling somebody."

"Here we go," Jen said.

"I don't have to if you don't want me to," I said.

"No, go ahead," she said.

"Go ahead," Mike said from the front seat.

"Maybe you should call that guy back at the museum," Penny said. "Maybe he's seen some spacecraft."

"Is that the nicest thing you could possibly think of to say?" Jen said.

"I'm sorry," Penny said.

Jen patted my arm. "Go ahead. Call anybody you want. It's a free country. I'll join our fellows up front, give you some privacy."

Jen leaned forward over the back of the seat and put an arm around Penny and an arm around Mike. "So, what's up guys?" she said.

I dialed our number at home thinking I'd check for messages as a first step, but the radio waves got crossed up or something and I ended up connected to a guy on a Continental Airways flight from LA to New York who was trying to call his mother in Akron. I told him I'd never talked to anybody on an airplane telephone before. I told him we'd been driving across New Mexico, that we'd been to Roswell and to the UFO Museum in Socorro, and that we were headed into a place called Pie Town. He told me he thought he'd seen a UFO once, down in Costa Rica, but he wasn't sure. He told me his mom had a sixth sense about the paranormal, out of body travel, the Rapture, mind locks, all that stuff, and that she was always sending him those covers off the *National Enquirer* or the *Star* where they make babies the size of houses, or put beautiful models' heads on giant snake bodies. "She thinks it's all true," the guy said. "I tell her 'Mom, it's trick photography,' but she won't buy that. She says that things are happening we can't even imagine, that the world is a constantly developing eruption. She says we'll be lucky if we last until the turn of the century."

Outside the car window the night was black and moving fast. There was crackling on the phone and the connection ratcheted in and out. I listened to static for a couple minutes, sat there waiting for things to come clear. After a while it was just a dead line and I was there with the cell phone stuck to my ear, listening. I was thinking maybe this guy's mother wasn't that far wrong.

(1995)

ELROY NIGHTS

The young man who lived across the courtyard from me was always elegantly dressed in expensive clothes, good shoes, his hair well cut and his face cleanly shaven. He was, precisely, dapper. He drove an older Cadillac convertible in periwinkle blue, and seemed a little too intent on having his way. He appeared to be lonely. I rarely saw him with company. Mostly I saw him crossing the courtyard from the parking garage, carrying a handsome leather case, his heels clicking on the faded tile. Then I would hear the screech of the elevator doors and the tired whine of the car as it rose to our floor. My apartment was on the third floor as well, directly across the court from his, and while I used my windows a good deal, his blinds were never open.

We had a new tenant in the building, a woman named Eileen Wiesatch. I met her when the landlady introduced us on a Saturday morning in March. Eileen was a TV producer for the local NBC affiliate. She worked on the news, I gathered. She was an attractive woman in her early thirties, small, with close-cropped hair, and she wore casual clothes—jeans and mannish dress shirts, an elegant sports jacket. It may have been cut especially for a woman, but it did not look as if it had been. It occurred to me that she might buy her clothes in the boys' department at Saks. It was a nice look—comfortable, casual, and, at the same time, a little daring. She was hidden and exposed by these clothes.

I assumed Mrs. Bolton, who was our landlady, introduced Eileen to the other tenants, just as she had introduced her to me. I was Mrs. Bolton's oldest tenant in two senses—the one with the greatest tenure in the building, and the oldest. Mrs. Bolton and I were contemporaries, in fact, so occasionally we would have dinner together—a casual arrangement. I would see her in the courtyard or in front of the building, and she would invite me to dinner or I would invite her. We would have a pleasant hour and a half, with wine and salad and gossip.

It was one of these dinners at Mrs. Bolton's that Edward Works, the young man who took too much care of himself, interrupted when he arrived to complain about Eileen Wiesatch, who was, according to him, filling the hall outside her apartment, which was immediately adjacent to his, with boxes, packing materials, crates, and a general run of garbage that he thought ought to be taken immediately to the Dempsey Dumpster behind the building.

Mrs. Bolton invited Works into her home and introduced me. "Elroy Nights," I said, shaking his hand. I said I'd seen him before, and was pleased to finally meet him. As the grand old man of the building, I said, I was pleased to have him with us.

"And I am pleased to be here," Edward Works said. "Except for this little difficulty with the new tenant who doesn't seem to want to play by the rules."

"She just moved in," Mrs. Bolton said. "Don't you think we should give her a week or two to get settled? I'm sure we can have Rupert take that material out of the hall."

"We should have the young woman take care of it," he said. "She should dispose of the mess as soon as it comes out of her apartment."

"Of course you're absolutely right," Mrs. Bolton said. "Still, a little tolerance is sometimes a kindness we can afford, don't you agree?"

He drew a large breath through his nose at this point.

Seeing Edward Works up close was interesting. Most often when you see a person that close, you see, among other things, the flaws in their presentation—the ties don't quite match the shirts, the shirts have hairline wrinkles in the collars, the belts are off center, the shoes are scuffed, the sewing on the trouser cuffs may have come undone. Any number of small details give us away, conspiring to suggest just how much of our "self" is manufactured, just how far we are from the person we want to present for public consumption. But in the world of Edward Works there were no errors, there was not a single hair out of place, no choice was even slightly mistaken, no bit of fluff or dander flawed his suit. His shirt was impeccably pressed and arranged. His trousers were creased to perfection, and his shoes, which looked very English, had a lovely warm polish. He looked so good that he was enormously out of place in Mrs. Bolton's living room, which was chintz and Naugahyde and small, thick with bad Impressionist prints in gaudy golden frames. In that setting Edward Works was a cutout, an image from a magazine, an exquisitely coiffed and prepared figure dropped into this too-comfortable, too-carpeted, too-worn apartment.

"I could help with the boxes," I said to Mrs. Bolton. "If they aren't too large."

"You'd do that?" Mrs. Bolton said. Then she froze a second, and then made a cartoon expression, blinking and twirling her eyes at the same time—the kind of thing a character does when hit over the head with a frying pan. "Of course you'd do that. Why am I even asking?"

I smiled and said, "Well? You never know, do you?"

"That's right," Mrs. Bolton said. "Exactly."

"So whatever you want to do," Edward Works said, snapping his wrist out so he could look at his very expensive, very small watch. "I have a meeting, so I guess I'll leave it to you." He rearranged his cuff and turned for the door. Over his shoulder he said, "I genuinely appreciate your help with this, Mrs. Bolton." He did not look back. He opened the door, walked out, and let the door close behind him.

Mrs. Bolton and I stood in the living room a moment before returning to the dining table where our food, looking a little forlorn, remained. As we sat down Mrs. Bolton said, "I think I've lost my appetite."

"No. No, you haven't," I said. "You are profoundly hungry. You will eat and eat until you can eat no more. I will help with Eileen, and Mr. Works will be happy again."

"He is a strange bird, isn't he?" Mrs. Bolton said.

"I've noticed," I said. "He seems altogether too well kept up."

"Exactly. Exactly my thought," she said. "Has he nothing better to do than dress and polish and do his nails?"

"I missed the nails," I said.

"They're gorgeous," she said. "You must have a look." She was grinning now, reaching for her fork, beginning to toy with the salad again. "When we finish here, let's take a walk up to Eileen's place and see just how bad the situation is."

"Excellent plan," I said. I was looking at my salad, where two halves of a boiled egg stared at me out of their leafy green pasture. I thought them very handsome—big yellow eyes, lovely milk-white flesh. Just looking at them reminded me of the peculiar taste of boiled eggs, a taste I'd savored since childhood. There was special pleasure in the damp dryness of the yolk held in that cooled, almost gelatinous white. I had discussed this with Mrs. Bolton on several occasions, and we had agreed that boiled eggs were best served slightly cooler than room temperature. Not cold, precisely, but slightly chilled. So whenever we dined together I could be sure the boiled eggs would have been held in the refrigerator for half an hour or so before serving. I took up my fork and inserted the tines into the yellow of one of the egg halves, then extracted the yolk whole, holding it at the end of my fork between us.

Mrs. Bolton raised an eyebrow and then smiled, closed her eyes, and nodded. "You go ahead," she said. I salted generously and popped the yolk into my mouth.

·

Eileen was wearing a halter top and very short shorts, and she was in the hall arranging boxes that were lined up along the carpet, stacked four or five high. She had made a mess of things, there was no question. She greeted us warmly, shrugging at Mrs. Bolton as if to say, You said I could stack my things out here, as if she were apologizing and complaining about herself, all at the same time.

Mrs. Bolton said, "Yikes."

"Elroy Nights," I said, reminding her and extending my hand.

Eileen nodded. "Of course."

"I'm kind of across the courtyard here," I said, pointing in through her front door toward where my apartment was. As had been the case when I was first introduced to Eileen, I was a little stunned. She looked too much like somebody you'd see on television, like all the young women who operate cable news programs, and who seem innocent and randy at the same time. Eileen had the look—all lovely skin, fresh hair, eyes that sparkled, perfect features, slender shoulders, small breasts, smaller waist. She was a type. Had I not known she worked for NBC, I would have thought she was a model. She took my hand when I extended it, and her grip was bony.

"Pleased to see you again," she said. "I've been trying to figure out which are your windows, actually. And I've talked with Mrs. Bolton about you as well." She said this with a certain flash in her eyes, a good joke.

"Oh, yes?" I said, turning to Mrs. Bolton. "And what has she said?"

"She maintains that you are the real deal," Eileen said, smiling and glancing quickly at Mrs. Bolton as if they shared a slightly different version of this.

"I'm sure I'm flattered," I said.

Mrs. Bolton patted my arm. "We've had a meeting with Mr. Edward Works," she said to Eileen. "Your neighbor. He seems to think there is too much, uh," she paused, looking at the debris in the hall, "*stuff* here. We were wondering if we might help you get it downstairs."

"We could do it together," I said.

"He's a little worm, isn't he?" Eileen said. "Edward Works."

Mrs. Bolton and I both regarded the ceiling at the same time.

"No, I don't want you to do it. I'll take care of it, don't you worry," Eileen said.

"But we want to help," I said.

"Sorry, it's not happening," she said. "I'll take care of it. Don't give it another thought, please. It is a mess. I wish it weren't, but I can take care of it. I'll speak to Mr. Go Down Moses as well."

"I should say in his defense that Mr. Works's mother died just two months ago," Mrs. Bolton said. "I think it hit him harder than he imagined it would."

"His mother died. That's right. I remember you telling me that," I said.

"That's a terrible thing to have happen," Eileen said. "I'm sorry to hear that."

"Losing your mother makes you feel disconnected from the world," Mrs. Bolton said.

"That's only true, of course, if your mother is someone with whom you are connected," I said. "Don't you think that's so?"

"Not at all," Mrs. Bolton said. "I think your mother tethers you to the world in a way that no one else does."

"How did she die?" Eileen said.

"It was a car accident," Mrs. Bolton said. "She was driving a car on one of the freeways—I believe she was on the way to meet Mr. Works for lunch—when her car was hit by a truck, one of those huge trucks that carry the great pine logs. She was decapitated. Like Jayne Mansfield."

"She wasn't really decapitated, I believe," I said.

Eileen made a face. "Well, in any case, I guess he has reason to be upset. It's too bad we have to live with such things."

"Exactly," I said. "I spend a great deal of time thinking about things that I would like to correct in my life, things I would change if I had the opportunity to do them over again."

Mrs. Bolton and Eileen both turned to me expectantly.

"Well, I do," I said. "I would like to go back in time and try again. Like my father's death. It's ten years ago now, but we were not as close as we had been. He lived in Atlanta, in a small house, alone. I talked to him on the phone often, but I don't think I was as loving as I might have been. He was quite sick the last years, and I don't think I did enough to help out."

"I'm sure you did fine," Mrs. Bolton said. "But I know what you mean. We all have our regrets."

"Count me in," Eileen said.

"Still," I said, "there are two or three times in my life that I would really like to go back and do over again. A moment when I wish I'd been somewhere I wasn't, or done something I didn't, a moment that might have significantly changed things. I just never paid sufficient attention. My dad's death was one. If I'd done it better, been there with him, helped out a little, well, his death might have been avoided, or at least made less terrifying for him. He might have had one of those good TV deaths where the person is ready. But he didn't. He was discovered by the plumber who was coming to the house to work on the toilets. Dad had a lot of complaints about toilets, had lots of trouble with them. So the plumber was called and when he arrived my father was dead, sitting in his chair staring at a television set tuned to the preview channel. The plumber told me. He was very specific. But I think if I had been there, if I had been with him, if I'd been kinder and tried harder, maybe he wouldn't have died that way."

"Well," Mrs. Bolton said, touching my arm. "Maybe it wasn't as bad as you imagine. Perhaps he just sat down to watch a little television and sort of dozed off."

"Yes," Eileen said. "Maybe he just stepped into the next world. Right as rain. The most natural thing in the world."

"I suppose it could have happened that way, but I do not think that it did. He was inclined to torment himself about almost everything. He found trouble wherever he looked. He found things done wrong, people doing things wrong, people not trying hard enough—he found things to complain about. And while the complaints were always directed at other people, I always had the sense that he was really complaining about himself. Cloaking his own inadequacies by pointing to the failures of others. He was easily exasperated."

Mrs. Bolton rearranged some of the boxes against the corridor wall. "Yes, many of us are easily exasperated. Mr. Works, for example. He's exasperated with our young friend here."

"And I'm exasperated right back," Eileen said, smiling.

"Oh, pish," Mrs. Bolton said, laughing at Eileen's joke.

"I would be exasperated with him," Eileen said, "if I were the exasperating kind. No, that's not what I mean."

"That's okay. We know what you mean, dearie," Mrs. Bolton said. She rubbed her gray hair, tucked in a tight bun. She loosed it as if to freshen herself.

"There are not many times in your life when you can make a real difference," I said. "Dad could have used some companionship, a friendly son to take care of him, to sit with him, to get what he was about, to like him in spite of himself. I mostly talked to him on the telephone. So I could get away quickly and easily. Shed of him, I didn't have to think about him all the time. That was easier. I called him often to chat about what was going on, to hear his medical problems, but see, by calling I didn't have to see the problems, didn't have to deal with them. We had a woman from Catholic Health Services—"

"I did that with my mother," Eileen said.

"What?"

"Took her to look at nursing homes, had people in to take care of her. Everybody does that."

"I just went along with whatever he wanted," I said. "Encouraged him, whatever he said. I didn't give it that much thought. I figured he wouldn't listen to me anyway."

"My mother always wanted to figure out her future," Eileen said.

"How old a woman was she then?" Mrs. Bolton said.

"Mid-fifties, I guess," Eileen said. "She still had a house in Baltimore."

"Oh, so you're from Baltimore?" Mrs. Bolton said. "Why didn't I know that?"

Eileen looked at her and raised an eyebrow. "Don't look now, Mrs. Bolton, but I believe you did."

"Well, of course," Mrs. Bolton said. "I must have misplaced it. Just one tiny bit of information misplaced. Nothing to worry about."

"He was kind of a tyrant," I said.

Just then the elevator clinked to a stop down the corridor and the doors hissed open, and Mr. Edward Works stepped out and started toward us down the carpeted hallway.

"Speak of the devil," Mrs. Bolton said, Groucho-Marxing her eyebrows.

"I think I'll just step back inside here," Eileen said, backing into the doorway of her apartment.

"Come right back out here," Mrs. Bolton said. "I want to introduce you."

"He was kind of a bore, too," I said. "He couldn't help it, but the truth was that's what he'd become. He was plenty ugly in those last years."

"Maybe that's what we all become," Mrs. Bolton said, eyeing me.

She turned around just in time to catch Mr. Edward Works by the elbow. "How are you, Mr. Works?" she said.

"I'm fine, thank you," he said, drawing his elbow away from her unsuccessfully.

"I want you to meet Eileen Wiesatch," she said. "She's new in the building. Just moving in, as you can see."

Mr. Works gave Mrs. Bolton a look as cross as any I'd seen in quite some time. Then he stepped forward and extended his hand to Eileen, who took it and smiled, saying, "Hi. How are you? Glad to meet you."

"Edward Works," Mr. Works said. "I'm just down the corridor here."

Eileen nodded, still holding his hand. "Yes, I know. I do want to apologize about all this mess I've made in the hall. I'll have it straightened away in a day or so. Do you think you can put up with it for that time?"

"Of course," Mr. Works said. "I hadn't even noticed it. I'll be happy to help if you need a hand."

"That's very kind of you," Eileen said.

"We were talking about things we would have done differently in our lives if we'd had the opportunity," I said. "Things we'd like to go back and correct."

"Go back?" Mr. Works said.

"Yes," I said. "Go back in time. How things might have been different if we were at a certain place in a certain time, and how now we might actually like to go back in time and be at those places at those times."

"Ah," he said, nodding.

"Time travel," Mrs. Bolton said.

"Yes, I see," Mr. Works said.

"I was talking about my father," I said. "I find that as I get older I think more and more about him, what his life must have been like after the children were grown into middle age and my mother passed away and he was living alone."

"Eileen's come to us from Baltimore," Mrs. Bolton said.

"That toddlin' town," I said.

Behind Mr. Works's back Mrs. Bolton gave me a vicious shake of the head and a grimace, as if telling me to behave myself. I shrugged at her and smiled. I thought what a lovely woman she was—generous, sweet, absent malice.

•

At two o'clock in the morning I was sitting at my window. I'd been watching a movie on HBO and was now having a bowl of cereal and watching the tree limbs blow in the breeze. There was rain headed our way.

I looked down into the courtyard, and something there caught my eye. Mr. Works and Eileen Wiesatch were sitting together on a bench and smoking cigarettes. The breeze carried the smoke from the cigarettes away. They appeared to be laughing. Laughing there on the bench, their arms strewn about, their knees propped up. They were in animated conversation.

I thought about a young man I had known some years before. He was a student at the university and lived in our building. I knew him only slightly, by Mrs. Bolton's introduction, hallway conversations, a rare chess game on a Saturday afternoon. He was on the sixth floor. One night, very late, he apparently had a wretched argument with his girlfriend. I heard the fight, but, like the others, ignored it. Two days later we discovered that he had committed suicide that night.

Sitting at my window, watching Mr. Works and Eileen in the courtyard, I thought about that young man, and I wished that I had gone out of my apartment that night many years ago. I wished that I'd gone down the hall and up the elevator and knocked on his door, and interceded somehow. I didn't know him well, but I knew him well enough. He was a friend of mine. Sitting at my window, watching the clouds go across the sky, spooning my cereal, what I thought was, I could have stopped him from killing himself. Practically anyone could have stopped him from killing himself. Of course, he might have done it later, but how can you know? How can you be sure that if you get him through one threatening nightmarish evening that he will ever get that close to suicide again? How can you be sure you have not saved him? One tiny joke, one gentle gesture, one little cuff on the back might have been enough to get him through the night, through the impulse. One of anything might have worked.

(2000)

THE BIG ROOM

Jen and I were driving through New Mexico with her father, who was a retired insurance guy just a few years older than me, a tall, thin guy with a swatch of white hair that slipped across his scalp as if it had fallen there from a tree. Jen thought this trip would be a good way to introduce me to her father, but on the second day things remained a little stiff, and Jen was still interpreting.

It had been raining most of the day, and when we drove into Carlsbad, New Mexico, late in the afternoon, the streets were flooded. It turned out we were some distance from the caverns, which I thought were right outside of town, but which were actually twenty-five miles south. The sun was nearly down, but there was still light buried in the thick clouds patrolling above us. The water washing over the curbs in town was metallic copper, reflecting clouds and sky together. We stopped at a four-way, then took a left onto a road that headed toward the caverns. We didn't get far. Jen signaled and pulled into the Holiday Inn, then went inside and registered for two rooms side by side on the second floor. We parked and carried the bags up, then stood for a couple minutes on the concrete balcony, talking about dinner. Jen wanted room service, and that was fine with me, but Mike wanted to go for Chinese.

"Not me," Jen said, going into our room. "You guys go ahead. I'm resting. I'm taking a shower and watching TV."

"What about it, Del?" Mike said.

"Sure," I said.

Jen gave her father a little kiss on the cheek, only the second time I'd seen her do that, and went into our room.

Mike gestured for me to follow him into his room. I didn't want to go, of course. I wanted to go in with Jen and relax and flip through TV channels, but these moments when you're supposed to have the conversation with the girlfriend's father always arrive, even at my age.

Mike tossed his suitcase on one of his beds and sat in the wonderfully generic chair next to the generic table, slapping the arm of the second chair. "Take a seat," he said. "I've been looking forward to having a chance to get with you one-on-one, know what I mean? Know what I mean, Del?"

"Sure," I said.

"So you're teaching at the college over there in Biloxi? And teaching is something you like to do, is that right?" Mike said.

"I don't mind it," I said. "It's good work. It's worthwhile work, sort of. In a small way. It's interesting, pays the bills."

"It's a fine career, teaching," Mike said. "It's a real commitment to society, to giving something back. You shouldn't short yourself about this."

"I'm not shorting myself," I said.

"Well, I mean, it's important," he said.

"Yes, I guess it is," I said.

"These kids need to be educated. Even Jen needs to be educated—she's got her degree, but she could use another one. Another degree never hurt anybody."

"We talked about that," I said. "About her going back to school, getting a graduate degree. Maybe art, we were thinking."

"You talked about it?"

"Yep. Sure did."

"Huh," he said. "Think of that."

I noticed there was a spot on the arm of the chair where somebody must've stuck gum or something, and then somebody else had come along and scraped it off, leaving a little around-the-edges residue.

"Well, we can't all be tycoons, Mike," I said. "Some of us just stay in the shadows, sneak by. Skirt the edges, economically speaking."

"It's not economics I'm worried about, Del," Mike said. "I don't know how to get into this, but perhaps I'll just come out and say it, okay? As I understand it, you're about—"

"Forty-seven," I said. "But I think young."

Mike did a polite laugh. "Anyway, what I was wondering was, see, I'm fifty-three, and there you are with my daughter, and she's twenty-six or twenty-seven—"

"Seven," I said.

"Right. So, doesn't that seem a little odd to you? I don't want to be forward about this, and I don't want to cause trouble, but it worries me, I don't mind telling you. I mean, I figured it would be best to tell you straight out like this, man to man."

"That's kind of you," I said.

"What?" he said.

"Not beating around the bush," I said. "So many people these days beat around the bush, the poor bush doesn't have a prayer, know what I mean, Mike?"

He yanked at the leg of his pants. "Not me, not my style at all, but I'm already retired, so I guess I wouldn't. Know, I mean."

"Well, Jen was a surprise to me, too," I said. "I'm divorced, and at first it was just a friendly thing, and then—"

"That's not the way Jennifer said it was," he said.

"What's that?" I said.

"A friendly thing," he said.

"Well, I meant it wasn't serious. I didn't know it was serious," I said.

"Nooner?" he said. He winked at me then, one of those winks where the message is "Know what this means?" I was not doing as well as I would have liked.

"No, no—not what I meant. I just didn't know what was going on. Now that we've been together a couple of years, well, we're comfortable together."

"Well, the both of you are comfortable, then," Mike said. "That's worth something."

He was around behind the chair now, leaning on its back, his arms folded. He was picking at his teeth with the nail of his thumb. "Comfortable. I like to see that, but I'm not sure. I mean, I'm wondering if you might—I don't want to be pushy here—sort of stand to one side, or try that, so Jennifer can go on with her life. Unless you see yourself as, well, you know—"

"Permanent?" I said.

"Right," he said.

"Well, I see that, yes. She sees that, I think. So that's why I don't get off to one side, as you say. We're sort of keeping company in a serious way."

"Keeping company. Now I haven't heard that since I was a kid, when my pappy used to talk about that. I think he used to talk about keeping company. That's nice, the way you use that," he said.

"Well, thank you," I said.

There was a long pause while he picked his teeth and looked down into the seat of the chair, which was beige. Then he straightened his arms and looked at the TV. The TV wasn't on.

"That Simpson thing's a mess out there, I'm telling you. I don't like it. You think he did it?" he said. "The police seem to think he did it."

"Yeah, that's right," I said.

"I don't know—you know that dog and everything, that dog found them," he said.

"Yep," I said.

"I don't know," Mike said, doing a little tight stretch with his shoulders, trying to move them forward. "I guess I'd better jump over and say good night to Jen. But I'm glad we had this talk. I mean, it didn't go all that far, but I feel better, anyway. We've had a little talk and maybe we could have another one later, you know? Build up to something."

"Sure," I said. "That'd be good for me."

"Let's schedule that. Let's pencil that in. After golf. You play golf?"

"No, I don't, really," I said. "I played golf when I was a kid, as Jen may have told you. I was on the golf team in high school. We were pretty fair golfers there in Houston at high school. But since then, I haven't played much. Golf's not my game, really."

"So what is your game?" he said.

"Well, I don't really have a game," I said. "When I was younger, I liked various games. I liked archery."

He gave me a look when I said archery.

"Well, I can't help it. I liked it," I said. "Shooting those arrows, that was fun. They shot across and hit those targets. Football and baseball, of course. I played Little League. Played grade school football."

"You didn't play high school?" he said. "You're a big guy—probably a big kid, weren't you?"

"Well, yeah, I was, but I didn't," I said.

"Why didn't you?" he said.

"I didn't want to," I said. "I decided in eighth grade that I didn't want to play football. I had an idiot coach."

"Everybody has an idiot coach in eighth grade," Mike said.

"This guy was sort of Vince Lombardi with that gay-jock conflict thing going. He had us line up and smack each other in the face before games—that sort of thing. Slug each other in the stomach as hard as we could. Get one kid to jump on another kid. That was always me, the one getting jumped. So I quit."

"Bet he didn't like that," he said.

"He told the other kids I was scared. Called me names. I saw him once a few years ago in a surplus store with his friend. I'm bigger than he is now, so I don't expect he'd call me anything if he recognized me. It was the Catholic school deal. This guy was still closeted. Liked to watch the little boys shower."

"So that's when you turned to archery?" Mike said.

"I didn't *turn to* archery. I was just interested in archery," I said.

"Were you any good at it?" Mike said.

"No," I said. "Bowling. I was pretty good at bowling. Now, there you go. That's my sport, bowling."

"I always hated bowling," Mike said.

We went to our room together, and after Mike said good night to Jen, he gave up the Chinese food idea and decided to get a sandwich in the restaurant. I said I'd pass and Mike didn't seem to mind, so I let him out of the room and locked up after him.

The comforters on the beds were abnormally plump. The television was a brand-new bottom-of-the-line RCA. I popped through the channels while Jen went into the bathroom and turned on the shower, then came out and started to undress. I liked to watch her dress and undress because she always acted like she was alone. That made it sexier, as if I was watching her strip on television, or I wasn't there at all and she was just changing, getting ready for bed, or for a date—as if she were completely vulnerable. And I liked how she handled the clothes when she took them off. She was neither too casual nor too precious with them. She put them down carefully but not too carefully. She folded her jeans, then folded them again. She draped her shirt over the back of a chair. She put her socks and shoes at attention at the foot of the chair. She looked good in her underpants. She looked healthy and young and a tiny bit awkward. Her skin was only lightly freckled. Her back curved in a pretty way. Her breasts were small and delicate, suggesting adolescence, just hinting that way. Her knees had pretty little wrinkles.

She slid her hands through her hair to freshen it, then stretched out for a minute on the second bed, her hands by her sides, her eyes shut. I got up and went into the bath to turn off the shower for her, and stopped to kiss her forehead when I came back, then sat down and started going soundlessly through the channels again.

"Thank you," Jen said, without opening her eyes. She reached down and pulled the flap of the comforter up on the side of the bed and over her chest and legs.

"Do you want me to wake you?" I said.

"Yes," she said. "Forty-five minutes. No more than that."

I switched to CNN and watched various muted lawyers in studios talk about the Simpson case. Earnest questions were asked by the news anchor (his face gave him away), and earnest answers were given by the consultants. In the courtroom replays, I spent a lot of time staring at Marcia Clark and the thing on her lip, the mole. I was glad I didn't have to listen to her shrill, officious, self-righteous version of justice.

I must have come in late on the Simpson report, because soon after they were on to Rwanda. The most horrifying pictures imaginable, thousands of people in a burned-out, mud-caked landscape with diseased water seeping in dark pools, the kind you see animals wallowing in, flies and bugs and people on the ground curled up suffering, wrapped in rags, smoke rising on the horizon, trees stripped of limbs and leaves, sagging huts, tents, people on stretchers, people being pulled by mules, ghastly, freakish, grotesquely maimed people wandering through the filth. Six one-armed boys in matching brown shorts. I wondered why we weren't more active in Rwanda. People all over the country, all over the world, were thinking exactly that thought, but none of us were doing much—we were going to wonder and wait for the next news story. I rattled through the usual arguments about going over there and not going, and all of them seemed designed to make me feel more guilty or less guilty. Only the simple *go* made any sense, so I took credit for being able to recognize that, but then decided the recognition was another rationalization, another trick. Then I figured I was too hard on myself, I couldn't be expected to do everything, or even any particular thing, and that all the guilt was itself an easy out—learned in Catholic boyhood.

There was nowhere to go with the cycle of guilt and relief, so I started wondering why the country hadn't done something about Rwanda. The massacre had been going on for months and months. I'd read about it in the papers, seen it on the news, it seemed like four or five months before. Eight months. How was it that a country, a powerful country, a country committed to decency, compassion, and kindness, routinely sat on its hands while tragedies unfolded? Again and again.

The pattern was the same. First a few little stories in the press, then more stories, and pretty soon earnest concern, and then grave concern, and then elaborate grave concern while many things were thought of and many people died. And then the crisis took a turn for the worse, and there was even graver concern, and there were more deaths and more stories. And then the crisis took an additional turn for the worse, and perhaps a third, and the process was repeated until what we were fed on the nightly news was a scene of incomprehensible agony. That's when the camera people did their lovely, lingering close-ups of the survivors, the new pictures matched with the hugely solemn voice-overs of the announcers.

I wondered what they thought of the camera people.

The eyes of these survivors always showed an inexplicable determination to live. I looked at them on television and thought, Why aren't you dead? How do you manage to want *not* to die? In that hotel room in Carlsbad, I wondered what I would want in their shoes.

Then it struck me that if they were in *my* shoes they would be sitting in a swanky Rwanda hotel watching me on their big screen TVs as I slogged through a urine-and-feces-strewn America, and they'd be thinking how bad they felt for not helping me out, they'd be wondering why their country didn't do something. They'd consider doing something ineffective and insufficient themselves, like TV news reporting of the tragedy in America, or gathering medical supplies, or writing torrid op-ed pieces in *The Rwanda Times*, or just feeling guilty about not doing anything—the usual tricks we play on ourselves so we feel less guilty about good fortune. I figured they wouldn't lift a finger and they'd wonder about that look in my eyes.

"He's a really nice man," Jen said. "He feels he's missed something. He hasn't, as far as I can tell, but he thinks it, anyway. He's so cut off from everything."

We were in the Big Room at Carlsbad Caverns, a space the size of several Astrodomes, as the literature was eager to point out, seven hundred feet underground. Mike had gone on ahead of us. Jen couldn't see too well, so she was holding on to my arm as we walked the path. It was cold in there, too cold to be comfortable.

The other cavernites were running around taking snapshots of every weird-shaped chunk of rock they could find, using their point-and-shoots to good advantage, so there were flashes everywhere. Curious formations dropped out of the ceiling, grew out of the floor. The path, lined with a foot-high pipe railing, rose and sank as it weaved through the cave.

"What'd he miss?" I said to Jen. "What does he think he missed?"

"By my reckoning, it's Sting, mostly," she said. "He got married thirty years ago and lived the right life as long as he could. After the divorce he lived more of it. He's been in it all this time. And here you come along with his little girl."

"So?" I said.

"Produces doubts," she said. She grabbed my arm as we went up over a rise next to a rock formation that looked like a giant breast. The room was full of echoes. We could see the silhouettes of people on the other side of the cave coming back along the end of the same trail we had just started on—it looped around the perimeter of the Big Room. Every word spoken in the cave rippled around the rocks. It sounded like nighttime, flooded with delicate echoes and little bits of laughter and the odd drop of water into a standing pool, the footsteps fast and slow, children running on the path, people talking in foreign languages explaining the sights to one another, the wheezing of thirty-five millimeter autowinders.

"So what do you want me to do?" I said. "You want me to apologize for being older?"

"Oh, are we *older*?" Jen said. "Is that how we think of ourselves today?"

"Okay, forget I said it," I said.

"Does all this stuff look phony to you?" she said, waving at the rock structures growing out of the ceiling and out of the floor. "Does it look a little bit like papier-mâché in here, or is that my imagination?"

This had been bothering me, too. Maybe it was just because we were in the Big Room, the one easily accessible by elevator seventy stories below the visitors center, and that we hadn't walked in through the natural entrance, down through the Bat Cave, Whale's Mouth, Devil's Den, Iceberg, Green Lake, Queen's Chamber, and the other evocatively named rooms and halls of the natural path down to the Big Room. Or maybe it was that they'd over-cleaned the place, what with the lamps and pathways and signs and the little multilingual hand-held, tape-recorded personal guides that rented at the visitors center for four and a half dollars. Whatever it was, the cavern looked too well groomed for me, too much like a life-size model of a real cavern that might be somewhere else, hidden away, out of public view, inaccessible save to government scientists, leaving this cleaned, polished, carefully manicured national park service engineer's idea of Carlsbad Caverns.

"Yeah, looks phony," I said. "But these big guys do look like walruses, don't they?" I was pointing to walrus-shaped rock formations.

"Some do," she said.

We were just then passing a place on our right called Mirror Lake. The cavern keepers had put an upside-down lighted sign just above this tiny puddle, so that when you looked into the puddle the words "Mirror Lake" appeared right-side-up and rippling on the surface of this bit of water. The pool couldn't have been more than eight feet across, two feet deep, but in the Big Room of this putative Carlsbad, it was *Mirror Lake.*

"This is what you mean, right?" I said.

"Yep. I could do that in my tub."

"Well, so much for silent chambers and timeless beauty," I said.

"I think we've been deeply injured by our time," Jen said. "I really wanted this to be wonderful. If you repeat this, I'll deny it, but this morning when I got up, I was excited about coming down here. Maybe if there were a little more dirt around, if we tripped on rocks and stuff?"

"That would help," I said. "Maybe you should go down into the unexplored part. If you're young and energetic, and you are, and you pay the ten dollars or whatever it takes, you get to see an unspoiled, un-dioramatized version of a cavern."

"Do you suppose they've got all this dramatic lighting down there?" Jen said.

"Go back two spaces," I said. "Excessive ridicule."

"Sorry," she said.

"After you factor out the trails and the lights and garden-club beautification, it's still okay, isn't it?" I said. "It really is kind of remarkable."

"Yes, of course it is," Jen said. "You didn't think I was saying it was *un*, did you?"

"Who knew?" I said.

"I'm saying I wish it were a little more undisturbed. And I don't think the theatrical lighting helps much. In fact, it kind of hurts. It's hard to see anything down here. Ordinary lighting would be better."

"You're the matter-of-fact kid, aren't you?" I said.

"So what if I am?" she said.

"You can't blame them. It's a precious national resource. All precious national resources are lighted this way. Have you ever seen the Washington Monument? The Lincoln Memorial?"

"We live to decorate," she said.

Jen sat down to rest on a stone bench in the middle of the cavern. I sat down beside her. The bench was cold. A Chinese family was there with us, speaking in hushed but rapid Chinese. A plump mother, a diminutive father, and two gorgeous, lanky, silk-haired Chinese girls in their teens. The parents were eagerly discussing the scenery. One of the kids was staring at her hand, and the second was reading what appeared to be a comic book, using a flashlight the size of a Pez dispenser. A tall guy, an American, came up behind us and was talking to the people he was with, telling them all about the cavern, explaining everything, challenging the people in his party to answer questions: When was the cavern discovered? What was its principal value then? When did it become a national park? What is the role of water in the formation of the rock structures? How many million years ago did the mesa out of which the canyon carved itself come into being?

Jen poked me in the ribs with her elbow. "Quit staring," she whispered. "He's going to call on us."

We got up and walked along the trail past some kind of wire ladder that dropped out of sight into a hole in the cavern floor, then past another hole called the Jumping Off Place, then past a hole called the Bottomless Pit.

"Throw yourself in," I heard somebody say.

"This pit isn't bottomless at all," somebody else said. "Look. It's only one hundred fifty feet deep or something."

"Is not," somebody else said.

"Read the sign," somebody said.

It was much darker and colder in this part of the cave. We hurried along the trail, arm in arm.

"How is it you know so much about what Mike's thinking?" I said.

"He talks to me," Jen said. "In dad language. He's my dad."

The smart guy had come up behind us again, and he was doing a quiz on bats. "So how do they manage to hang upside down?" he asked his kids. "When they're sleeping?"

"Yeah," one of the kids said. "How do they do that?"

"Magnets," another one of the kids said.

"Don't be smart, Junior," the father said. "The answer is that when a bat hangs upside down with its feet closed onto something, its feet are in their natural condition, just as our hands are when they are open. See? When our hands are open, they're relaxed, and when a bat's feet are closed, *they're* relaxed. It's as if our hands were closed when they were at rest, but for the bat, relaxed is closed and open is working, like our hands would be if we were grabbing onto something. Do you see? When the bat relaxes, its feet close."

"You mean bat feet are like clothespins?" one of the kids said.

"Like clothespins," the father said, obviously a bit flustered. "Well, I guess so. Yes."

We stood aside on the trail and let them pass. We were looking at a small tableau, draperies of stalagmites and other formations called soda straws, which made up an attractive altar-sized indentation off the main path.

"Those little ones look like prairie dogs," Jen said. "See that one there?" She pointed to a little knot of rock that looked like a prairie dog standing on its hind legs. "They're just gathered around listening to Prairie Dog's Home Companion."

"We've got to get out of here," I said.

"What? You're not having fun?" she said.

"I'm freezing," I said.

"What about all these wonderful national rocks and these crystal growths and all these astonishingly beautiful and delicate objects?"

"I'm buying the video," I said. "Let's speed it up, okay?"

And that's what we did, taking the rest of the trail at a near trot, passing up the smart guy and his kids, the Chinese family, some other people we'd seen along the way. We even passed Mike, who was leaning against some rocks, looking up at the ceiling of the Big Room.

"We'll be in the lunch area," Jen said, as we went by him.

"Okay, great," Mike said. "I'm going at my own pace, and I think I'm going to be all right—you kids enjoy yourselves."

"We may be topside," I said, pointing up with a thumb.

He gave me a thump on the shoulder, and Jen kissed him loud on the cheek, and then we moved on fast. The lunch area was a hollowed-out part of the cavern with a fifties-looking concrete concession stand at the bottom of it, the architecture reminiscent of Frank Lloyd Wright's Johnson's Wax office building. We shared a quick Coke and a candy bar and then got in line at the elevator, waiting to go up.

"This is like the minus seventy-fifth floor, right?" Jen said, as we were waiting.

A bald guy in front of us turned around with his video camera, videoed us. Jen made some faces for him and introduced me as Jack Ruby.

"You remember Jack Ruby, don't you?" she said to the video camera.

The bald guy stopped shooting and stood up. "Sure. I saw the movie, kind of a mob intermezzo."

"You look a lot like Tom Noonan," Jen said.

"You should see how I feel," the guy said.

When we got back up to the visitors center, we stopped at a trinket shop, and I bought a transparent red comb with Carlsbad Caverns engraved in its spine. Jen bought a chrome and red and white decal. Then we went outside and sat on a stone fence in the warm and gentle sun. It was perfect up there. This little breeze was around.

(1995)

HARMONIC

You are online, looking at the three-month chart of a favorite stock, when a car hits the tree in your yard. At first you are afraid it's your daughter, Trinity. It is two in the morning, and she's out as usual. You look outside; it isn't her. You are relieved, but the car is burning, flames are running up the tree. You rush out but can't get close. There are already sirens in the distance. Traffic stops, people come out of houses—everything happens quickly You stand nervously in the front yard, keeping your distance from the car, talking to neighbors, all of you gawking. Your numbers grow. People sort of materialize, *Star Trek*-style. In a couple of minutes the cops come sliding in, their sirens shut down.

The street fills with hoses and lights, cops, fire trucks, firemen, radio static, shouted orders. Bystanders. The burning car is at the center of things. The firemen douse the flames, and the street fills with smoke that looks like train steam. A dozen guys in rubber coats and big boots, in yellow slickers, carrying axes and flashlights, stand in little groups, smoking. Other guys move around, talk, point lights at people and things—the mailbox, a tree stump, a car in a driveway, two kids on the lawn next door. Some cops scour the grass, their flashes weaving like inverted search-lights. They're looking for scraps, parts of the car. The car is wrapped around a two-foot-thick pine. The car and the tree smolder. The fire really is almost out.

Someone recognizes the car. It belongs to a neighbor, a young woman who has recently moved to Lakewood. You don't know her name, you know her only to wave to when she walks the loop around the little lake. She always wears red shorts and a navy blue T-shirt when she walks. In the crash she has on a soaked white dress. She has been shot through the windshield, no chance to survive. The car is half its original size, bent like a horseshoe around the tree. It's smoking, giving off occasional small jets of flame, all the glass busted out.

It's cold. Everyone's breath comes in silver streams, caught in the lights circling the yards of the houses. You go back and forth at the edge of the street, toward the car and then away, closer each time. You know people who have lost limbs and children in car crashes. Your friend Mary was broadsided by a delivery van doing sixty. She caught a chrome bumper in the ribs and was crushed. Her car went seventy feet through the air and landed in a display window.

The scene hisses. Reflective yellow strips catch flicking lights. Water standing in the cold, cold grass squishes underfoot. Engines lope, generators rattle on the trucks, circling lights click quietly on the roofs of police cars.

The driver is half out the windshield, face down against the metal, bent at the waist. Her white dress is twisted, stained, and her hair is black, wet, long, curled. You've seen it before, this kind of thing, bodies beside the road covered in sheets, but in front of the house, looking at the girl who has driven her car eighty miles an hour into a stately pine, who came up the long gradual rise from Case Avenue accelerating hard and went straight into the tree, that makes you want to cry. No one is ever safe.

•

You have always been interested in how dead people look. This woman coming out of the windshield looks broken. You're scared because the game has suddenly changed, something huge has happened, something so strange another world opens up, like when you were a kid and your parents got into a fight and you had to go to your room and wait, just stay out of it, hide from it, because the world had cracked apart, come loose from its moorings, and the night had become a dangerous time when anything could happen.

You wonder: had she known the tree was coming, had she aimed at it, or did she just abandon control, knowing that sooner or later something would stop her? You imagine those last seconds—engine screaming, car leaping ahead. Had she left it to chance, or had she tried to make the curve? What did it look like to her, through the windshield, those last seconds as the tree swept toward her faster, larger, inevitable?

If only she'd made it to tomorrow. The world seems different picking up the kids at school, coming home from the grocery, stopping at Blockbuster—with cars and people under control the world moves in an orderly way.

•

Your wife has gone to bed and left you at the computer peering at graphs of stocks. You are studying Harmonic Lightwave, something you bought at Ameritrade after Stewart persuaded that little fat guy to buy, after the spiritual centering class turned into a stock fantasy and "eight bucks" became a mantra. Like everyone else you opened an account before realizing you had no clue what to buy.

Your daughter, Trinity, is nineteen. You and your wife have different views on how Trinity should be treated now that she is in her second year of college. You believe more should be expected of her—more discipline, more participation in your life at the house—that she should be treated as an adult. Your wife says Trinity is still a kid. "The teens last longer these days," she says. "Until their late twenties." To ask Trinity to behave "responsibly"—she puts it in finger quotes—would just force her away from you both.

So Trinity goes where she wants and does as she pleases. There is no curfew, there are no rules, she has no responsibilities. She has the white Mazda you gave her on her seventeenth birthday, and keys and credit cards and a license to come and go as she sees fit. Usually she's home by four a.m. She and her friends go to the bars, to people's apartments, they crowd into booths at the Waffle House in the early morning hours, call each other all the time, leaving cryptic messages in code on those hard little colorful pagers they carry, or they used to carry—recently Trinity has upgraded to a new cell phone and given you instructions not to page her anymore.

Harmonic has had a bad day. It is down seven and an eighth on volume. You are thinking of putting in a sell order when you hear the skidding tires. Headlights swing past the window of the small dining room you have converted into an office. There is an explosion right outside. You think of a water heater exploding, but it is too large and too close. You think: shotgun. You think: car crash. You know instantly and just hope the others. There is a second explosion, smaller but still deafening, an eerie yellow light blooms outside the miniblinds. You feel some sudden indescribable fear.

You live in a small community on a tiny lake. Eighty houses, and yours was one of the first, though you've had it only two years. You bought from the original owner. You have a lovely lawn, elaborate beds and gardens, a deck that overlooks the lake. You often sit out in the evening, when the weather allows. The lake is so small you could hit a golf ball across it. You've never done that—you aren't a golfer—but friends have said as much. Your neighbors are people who never seem to leave their homes.

The house is still after the explosions. It is always quiet when Trinity is out, sometimes eerily so. Your wife is used to Trinity's noise—always banging up and down the stairs, raking the TV or stereo up, talking too loud on the phone. You can never quite hear what she is saying, but you can't escape her voice, either. Your wife finds the quiet unnerving. You savor it.

Finally you scissor open the miniblinds. The burning car is two hundred feet from the window. Your stomach feels large and hollow as you stare between the blinds at the fire, the creased metal, the tree, the smoke.

•

You say to your wife, "I have found that we are not all that tolerant of others, generally. We nod, we smile, we are a little bit polite, but mostly we are eager to return to our homes, lock the doors, play with our dogs, watch our TVs, and live in that tiny circle of confusion where we have some influence."

•

Standing in the yard with the cops, listening to the radios and the muffled voices of the men and the noise from newspeople who have arrived, watching their bright flashguns, there is a curious sobriety to the scene, a quiet framed by emergency, as if someone has suddenly turned on the lights in the middle of a wicked party. The air is thin and brittle. People move hesitantly and they are dressed foolishly. Who are they, and what are they doing? Why are they so suddenly restrained? Do they feel what you feel?

Cops wave away accumulating traffic, sort out their duties, marshal the bits and pieces of the wreck that have flown off across your yard.

You hear footfalls in the street, boots scuffing the gravel at the curb, rubber boots sloshing on the soft grass in the yard. Traffic is blocked for a good distance in either direction. A fender is pulled out of the ditch and leaned against the white wooden post of your mailbox. Three cops in leather jackets walk three abreast from one edge of the yard to the other, their lights flashing on the ground in front of them. A big guy in a slicker turns people around, sends them on their way, directs traffic into and out of the driveways. This cop wears a jacket that says POLICE in big reflective letters, and he looks as if he is heading in your direction. Listen to the soles of his shoes as they slide across the concrete toward you. Nod at him as he gets closer. Step back into the yard and listen to wind slip through the trees overhead.

The cop says, "You live here?" flicking his flashlight toward the porch. "Yes," you say. "Too bad," he says, and he turns, stands there with his back to you. You nod and stare at the glittering letters on his back. You listen to the cops talk—their short little remarks, their rough laughter. You try to make out what they are saying.

(2000)

MONGREL

Riva Jay felt free steering the big Cadillac convertible, top down, along the Florida coast highway with the Gulf maybe fifty yards to her left. She was leaving in a hurry after a weary month in the town where she was born, and she liked the snappy sound of the glasspack mufflers, the wet wind popping around her head, all that empty space out in front of her. Riva was eighteen going on fifteen, that's what everybody always said, from the furry social worker, to the T-shirted truckers, to the cheap suits in the bars and the mooks she ran into in the day hotels. God knows what they all thought it meant—that she was too damn young, that she acted funny, that she pissed them off—it could've been anything.

When Riva was eleven her parents sort of died in a convenience store robbery. They ran the convenience store. Her daddy watched the counter and her mama watched her daddy, and the two of them had no business in the world being together in the first place. He was a southern boy from Plaquemines Parish in Louisiana, and she was from Long Island. From her mama's angle, Daddy was a born janitor, the pure cause of her decline from the day of their marriage forward. But one day three Mexican boys with skinny little sideburns and pencil moustaches slid in and started to rob them and her daddy, well, he picked that moment to decide he'd had enough of just about everything. She never knew why he picked that time, or place, only that he was finished being on the bottom rung. He pulled an aluminum bat out from under the scarred counter and, quite naturally, that pissed off the Mexicans, who started making fun of him, fucking with him in Spanish, pointing their little guns around, and pretty soon everybody in the room was just as brave as he or she could be. They were practically on fire in there they were so brave. Eventually one gun went off, then another, and pretty soon they had themselves a full-fledged TV special, and pretty soon after that these Mexican boys, without a care in the world, were flying out of the place into their bright pink Pontiac Bonneville, and Riva's mama and daddy were tumbled down on the floor bleeding.

After that things changed around the house. Riva and her daddy grew closer, and Riva's mama was none too happy about that or anything else. By the time she was thirteen, Riva was daddy's little girl in ways that all of them knew were wrong, and when her mama came home early one weekend afternoon and found Riva bathing Daddy, well, then *she'd* had enough. The husband tried to explain but Riva's mother could not bear to hear the explanation, and instead fetched the gun they had bought together after the Mexican robbery, and plugged Riva's daddy in the forehead. Pop! Just like that. Then she turned the gun on herself, put it in her mouth, and snapped the trigger, calling a halt to the whole game. Riva, left alone in the bathroom with a sponge full of Dial soap, just knelt there amazed at how little the hole was where the bullet went into her daddy's skull.

After that Riva was shipped to her grandmother's in Lovine, Alabama, and that was real nice for a couple of years, though her grandmother had a habit of smacking Riva with her cane at every opportunity, sticking her with it, and poking her ass, and popping it against her breasts for no particular reason, admonishing her granddaughter to behave herself or she'd never find a decent man. "You keep these to yourself," she'd wheeze, snapping the thin cane across Riva's chest. "You remember what they're there for, you hear?"

But when Riva hit high school the boys just loved her to death, and being somewhat new to love, she returned the favor time after time, and after a while there were just too many boys, too much trouble, too many canings, and eventually Riva Jay ended up scheduled for three years in the Certification School for Troubled Youth. This was near Birmingham, a warehouse building on the site of a defunct chemical factory, and it was there she learned the true value of risk/reward analysis. She did school work in somebody's office and made her high school diploma in record time, and then, one night in 1998, she managed to wiggle out through a concrete pipe in the cellar of the main building, and she never looked back. Hitched her way around the South, crisscrossing it, until finally she was back home in the tiny coastal Florida town where she'd grown up—Quantum, population eight thousand. It was on the Gulf in that deserted stretch between Pensacola and Tallahassee, the only "Old Florida" that was left, that remained undiscovered by the developers, where nobody arrived, nobody left, and people had possums for pets. On tough nights in hurricane season the water ran right up into town and stayed there.

Though she'd only been gone a few years, nobody much remembered her, and she didn't run around trying to remind anybody. The town hadn't changed since she left—it was a blemish on the two-lane, a sneeze, a backwater, but like everywhere else the kids had taken over, frightening their parents, so Riva had a natural constituency, and hung with the high school crowd. She climbed their water tower, smoked in their train station, swam in a couple of creeks deep in the forested land north of town, and laid out on the satin white beach that ran a few miles along the highway. The town also had a Ford dealership, a ratty strip mall, a Snowball stand, a Quad Cinema, and the Gerald R. Ford High School, where all her pals sometimes gathered for drug sales and fist fights.

One day after she'd been around a while she took a walk to see her parents' convenience store, which was just a slab of concrete littered with broken glass and four-foot weeds, and an old storage building at the back of the lot where she'd been sent to play as a child. It still had the yellow door she'd helped her daddy paint, though the door was horizontal by now, hooked into the jamb by one twisted hinge. But now, just north of the place, there were tall cyclone fences peppered with KEEP OUT and MILITARY INSTALLATION signs, DO NOT GO BEYOND THIS POINT signs, and Riva was immediately attracted to the fence. The kids she hung out with told her there was nothing happening there, or whatever was happening they didn't need to know, that the camp was just an endless supply of obnoxious buffed-out guys who were always strutting through town in full camouflage gear—bright red skin and new tattoos.

She had a room at the Get Up & Go Motel and pretty quick landed a burger job at the DQ. Wasn't really a DQ. It had been a DQ years before, in her mama's day, but now it was a retro hamburger shop called Pattyland, which was Mr. Bob Rupert's idea of a cool retro hamburger shop name. Mr. Bob's wife was named Patty, and, as he explained to every customer who asked, a "patty" was another name for a hamburger. Mostly the customers knew enough not to ask. By the time Riva signed on it was just her friends asking, eager to hear Mr. Bob's absolutely straight-faced explanation. Nobody really knew if Mr. Bob was in on the joke or the butt of the joke, and he never let on.

A week into the job she met this guy named Tiny Furlong. He was real nice to her, but he was fifty and heavy-armed and queerly cocky, and he looked like the kind of guy who might try to pay a pretty girl to pee on him, so at first she gave him a wide berth. But then one night she was finishing her shift, messed up on weed and Crown Royal, and Tiny was in there being as sweet as prune pie and she figured she just did not care, she figured why not, so she shared a drink with him when there was nobody else around, and she sat and listened to his story, all about his ex-wife, his club called the Kit Kat, which was once a great place, but by now was just a dim-light dive with a handful of old guys sitting like stones at the bar. And listening to this story, Riva felt bad for Tiny Furlong because his story didn't seem that far off hers, really, it had different people, and places, and things, but still somehow it was just the same story as hers.

Right about then Tiny said, "I don't want to offend, but I have to tell you that I am *stung* with your great pubescent beauty." And he reached out and rested a baseball-glove-size hand on her thigh as they sat on the stools there in Pattyland.

"Really," was what Riva told him, but than she just swatted the hand off her knee in a friendly way, like she was being playful, which was a clear case of mixed signals, and Tiny, who was not a man without memory and experience, got the deal right away. He went on talking about his troubles while he was helping Riva close up. And then he told her about his Cadillac, and he said, "Wait'll you hear her. I just got a pair of new glasspacks on her and she sounds like a big dog breathing hard."

"*Really*," Riva said, clicking off the lights there at Pattyland.

And then they crunched across the shell lot to his car and he let her in and drove slowly down the highway, which was also the town's main street, the Cadillac's exhaust hammering and thudding in equal measures. Tiny took her for a look at the Kit Kat, which she noticed right away was on a nice piece of property right across the two-lane from the beach. It was about two in the morning and he stopped right in the middle of the highway and said, "There she is," sweeping his hand the way people do when they're showing off stuff they're not quite sure they should be proud of.

So they sat there a bit and drank out of a bottle in a bag and pretty soon Tiny was saying maybe they could live together, that she needed a better place than the Get Up, and Riva was thinking that Tiny seemed like not the worst guy in the world, and he told her that he had "a heart of gold where Little Riva Jay is concerned," which she figured was overstatement. But then he said, "Listen, I'm ready to be whatever you want me to be," and when he asked her how she felt about that, Riva said, "You're ready so soon?" but then felt perhaps she wasn't taking his rapture seriously enough, and she said, "Tiny, I love you for the man you want to be, and I love you for the man you almost are," and he was hugely touched, heart-wrenched, and got tears coming straight out of his eyes while they were still parked in the middle of the road, and Riva felt worse yet, realizing that he probably didn't get out much and probably hadn't seen the movie.

She felt bad and she'd had enough puppy love for one night and she asked him if he was serious, trying to shut him off, and Tiny said he was "as serious as bacon," which was something she didn't exactly get, but didn't let disturb her, either. She figured Tiny was a good bet for meals and a roof, and that to get them she would not have to degrade herself too utterly, so she right then and there took him up on the offer to share the apartment over the Kit Kat, to be his friend, to maybe help out around the club from time to time, to wash and to fold, and even cook a meal from time to time, a skill she has not yet acquired but recognized when she saw it on television.

As they parked the Cadillac and went into the club, up the dingy stairs to the apartment, Riva could only imagine her future—suddenly she was her mama and daddy all over again, and the end was a melee of hot Mexican lead. Tiny's apartment was exactly the rat hole she anticipated, but from her new room she could see the white ridges of the Gulf out the window and she reminded her skittish self that she'd seen worse rat holes in her day. She figured it would be fine just as soon as she got things straight with Tiny, so she sat him down and said, "Here are my rules."

And he nodded, looking up at her, surprised by the good fortune of having her there at all, and disinclined to interrupt her.

She said, "I am not pulling your pop, okay? I am not cooking. I am not cleaning. We got to get a girl in for all that, okay? Are we clear?"

"Crystal," he said, instantly extended a hand to seal the deal.

Then they slipped back to the motel to get her things, stopped at the convenience store for Cokes and chocolate bars and pork rinds, and moved her right on in.

Riva figured that he thought he'd keep her around a while and then fuck her silly when she wasn't looking, when her guard was down, but her guard was never down, and she could be as mean as a witch if she had to. When bed time rolled around that first evening he appeared in her doorway to say goodnight, outfitted in curious brown pajamas.

From then on he was kind of a mystery to her. Tolerant but distant, sometimes gruff and withdrawn. Fatherly in some old-fashioned, slightly tormented way. He was full of instructions and directives and lectures, none of which made much sense, and this was like magic for Riva, exactly what she wanted. By the middle of the second week everything seemed settled and she felt as if she'd been there a year.

She was hanging at the club nights, making fun of Tiny in front of his buddies, teasing him in an oddly intimate way in spite of their lack of any intimacy whatsoever, telling his pals that Tiny was a dead guy, that he probably never was alive in the first place, and that any one of them could have her for a nickel. Tiny got a kick out of it, got mileage with his pals for having the teenage live-in companion, and, figuring that what they didn't know wouldn't hurt them, he said, "She's got some kinda mouth on her, huh?" and then did his silly shit grin while they all rolled their eyes, eight eyes circling the premises in tandem, and reset their bony asses on the stools. For Tiny that was just the kind of respect he'd wanted to produce in others since the eighth grade, the last grade he ever saw, so he was happy. He fought with Riva in public, ignored her in private.

From her point of view this was ideal. They got weeks into it, going on a month, and they even had some fun together, watched some TV, ate take out food, drove in the car. On one special night she got a couple of her high school girlfriends to come over and they all got down to their panties and T-shirts, and watched movies with Tiny, who thought the world had come to a sudden, spectacularly satisfying end.

When they were alone he cooked Riva's breakfast and dinner, bought the cigarettes, told her how the arrangement was "working out pretty well, really," and she thought he wasn't that far wrong. She didn't mind living over the bar, walking the beach, going down every night and hitting the jukebox, and then, when the regulars had cleared off, going out to claim that highway as her own, standing there in the middle of the dark night, sliding her soles a block toward town, a block away, the wind pushing at her and the water coughing up on the beach and the sand sliding across the road like some kind of mutant organism on some new science fiction TV show that was almost as good as some old science fiction TV show that they'd finally let go off the air after running it into the ground maybe three or four years too long. It was not too bad at all in the middle of the highway out there, in the weather, whatever it was, standing there, a couple of bare bulbs slung across the front of the Kit Kat spraying all the light there was except maybe the blinking yellow a half-mile down toward the center of town. So it looked to her as if she'd finally found a setup she could live with, a little bit of shade in the burning sun of her life thus far, a La-Z-Boy in the doublewide of her dreams.

But suddenly, things started going to Tiny's head. He gave up his lectures and told her she made him feel like a kid again.

"Why shouldn't I?" she said. "I'm like, *seventeen*, and you're in the market for coffins." But that didn't slow him down, and day after day he pressed the point of his newly blossomed love. She did not want to hear it because Tiny was real and Tiny was true, and the more he declared his love the more he seemed like a meatball she would rather not have rolling around on her plate. For Riva he was fine as long as he stayed in his cage, but when he wanted to Romeo her every fifteen minutes, and when he told her she was the sun and the moon and the stars for him, well, it made her feel bad, like she was something small that left a trail wherever it went.

She tried to tell him, again and again, in thought, word, and deed. She tried to make it clear, but this new Tiny would not stop, and pretty soon he pledged his endless love in no uncertain terms, on bended knee and etcetera, confessing to Riva that she was every-thing to him, that when he was mean and unkind and punishing and tough, he was just trying to help, and besides, he was trying to cover up his fear of losing her, and then he said that she was his Blessed Virgin Mary herself, no sacrilege intended, and would she marry him?

All this made Riva a little sick to her stomach. She preferred his disinterest, bad treatment, she preferred being just more crap dirtying up his drawers, or the kind of white trash that decent men used for a rag sometimes—the stuff she'd heard since childhood and with which she was familiar. Suddenly Tiny made her nervous and she hoped for a change, a reversion to type. But that did not happen, and after seven ragged days and nights of Tiny's desperation, she'd had enough.

One night when Tiny went downstairs to close up the bar, Riva knew that it had all gone wrong in some terrible way, that it was done, and she thought that she might take a quick shower while he was downstairs and then hitchhike on up the coast. But he was too quick for her, and too demanding, and when he came upstairs from the club he was worse, blubbering, telling her how much he loved her and how much he needed her and how he wanted to marry her and make an honest woman of her. She steered him into the kitchen and sat him down at the table, dropped a bottle of Jack Daniels in front of him, and said to him that she was already right then just about twice as honest a woman as he would ever want to meet in his entire life. She said, "There are things out here in this world that you do not want to know, Tiny Furlong. There are crimes too ugly to be put on television, things we do to each other that would burn the skin off of your face. We can't trust each other. We are only good for each other when we can keep a civil distance between ourselves. You are too kind a man, too good a man with too much affection, too much desire, too much hope." And then she pulled out of her backpack the handgun her mama and daddy had bought many years before and she gave Tiny Furlong a small hole just above the bridge of his nose, and he took it with his eyes open and a loving smile on his face, and when it was all done Riva figured she was about finished with the town of Quantum, and she boarded the Cadillac, lowered the top, and spun out into that silent night.

(2022)

THE LESSON

Gil and Harold worked together at the Jitney Jungle grocery store in north Biloxi—that's where they met. Gil was from Tarzana. His family moved to Mississippi when he was in his early teens. His father did something for NASA, so they moved to Picayune, just outside the NASA complex. Later, Gil had gone two years to the George Tyler Community College in Belhaven, and then, when the casinos came in on the coast, he had moved down.

Harold was a local boy—skinny, gangly, tall, awkward, slow. He was born and reared on the Mississippi gulf coast, mostly by his mother after his father left when Harold was five. His mother had worked for the county court as a stenographer. After high school, he'd gone straight to work for Colonel Sanders.

Gil and Harold shared a distaste for the manager, Clovis Heimsath, who was from Alabama, and who always seemed to enjoy giving them more sloppy work than they could handle.

They were stocking and fronting the canned vegetables. "I feel like we ought to handle old Clovis," Harold said, wagging a can of beets at his Gil. "We ought to can him, what do you think?"

"That's a big amen," Gil said.

"We're going to need a sealer," Harold said, giggling. "We're going to need a butcher's saw."

"Use the one in back," Gil said.

"I seen this one on television," Harold said. "They cut off parts whole. Like hands and feet and legs and arms. We're going to need mighty big cans to put his arms in."

"We'll cut 'em up and run them through the grinder, have us some ground Clovis. We can design some labels in that computer system of his."

"We ought to do Margie, too," Harold said.

Margie was the head checker and Clovis's favorite—a little bit of a looker. Her uniform was always cleaner than everybody else's, and she always looked sexy in it. She always had that top button open, and the uniform was real smooth over her backside.

"No, maybe not Margie," Gil said.

"You got the burns for Margie," Harold said. "That's what it is."

Just about then Clovis and Margie turned onto the aisle. Clovis touched Margie's arm and stopped her. They were about ten feet away from Gil and Harold.

Clovis said, "Now ain't that pretty? I like to watch a man work."

Margie smiled and waved hello to Gil and Harold.

Clovis put one hand up against a shelf, disturbing the corned beef hash. "Look at them skittering around up there," he said. "You ever see two gerbils in a cage—how they go round and round?"

"Hey, Clovis," Margie said. She gave him a play slap on the shoulder.

"Yes sir, boss," Gil said. "Whatever you say, we're after it. We're doing our job here. We're smoking these cans."

"I've been thinking about getting them one of those wheels," Clovis said. "Let them run around on that for a while." He put his arm around Margie's waist, around the white plastic belt that cinched the pale pink shirtwaist uniform, and guided her between Gil and Harold.

Gil and Harold watched them go, watched them down the aisle. When they got next to the Libby's at the end of the aisle, Clovis let his hand slip down over her butt. He didn't even turn around to see if Gil and Harold were watching, he was that sure.

When they'd gone, Harold said, "He's going to do her, right now."

"No," Gil said. "I don't think so."

"He's going to do her," Harold said. "He's taking her back to Meat. He's going to take her apart."

"She looked kind of unhappy," Gil said.

"You got to pay the price to be head checker," Harold said.

They did more cans until Harold came to the small white round potatoes and decided he needed some more from stock. "I'm going to the back," he said.

"What do you mean?" Gil said.

"I need more potatoes," Harold said. He dusted his hands on the seat of his pants.

"Sure," Gil said. "Everybody knows."

"If I happen to see something while I'm hunting potatoes," Harold said. "Well, be that as it may. That's just an accident."

"Get caught and we're slimed," Gil said. "I need the job."

"I ain't getting caught. I ain't doing nothing," Harold said.

"Maybe I ought to come," Gil said. "Keep you honest. Keep you clean."

Harold did an awkward dance toward the back and started singing the Mr. Clean song, but he had trouble remembering details, so he just repeated the 'Mr. Clean, Mr. Clean, Mr. Clean' refrain and did the big fairy-like sweep down the aisle.

"Shit," Gil said, getting off the overturned red plastic milk crate he'd been sitting on. He liked the grocery store, liked the order of things, liked the variety, the people who came and went—he thought it was all pretty. He liked the job and the miniature apartment he had on Crouch Street and the new TV he bought at Cowboy Maloney's Electric City, out on Pass Road. He liked just about everything about his life, and as he watched this six-foot-five bean pole dance toward the back of the store, he began to fear that his whole life was about to change.

Gil found Harold in the narrow, dark-paneled hall leading to Clovis's office, doubled over and peeking into the room through the hole where the second door lock had been. Without turning around, Harold waved an arm at Gil, telling him to stay quiet, stay quiet.

"What're they doing?" Gil whispered.

Harold flattened his palm over the hole and turned. "This is *exactly* like that *Red Shoe Diary* show," he said. "He's wonking her right here. She loves it."

"Lemme look," Gil said.

"No, you don't want to take no look," Harold said. "You're too busy. Get out of here. Go rack them cans."

"I'm taking a look," Gil said. He put a hand on Harold's shoulder, gave a little tug, but Harold was surprisingly strong and didn't budge.

"Get on out of here," he whispered to Gil. "You're making too much noise." He bent down to the hole again, and pretty soon he was making little grunting sounds as if in time with what he was seeing. Gil leaned against the paneling and slid down the wall.

"Come on, Harold," he said. "Fair's fair."

"My ass," Harold. "You got a dollar?"

"You're going to charge me for a look?" Gil said.

"Get that dollar out here," Harold said, grinning. He went back to the door lock and pressed his face against it. "Oh, baby," he said. "Oh baby, oh baby, oh baby."

"Shit," Gil said. He went into his wallet and got out a couple of bills. The compressor on the big freezer compartment just the other side of Clovis's office kicked on, and everything in the placed started to rattle and hum.

"They're going round the world," Harold said.

Gil grabbed Harold's shoulder and shoved a dollar into one of his hands, tried to push him aside, but Harold wasn't giving up this part.

"Scoot, boy. Get away."

"C'mon. I gave you a dollar," Gil said.

"Price's going up," Harold whispered. "Whooee. You go girl. Uh-huh."

Gil yanked at Harold but couldn't get him to move, and in a few seconds more Harold gave up the hole, leaned back against the wall, and shivered all over. "Holy Jesus," he said.

Gil jumped forward, bumped his head into the door jamb, tried to center his eye over the old keyhole. All he saw was Clovis standing by his desk with his shirt on but no pants. He had a lot of hair on his legs.

"Where's she?" Gil said.

"Probably the head," Harold said. "It's over. She left."

Gil kept his eye at the hole, twisting left and right, trying to see more of the room, trying to find Margie. "I don't see her," he said.

"She's in there," Harold said. "Hang on a minute. She'll be out. Maybe they'll go again. Gimme another dollar."

"I ain't giving you squat," Gil said. "They gone. They ain't going to do nothing more. I'm just picking slag here."

"Boy, she is fine," Harold said. He was rubbing his eyes with his thumbs. "Mmm. Hard-working woman."

"Don't start up, okay? I ain't seen nothing. You're just giving me nothing."

"Keep your eyes on it," Harold said. "She's bound to come out."

Clovis pulled up his trousers and tucked in his shirttail while peering out the head-high glass that let him watch the whole store from his office.

"We better get going," Harold said.

"I ain't going anywhere till I see her," Gil said. "They can walk right out this door, and I'll be standing here telling them hello."

"They're coming," Harold said.

"I don't care," Gil said. He kept his face pressed to the door.

Clovis's office was a mess. It was a crummy storeroom with a steel desk and stacks of paper around. There were stacks of flats of canned foods, and little eight by twelve plaques on the wall. Clovis stood tall in that room. As Clovis straightened his clothes, peeped out into the store through the mirrored glass, Gil thought that Clovis didn't have a bad deal at all. Like everybody, Clovis got paid for getting in out of the rain, only he got paid more, and got special privileges like Margie, and got to make fun of stock boys like Gil and Harold. As Gil watched, the idea of cutting up Clovis into little parts suddenly began to seem more appealing. He imagined draping Clovis over the butcher's saw and shoving him through the band so that his leg buzzed off. He heard the sound of the saw stripping through his skin and hitting the bone. He pictured the blood showering out, jetting everywhere. He thought about running an arm through that band saw, just like a two by four, zipping off a hand. Maybe he would throw the hand at Harold, something like that. But Harold wouldn't be paying attention, he'd be over in the corner humping Margie, who'd be squealing.

"What's happening?" Harold said. "Let's go."

"She ain't come out yet," Gil said.

"Why don't you ask her about it later," Harold said. "We're going to get our ass caught if you keep standing in that door like that."

"I wouldn't mind sawing him," Gil said. "But not her. I mean, I want to *do* her, but I don't want to saw her up after."

"You're crazy," Harold said. "We ain't sawing anybody."

Gil turned away from the hole, looked at Harold who was sitting on the floor, his immensely long legs jacked up in front of him. "I know that," Gil said. "But you're the big talker. You wanted to put 'em in cans."

"I'm gone," Harold said. He struggled to his feet and limped down the hall. Gil turned and pressed his eye to the hole one more time, saw Margie come up to Clovis's desk, straightening her uniform. When she turned and headed for the door, he beat it down the hall, then cut left and went around to the refrigeration room. He broke open a carton of ice cream sandwiches, took one, peeled and ate it while he waited for Clovis and Margie to clear.

Gil and Harold and Margie had lunch together at the McDonald's by the gas station out on the corner of the shopping center. They sat in a booth by the window watching the cars go by. Margie was as happy as could be. She waved a French fry at Gil and said, "I hear you boys were watching."

"We were," Gil said. "Well, he was. I was more or less by-standing."

"I seen it all," Harold said.

"You mean you didn't get to see?" Margie said to Gil.

"Saw you straightening the uniform," Gil said.

"That's not too much," she said.

"I thought it was pretty good," Gil said.

"You're a sweetie," she said. "Natural born."

"I got two dollars out of him," Harold said.

"To tell you the truth," Gil said, "I saw more than I wanted. You and Clovis, I don't know. I'm troubled by it. I wish you wouldn't do it anymore."

"What is this? A declaration of love?" Margie said.

"Hey, boy," Harold said. He looked like a giant basketball player in a yellow kid's booth there in the McDonald's.

Gil said, "I just think it's unsightly, you know? It's kind of beneath you."

Margie smiled real prettily, powerfully. Like a woman will. "Well it *is* a declaration of love," she said. "What do you know."

Gil knew she was right and he was proud of himself for saying what he had. There were thunderstorms all that afternoon, and everyone who came into the store was sopping wet. Margie seemed perky behind her register, chatting and laughing with all the customers as she pinged the bar codes over the reader. Gil was all around the store, working the shelves, the stock, mopping the back, sacking. Whenever he could, he went and sacked for Margie, just so he could be close to her. Clovis was gone most of the afternoon but came back around five and even manned a register. They got the five-to-six rush and then things started slacking off, and by seven the place was near dead.

A little after seven, Gil came to the front after resetting the bananas, apples, and oranges in the produce section. Harold was over there watering things down. Gil caught Clovis and Margie chatting by her register. Clovis had his back to Gil, and as he came up he heard Clovis say, "Let's take a little trip, what do you say?"

"I'm tired, Clo," Margie said. "It'll keep."

He jangled his keys. "I don't know. I think the Boss is ready to go."

She patted his shoulder and smiled at him. "Give him a chill," she said, then she waved at Gil. "Howdy, Gil."

Clovis turned, surprised that Gil was as close as he was. "What are you doing here, kid? You finished in produce?"

"Harold's handling it," Gil said.

"You mop sixteen and seventeen?" Clovis said.

"Sure did," Gil said.

"The new milk out?" Clovis said.

"Yes sir," Gil said.

"Why don't you go out front and round up the baskets then," Clovis said. "Margie and I have a little business." Margie made a face.

"It doesn't look like it to me," Gil said.

"What?" Clovis said.

"Let it go, Clovis," Margie said.

"Sure, fine," Clovis said. He turned back to Gil. "Get the baskets, will you? Everything's fine."

"Why don't you get the baskets," Gil said.

"Hey, listen, hit your time card on the way out," Clovis said. "Have I got your address up there? Thanks for everything."

"Oh, come on, Clovis," Margie said. "Leave him alone. He probably needs the job."

"If he needs the job, then he shouldn't be mouthing off to the boss," Clovis said. "You need the job, Gil?"

"Not bad enough," Gil said.

Margie pulled Clovis down to her and whispered something in his ear. It seemed to go on for a long time. When Clovis stood up and turned around, he was smiling. "I get it," he said. "Okay, fine. If you don't want to do the baskets, fine. Ask Harold to go get the baskets, will you?"

Gil grabbed the microphone and switched on the PA at the register where he was standing. "Harold, come to the front, will you. Harold, to the front."

He looked up at the ceiling at the white painted corrugated metal and bar joists and air-conditioning ducts. Sometimes a bird or two lived up there. It was always a mystery to Gil how a bird could get in. When customers complained, they had to chase the birds and get them out. Once Clovis brought a BB rifle and they had taken turns shooting at a bird until they popped the glass on a case back in Meat. Then they tried herding it out, propping the doors open and running through the store with brooms, throwing things at the ceiling where the bird was sitting on one of the joists. He was still looking at the ceiling when Clovis put an arm around his shoulders and started walking him toward the rear of the store.

"You know, Gil," Clovis said. "Nobody's getting hurt here. You shouldn't get upset just because I have a little bit of good fortune. See, you've got your whole life out in front of you. Anything can happen to you, but I'm past forty. I've got a college degree, and now I'm paying for a couple of kids that don't like me very much, and

I can't sleep. At three o'clock this morning I was up watching *Lingerie Dreams II* on pay-per-view. And I'm a churchgoing man, so that made me feel bad, just like other things do. But we do things anyway, you know what I'm saying? Don't know why, don't seem to have much choice. You look at it one way, and I'm taking advantage of my high position here at the store. Look at it another way, I'm an old guy being treated kindly."

"That's a continental attitude," Gil said. "I've seen that in the movies."

"Well, yeah," Clovis said. "Maybe it is. But I tell you what, I'll try to keep it down in the future. How's that?"

"I think we'd all appreciate it," Gil said. He noticed how stiffly he was walking.

Clovis pulled off, patted Gil's shoulder, and turned to go up into his office. Gil stopped in the middle of the aisle in front of the packaged meats, idly straightening some rib-eye steaks and some filets, some strip steaks. Later on, when he went home that night, he would wonder what had happened exactly. He wouldn't be able to put his finger on it, but he would think he had either learned a lesson or missed a step, and not knowing which it was would haunt him for a very long time.

(1997)

TRICK SCENERY

You have a face like an old sack, like an old vegetable, and the scenery rolls along beside you—it might be some kind of film gimmick, you don't know. You're alone and the sky is colorless, the trees shallow and black-looking. You've got an old Chevrolet, thirty-eight, thirty-nine, a convertible, a roadster, steel gray and it doesn't shine at all. You're an older man, maybe forty, and you wear your hat cocked back on your head the way reporters always do in newspaper movies, and you want a woman. You're driving a long drive, lasting several hours at least, along unused highway through unspectacular countryside—dry, dark, in some way a burlesque of menacing countryside, the way it rolls by you as if painted on a movie flat. You're tired and you want a woman, because a woman would make all the difference in the world.

Even without sun the heat of the afternoon, of the early evening, is unbearable, aggravating. With a woman the trees would be pretty and black, silky against the neutral sky—a woman has the power to change things. But you are afraid that you will never have a woman to ride with you, to wear a cheap dress from a department store and sit with you in the old roadster for the long drive along the unused highway. Resigned is perhaps a better word. And not all women are pretty, not all women will wear dresses from department stores, and it is true that some pretty women do not look so good in cheap dresses, shirtwaists, nylons and rayons, polyesters, prints and patterns with colorful belts in string loops, daring bright solids—these make some women look like they wish they were other women.

You wear a black suit with pinstripes, perhaps chalk-stripes, and a crumpled snap-brim hat pushed back on your head. You wear a vest with the last button open over your belt buckle. Your suit would be perfect for a man with a blonde woman, a tall woman, her hair short and severe and only caressed by the wind (she would adjust the wing window on the front door of the roadster so that the wind would fly around her).

You see a film on television at the motel, get a late start because you wait for the film, then watch it from beginning to end sitting with your legs crossed on the unmade double bed in your room. The film is *The Tin Star* with Henry Fonda an aging bounty hunter rich in the lore of the West and of justice. You sit in your room without a woman and watch the movie on the fuzzy Motorola which the night manager says is the best set in the motel, and it isn't a wonderful film, but for you, for this moment, perfect.

You have to ask yourself why you do not have a woman. You are not a salesman. You are not a criminal or a businessman of any kind, you are a man on vacation, on a trip, with no particular destination but a strict timetable, a schedule for your return. And no woman, no bare arms to run fingers over in a festival of gesture and affection, no gently curved breasts to admire at midnight against the false brocade of a motel wall. The question is terrifying.

The radio in the Chevrolet is broken; you cannot sing.

It would be worse if you had a woman asleep in the car, a woman with sealed eyes and crooked neck, slumped beside you in the seat, her head twisted back and limp on your shoulder. A woman whose mouth in sleep became an ugly hole laced at its edges with blown hair, strands of which stuck and darkened in the beads of perspiration above the lip, stuck in the waxy gloss bordering the mouth.

So with your hat back and a curl of dark hair falling flat on your forehead above dulled blue eyes you drive, and the highway seems more endless than ever.

There is the sound of the motor of the Chevrolet, and the sound of the wind hitting the metal, and the sound of the thick rubber on the tar-filled road—these sounds dying in the night. The splash of your headlights on the road illuminates nothing.

The vacation is torment, pure and drab, but you drive and watch the wall of the landscape pass, and your three-piece suit is so beautiful. You wonder if you could not awaken the woman, wipe her face, offer her the red ball for her mouth.

(1987)

PART SIX

THE GREAT PYRAMIDS

It had been raining for three days. Wallace sat on the heavy brocade cover of his sister's bed watching the weather on television, the word "muted" in green in the upper right corner of the screen, waiting for his sister to come home, waiting for a call. He'd been working on a website for an insurance company, a job Kelly had arranged. They did freelance web design, the two of them together. He and Kelly had always gotten along. She was only a couple of years older.

The rain sounded like a TV somebody had left on real loud after a station had gone off the air.

Wallace's mother and father had died over a year before—one after the other, two weeks apart. Everybody remarked that it always happened that way. Wallace didn't know if it did or not, only that it had happened to his mother and father. He had dropped out of college and was living at home when his parents died. Later, his sister asked him to come and live with her, to keep her company. She was hearing voices, she told him. When she tried to sleep, she heard people breathing close by. He found this completely touching. A side of his sister he'd never seen. She'd always been successful, straight, the one who got everything done and right and on time. Now she asked for his help, showed him something he'd never seen.

Less than a month after his parents were dead, Kelly and Wallace moved into the house on Cork Street, a forties bungalow six blocks off the coast highway, wood siding and a pitched roof and window air conditioners, and inside a lot of heavy, old furniture left by the previous owners who had moved into an assisted-living facility in Biloxi.

Kelly bought the house, but she acted as if it was theirs, as much his as hers.

She was Catholic still, went to mass, prayed. Wallace figured she was lucky. He'd quit with the incense and stained-glass windows.

"You can do it that way if you want to," she said. "It's plenty fair."

He said he didn't doubt it.

He was comfortable in the house, though it was dark—the walls were dusty pastels, the windows had blinds and heavy drapes. There were thick padded carpets and the furniture was all oversize fake antiques. Knobby bedposts, shoulder-high chests-of-drawers, gaudy red-polished wood. He like living there because it felt like living in his grandparents' house, which made him even less responsible than he was in his parents' house, which was one reason he'd gone to live at his parents' house in the first place. He hadn't expected them to die.

The old couple that had moved out of the Cork Street house were making a new start, so they left everything behind. Kelly kept it all, and left her things in storage. She adopted the furniture—and the linens, the towels, the flatware, the dishes, all of the equipment the old couple had left behind.

Kelly called him from the casino. She worked part-time as a craps dealer, and was studying to deal blackjack.

"I'm coming to get you," she said. "We're going out. You stay in too much. You need to get out more."

"Fine," Wallace said. "I'll be here."

"I want to go eat," she said. "Do you want to eat?"

"Isn't it a little wet outside?"

"How about Chinese food?" she said.

Half an hour later she called again. This time from a gas station about a mile up the highway.

"It's pretty bad here, Wally," she said. "I had to pull off because the water is up to the top of the wheel opening. Everybody's splashing around and the guy running this place says there are snakes all over. I've seen a couple."

"You've seen snakes?" he said.

"Yeah. They look like tiny Loch Ness monsters," she said. "They float around in the water with their heads sticking out."

"Great news," he said.

"I'm going to wait a few minutes, then I'm going to try to come up and get you, okay?" she said.

"What if the car stalls?" he said.

"Then I won't get you," she said. "You'll notice. If I'm not there in half an hour, you come get me."

"Why don't I just come now? Bring the truck?" he said.

"That's okay. Would you mind?" she said.

"No," he said. "You sit tight. I'll be there momentarily." He hung up and thumbed the remote on the television, going through the channels looking for a quick update. The closest he could come was a disheveled guy in shirt sleeves with his collar loosened and his tie pulled down, waving vaguely at a chroma-key map of the coast. Wallace tried to punch the button to unmute the sound, but he missed and he had to punch a couple other buttons, and when he finally got the sound turned up, the station was in the middle of a bean commercial.

Wallace did a quick change of clothes and went out the side door and got into the big Ford truck that his father had had. They didn't use it very often, but it started right up. It was late afternoon, but it was almost dark as night outside. The street was shaded by giant oaks and the sky, where it was visible, was veined in pinks and pale yellows. Thunder cracked and ratcheted and thudded around in that sky. Lightning zigzagged every which way, as if it were the electricity in some maniac doctor's laboratory. The rain came down in gallons and sheets and crystal lead-colored stripes, spattering off the truck windshield, hammering the roof and the hood. He backed out of the driveway and got up in the center of Cork Street riding high. He left the window down and as he drove toward the highway he'd see that all the yards in the neighborhood were glistening, all the grass was knee-deep in standing water. The drainage ditches along the road were overflowing and occasionally he saw a woman in a house dress on a porch with a dog looking out a screen door.

Most of the houses had their lights on inside. Occasionally he could see people moving about or sitting in old overstuffed chairs, reading or watching television. He was barely moving along Cork Street in the truck. He'd give it a little gas, then let off the gas, and let the truck roll. He didn't want to stir up a lot of water and didn't want to get water on the brakes, thought it would be safer to just take it slow. He had a towel in the truck and he put it over his left arm on the edge of the window that was open. All the racket of the thunderstorm was kind of muted. The light had a kind of greenish cast to it. Not a bright green, but something dull. The light seemed almost like fatigue light—army green, lit from the inside, so it had a kind of luminous quality.

The wipers on the truck were clacking back and forth, but he still couldn't see much out front. A couple of blocks from his house a black dog came up on the driver's side of the truck and started walking with him, eyeing the front wheel as if trying to decide whether or not he need to chase this truck or bite that tire.

"What are you doing, Bugs?" Wallace said to the dog. "Why are you walking along like that? It's raining. Aren't you wet?" The dog turned his head and kind of squinted at Wallace, then went back to looking at the front tire. Wallace gave the gas a little squirt and the truck jumped ahead. The dog stopped in his tracks and then trotted up again to walk alongside. "We're going to have Chinese food. Would you like to come? I guess you don't feel so good about Chinese food, now that I think about it."

The dog lifted his head up and rolled his eyes back, looking at Wallace almost upside down.

"Sorry," Wallace said. "Why don't you go on home now. Go on." He waved his arm out the window at the dog, trying to get the dog to stop following him. In the next block he saw two kids in the front of a gray, clapboard house. They were inside a box that a refrigerator had come in. It was a Frigidaire and was on its side, open on the end toward the street, and the two kids were sitting inside. It looked like they were playing cards, but Wallace couldn't quite tell that. The headlights reflected off the flying rain. He could only see six or seven yards in front of him, and all he could see was glittering hash of water that kept falling, blown sideways, splashing off the road. As he came out from under the oaks near the highway, things lightened up. The sky was gray-white. He could make out the muddled shape of cars going by with their lights shining. Everybody was driving real slow, single file, trying to avoid the deepest parts of the flooded street. He snapped on his blinker and waited while a burgundy-colored Cadillac went by, followed by a modern car that he didn't know the name of, and then a delivery van. When they had passed, he edged out into the street, looking both ways elaborately. When he didn't see anything coming, he made the left turn and rode the crown of the highway toward the gas station where Kelly was waiting.

As he went down the highway, there were a few cars stalled in the median and a few cars pulled off on the concrete overlooking the beach, but mostly traffic moved smoothly. When he got to the gas station, he found Kelly standing under the overhang, chewing on a stick of red licorice. There were three or four other people huddled in the protection of the gas station. He pulled in and Kelly got into the truck, leaned over and planted a little kiss on the side of his mouth.

"Hello, my brother," she said.

He arched an eyebrow and swung the truck back into the rain. Kelly patted his thigh.

"Let's roll," she said.

"Where are we rolling to?" Wallace said.

"Out into the weather," she said.

He got back onto the beach highway. Everybody was driving real slow. Everybody was being real careful. All the cars kicked up little waves. The windshield wipers cracked back and forth across the glass, unable to keep it clear. At Fodor Road Kelly said, "Turn here. I want to go to this Chinese place."

"You could have given me some warning," he said, slipping into the center lane, hitting his signal.

The restaurant was called Shanghai Garden. It was a place they went once in a while. The food wasn't great, but it didn't have too many customers, and the people who ran it were very pleasant and friendly. The building was a converted convenience store, the front windows blocked with heavy red burlap curtains. Inside there was some carved-wood latticework, a few green leatherette booths, a wall of mirrors, and a buffet table that the restaurant never used anymore. The rest of the interior was painted all dark green with red trim and gold highlights. Here and there were white lanterns with red tassels hanging from the ceiling, and on the wall the usual assortment of dragons.

Wallace and Kelly took menus and seated themselves in a booth by the front window. The menus were stained. The tablecloth was dark green and stained and the place mats were paper, printed with the usual stuff about the Chinese calendar.

"Are you a dog?" Kelly said. "I can't remember if you're a dog or a horse."

"Horse," he said.

"Look at that," she said. "We're perfectly suited for each other. See here?" She tapped the section on his place mat under the drawing of the horse. "I'm highly compatible with the horse."

"Are we eating?" he said.

At one end of the room there was a giant rear-screen projection television hooked to a VCR, showing some kind of Chinese talent show.

"So here's what happened to me," Kelly said. "I've decided we need to go see where Mom and Dad are buried. We need to go see them."

Wallace was studying the menu, studying it hard. He didn't look up. "No thanks," he said. "Been there, done that. What about this lo mein?"

"Wallace," Kelly said. She reached across the table and touched his hand. "We need to go out there. We need to go together."

"Let's don't and say we did," Wallace said. That was some crack his father had picked up from some radio show, something he said every time he didn't want to do something Wallace's mother had suggested.

"We have to," Kelly said. She sat back and flipped open her menu, lying it flat on the table.

They ordered hot and sour soup, pot stickers, house vegetables deluxe, and lemon chicken, something Wallace always ordered when he went to a Chinese restaurant. They sat in the dark restaurant, listening to the rain, waiting for the food.

After a few minutes she asked him, "Do you think it's strange, us living together?"

He grinned at her. "It could be stranger."

"I know that," she said.

"I don't know," he said. "Does it bother you? Do you want me to move out? I can move out if you want me to."

"No, I don't want you to move out," she said. "I like you there."

"That settles it then," Wallace said.

Neither one of them had had a date since Wallace had moved in. Wallace used to have a girlfriend, a woman named Mindy. A thin, little stick of a person who studied fine art at a local college. But she had moved away, moved to Miami to study painting there, and Wallace hadn't heard from her in over a year. Kelly used to have a lot of boyfriends, at least that's what he thought he remembered from high school and when she started college, but since their parents died, she seemed to be content with him.

"So I talked to Eve," she said.

"Eve?" he said.

"The girl I used to live with in New Orleans. She's a social worker. And, well, here's what happened. She had this client who really loved Hillary Clinton, and when Hillary was going around the country promoting her book, she went to New Orleans to do a book signing and this woman wanted to go. My friend, Eve, agreed to take her. It was a deal where you bought a book in advance and then you stood in line and got to shake Hillary's hand. This woman, Eve's client, had some kind of brain damage, some kind of tumors on the brain or something and had had part of her frontal lobe removed when she was a child, so she was a little bit off center. Anyway, they went to the bookstore, and there was this huge line outside the bookstore, and this woman started crying because she thought she wasn't going to get in to see Mrs. Clinton. The longer they waited, the more hysterical she got, until finally Eve said, okay, I think we're going to get to see Mrs. Clinton, but what you need to do now is focus on what you're going to say to her. I think you ought to think about one question that you can ask Mrs. Clinton when you meet her and shake her hand."

"So your friend said to this woman that she had to think of a question," Wallace said.

"Right," Kelly said. "That seemed to contain the woman. She was really focusing on that. It was a pretty long wait, and about forty-five minutes later the line finally got back to them and they got to Mrs. Clinton. This woman grabbed Mrs. Clinton's hand to shake it. She started telling Mrs. Clinton how wonderful she was and saying that she was so excited about seeing her. She said, 'Mrs. First Lady, I just have to get down on my knees and thank you for everything you've done for mental health in this country. You and Mr. President have done so much for mentally handicapped people in this country.' The woman was down on her knees and my friend Eve was sure the Secret Service was about to swoop in and pick them up. The woman was crying and holding on to Mrs. Clinton's hand with both of her hands, and going on and on about how wonderful Mrs. First Lady was. She just wouldn't stop. Eve was leaning over trying to comfort the woman and trying to get her to stand up. Mrs. Clinton was standing there shaking her hand, but no Secret Service people came. Eventually, after a couple of minutes of this, Eve got her to stand up, got her to release Mrs. Clinton's hand, and they moved on. They left the store and the woman seemed perfectly happy and content, because she had gotten to do what she wanted. They got in the car and started to leave, and then the woman started crying again. My friend Eve turned to her and asked, 'Why are you crying? What's upsetting you now?' And the woman said, 'I forgot to ask my question.' Eve asked her what the question was and the woman said, 'Well, I wanted to ask why the navy makes people retire early.' "

Kelly said this in a childlike, plaintive way, and Wallace laughed a little, and then more, and then stopped laughing altogether and looked at his sister.

"I know," she said.

"Some things are so wonderful in this world," he said.

Kelly smoothed her place mat and rearranged her napkin, the glass, her utensils. Then she started on the lazy susan where the sweet and sour sauces were, where the soy sauce was, where the little chrome rack of Sweet & Low and sugar sat. When she got that straightened away, she started to work on Wallace's place setting. He pulled back the red burlap curtain and looked outside into the frizzy rain. Two police cars had pulled up and blocked the highway. Their lights were flashing and the policemen were out in bright yellow slickers directing traffic, detouring it off the beach highway. The glass rattled with thunder. Across the highway the water and the sky were indistinguishable. A single mottled gray ran all the way from the beach up into the clouds. There was no horizon. The water was relentless. The policemen were calf deep in it. The cars detouring off the highway plowed the water. The streetlight was blinking green. The trees outside were bent over and limp. They looked like they were tired of the rain.

The food came and they began to eat. Wallace started listening to the music being played in the restaurant—a peculiar Chinese techno-rave dance music, with a high-speed, insistent beat. The song sounded like German pop music with a few Oriental instruments tossed in here and there. He watched Kelly cool her soup in the large plastic version of the Chinese spoon. She seemed to him an attractive woman. A girl, someone any man would find attractive. She was attractive to him, though not in the way he was thinking about. She was so sweet, so gentle, so deeply invested in the parts of their lives, so genuinely invested. He wondered why he hadn't met anyone like her. He remembered a girl from high school—a smart girl who had a kind of simplicity and ease about her, a directness. She reminded him a little of his sister, but she was the last girl he could remember who had anything in common with Kelly. He tapped his mouth with his napkin and then slid out of his side of the booth and got into Kelly's side. She was startled and slid away from him.

"Shhh," he said, holding up a hand. He reached out and touched her hair, ran his fingers through it, the tips of his fingers through to her scalp.

"What are you doing?" she said. "Get back over there."

"I'm going in just a minute," Wallace said.

"Go on," she said and shooed him with her napkin. He pulled her to him and she resisted at first, but then perhaps sensing that he wasn't going to give up, she gave in and allowed herself to be pulled to him, and he kissed her softly on the cheek and then on her neck beneath her ear. He let his head rest on her shoulder a minute, then kissed her there and sat up and edged out of the booth. He stood alongside the table for a minute, took a drink of his Diet Coke, stared across the room at the big television.

From behind Kelly caught his hand, gave him a little tug toward his seat. "We don't have to go anywhere if you don't want to," she said. "It's just that I miss them. I still see them in my head sometimes. I can hear them talking. I can hear things Mother said to me. I can remember what her hand felt like when she touched me. I can remember the way her skin looked—almost translucent, filmy. I can remember the way she squinted. I just think it would be good if we went to see them."

"I'll go," Wallace said. "I'll go right now. I'll get the check and we can go."

"No, I want to finish this first," she said.

He sat down again, facing her. He had no appetite, but put two or three things on his plate, busied himself moving them back and forth, moving them clockwise around his plate. "How come you're not using chopsticks?" he said to her.

"No need to," she said.

"It makes for a more complete experience," he said. "That's what you told me."

"I think somebody must have told me once," she said.

He pulled back the curtain again. Outside there were more flashing, glittering, blinking lights. There were new policemen and there was a wrecker and there was a truck that had somehow jackknifed off the low sea wall. There were even some of those burning torches that are supplied in all emergency road kits. He could hear the buzz of the blinking Shanghai Garden sign mounted on the outside of the glass near the booth where they sat. Kelly pulled back the curtain on her side and looked out.

"*You long to see the great pyramids of Egypt*," Wallace said.

"What's that?" Kelly said.

"The last fortune cookie I got here."

"Hmm," she said, tapping the glass. "They couldn't beat this."

(2000)

GALVESTON

Rachel doesn't want to know what I'm doing. In fact, what I'm doing is about the last thing Rachel wants to know. We've been married five years, and for her it's been one tragedy after another, one disappointment after another, one distaste after another. We got married because we thought she was pregnant. We thought we loved each other. We thought the world was a place we could navigate together. But it wasn't that, it wasn't that from the start. It was just like it had been before we got married—messy, uncomfortable, crazy, stupid. I don't know whatever gave us the idea that it was going to be different.

The week after we got married her mother died, so we had to fly out to Utah for the funeral. We were there for four days, and I can barely remember what her father looked like. She has some brothers and sisters, I know, but I don't remember them much, either, except for khakis. They all wore khakis. It seemed that everybody in Utah wore khakis. I'd never seen so many khakis anywhere. I mean, there are khakis around when you're in your ordinary life—you see khaki, but not like this. Not on everybody, not without exception. I'll say this for them, though: in Utah they didn't press their khakis, which I figure is a pretty big step forward.

We camped out in the car on the way to Utah and on the way back. That was what was fun about the trip—sleeping in the car pulled over at a highway rest stop. We had a new car. The seats were kind of comfortable and went all the way back, so you could stretch out.

•

Rachel calls me at the office. "I want a divorce," she says. "I don't want you to come home tonight or any other night. I don't want to ever have to see you again. I don't want to hear your voice. I don't want to smell you. That's it. It's over."

Then she hangs up, leaves me there on the line. I hardly know what to do. Is this Rachel-whimsy? A sudden feeling that we aren't suited for each other? Has she been drinking? She does that at home alone during the day. She'll drink Jack Daniel's until she's blotto. Makes her feel things—she thinks she has ideas about the world then. She thinks she sees the world in a new, clearer way. It's not an unusual drunk, kind of routine. It doesn't happen all the time, either, but it happens often enough to make me think that there's more to it than just the odd discomfort, the odd unhappiness with our lives.

•

We have a bungalow on the corner of Decatur and Tenth. It's gray and was built in the forties and redone in the seventies or early eighties. It seems like a pretty nice place to me. Sometimes in the summertime we leave the windows open and turn on the attic fan, and it draws breezes through the house, breezes that remind me of nights at the beach. We lie on the bed together with these fast winds blowing over us. The smell of the place is kind of old—old wood, old flooring, old fixtures—and I'm reminded of the times I spent on the sleeping porch at my grandmother's house in Galveston, Texas, in the fifties. I don't think I loved my grandmother enough. I don't think I loved her at all. She was short and fat and talked a lot and smelled funny. She was wrinkled, wrinkled. She was kind of a big fireplace, a bossy woman who made my father into the pushover he was. I could never feature her with my grandfather, who was a lanky, easygoing, handsome guy. Not the kind of guy you'd see with some short, fat, wrinkled woman, ordinarily. She might not have been wrinkled all her life. That's a possibility. They had a black woman who cooked for them—I don't remember her name—Estie or Blattie or something. One of those member-of-the-family deals that make the race relations in the South a little less disgusting in practice than those in the North. I mean, they liked this woman quite a lot, and the woman liked them. Sure, there were limits and preconditions and expectations, but even with all of those, the people seemed to care about each other.

•

In Galveston in the fifties, there was more light than I have seen in any other place at any other time. Nothing seemed to be dark at all. Everything was baked white and bristling with reflections. Sand everywhere, bright awnings, green shutters, fast winds. It wasn't bad. I wouldn't mind being there now. I wouldn't mind ditching Rachel and moving back there and running a restaurant, maybe some place like John's, or someplace up on the seawall, or someplace downtown.

Before I met Rachel, I knew a woman whose father was from Galveston. The only other person I ever met whose father was from Galveston. He ran a lumberyard. She was a nice woman, quite smart. A little too well-to-do, maybe. I never slept with her.

•

On the trip to Utah, driving down the empty streets of small towns through the night, going out there, it was like we were riding toy streets and train sets and plastic towns, little towns that I had seen as a kid. The green of the grass was bright plastic green or the white of the bricks was viciously white or the roofs were bright red shingles. The streetlights in these towns seemed to be wasting themselves over these empty streets in the middle of the night. Stoplights stupidly going red, going green, going red. It was a silly business, but very beautiful. It was like we owned the whole place, like there wasn't anybody else around, and it was ours. Little cats would run across the street in the middle of the night, hopping almost. Sometimes we'd stop and have a look at them. They would be orange or black or gray tabbies. The early birds would be out—milk trucks, people in pickups, people coming home or going to doughnut shops. The air would be sort of not-quite-black, as if you could focus on it. The sky was true black with millions and millions and millions of tiny stars, and all the same size. It's not a business, the sky at night.

When you got out on the highway again it would be pitch dark, and your running lights would be all that lit the way. The odd motel on the side of the road was supposed to make you feel something, but we were at the point where we didn't feel a thing. We saw the signs and thought they were pretty.

•

You never think you're going to dislike someone you've been living with for years. You know so much about them, spend so much time with them working, trying to make things okay. The idea that you'll end up not liking them is strange, remote, like some ship you don't expect to come into your channel. Somebody you don't expect to see in the neighborhood. That's the way it is with Rachel and me. We go to bed at night now and can't quite imagine why we ever got together in the first place—what she saw in me, what I saw in her—it just doesn't make any sense. I don't quite hate her, but it might be worse than that, just not caring about her, just erasing her out of my life. She doesn't exist for me. She might as well be some woman in a Jeep Cherokee in a parking lot somewhere. She's not one of those best-looking women you ache for when you see them. But I don't ache so much anymore, anyway. There was a time, but that time came and went. Now I see like some camera.

A new woman is in a parking lot, and I can see that she's attractive, and, yes, I can see that her skin is lovely, and, yes, I can see that her hair falls beautifully around her face, her cheekbones are high, clear, defined. She has a few freckles across her nose, and she has lips that say they mean business. She has good, strong legs, thin, focused. She walks with determination, aware of her body, of herself, of the space she sculpts. You can see it in the way her arms move and the way her butt moves. I see all of this. I don't care. I watch her go into the store, and I don't care. There was a time I would have chased her around the store, stung and intoxicated, following her from aisle to aisle, from produce to crackers to napkins to frozen foods—all for another sweet deep drink of her.

But Rachel isn't that good-looking, that exciting, and even if I saw Rachel right now, I wouldn't follow her. We live in the same house, but she's just vertical furniture. She's a table or chair or closet door. I wonder if it's this way for other people, if they look at their husbands and wives this way. I wonder if this is how Rachel looks at me, wondering what the hell I'm doing here, thinking she doesn't want to see me tomorrow.

(2000)

TINY APE

Murray ran the car wash at the Sunoco station just off the interstate, where the highway curled down to meet the mall, for Big Willie Fryer. Willie was a Scandinavian guy, maybe six-six, three hundred pounds, not exactly fat, but not Mr. Olympia either. Just plain big. When he handled things—oilcans, trash barrels, crates—everything looked light as a feather. Pencils shrunk in his hand. Murray mostly kept track of the trash-kids that scrubbed the wheels and applied the scent and wiped the cars down after they ran through the Hogan, which was what everybody called the wash tunnel, though nobody could tell Murray why. Big Willie told him it was the name of the previous system, a felt-and-spray setup he'd ordered out of New Orleans when his father had the station back in the sixties. The Hogan had been replaced with an upmarket nothing-touches-the-cars system in the mid-eighties, so nothing there had the name Hogan on it.

Murray was thirty-two, closing on three, and was happy to have the new managerial position, especially since he'd been ready to sign on to wipe cars himself. He'd shown so much initiative in the interview that he'd shot up through the rank to wash manager and had an office he shared with Ted Kiowa, the mechanic who ran Willie's garage section and who was not Native American, thank you, and Lillian Range, who ran the gas section. This idea of middle management knocked Big Willie out. He'd read an article about the advantages of spreading out responsibilities in small businesses in *Entrepreneur,* and had decided to apply it across the board at his Sunoco.

Murray was in the wash business because he'd lost a couple of jobs, much better jobs, white-collar jobs—one as an architect with his own practice, another as a draftsman for Rollie Odom Associates, the firm to which he'd sold his practice when he had to turn everything liquid to pay for a three-month gambling binge in which he'd managed to lose about sixty thousand dollars, most of which he didn't have. So there went the house, the mortgage, the car, the tiny savings, the computers, books, stereos, TVs—everything Murray could get a dime out of. And, after all that, Odom was kind enough to pay a little something for Murray's office equipment and a couple of clients, and kinder still to give Murray a temp job drawing changes into the standard house plans that Odom used to fulfill his clients' dreams. But Odom wasn't altogether in the charity business, so, quick enough, Murray was looking, and quick after that he was in the car wash business with Big Willie.

"You a gambler, that it?" Willie said when Murray walked in with the help wanted sign Willie'd put out.

"Was," Murray said. "Learned my lesson."

"Everybody says," Willie said.

"I need the job," Murray said. "I'll work at it."

"Drying cars," Willie said.

Murray nodded.

Willie stared at him for a minute, then raised his hands in a gesture of resignation. "You can have it. I got some plans you might fit into. You some kind of salesman in a past life?"

"Architect," Murray said. "Mostly houses, some supervision."

"Start tomorrow," Willie said.

•

Murray celebrated his first paycheck at the Lady Luck Casino, but he didn't celebrate very long, and about nine o'clock he was standing outside the Lady Luck watching the nine o'clock show of the fire-breathing dragon.

He leaned on the thick red pipe railing, and when a clean-enough-looking woman came and stood about ten feet away, he smiled and said, "Winner or loser?"

"Who's asking?" she said, without even turning to look at him.

He liked that, liked it that she spoke straight out into the wind in front of her, made no effort to be sure he heard, did not care what he looked like—wasn't even interested enough to glance.

"Loser asks," he said. "Three hundred and change. I was up, but . . . you know."

Now she looked. She had the usual straight black hair in a kind of bowl cut they got from the movies, the usual how-ugly-can-I-get body stocking in meal-brown, the usual heavily patterned miniskirt, the regular open-collar sleeveless T-shirt with another flowered shirt over that but under the black jacket. She had the usual boots, black, laced on brass eyes.

"You look like a loser," she said to Murray, who was in chinos and a pullover.

"Yeah, well, you look like Bruce Dern, so you want a drink or what?"

"I want a drink all I gotta do is crawl through the door over here," she said, wiggling an arm toward the casino.

"That's what I'm saying," he said. "We go together. Have a couple drinks, check the action. See what you bring me."

"That's my job in life," she said. "To bring you something."

"You know what I'm saying," Murray said.

"I'm catching the dragon," she said.

"I can wait." Murray lit a smoke and turned away from the dragon, looking back across the inlet between the Lady Luck and its six-story parking garage toward the Grand Casino Biloxi. It was Sunday. He thought he was going to get lucky, felt it settling in his bones. He slid a little left seeing if he could catch a scent off her like off the cocktail chicks in the casinos. Sometimes he'd sit at the quarter slots playing real slow and drinking fast just so he could brush the babes in push-ups and scarlet hose who did the serving.

Didn't they know better? He was at the quarter slots, for Christ's sake. Didn't they teach these high-bra girls anything?

He liked to call them over with his eyes, raise his brow a bit, or catch them looking his way and torque his head to one side just a little. That brought them straight away. He'd put a five on their little trays and ask for Coke and Jack, knowing he wouldn't get it in a million years, but it made him feel better to call it by name, to make them think he thought they were taking care of him special.

The big dragon music was coming up now. All that tinkling and gonging and Oriental nasal stuff, and the smoke was beginning to roll out from under the garage-size fake rock the casino built that housed the fire-breathing dragon. The families were all gathered around on the walkways, fathers itching to get back to the machines or the tables but pulled out to watch the hourly display by their wives, who were ready to leave.

"Name's Patti," she said, "I work here, you know."

"What? The Lady Luck?"

"Yeah. I run drinks. I've seen you in there dicking with the tiny slots—you're not big money, are you?"

"Little money," he said. "But I'm a swell guy."

"What's that mean?" she asked.

"Means I've got a job, I don't smack women, I clean up after myself. You know, Cary Grant."

"My luck," she said, flicking her cigarette into the army-green water. "Listen, I gotta get in costume and do a half shift, eight to two. See me after, huh?"

"No shit?" Murray said. This was big news to him. He'd hit on hundreds of women around the casinos, maybe dozens, anyway, but never gotten a flicker. He was so bad it'd become a no-expectation game. He carried it on only out of habit. "Maybe I'll come back and play some slots or something," he said. "Try the crap tables. You really going out with me later?"

"You can take me to breakfast," she said. "Anywhere you want."

So she went inside the Lady Luck, and Murray went home and took a bath, changed into his clean black jeans and a high-fashion J. Crew T, sprinkled himself with deodorant and cologne, and drove back to the casino a little after one. He played some Double-Diamond machines and hit a four-hundred-dollar payout, then cashed out and wandered around dropping twenties into other machines that took them without looking back.

He was pushing a rumpled hundred into a ten-buck Red, White & Blue in the Slot Salon when Patti slipped by behind him and asked if he wanted a cocktail. She had on the short black skirt, the scarlet hose, the white blouse. She draped her hand over his shoulder.

"You bet," he said. "You near done?"

"That's the bad news," Patti said. "They want me to go all night. Two girls are down with the flu." She nodded at a fat guy sitting all over his stool in front of one of the five-dollar machines. He was shaking his arm at her. "Let me get this Dumpster's drink and then I'll take you on break with me, that be okay?"

"Perfect," he said. "Better and better."

"See you cleaned up," she said, dragging the hand across his arm as she moved toward the fat one. "Nice going."

They screwed for the first time on her break in a closet on the third floor of the casino, a section of the place that was under construction, where they were adding some new offices. She sat on a sawhorse, rolled the tights down to mid-thigh, and got her ankles up over his shoulders. He worked with his jeans on.

•

Murray got her for breakfast at six in the morning. She met him in the parking garage, still in uniform. "Let's run by my place so I can change," she said. "Then Buck's, okay?" Buck's was a pancake house off Highway 90, the beach road.

"Maybe I can help you change," Murray said. "You can just stand there, and I'll do all the work."

"Put a bag in it, will you? I'm awake twenty hours. I'm running down. Tumbling you is the last thing I want to think about."

"Maybe it's the outfit," he said.

"Maybe you're a cheese head," she said. She reached out as if to pat his hand but just patted the air near his hand. He felt the breeze.

Her apartment was a second-floor unit in a set called Ocean View Apartments, and there was a view—you just had to struggle to get at it. The metal railings rang as they went up the concrete steps. She was in 214. The rooms were small and dark, paneled, with rent-a-junk furniture. Stupid magazines were around, bent back, rolled up. She was reading a lot about the O. J. Simpson case.

"Help yourself to the kitchen," Patti said, heading into the little hallway that led to her bedroom. "I'll be back in a nip."

The kitchen was wood-look vinyl on the cabinets and a dark brown refrigerator with a plant dribbling off the top and down alongside the hinges. She had good refrigerator magnets—a TV dinner, a roll of Tums, a tiny cherry pie, and a manger scene. "I like your magnets," Murray shouted back into the hall.

"What?" she said, coming out to the edge of the living room. She had jeans on and was holding a T-shirt in front of her.

"I'm a fridge-magnet guy," he said. "I mean, I always study them. I don't collect or anything—I hate people who collect things—but I pay attention. Yours are good."

She gave him an eye roll and said, "Thanks. I spent ages picking them out."

"It's just something I'm interested in," he said.

"Life on the edge," she said. She stepped back into the hall and threw the T-shirt over her head. "You ready?"

"Ever," he said.

She grabbed a green sim-alligator purse that was strung over the back of a Gnu chair in the living-dining-combo room, and went past him headed for the door. "C'mon, Dingy," she said. "And what's that smell you got on? Are you wearing some damn men's cologne or something? Jesus—you smell like a camellia."

"Thanks, honey," he said. "Hang on a half minute while I tend to business." He pointed back to the hall and went that direction at the same time, hunting the bathroom. It was close and lilac. He dropped the shirt and washed down fast with water from the tap, trying not to get it all over. Then he tapped dry with a floral towel and got her Suave out of the medicine cabinet. Then he put his shirt back on and flushed the toilet.

The light was still lazy when they left Patti's apartment, and the air was thick the way Gulf air gets on hot, still mornings. They toured Beach Boulevard headed west, toward Pass Christian, where Buck's sat on a miserable little spike of sand that ran out four hundred yards into the Mississippi Sound. The land wasn't there, really, or wouldn't have been unless the Mississippi Corps of Engineers, or whatever they were called in Mississippi, hadn't poured enough concrete around it to build a couple of replicas of the Great Pyramid. They did this in chicken-wire boxes about a foot square and three feet long, then dumped these giant concrete blocks helter-skelter all the way around Dogleg Point, which was the name the locals had given this particular piece of land because it was shaped like same. Buck's was out toward the end, far enough out so that the noise from the highway went way down, and car tires crunching in the oyster-shell lot were the only thing that disturbed the constant light clap of the water.

(2000)

RAIN CHECK

Hoping for quick intimacy, I start telling Lucille things I'm afraid of. It's a late dinner, our first meeting, a date arranged by a friend of hers who works in my office, and we go to the restaurant Lucille chooses, a place called Red Legs, where all the waiters work in dresses. "It's antebellum drag," she says. "Isn't it crazy?" Red Legs doesn't look very antebellum to me. It has a low ceiling and, along one wall, a thirty-sheet Coppertone billboard of a very tan girl. There's tropical flavor, too—a couple of dozen giant dead banana plants. Lucille says she's not afraid of anything, so I shut up about loneliness.

Our waiter, a stumpy guy wearing a satin hoopskirt, stands about two feet from our table, dangling a menu in each hand as if he were holding freshly dressed chickens by their feet. He has a diseased-looking black beard floating over his chest. "Do we want to see a menu?" he asks.

Lucille tries to swipe one from his hand, but he jerks back out of reach. "Great," she says. "Let's see the menu." She looks at me as if I've already failed to perform.

I hold out my hand for the menu. "Send the cocktail waitress, will you?" I'm careful not to look at the waiter.

When he's gone, Lucille says, "I've been seeing this Oriental guy—he's only twenty. How old are you?"

"Forty in December."

"Damn," she says. "Forty." Then she ducks her head behind the menu. "I guess that's not so bad. My dad's about forty, maybe forty-five, and he's all right."

I smile at her menu. "It's not as bad as it's said to be. Where's your friend tonight?"

"Who? Oh, Wang? He's out of the country. He had to go to New Guinea or someplace. Did I tell you he's from Oklahoma? I don't know how they got all these Orientals in Oklahoma, but they're there. I think it must be the oil—they're good with oil is what Wang says."

There's a red bug with two black dots on its back near the edge of the table, crawling toward me. I try to flick it casually in the direction of the nearest banana plant, but my hands are cold and I mush the bug into the tablecloth.

Lucille comes out from behind her menu. "What's that?" she asks, pointing at the small stain by my hand.

"Nothing." I pull my napkin out of my lap and wipe at the mess, which makes it a little better.

"Oh," she says.

After some more difficulty with the waiter, we get the dinner. Lucille gives me a play-by-play of her off-again, on-again romance with the Oklahoma playboy Wang. She keeps apologizing for boring me with his exploits and opinions, but she doesn't stop. By midnight I feel like Wang's mother.

I'm trying to finish the lemon-yellow dessert soup the waiter recommended, when Lucille starts showing me the bruises on her shoulders. "He's real good," she says. "But very Oriental, if you know what I mean."

"Uh-huh," I say, looking around for the waiter. I finally have to stand up to get his attention.

"How was the duck?" he says when he arrives.

I point at the check, but he doesn't want to give it to me; he keeps writing on it and looking off toward the kitchen, then writing some more. It's late and there isn't anything going on in the kitchen as far as I can see; they've turned off most of the lights in there.

"What duck?" I say. We didn't have any duck; he must have us mixed up with somebody else.

"The duck. You know," Lucille says. She nods at the waiter and fingers the skirt he's wearing, pulling him closer to her. "The duck was excellent; we loved it. You got meringues tonight?"

He puts away the check. "So you want the meringues? You want the soup and you want the meringues too."

Lucille smiles and says, "Wavy ones. Okay?"

When the waiter turns to me, I nod and say, "Okay on the meringues."

We wait in silence for him to bring them, and when he does, Lucille asks me how I like them and I say, "They're wavy."

The waiter returns and drops the check into my hand. I give him Visa, then ask for it back and give him MasterCard, because I don't usually use Visa; then it dawns on me that Lucille might think I've got some problem with Visa, like I'm over limit or something, so when the waiter leaves I say, "I really hate Visa, don't you?"

"Hate Visa? Why?"

Before I can reply, the waiter is back. "Listen, we're out of MasterCard charge slips. Would you mind going ahead with the Visa?"

I shrug and bend forward to pull my wallet out of my pocket, and while I'm doing this he says, to Lucille, "I'm really glad you enjoyed the duck."

"The duck was superb," I say, handing him the Visa. He's not getting me twice on the duck.

Outside it's raining and everything is glittery—the lights, the glass slabs in the storefronts, the car tops. Even the street is glowing like some street in the movies.

Lucille says, "Let's take a walk, okay?"

"Sure," I say. "Why not?" I can walk, I know how to go for a walk.

So I start off, and Lucille, who's two or three yards ahead of me already, stops and pivots on her heel and says, "What in the name of Jesus are you doing?"

I flip my arms out to one side and say, "Dancing, I'm dancing. What are you, the only woman in America who doesn't know shine about going for a walk?"

"I've done all right in the past," she says. "Besides, Wang and I spend a lot of time in the Lagonda."

So we walk a couple of blocks, and the rain starts coming harder. We stop for a minute in the doorway of a place that sells kitchen appliances and watch a few cars go by. Finally I say, "Maybe we ought to get back to the car?"

"It'd be drier."

"You want me to go get it? Pick you up here?"

"Would you?"

Lucille is very pretty when she's pleased, so I splash back toward the restaurant and the car, thinking maybe I should take a harder line with her, maybe that's the problem. But when I get the Pontiac and pull it up to the curb by the appliance store, she's not there. I get back in the car and drive up and down the street a couple of times, a couple of blocks each way, but I don't see her. About the third time I pass Red Legs, there she is under the awning, waving at me, so I turn the car around and pull up.

"I had to make a call," she shouts when I roll down the window. "Have you been looking long?"

I motion her to the car, and she comes over and leans in the passenger-side window and says, "I want to ride in back, okay?"

"You what?" I laugh when I say it, but by the time she figures out I'm not pleased, she's already in back and making chauffeur jokes.

"Sometimes," she says from the back seat, "when Wang is reading the sports section in the morning, you know? We'll be sitting there at the table and he'll have the sports flattened over his cereal bowl and I'll watch him until I can tell he's interested in some article, and then, real quick, I'll turn the page, you know? It's funny."

"It is funny. Where do you want to go?"

"Across the river. I want to go to the zoo."

"Zoo's closed, Lucille."

"So what's the big deal? Open it up, why don't you? Ram the gates."

"No, Lucille. I don't want to drive across the river, so maybe we just go home, huh?"

"I always go home. Wang takes me home all the time. I want to stay out and do stuff."

"Blow up the zoo?"

"Yeah. What's wrong with the zoo? What, you hate animals or something?"

She must be down on the seat; I can't see her silhouette in the rearview mirror anymore—just the back window plastered with thousands of tiny colored water bubbles. She's quiet for a bit, so I drive around the neighborhood where we ate, past the City Hall and the Federal Building, alongside Tornado Park, with its neon scale replica of the 1947 tornado, dedicated to the victims, through the Peter J. Lamilar Memorial Tunnel, which bypasses the Fourth Ward and brings us out in an old residential district on the South Side. I'm a little nervous, because she's so quiet.

"You okay?" I ask. I turn around and see her balled up on the back seat. "Hey, Lucille?"

"This is our first date," she says softly. "And already you hurt me."

We're on a brightly lit tree-lined street, going slow. "What do you mean, hurt you?"

"Hurt me—you know." She's crying now, and I can barely hear her through the sniffling. "I don't know why you couldn't just do what I wanted. It wasn't that big a thing. Just because you're old, you don't have to take it out on me."

I turn the car around and head back toward downtown. "What're you talking about?"

"Zoo," she says. "What's this rag back here for? Can I use it?"

"Help yourself."

"And that's not all," she says. Then she blows her nose on the hand towel I keep under the seat of the Pontiac so I'll have something to wipe my hands on if I have to change a tire. I make a mental note to stop at the Kmart tomorrow and get another towel.

That's what I'm thinking about when we come out of the tunnel and the car starts skidding across the street, I can't get control of it. We go through the red light, and a truck slams into the front fender of the Pontiac, sliding us up over the curb into a room-size blue plywood Salvation Army drop.

"Kowabunga!" Lucille says.

"You hurt?" I switch off the ignition and lean over the seat back; she's on her knees in the foot well, her shoulders wedged in between the rear cushion and the back of the front seat.

"I'm doing great," she says. "I'm having the time of my life."

The guy from the truck is out in the road hammering on our window with his ring. "She hurt?" he says. He's a kid about twenty-five; he's got long hair in a ponytail down past his shoulder blades. I get Lucille loose and sitting up in the back seat, and then get out of the car to see how bad the wreck is.

"Skylar," the kid says, sticking out his hand. "Baby Skylar. Listen, it's going to be all right."

His truck is still running, sitting sideways in the intersection, the wipers clacking back and forth, a cone of gray-white smoke pumping out of the exhaust. It's an SPCA truck.

"The city'll pay for everything," he says. "All we gotta do is tell the cop you had the light."

"Right."

Lucille joins us in the intersection, walking a little unsteadily. She wraps her arm around my waist for support. The kid explains the deal to her just the way he explained it to me, and she says, "That's not what happened. This one went through the damn light sideways is what happened."

"He knows that," I say.

A big dog presses his snout through the open wing window in the passenger door of the truck and barks twice, then stares at the three of us standing in the middle of the empty intersection.

"That's Collingsworth," Skylar says.

Lucille waves at the dog.

There's a four-story apartment building backed up to the edge of the block where the tunnel ends, and now there are people opening windows and shouting to see if anybody's hurt.

"It's okay," Skylar shouts back. "Call the police, will you?"

"Call 'em yourself, Motormouth," somebody says. Then somebody else says, "Oh, shut up, Ralph. I'll call them."

On another corner, above the all-night blinking sign on a cut-rate camera shop, a woman who looks as if she's covered in sequins pulls up a window and thrusts the top half of her body outside. "What in the goddam hell you kids doing out here?" she yells. "It's four in the morning and people are trying to sleep."

Lucille shoots the woman the bird and shouts, "It ain't much past two, Fatso, and if you were trying to sleep I'll feed you for a month, even if I have to get a bank loan to do it."

The woman screams something obscene and slams her window so hard the glass breaks and tinkles into the street like a Taiwanese wind chime in a fast breeze.

The three of us sit down on the curb beside my car to wait for the cop. The rain has let up, but there's still a mist, and while Lucille and Skylar talk about rock bands, I remember that rain like this is supposed to be a great pleasure.

It takes three-quarters of an hour for the cop, who looks as if he's about thirteen, to get to the scene, and another hour to do the paperwork with his stubby yellow pencil, so it's almost four when we finish with the accident report. Lucille gets in the front seat of the Pontiac, and with the help of the two guys outside we get the car loose from the Salvation Army box and into the street.

"That was fun," she says as we drive away. "The car's not bad, is it?"

"Could've been worse."

She takes something from her purse and holds it out toward me—not right in front of me but over to the side and low, so that at first I just see her hand coming at me and I flinch. "Silly," she says. "It's only a mint. Don't you want it?"

I take the mint and eat it fast.

"Don't you like the way everything looks in the rain?" she says. "So mysterious and Latin American?"

"It's fine. It's really fine."

"So what's eating you? You don't have to jump all over me because you had one tiny little wreck. Jesus."

I watch the road. "I pay my way. Some women even like me."

"I like you," Lucille says. "I do. I'm not slumming, if that's what you think."

We have to go slow, because the right front wheel feels as if it's about to fall off. There's a terrible scraping noise whenever I turn a corner, so I try to calculate the straightest route to Lucille's house from where we are. She helps by describing a shortcut that sounds like the Lime Rock racing circuit.

We get to her building, and I get out to walk her to the door just the way I've been walking women to their doors for better than twenty years. In the arched recess in front of her building she says, "Do you want some breakfast?"

The invitation sounds tired but sincere, so I say, "Not now. Maybe I'll take a rain check."

"A what?"

"Another time."

Then, with the garbage men going up and down the street singing some kind of lilting reggae tune, and the cans clanking around and rolling in the gutter when they're thrown from the truck back toward where they were picked up, Lucille says haltingly, "So. What about a shower?" I give her a long look, letting the silence mount up. I stand there with her for a good two minutes, without saying a word, trying to outwait her, trying to see what's what. It's five o'clock and the light out is delicate and pink. The garbage song dies off up the block, and half a dozen fatigued-looking kids in matching jackets pull up in a green Dodge and pile into the street, making catcalls and whistling and pointing at us. She smiles at me as if she really does like me. Maybe we've been there longer than two minutes, but when the smile comes, I see her lips a little bit apart and her slightly hooded eyes, and she traces her fingers down my arm from the elbow to the wrist and stops there, loosely hooking her fingertips inside my shirt cuff, pinching my skin with her nails.

(1982)

Autobiography Of

—Can't talk now. Busy.

—Doing what?

—Writing my novel.

—Still at it, you?

—Nothing left to do.

—What's it about?

—It's about you, he said.

—Oh yeah, sure.

—Really.

—About me?

—You and me, he said.

—Us, then.

—Right. That's right.

—What're we doing in this novel?

—Talking.

—About?

—The problems.

—Which ones?

—As they exist.

—Ah.

—I don't want to be here, he said.

—Who does? Not me, either.

—Because why?

—Got nothing. What am I doing in a novel?

—Reaching out.

—Hate that.

–Me, too.

–Imbeciles.

–You said it.

–But us, too. I mean—

–I know what you mean.

–I mean we're imbeciles, too.

–Duh.

–Should have been scientists if you ask me.

–Face down a single, definable project.

–Exactly.

–None of this broad brush stuff.

–Right.

–I'm waving my hand like a broad brush.

–See that.

–Looks brush-like, from this vantage. As on a wall, for example.

–I see that.

–Painting up a storm, I am.

–You should've been a painter.

–I was one. Once.

–Yeah?

–Shows and everything. Got bored after a time.

–Here?

–New York. Late sixties.

–Color field painting.

–No, that was earlier. Concept stuff.

–Oh Jesus.

–Yeah, that's what everyone said.

–Tiny idea, just that one tiny idea. Beat to death.

–Still, was an idea. Was something.

–What?

–A kind of guidance. A suggestion.

–Silly shite.

–That, too.

–Kosuth and Larry What'sit, and Hobbler, and the Spiral
 Jetty guy.

–Smithson. He was doing something else.

–Something spiral.

–Exactly, but they confused it with.

–Always do that, they.

–Nature of the beast.

–Huebler, that was his name.

–And the Brits. Art and Language.

–Remember it well.

–How could you forget?

–A romantic period.

–Bloody hash you ask me.

–I did tape.

–Tape?

–Yeah, on walls. And that stuff you put in drawers. Also on walls.

–Marking territory?

–I suppose. Making a mark.

–Somebody got famous for a minute doing tape.

–That was later and wasn't me. I'd moved on by then.

–I remember. You sent me one.

–Replacements.

–Right. Instead of making something I did X.

–X?

–Buy stuff, mostly. Pictured. TV, etc.

–You bought a TV?

–I said I did.

–But you didn't really?

–For me to know, he said.

–Fox.

–Don't get it, he said. What's a fox?

–Animal, of course. Little, red, etc.

–So what brings you here today.

–Cookies. Wanted some cookies.

–Know what you mean.

–Chocolate chip, oatmeal raisin, brownie cookies.

–Basic rations.

–Diabetic.

–Well, there are worse things.

–Burn through 'em.

–Yep.

–Eat 'em up and move on.
–Better 'n bread. Bread'll kill you.
–Don't like fish that much.
–Slice them open. I hate that.
–In half.
–What I mean, he said.
–Down the belly.
–Seems cruel, doesn't it?
–At minimum. Should be another way to attack them.
–From the side would be kinder.
–More humane.
–Yeah.
–Sorta what they're after anyway, ain't?
–The what you call it—fillet.
–Scrape the damn scales.
–It's a mess. I give it up.
–*So* what happened after the concept stuff?
–Returned to a former life.
–School?
–Music. Had a band.
–Had?
–Was a member of.
–I don't want to be here.
–Said that.
–Well, maybe I could go elsewhere.
–Do what?
–Play music like you.
–I was the worst. I was the concept guy.
–Couldn't play a lick?
–That's it. Was embarrassing.
–Somehow you faked it.
–They were generous toward me.
–Who, the audience?
–The others. Players. They could play.
–Made up for you, covered for you.
–Yep. I had a certain utility.
–Oh yes.

—I could play dog. Get the dog riled up.

—Dog was in the band.

—Sure. He was the best thing in the band.

—What'd he do?

—Howled, of course.

—Barked?

—Sometimes, when he had a mind to.

—Scratched? You mic'd him scratching?

—Precisely. Cage would've.

—If he'd thought of it.

—Friendly thing, the dog.

—They are that.

—Yep. Unlike some other species.

—A raw nerve there.

—Indeed. Flight out of Egypt.

—What the?

—Mary said that.

—Magdalene?

—No, the other Mary. Still out in Ohio.

—A dear soul to be certain.

—I'll say.

—So the deal is the wife left me again.

—How many times now?

—Uncountable.

—I know the thing.

—Unsettling.

—They do that.

—Mind of their own and all that.

—Exactly.

—I don't mean to demean.

—Of course not.

—You understand?

—I do. Utterly.

—Things get out of control.

—Blow up.

—Magnify.

—Catastrophize.

–Every time. It's unfortunate.
–There's a limit, though.
–How do you mean?
–Beyond which, etc.
–To be sure.
–They will act, by God.
–Just so.
–I don't hold it against them.
–No! Absolutely!
–A necessary escape valve.
–Perfectly correct.
–A valve is a wonderful thing.
–Lets stuff in, lets stuff out.
–The ideal form.
–Theatrical.
–Just so.
–And religious, too.
–What would we do without.
–Just so.
–That which washes all our skins.
–Sins?
–Sins also, he said.
–There seem to be fewer sins these days.
–By God! You have it right!
–You've noticed, too?
–Yes! Thought it a hundred times.
–All those sins we were warned about as children.
–Exactly.
–Touching, thinking sins, looking sins.
–Wanting sins were the worst.
–To want, Oh my God.
–Seven and seven.
–The Gold Standard.
–Not too many, not too few.
–Loved the box, though. Solace.
–A great relief.
–It has vanished, now.

—Shame, that.
—Isn't it?
—They ought to bring it back.
—I had impure thoughts thirty-nine thousand times since my last.
—Last week, you mean.
—Exactly.
—The little red bulb over the door.
—Exquisite.
—The kneeler.
—Wonderfully rubberized.
—The diagonally crossed wire screen.
—The shadow beyond.
—The smell—wood, incense, candle smoke.
—The fat man beyond.
—His hand in silhouette covering his face.
—Discreet fellow.
—Of course.
—And listening intently.
—They were all different.
—Some earnest, some blithe.
—Saying rosaries in the catbird seat.
—Barely listening.
—File it all away.
—Some tried to talk to you.
—The worst.
—Reason with you.
—No, those were the worst.
—Some withheld the absolution.
—No, *those* were the worst.
—Kinda went against the whole deal.
—They should have washed those guys out.
—Rotten apples.
—They were going to help you no matter what.
—Click click of the big rosary beads.
—Unforgettable.

(1990)

SPOTS

Cheryl was fourteen years younger than me and a hundred pounds lighter, my new girlfriend of a month. She'd bought a carving knife at Kmart, a serrated cut-anything deal like guys demo on TV, slicing aerosol cans and sawing finger-size bolts that hold flywheels on generators. She was playing with this knife, cutting things for fun—a book I liked, a shoe-polish bottle—and waving the blade at me to make a point, which was that I shouldn't have been messing with my brother's wife, Susan, the week before while my brother Knox was out in California on his annual visit. She was right, of course. The playing around didn't amount to much more than teasing, some little body wrestling, but I regretted it already, for the right reasons and the wrong ones. Cheryl regretted it, too. There wasn't anything I could do about it, though, and I was trying to get it behind us.

"You haven't told me everything," she said, training the knife tip on my chest. "Not the whole story. Knox told me his side, and his side makes you guys look slimy, especially you. At least Susan was upset about him going off to California."

"The whole deal is I said I'd always liked her and one thing led to another," I said. "That's all." I waved and reached for a banana that was turning black on the counter. "At least we had enough sense not to go to bed."

"Yeah, that's a big deal. Thanks. Besides, how do we even know that? Can you prove it? What if you two just agreed to say that and stick to it? How would we ever know any different? Why don't you just say how close you got, in detail, describe all this rolling and tumbling shit, and that'll be that. Just go ahead and tell me."

"I don't want to do that," I said. "I don't see that helping anything."

"Blah, blah," Cheryl said. "It's really great being your new friend. Really. If I'd known what you were like, I'd have stuck with the last bozo I was with, that fat one with all the hair down his back."

"C'mon. Susan and I go way back. We like each other," I said. "There's this natural affection. We just let it get away from us a little."

"Yeah, a couple hundred times. You tell me you have to stay over because she's nervous, and I just buy it. I'm over here watching TV. Jesus." She shook her head and took another swing in my direction with the knife.

We were in the kitchen. It was tiny, things were tight. Cabinets were full of cookery, spices, electronic aids. Her stuff was all over, stuff she'd just brought, packed in, crammed onto the countertops.

"It wasn't anything," I said.

"Yeah? What, you hugged, kissed? That it? Never got your clothes off, right?" She swerved the knife at my shirt, then my pants, then did it again, not seeing that I was headed for the refrigerator, and accidentally caught my cheek. I got a slice from my ear to my chin and forward.

I was surprised more than hurt, startled by blood scattering down my neck. The cut wasn't deep, I couldn't imagine it being deep, but it stung and bled like crazy. I grabbed a paper towel roll and used the whole thing to mop my face.

Cheryl screeched for a second, holding the knife out in front of her, then suddenly stopped, as if realizing she was in some kind of fright movie act. She said, "Are you all right?"

"I think so," I said. "It's not that bad, I don't think."

"I'm really sorry," she said, her body curling down on the word, as if to demonstrate how sorry she was.

"Not that bad," I said. "It wasn't that hard, was it?"

She got another roll of paper towels and reeled off big swaths she used to wipe my shoulder and shirt. I bent over the sink, dropping blood onto the metal.

When the phone rang I said, "Will you get it?"

"I don't want to answer," Cheryl said. "What if it's Susan? What if it's for you?"

I wedged her aside and reached the receiver mounted on the wall by the kitchen door. "What?" I said into the handset.

I listened for a second, then shut my eyes and handed the phone to Cheryl. "It's your mother. Tell her you sliced me up, and we've got to call the hospital."

I leaned over the sink again, watching the blood, which was slowing some, thread its way into the running water and slide fast into the drain. There were white specks in the drain, and I couldn't figure out what they were. I was trying to think what we'd eaten that would end up these tiny white bits in the kitchen sink, and, at the same time, I was soaking towels in faucet water, pressing them to my chin.

Cheryl was calm on the phone, chatting with her mom. All the time she kept wiping at my neck. She said, "I just cut Del accidentally with this knife and he's bleeding some, but we don't think it's that bad, at least we hope not." Her mother must have missed it, and Cheryl repeated it right away, louder. "I just accidentally cut his face with a knife. We were playing around, and I cut him. He's bleeding now. We probably have to go."

She listened another half minute, then hung up the phone. "You ready? We'll go to St. Christian's, okay? They have an emergency deal."

"Urgent Care," I said. "They're quicker." I had my head turned sideways, cut side up, trying to stem the bleeding.

"Yeah, but they're like vets," she said. She was leaning on the counter next to me, twisting her head around for a better look. "They're going to have to stitch the hell out of this."

"That's great news."

She said, "I didn't mean to do this, you know. I was just playing around. I wasn't playing around about Susan, but the knife stuff . . ."

"You didn't mind sticking me."

"Oh, come on. Like I really want to slice your face in a million pieces."

"Okay," I said. "You didn't mean to hit me."

"Later I want to rip skins off rabbits and stuff. That's me. Carjack some Cherokees, okay? Spit at people, crash store windows, whatever. I want to be modern, sleep with my brother's wife, you know."

"Fine," I said. I was bleeding, but it was slowing down. "Can you hand me a towel?" When I pulled the paper towels off the cut, blood only bulged out, making a line down my face, dripping off. I pointed at the cut. "Would you get with it? Are we going to the doctor?"

"Fine," she said. "If you think it's necessary."

I was mopping with the towel she'd handed me, going into the next room looking for my shoes.

"I'm sorry," she said, following me. "I'm nervous, I think. Are we going? What're we doing?"

"Have you got keys?" I said.

She shook the keys.

"Okay, let's go," I said. I was at the door.

Cheryl was driving, fast but not too fast, whipping her head back and forth checking cross streets. "I didn't really cut you," she said. "Maybe if I was Mexican, I'd have cut you. White trash, cut you. Middle class, no. Too many jobs, too many cars—I can't cut anybody. Unless I go crazy, and then I can cut shit out of whoever—there'll be an explanation. If I'm not crazy I can only screw around in the kitchen and nick you a little by accident." She stopped and tilted her head looking at me. "You know, this might look pretty good after a while. Before it heals up."

"It's going to look like a cat scratch," I said.

"Way too big. You're getting lots of compliments on this at the shop. They'll regard you with a new respect, maybe even fear. It's just what you want."

•

At the emergency room a tiny doctor, an Asian, took a look at my face, then looked at Cheryl, then back at me and just shook his head. His black hair was shivering. He pointed to some plastic seats in an examination room. "I'll be back," he said. "Keep the towel on it."

Then he left. Cheryl sat at the opposite end of the room. It was cool in there, lots of aluminum and shiny steel.

"How's it feel?" Cheryl said.

"It doesn't feel," I said. I took the towel off, tossed it to her, then unspooled paper towels from the roll she'd brought, folded them, dampened them under the faucet.

"If you're thinking I did this on purpose you're crazy," Cheryl said. "I just wanted you to know that. I don't like this Susan stuff at her place, or in the fucking elevator, the two of you riding up and down like teenagers watching the sun go down, but I'm not crazy."

"I told you I don't think it was on purpose. I think you slipped."

"Right," she said. "But that was stupid for you guys to do that in the elevator."

"I was leaving," I said. "She didn't want me to leave."

"What's this, no-fault sex? How do I know that's where it stops? Wouldn't you rather have this really open relationship, tell each other everything—that way it'd be easy for the other guy, you know?"

"We have that," I said. "I told you everything."

"Sort of. I'm thinking seriously open. Who I think about when I masturbate. Everything. It'll be great. We'll tell the truth. We'll tell more truth than anybody ever told before."

"Fine," I said, pulling the towels across my face.

"And we won't have to pay too much attention, because everything will be up on the surface. We won't have any peculiar or difficult thoughts, either, you've got to promise that. It'll be like CNN."

"C'mon, Cheryl. Settle down, will you?"

"Let's go on Arsenio, anyway," she said.

"What?" The bleeding was slow, almost stopped. I smeared it with my finger, then blotted with the towels.

"He's black, he's modern, he's happening, he's huh-huh-huh." She made the grunting noise and did that business circling her arm.

"He's canceled," I said.

She slumped on the stool. "I know. He's going to be. He's bad meat. He's over—I know that. It's fast out there. What do I think, they're going to wait for me?"

"Jesus," I said. "Put a rag in it, okay?"

"What a romance this is," she said. "Here we are in the middle of the night at the hospital, and you're telling me that. What is that?"

"You're babbling," I said. "We're trying to get my face fixed, and you're raving about Susan and sex and I don't know what."

"Hey," she said. "It's not sex, I got plenty of that." She got up and leaned against the wall of the exam room, popping her shirt snaps, loosening her pants, and slipping her hand down under the zipper. "All you have to do is watch. Every man I ever met wanted to watch. Get over there, stand this way, stand that way—"

I shut the door and stood in front of the little glass porthole so nobody could see in. "Please, Cheryl. Christ. What's wrong with you?"

She was like, "Do this, do that, move this way, rub it, finger it, squat, bend over, twist that, squeeze it, hold 'em up, pull it this way, lick it, bite it, hold 'em apart, rotate, ride it way up, kiss it—every man I ever met. That's the kind of babbling I get. You're no different."

"I agree," I said. "Fine. Just get dressed. Snap the little snaps."

"I don't know what happened to the old days when people felt things for each other, touched each other, cared for each other—I had better sex in high school than I've had since."

"If that's what you think," I said. "Just button up for the here and now, okay?"

"What, am I scaring you like this? Hey, we can tape it and sell it to Cinemax. We'll be ahead of the curve," she said. She closed her pants and started on the shirt.

"What's with all this?" I said. "Have we been sticking a little too close to *The Week in Rock* or what?"

"Well," she said. "Being modern is making a difference. It's having our voices heard."

"You gotta have one of the nine recognized voices to get heard," I said. "And it's gotta be saying one of the nine recognized things. Outside of that you can forget it."

"There you go again," she said. "So what are the nine things?"

"Check your local listings," I said.

"See, when you say stuff like that you sound like Susan," she said, sitting again. "I mean, I can take a certain amount of cynicism, but after a while it's as phony as anything else. It's just depressing.

Besides, I pick and choose the stuff I pay attention to. I don't buy it whole."

I opened the door and stuck my head out, then redampened the paper towels. "Thank God for that," I said.

We had been in the examination room for about ten minutes when a nurse came in, took the towel pack off, dabbed some Mercurochrome on my face, pushed the towels back into place, and told me to go home.

"I thought he was coming back," I said.

"Who?" the nurse asked.

"The doctor," I said.

"We saw a Japanese doctor," Cheryl said to the nurse. "Short guy? Black hair?"

Right then the Japanese doctor came in. "What's going on?"

I said, "I don't know. The nurse was thinking I was ready."

He said, "No dice. We've got to do a few small stitches. We're very well trained in stitches, but we've still got to practice sometime, don't we?" He grinned at Cheryl.

The nurse went to get some things the doctor needed, and, meanwhile, he washed his hands in the metal sink, whistling something I couldn't figure out. He had me sit on a low white stool and cleaned the cut with cotton and alcohol, then shot my face in three places with tiny bursts of anesthetic from a yellow plastic syringe. When the nurse returned he took twelve black stitches at the front end of the cut along the curve of my chin.

•

When it got to be four in the morning, and I still wasn't asleep, I decided to clean up the kitchen. I wiped the counters and the floor, rinsed the sink with soap, then alcohol, packed up all the garbage I could find in the house, and took it out to the Dumpster that was at the back of the property, across the parking area from the building.

The street that ran alongside the condo dead-ended into Highway 90. It was a quiet, tree-shaded, narrow street lined with a couple of old houses and a bunch of rental townhouses. There was a flash of heat lightning as I carried the garbage bags across the parking lot, and then the sky looked a calm, midnight blue. I flipped the two bags, one after the other, into the Dumpster, and I was standing there looking distractedly around when all the streetlights, and the porch lights on the buildings across the street, suddenly flashed off. There wasn't a noise, just the sudden withdrawal of the light—I could still see, of course, but the buildings were all faced in shadow, were almost silhouettes. It put me on edge, gave me a pleasant but slightly nervous feeling, as if something might be happening. It was like one of those movie scenes where the intruder, before he goes in, cuts the power to the house where the woman is hiding. It was silly to think about it at all, but the anxiety was pleasant, so I stood for a minute there on the blacktop, arms crossed, scanning townhouses across the street for a clue, a movement, anything out of the ordinary. There was nothing. I waited another couple of minutes, then started on a walk toward the highway and the beach. The air was peculiar, the way it just hung, motionless, drifting off the water, and the only sound was the faint hiss of little breakers running over rock jetties. There weren't any cars on Highway 90, and only one streetlamp burned about a hundred and fifty yards down the road. I stood on the corner in front of the condos and looked up at our place, the dark bedroom where Cheryl was sleeping, then walked out into the middle of the empty highway and crossed to the beach side where the sand was gritty under my shoes, then came back, looking all around, soaking up everything. With the lights out things seemed to have lost their power. It was like nothing was holding anything, the resistance was gone, that little pressure that's always against you, obliging you, keeping you in place. I thought about calling Susan on the telephone, about walking up the beach highway until I found a pay phone that was working and giving her a ring. That seemed like a good idea, and I started walking. I thought if my brother Knox answered, well, I'd ask him how he was, and then I'd ask to speak to Susan. Just straight out. Just like that.

(2000)

CLEANERS

A little over a week later I talked to my father on the phone on Monday night, went through the usual routine with him, the catalog of his ailments, the complaints about the woman who was coming in every day to help him out, the problem he was having with his testicles, how they were raw because he spent so much time sitting and he never moved much. I made some joke about that, and he laughed and made some other joke himself, laughed at that, too, so altogether it was a better conversation than usual.

Then Tuesday morning the nurse from the service called and said, "There's been some trouble with your father." I figured he was sick or something, maybe he had to go to the hospital, but then the woman said she had come in that morning and found him tangled up on the floor, his knee cocked through the scissors-like legs of an overturned TV tray. And then she said my father had died.

"He died?" I said.

She repeated the explanation and then gave the telephone to a policeman who said he was there overseeing things, and wanted to know if I had a preference in funeral arrangements. I didn't. I gave him the name of the only funeral home I knew, some family-run Catholic place I remembered because I'd been to grade school with one of the children. I asked to speak to the nurse again.

"He went peaceful, Mr. Ray," she said. "He was comfortable. I prayed for him."

"I thought he was twisted up in a TV tray," I said.

"Well, he was. But he was okay after that, and then he went to rest and when I went back he wasn't breathing."

"So he was alive when you got in this morning?" I said.

"Yes," the woman said. "He couldn't answer the door because he was caught in that table thing, but once we got the security people and got inside, we put him on the bed and he seemed to be fine. He was very peaceful then, very relaxed and comfortable. The television was on. He was trying to watch a tape, I think, but it wasn't running."

"After you put him on the bed, you mean?"

"No, before. That's what he'd been doing, trying to set up that *Sound of Music* tape he liked."

"That's when he got caught in the TV tray?"

"I think so, yes," she said.

We went through it again and then I said I'd be driving over the following day and I asked her to tell the complex manager to leave a key for me.

As soon as I got off the phone I called my mother.

Telling her wasn't hard because she seemed to know what I was going to say from my tone of voice. When I heard her crying on the other end of the line I felt stupid for having called her instead of driving across town to tell her in person, but as soon as I said something about coming over, she said, "That's not necessary. I'm fine." And her crying stopped.

"I thought I'd go over there tomorrow," I said.

"Fine," she said. "I'm coming with you."

"I know," I said. "Do you want to stay over here tonight? I could come get you now, and then we'll go when we get up."

"What? No," she said. "What is it, an eight-hour drive? Get me in the morning. That'll be fine. And give me the woman's name, the one you talked to."

•

Wednesday morning was crisp and chilly, a dry cold. Highway 10 wasn't crowded. The speed limit was seventy, so I drove just under eighty. Mother wasn't crying, but her eyes were ringed and puffy.

"I'm not looking at the body," she said, as we passed Hammond, Louisiana. "They'll ask us, and I'm going to say no. You can if you want to, but I think it's ghoulish. You don't think that's terrible, do you?"

"No," I said. "It makes sense."

"Some people want to see. They want to spit in the eye of death, but not me. I can't do anything for him now. I had my chance."

"You did plenty, Mom," I said.

"Maybe. I don't know. I shouldn't have left him there alone, that's what it is, really. That's what I think. I should have made him come over, or stayed there with him, either one."

"He could've come," I said, trying to remember the last time I'd seen my father—it must have been the summer after she moved. When she came, he thought about coming, too. I remember thinking he wanted to be coaxed. We did some of that, but not enough to get the job done.

"I think I discouraged him," she said.

"No, you didn't. You begged him to come."

"It doesn't do any good to lie about it, Ray."

"I'm not lying," I said. "I'm just trying to remember. You wanted him to come, and only sort of reluctantly came yourself after he said he wasn't. Besides, you were supposed to get things straightened away, weren't you?"

"It shocked me when he didn't come," Mother said. "I was sure he'd come in the first six months. That kind of hurt."

"He was going to come," I said. "He talked about it all the time. He missed you so much, but he couldn't get off the dime."

"I missed him."

"I was thinking about how he smelled," I said. "Like if you threw his shirts in the laundry with yours you got that scent of him? Sometimes I think I smell like that now. The sheets I sleep on or something."

She said, "I hate when people die. When I die just dump me out the door, will you? Put me in a Hefty Lawn and Leaf sack and drag me to the curb." She stared out the window of my Explorer. "What would he think if he saw us speeding over there right now?"

"He'd think it was fine," I said.

"No," she said. "You know better than that. He'd think it was a waste of gasoline, he wouldn't like it."

"He'd say that, but he'd want us coming."

"He had a hard time being ordinary, Hopper did. Never quite made it up to that. You're taking right after him."

I shook my head and locked the cruise control at seventy-eight. I didn't want to take care of my father. I was nervous, as if the bad news wasn't at hand, but was still out there. As if we were driving to Houston for further medical tests to uncover my mother's lung cancer or heart disease. When things were quiet in the car, the thought "My father's dead" rang over and over in my head until the phrase was like an echo. Then, when I was able to forget for a few miles, I'd suddenly realize I was thinking about something I wanted to tell him when we got to Houston.

I hadn't suspected that he was about to die, but now that it had happened, I was sure I'd known. It was obvious from the complaints, the nursing service, the difficulty he had keeping track of his pills, the way he sometimes seemed out of his head if my phone call caught him after a nap.

When Mary's sister was killed in the car crash, it didn't feel like anything. We were friends and it was nothing, like she'd been erased. The police woke us at three in the morning and I was all business. Up and dressed and getting Mary going and heading for the hospital and then, when the sister died, making the arrangements. I thought it ought to feel worse, but it only felt like stuff to do. So I took care of things. I thought I'd cry later, but never did. Weeks went by, months. I didn't even miss Mary's sister, really. What was different was that I didn't talk to her the way I had, didn't sit down with her and chat. Otherwise things were the same. She vanished. It didn't matter.

The same thing was going to happen with my father. I wanted to do it right, to feel sad, but I didn't, really, I felt taut and tired, and I had to drive all the way to Houston. Some inevitable thing had happened. I didn't want to mess with funeral directors and cemetery guys. I didn't want to smile and act lost and accept their condolences. I didn't want to nod and be nodded at, knowingly, when I was already looking forward to having it done with, being finished with him.

I thought I might miss the telephone calls, his gravelly voice and the endless litany of small troubles—bowels, bankers, difficulty seeing and walking, bad food, the day nurse who spoke no English—the complaints about everything and everyone, leavened occasionally with a recognition that he was being self-indulgent. And I would miss the hesitant questions about my mother—how was she, why did she not call him more often, did I think she still loved him at all? That was the part of him I loved most.

Mother stirred in the seat next to me. "Stop at the next rest station," she said. "I need to stop. Okay? Have you got any Kleenex in this car? And what is this about you people losing money at the casino? Mary said five thousand dollars."

"We've lost a bunch," I said.

"Is it that much?"

"Yes, maybe more. We didn't exactly keep track."

"So. Up jumps the devil," she said. "You're a nut. Are you having some kind of spiritual problem? Is the marriage okay? What is it?"

She looked out her window as a bright chrome eighteen-wheel tanker truck passed, distorting the reflection of the Explorer in its curved side.

"We're fine," I said.

She waved me off. "Never mind, don't tell me another thing about it, I don't want to hear. Whatever it is, it'll make perfect sense to you, and no sense at all to me. Can you afford to lose that much money?" She tapped the window pointing at a rest stop we were passing, a place with concrete pavilions and a glass-enclosed visitors center. "Hey," she said.

•

My father had turned the downstairs of the condo into a private nursing home—a single bed, a chest of drawers, a chair, a TV, the dining table, a collection of plastic containers, a carton of Depends, a box for his pill bottles. He had the living room furniture piled up in the dining room. It was pitiful. My mother sniffled and crunched a tissue, and I stared at the room. Someone had cleaned things up after my father's death. There were sheets and pillowcases folded neatly on the end of the bed. The magazines were all straightened, as were the books in the single row alongside the bed. The dishes were clean. Everything was put away. There was a note from the nursing service woman, in a childlike scrawl, repeating the story of how tranquil my father had been at the moment of death. His wallet was in the middle of a dining table cluttered with bills, letters, manila folders, unopened mail, small tools, two boxes of ballpoint pens.

Mother said, "This is not what I want to see."

We sat in the chairs in the converted living room and had drinks. We didn't talk, just sat and absorbed the situation, drank, rested from the drive.

When her drink was half gone, she said, "This is something, isn't it?"

"It looks lonely as hell, doesn't it?"

"He died right here." She waved at the TV tray which was back in its place alongside his favorite chair. "Do you feel that eerie thing? Like his presence? I don't know. He's not coming back, is he? He wasn't such a bad guy. He was difficult, but that's okay for a man to be. Better that than too easy. It wasn't much fun when he was on your case, though."

"I think he meant well," I said. "He never meant anything but well."

"That's the truth. We'll put that on the headstone," she said.

My shoulders hurt. In the room it felt as though time had stopped moving, everything arrested, frozen, held that way. Nobody that had to do with us would ever move around in that condo again. It was a dead place, and at the same time we still had to spend a couple of days there. I felt the weight of my father's death and that place dragging on my shoulders. I wanted to go to sleep, to get out of there by whatever means. I said, "He was fine. He didn't deserve to die, though I guess that's stupid, who does? Last time I talked to him he was telling me about a rash on his testicles."

"I think you should keep that to yourself," my mother said.

"Maybe I'll go upstairs and take a nap," I said. "Will that upset you? I'll think of something smarter to say afterwards."

"You don't have to think a thing," she said. "It's just that this is worse than I anticipated. It's gruesome."

"Don't think about it," I said. "I'm sorry, Mother." I got up and stood behind her chair, then wondered why I'd done that, wondered if it was because I'd seen it in a hundred movies, on a thousand TV shows. *The Comforting*. I put my hands on her, on her shoulders, on the sides of the tops of her arms, I stroked her hair, leaned down and kissed her cheek, seeing each of the gestures in my imagination before doing it. "It's okay," I whispered.

She reached up with her left hand and patted softly the side of my head. "Thank you, baby," she said.

There were three bedrooms upstairs. One was a guest bedroom that I had always used when I visited. It had twin beds, a TV, a night table with an electric clock on it. Some boxes of my father's business stuff were stuck in the corner. There was a walk-in closet. I stretched out on the bed, put a washcloth over my eyes, and folded my arms across my chest. The pillow was foam rubber, old, uncomfortable. I thought I remembered it from childhood, but that might have been wrong. It had a ridge that hit right at the base of my neck. I listened to my mother in the master bedroom across the hall, her old bedroom. She was opening drawers and closets, moving stuff around.

Then she knocked on my door. "Come in," I said.

She stepped into the small bedroom and sat on the edge of the second bed. "I know you think he was horrible to me," she said. "But I gave as good as I got most of the time. He was crazy, like he always thought he was right, always thought things should make sense, thought you could find a right way or a best way for things. But that was a luxury for me. Another reason to love him."

It was dark outside and the flood lamps from the adjacent condos shot in through the mini blinds. There was dust swirling in the shafts of light.

She said, "It could've been much worse. He was scared at the end. He had nowhere to go, nobody to turn to. What was he going to do? I think it made him feel better to take it out on me, order me around, say I was crazy."

"You are crazy, aren't you?" I lifted the washcloth off my eyes to squint at my mother.

She smiled in a way so faint that it barely disturbed her face.

Strips of shadow from the blinds crossed the ceiling and peeled down the walls of the small bedroom. Mother scooted up onto the other bed, straightened her skirt, wiggled her feet in their white canvas shoes. "Sure I am," she said. "And I don't want to go out there alone."

"There's a lot of work," I said.

"You know what? I was thinking we could call somebody and get it packed and shipped back without ever getting into it. We could get into it later."

I adjusted the washcloth and thought how wonderful that would be. It was as if suddenly we didn't have to have the surgery after all. I got a chill running my spine. "You think we can do that?"

"We're the boss," she said. "I'll store it at the house, or get a place."

"He wouldn't approve," I said. "Hopper would want lists, plans, details, diagrams. Research. The whole deal. Of course, now that he's dead, he doesn't want a thing."

"That'll do, Ray," she said.

"I was trying to help," I said.

"It'll be good. It's cleaner. We never have to see the body, they take care of everything, we don't have to tear it all down, we just call them and get it done."

I sighed. "Well, I like the idea, but who is 'them'?"

"You know, when *my* father died it was a mess," she said. "He died in the house. Lots of boiling water, steam everywhere, heavy air, thick drawn curtains, constant scrubbing floors, washing bed linens and his bed clothes, relatives milling around, doctors coming and going."

"Dickens," I said.

"I can't imagine going through Hopper's clothes, choosing this and that," she said. "His things. We'll keep everything. I'll call Bekins tomorrow, we'll meet them and get it set up, and that'll be that."

Tension jetted out of my shoulders. I rolled my neck back and forth on the pillow. What a wonderful thought.

"I don't want to stay any longer than we have to," she said. "Although, I kind of wish he were here telling us what to do."

"I was thinking what if he was on his way back from the doctor. And you two were going to watch a National Geographic Special 'The Big Cats' at ear-snapping volume. I used to come up here to hide from the noise when you watched TV."

"Wait till you can't hear," she said.

"He was kind of a freak on that volume."

"Who isn't a freak some way or other? For me he was like a guiding light, you know? That kind of thing. God, I hate this." She got off the bed and split the blinds with two fingers. "Your father was good to me most of my life. You can't ask for more than that."

"You know, I guess."

"Yes," she said. "But I can't stand being here, it's making me nuts. I shouldn't have left him. That was wrong."

•

Mary called late to find out how things were going. I got the phone downstairs and filled her in. "We're calling the movers and bailing out quick," I said. "That's what Mother wants to do. She feels guilty about his dying."

"Like she should have made him move or something?"

"Yeah. I didn't do much either."

"Like he really listened to you, Ray," Mary said.

"I could've tried harder."

"So what's it like otherwise?" she asked.

"Nothing. Empty rooms, like we're waiting for somebody to come home. He turned the downstairs into a homemade hospital or something. It's awful."

"What's that mean?"

"He had everything pushed out of the way, only functional stuff around, pee pots everywhere—he was having some bladder problem I guess. He was living in this one room down there, had a dresser, a TV, bath—like a hospital room."

"I'm sorry," she said. "So are you okay?"

"I'm tired. He's gone. Sometimes it seems like a joke and he'll show up any minute. Getting somebody else to handle everything is a relief. I guess we're doing the burial and that stuff, I don't know."

"You want me to look for storage places?"

"Yeah, if you would. That'd be great. Out by Mother's. Is RV doing okay?"

"Boy trouble with Jeff," Mary said.

"Oh yeah? Have we met Jeff?"

"No. And Randall got a Vespa, so she wants a Vespa."

"I thought they wanted cars."

"Randall already has a car. This is something to play with."

"I see," I said. "Who's Randall?"

"He's like, *there*, when she chills," Mary said. "That's what I hear, anyway."

"Oh. Cool."

"What about the funeral?"

"We don't speak funeral," I said. "Cremate and hide the ashes. Nobody leaves the house. No service, no marker, no nothing. We'll be back there in two days."

"Well, that'll be good. Being back."

"I guess. There's something about him not being here," I said. "He can't scowl at what you say. I have this urge to poke into things, see what's what. I can move stuff with impunity."

"Hmm?" Mary wasn't listening to me. She was carrying on a conversation on the side. Then she said, "RV wants a word with you."

I listened to the phone being passed. Then RV said, "Hey, Ray."

"How are you, doll?"

She sighed. "Okay, I guess. Randall's Vespa is really cool. It's real old. Maybe I'll steal it and take you for a ride sometime. I'm sorry about, you know—everything."

"Thank you, sweetie. I miss you."

"Yeah, me too. Nobody's ragging on me about my room, my homework, and my clothes."

"I love your room, homework, and clothes," I said. "I dream of them."

"You're a sick pigeon," she said. "Here, Mom. Your husband's being sick on the phone."

"Am not," I yelled into the handset.

"They're going to another party tonight," Mary said, when she came back on the line.

I was staring at the furniture in the living room, at the way my father had changed things to fit his new life.

"All this furniture is so still," I said. "It's a death watch."

"I'm sorry, Ray," she said.

"Thanks," I said. "I mean, talking to him on the phone he complained about everything, but seeing it firsthand is different."

"It's bad enough without feeling guilty," she said. "Forget that, will you?"

"Yeah, I know. Is there any other news?"

"One of the cards is over limit," she said. "The Chase cards? Forget it."

"Get another one. Bank of America. Bank of New York. First National Bank. Supplies are endless."

"This is not a healthy attitude, Ray. Maybe we should go back to architecture."

"Can't," I said. "Coming into Houston I realized that building is aggression. New parking garages, pint-size office buildings, freeways—they're all explosions in the center of otherwise entirely satisfactory settings. I don't know why I never saw it before."

"Maybe this isn't the time," she said.

"I haven't been working much for a while, anyway. Or hadn't you noticed?"

"I noticed. That's why I brought it up."

"We'll probably get something from the estate," I said. "That'll help. Not much, but we can pay some on the cards."

We said goodnight and I put the phone back in its charging cradle, then sat on the edge of my father's bed, looking at the living room from that vantage, trying to see it as he had. It looked as if everything in the room was leaning toward me just slightly, just enough to notice. In a few minutes I lay back on the bed and closed my eyes. I heard stuff outside—buzzing streetlights, cars coming and going, chirps of security systems set, footsteps on the walk, muffled young voices in animated conversation passing outside my father's door.

•

Mother had the knack. The next day people from the funeral home, the cemetery, the moving company, the condo rental agency, the Goodwill, the Sisters of Our Savior Mission, and several other helpful organizations started arriving at noon. They were mostly men, fortyish and in smooth suits who got confused with all the papers they needed to get signed.

I sat at the dining table eating a sandwich I'd made from roast beef and white bread from the deli section of the local grocery. The guys doing the helping were constantly pointing at spots my mother was supposed to initial on their papers. They'd tap the signature lines with their Cross ballpoints. I scanned a brochure called *Finally, An Island of Rest* while the cemetery man, Steve Walker, a blond and too-healthy guy in his late thirties, talked perpetual care, interment exclusions, monument privilege restrictions, lawn crypts, the merits of Urn Garden versus Columbarium Niche.

The funeral director brought an aluminum suitcase filled with photographs and color samples and swatches of coffin cloth. He was prepared no matter which way we wanted to go. The moving guy spent an hour going around the house touching things and making notes, while his associate put green numbered tags on all the furniture, lamps, appliances—anything that was to be packed individually. The Sisters of Our Savior representative was a younger man, dressed the way priests use to dress when they ventured off church grounds, only he looked like a skinhead, so you either couldn't take him seriously, or you had to take him so seriously that it was scary.

Most of the people talked about death, but looked as though they were more interested in beach volleyball and Eddie Bauer. All were men, and every man was practiced, efficient, helpful. Not one was unctuous, oily, lubricated, or waxy.

During a break in the action I said, "Whatever happened to stereotypes? This is quite a show you whomped up."

"Thank you," Mother said. "It's my 'Baked While You Sleep' background. We'll be gone tomorrow, day after at the latest."

"No wonder everybody loves you. When we get back, I'm driving you around to look for that Larroquette guy you were so interested in. We're going everywhere. No stone unturned."

"We need a storage place. You can drive me around to look at storage places."

"Mary's looking."

"Oh yeah? Good."

She waited for the next visitor reading the material left behind by the last. Mother was still handsome. Her skin shined and her hair was salt and peppery, off the shoulder in a fifties way she'd worn since I could remember. There was something winsome about her, even in her sixties. I had a hard time thinking of her and my father together, meeting at college, dating, going out in Galveston, lingering along the boardwalk, or partying at Sui Jen, an ancient dance hall that teetered out over the water back then, until some hurricane got it in the mid-fifties. I'd seen photos of them in my father's 1953 Studebaker, waving at the camera, looking daffy, driving off from my grandparents' house. He was the drummer in a jazz quartet that played around, and my mother was never too far from the bandstand, smoking cigarettes and drinking her bourbon so slowly that the glass never seemed to change. Wearing black tailored suits with white piping. There were crazy parties—ones that ended in car games that nearly killed all participants, or in the good fun of hanging people upside down off the fourteenth-floor penthouse garden of the Milam Hotel up in Houston, or in gunshots over in the fourth ward. I had heard the stories as a kid, retold with fondness and delight over Sunday dinner, or when old friends who only showed up every couple of years came to visit. I knew my parents more from those stories and from photographs and eight-millimeter home movies than from memory. These were events or afternoons caught forever, showing me what it had been like. I couldn't pinpoint when the photographs and movies replaced my own real memories, and I had a few schematic recollections independent of the pictures—something at grade school with a lay teacher, a spanking I'd gotten for lying about some cookies, shooting arrows in the yard—but mostly my memory was snapshots. I'd see a photo of the house we lived in when I was ten and recognize the furniture without actually remembering it. I couldn't imagine what it was like to sit in that chair doing my homework, as I was in dozens of pictures, or to be on the kitchen cabinet talking to my mother, as I was in others, or to be playing with Christmas toys. I said I remembered, but what I meant was I remembered the pictures. Nothing in them had heft or dimension, they were all signs, images I could identify but not give life to.

"We were finally talking about him coming to Mississippi," my mother said. "Hopper wasn't ready, but he was getting closer. I mean, what was he going to do? Sixty-eight—a new romance? I thought he'd give in and move this year. If he didn't I was going to come back here." She was swiveling my father's wallet in circles on the dining table. "I thought we'd visit a few times, then, gradually, you know . . ."

"He always asked me about you," I said. "How you were and everything."

"Who else did he know? Everybody else who lives around here is thirty. Maybe the gal two doors down on the other side of the walk who used to bring the potato soup. He might have taken up with her, I guess. But she died a while ago."

My mother was staring out the sliding glass doors at the narrow patio overgrown with wisteria. Bees buzzed vigorously among the blue-violet flower clusters that hung off the vines. A Weber barbecue grill I bought them one summer was out there.

•

It wasn't as easy as Mother said it would be. She decided we had to go through Hopper's papers, the stuff in the backs of the closets, the china, the books, the family records, photographs, and the rest of it. I went to the U-Haul store to buy a few boxes and found this six-inch wide green plastic wrap in a five-hundred-yard roll. The plastic stuck to itself, so you could wrap anything with it. It was like industrial strength Saran Wrap on a handle. We spent a day or two sorting, boxing, wrapping, reducing my father's life to its simplest parts. And since he'd kept files for bills, insurance, Social Security, investments, medical expenses, and so on, the only thing left untended was his wallet, which was curiously alive, as if waiting for him to fetch it. It was a bulging black thing stuffed with cards and bits of paper, cash, a flat key that we didn't know what fit, a fingernail-size chip of mica, an old St. Christopher's medal engraved on the back with his mother's name. The wallet seemed wholly personal; the one thing that kept him alive. I tried putting it in the boxes we were packing, but every time I got it in a box, I had to take it out and put it back on the table. In the end, I carried that wallet with me on the ride home.

(1998)